I0643402

THE SEVEN SPIRES

RUSSELL ARCHEY

5 PRINCE PUBLISHING

Published by

5 PRINCE PUBLISHING & BOOKS, LLC

PO Box 865, Arvada, CO 80001

www.5PrinceBooks.com

ISBN digital: 978-1-63112-250-7

ISBN print: 978-1-63112-251-4

Cover Credit: Marianne Nowicki

For Symphony and Carter...
who deserve all the magic in the world.

ACKNOWLEDGMENTS

A lot of hard work went into making my first book a reality—and not just my own.

To my wife, Jennifer, who has always supported my endeavors no matter how far-fetched, crazy, improbable, or irritating.

Thank you, 5 Prince Publishing (and especially Bernadette Marie) who have played a massive part in helping make this step in my life and career a reality and being absolutely amazing during the process.

To Cate, my first editor: I appreciate your art, your craft, and everything you do to make my book its absolute best. You're worth your weight in gold.

Finally, to each and every person who reads this book, whether you liked it or not—thank you.

THE SEVEN SPIRES

THE MAIDEN OF EMRALLT

This would be the first of many trips for her to the great tower this season. Her best memories were those of cresting the last green hill and seeing the Emerald Spire rise like one great tree reaching for the sun.

It stood above all the surrounding forests. Though the trees in the lush realm of Emrallt grew large and strong, they still paled in comparison to the ancient, mysterious, and beautiful structure.

She would always pause at the crown of the hill, overlooking the road playfully winding and rolling, like the waves of a gentle river. The forests on each side were leafy shores providing shade and rest. She loved the journey to the capital city, Emerald Arbor, each and every time.

Along the way, she would gather an assortment of the many and varied blossoms that grew along the roads and in the fields. Sometimes she caught herself venturing farther off the road than was prudent, and would end up at staying at a small traveler's inn after losing too much daylight.

It wasn't without purpose, however, as the bouquets, corsages, perfumes, and preserved and scented trinkets she would fashion from them brought in plenty of coin for the young Maiden.

It was at the last stretch of paved cobblestone road leading to the city surrounding the tower that she would stop and take in a final glance of the spire before entering the city.

The continent of Septer was home to seven great spires. Each uniquely magnificent. The Maiden had only ever seen the one of her homeland: the Emerald Spire. Surrounded by the capital city, the spire was a sight to behold.

She would marvel at the large, open-air balconies that stretched from the sides of the spire, like branches. Her neck would have to crane almost painfully to see the very top where the great, green emerald, large enough to hold ten men, sat cradled on an ornate, carved dais overlooking the realm. Or, so she was told. The first two stories were open to commoners and nobility alike. Beyond that, only nobility and royalty could pass.

She passed below the great arch leading into and out of the public square beneath the spire. Massive roots grew from beneath the rich soil and naturally curved into an arch, covered in the largest blooms in the kingdom. Some said the roots were attached to the spire itself and were just as ancient. Both had existed as long as recorded history, and the means of their construction were entirely unknown; even their kings knew not how they came to be.

The spires were ancient and arcane. Each realm had a spire and each spire, a kingdom. Each of the seven monarchs knew that the spire of their respective kingdom was in their charge. However, the spires held a mysterious power all of their own, and it was believed that the kings and queens served the spire, as much as their people served their monarchs.

The Maiden had overheard scholars in the libraries and gathering halls discuss such things, but never paid them much mind. The only bit of information that struck her was that the language written on the city arch was dead and gone—perhaps belonging to an ancient elven dialect or an extinct people. The tower itself, well, it was fashioned like any structure. A truly magnificent one, but still had halls, rooms, stairwells, and all the markings of any other architecture. The uniqueness of this spire was that it appeared to be carved into a still-living, colossal tree. The city of Emerald Arbor had sprung up around the spire throughout its long history. The Maiden never cared to call it home—but she loved to visit from her home in the countryside.

To the Maiden, Emerald Arbor was a good city filled with good people. She had not met a bitter soul among them in her years here. The city guard ensured that any who brought harm to others were swiftly escorted to the subterranean dungeons of the Deep Briars. There were alleys to be avoided, this was true, and unseemly districts not to tarry about in, but they were few. Though, as of late, some streets seemed to bear larger shadows.

Today, the city was particularly alight. Every knight in the realm was there to attend a tournament to be held later in the afternoon. Multiple skills would be tested: swordplay, archery, and the joust. It was all there. The Maiden looked forward to seeing them in their armor and livery of varying colors, jockeying for superiority. It was all mock combat, but once in a while a competitor would feel slighted and a duel may take place. No lethal combat was allowed, but, the Maiden had to admit, she found all of it quite thrilling.

The Maiden was content to casually walk the cobblestone paths of her favorite plaza. The orange and white goldfish of the largest fountain seemed to know that she brought crumbs. They swam to her en masse and bobbled in the water awaiting their meal.

She was anxiously anticipating the start of the tournament. As she often did when she became nervous, she hummed to herself the songs her mother used to lull her to sleep with. They were nursery rhymes mostly, but they had always soothed her, even now. The one that currently repeated itself in her mind was the refrain of *Sleep Little Light, Little Child*.

It was among her favorites and comforted her in life's

tougher moments. She swirled her fingers in the cool waters. The fish nipped at her lithe, lovely hands. She continued singing quietly to herself and listening to the soothing babble of the fountain, when she heard the heavy clop of horse's hooves. She looked up casually and her gentle, calming voice caught with a slight squeak.

As she looked up, an Emrallti knight was already halting his horse near her, its hooves clomping and the beast snorting impatiently. He was resplendent in his armor of steel engraved with a large, spreading oak tree—the symbol of the Emerald Realm. His armor was thoroughly polished, giving the steel a look of molten silver. She noted that despite the brilliant sheen, his armor was marred by scratches and pockmarks that could not be removed by simply polishing. These could have been removed by any armorsmith—why did they yet remain?

"Such an odd habit," he said.

When the Maiden looked up at him, he smiled to hide his surprise. This girl in commoner's garb had the bearing and beauty of royalty—a queen in a commoner's dress. Her auburn hair fell freely around her graceful neck and shoulders. Her eyes were as blue as the great sapphire of their neighbors to the north and he fancied they could match it in size. One could have plucked the very blossoms from the trees and they would feel withered and frail compared to her lips.

When she realized he was joking and that she might have just made them both look foolish, the Maiden hung her head timidly and looked back to the pond.

"What would that be, sir?"

The Knight regained his senses and realized he might have appeared rude. He smiled at her again in reassurance.

"Serenading the fish," he said with a laugh. "Might I ask if they sing back?"

She smirked and continued to look into the pool.

"Wouldn't that be interesting? It's just a cradlesong—one my mother would sing to me. You're competing today, I assume?"

He nodded humbly. "Yes. Any knight worth his armor competes."

She smiled and reached out to his lovely brown stallion to pet it gently on the nose. It snorted contentedly. She had always wanted a horse to call her own but her family could never afford more than their old mule.

"Will you be at the games, my lady?" the knight asked.

"I will—I greatly look forward to it each time," she replied, smiling up at him.

The Knight patted his horse, which was adorned with the trappings of his station. Small green and gold Emerald Arbor pennons fluttered about the animal. This knight served the King of Emrallt, himself. He removed one pennon—a deep green triangular piece of cloth with a silver oak tree emblazoned upon it.

To her surprise, the Knight offered it to her. The Maiden, her mouth unknowingly agape, slowly accepted the gift from his hand. She looked up at him, shocked.

"Will you cheer for me?" he asked, seeing the look of gratitude sparkling in those sapphire eyes.

"Of course—thank you," she said, practically beaming.

"My lady," the Knight concluded with a gentle nod.

He bade his horse forward and trotted away in the direction of the tournament grounds. The Maiden was struck with awe and wonder at her luck. He was certainly handsome, and in his armor, he looked invincible. She certainly hoped he would emerge the victor today.

The Maiden looked at the Knight's token. It was a simple, but beautiful, gift. It was finely crafted. The cloth was exquisite; only silk would feel better to the touch. She would keep it with her always—perhaps it would bring good fortune.

2

THE EMERALD SPIRE

The few hours until the games passed quickly after her meeting with the knight. She could hear the bustle of the tournament grounds growing and made her way there. The people voiced their excitement and it buzzed about the crowd. The Maiden found a place near one of the seating areas that she could climb upon and watch—the seats themselves were full and she could not find a place even for her small frame to fit.

She looked about and saw all of the knights gathered together near a particular area. Only the knights were allowed to compete and, despite the occasional bruised ego, the competition and rivalry was part of the camaraderie of the group. They were the realm's best, after all, and served a single purpose—to protect the royal family.

She recognized her knight among them, as they had not yet donned their helmets. As fate would have it he happened to look over her way. She smiled and waved at him, his token in her hand. He noticed and returned her greeting. Then a man in official-looking attire approached the knights and they all turned to listen. After speaking with them for a moment, they departed to make final preparations for the games.

Trumpets sounded, signaling the start of the tournament and the people cheered even louder, building to a great roar of anticipation. The same gentleman who had spoken to the knights stepped upon a podium near a guarded section of seating flanked by armed men in breastplates and kettle helmets. Here the king and queen took their seats along with family and honored guests, surrounded by heraldry and banners of all kinds.

The gentleman raised his hands to calm the crowd which, after a few moments, eventually quieted enough for him to speak.

"My lords and ladies, I am honored to present Their Majesties King Brennen and Queen Alma of Emrallt, the Emerald Realm, and their guest of honor, the Prince of Avallonis, of the Sapphire Realm."

The Prince turned and bowed graciously to the king and queen, and the people cheered again. When he had turned back to the audience, they all quieted.

"And now, let us begin the games," he said with enthusiasm, to which everyone responded with more cheers.

He introduced the first two riders. They appeared similar to the Maiden's knight but still different. They were both from Emrallt, so their horses were adorned with unique patterns on the banners to differentiate them. The knights' armor was the same, however; pure polished steel that must have reflected the light of the sun into their enemy's eyes. Matching green surcoats covered chainmail underneath.

They carried their greatest weapon used when in battle—a lance nearly ten feet in length. It was a blunted tournament lance but was no less intimidating. The Emrallti knights had used them in past battles which had led to a common epithet for them among other realms—Emerald Lancers. Each realm had its own knights to protect their king and lead the way in battle, and these were the best of those belonging to the Emerald Spire.

The two knights worked their horses into a frenzy. At the mark, the two charged one another on opposite sides of a partition. They held their shields protectively and aimed their lances in hope of striking the opposing rider to the dirt.

At the height of their charge, the two met—lance to shield. After an explosion of shattered lances and shouts from the crowd, both yet remained seated. However, one was more visibly affected by the blow. He lurched in his seat, seeming for a brief moment as though he may tumble to the ground. He gripped the front of his saddle, stretched his neck from side to side, and trotted his horse back to his squire—all to mixed boos and cheers from the crowd.

The knights readied themselves for a second charge. Both lances broke again, but this time, one of the knights was thrown from his horse. To the shock of the crowd, it was not the knight who had suffered the previous blow. The winner of the match raised what remained of his lance into the air and shook it victoriously. The fallen knight was helped to his feet and he shook his head in disappointment as he departed in defeat.

During the second bout, the Maiden cast a glance to the king's stand. She was curious about the Prince from the northern realm of Avallonis, as many common folk were. He was younger than the Knight but still older than herself. He held his head high in royal fashion, though he did not have the look of one who was self-righteous or conceited. Judging by the stern weight in his eyes—of sadness or not, she couldn't say—he seemed to be trying too hard to look like a royal visitor. Though, he did appear to be genuinely interested in the games.

Her eyes must have lingered too long, for he caught her looking his way and smiled at her before she could turn back to the knights. She felt herself blushing and looked away to focus on the games.

The next contenders strode to their starting positions. She recognized the Knight among them—the pennon he had given was missing from among the others. He sat stoically awaiting the call to charge. She waved and shouted for him amidst the cheering crowd. He noticed and lifted his lance in salute to her.

The knights charged one another. Their horses raced forward and kicked up dirt and hay into the air. In but a few thundering moments they were upon one another. The sound of shattered lances cracked the air once again. A large man moved in front of the Maiden and blocked her view. A gasp from the crowd had her tip-toeing and twisting to see around the large-framed man before her. She climbed a little higher, fearing to see her Knight unseated and being helped to his feet.

Instead, she saw him on the back of his horse hefting his lance victoriously. He had knocked the other rider from his horse and won the match in a single charge. The crowd began cheering and she joined them.

It was a magnificent day.

3

ALLEY RATS

The Maiden heard the clanging of bells in the distance. The city's clocktower was signaling the late afternoon. She sighed inwardly and desperately longed to stay for the remainder of the games. However, her family would be waiting for her to finish her other duties about the house and garden. They would also need what coin she made for her day's work selling her wares.

Before departing the tournament grounds, the Maiden noticed that the Prince was absent from his seat next to the king and queen. Oddly enough, the royal family was still present—she assumed they would accompany the Prince wherever he went; he being a royal guest.

She thought little else of it—royal problems for royal people—and decided to make her way home. She walked quickly through the empty streets, most townsfolk attending the games, and took the swiftest way she knew through the city.

Upon turning a corner on the edge of the markets she stumbled onto a peculiar sight. Two cloaked figures were looking into the windows of a shop. The Maiden glanced about her and saw no one was nearby. She felt she should leave the situation be, but these could also be nothing more than hungry children, judging by their size. She had sold many of her trinkets and other items that day and could spare some coin for them.

"Hi, there..." she called out hesitantly.

The two figures spun around to see her and she caught her breath. They were ratlings—she saw their wrinkled snouts and irregular, yellowed teeth that stuck out like ugly thorns from their mouths. They began yelling in a guttural, chittering language and chased after her.

She cried out and began to run, hearing the rapid pattering of clawed little feet behind her. One of them darted up and along a wall with great agility, digging their claws into the rough stone and wood of the houses and shops to cut off her escape. She turned and found the other way blocked as well. The two of them approached her slowly, cornering the Maiden against two adjacent buildings.

She knew better than to call for help. The city was all but closed down due to the tournament and none would hear her. The small, ugly, and vicious little things stalked toward her—whispering to each other. Their faces were a cruel amalgam of rodent and human, with a long, blunt snout attached to a sloping forehead and large, black eyes. She saw the scars on their faces crumple as they sneered at her. One of them watched her with a blind, milky-white eye.

Their noses stretched out to her and twitched quickly as they smelled her. She could see long, thin whiskers near their nostrils. They looked at each other and spoke in their language again—a wretched piping of squeaks and growls. She could not understand them and it only worsened her fear. She could smell them from where she was standing—a sour odor that she couldn't tell was from sweat or sewer or both. The air stood still and all was quiet about her. She felt if she were to yell for help that the sudden noise would quite possibly startle them enough for her to escape.

Before she could even take a breath one of them spoke to her.

"Y—you make flower scents," it said in a gravelly, broken tone. She nodded her head.

"Yes—yes I do," she answered meekly.

She saw a hand—fur-covered, bony, with sharp, dirty claws— reach out to her.

"Give," it said sharply. "Give, and we let you go."

She saw the half-blind one shoulder its way past the other and draw a rusty dagger from beneath its dingy black robes.

"Now," it hissed.

The Maiden quickly searched her person for any scents or trinkets she may have left. Her heart sunk when she could find nothing. She had sold them all. Her good fortune seemed to be turning.

When she stopped looking so frantically the two ratlings sneered. The half-blind one grabbed her dress and yanked her forward. It sniffed her again.

"I make pretty face not so pretty, maybe?" he threatened, raising the knife.

"I have gold," she offered, "I sold all my scents—but you can have the gold," she said, remembering her profits for the day.

The one that held the knife curled its lips at the offer then seemed to ease its grasp. The other shoved him violently.

"Fool, stupid! Moss Blossom want the scents!" it said.

The Maiden assumed that the other one was referring to itself when it mentioned the name "Moss Blossom". She also noted that Moss Blossom was more slender, had a higher-pitched voice, and wore several earrings made of copper and tin. Moss Blossom was a female.

"Moss Blossom…" the Maiden muttered.

The slender ratling looked over, bared her hideous teeth, and sniffed derisively at her. The Maiden opened her hands and showed the ratlings the small number of gold and silver coins she had earned for her work.

The half-blind one seemed particularly interested. His good eye opened wide and he began to take the money. Moss Blossom snarled and slapped him.

"We get coin—Moss Blossom want scents!" she shrieked.

She took the rusty knife that now lay on the ground, sneering at her partner who was groaning and holding his face. Moss Blossom then began to make her way back to the Maiden.

"You no give—I take," Moss Blossom snarled.

In the flicker of an eyelash, a large rock struck Moss Blossom in the head. She squealed and fell to the ground, clutching where the rock had hit her. The Maiden looked up to see a slightly familiar face approaching them quickly—the Prince of Avallonis was approaching with his sword drawn.

He walked to the ratlings and pointed his sword at Moss Blossom.

"Do you know what this is?" he demanded of them.

Moss Blossom looked up and saw the tip of the blade pointed directly at her head. "Sh-sharp..." she stuttered.

"Yes," the Prince replied, "very sharp."

The Prince saw the male rising to its feet, but still nursing his swollen face. He then shot Moss Blossom a fearsome look.

"Leave—before I have you locked in the Deep Briars," the Prince threatened.

The two ratlings ran away without protest and were gone quickly—scurrying swiftly into the small space between two buildings.

The Prince approached the Maiden and looked her over, trying to see if she was wounded. She attempted to straighten her dress and get the dirt and grime from it. It was of little use—it would have to be washed, but she was still quite embarrassed.

"Thank you, m'lord," the Maiden said, clumsily.

He smiled warmly at her. "What are you doing out here, miss? I'm not overly familiar with Emerald Arbor, but it would seem to me there are much better districts to shop in."

She blushed in shame. "I thought it was a shortcut—I'm making my way home."

The Prince gave her a reproachful look, although it quickly became apparent it was in jest. He then retrieved a small blade from his boot and offered it to her along with its small leather sheath.

"Majesty, this—this is a fine gift. I can't—" she began, but the Prince interrupted her before she could protest further.

"I insist," he said. "I may not be able to escort you home, but I can help you get there a little more safely—and just as quickly as any shortcut."

Escort— yes, where was his escort?

"Your Grace, if I may ask— where is your guard?"

He smirked and look over his shoulders.

"I ducked them," he chuckled. "They're probably quite upset. But, I wanted some time to myself. Good thing, right?" he said with raised eyebrows.

He led her in the direction from whence he'd come and she saw his horse there, waiting.

"I heard the little beasts making their threats. I dismounted here. Didn't want them making any rash decisions."

"Your escort still hasn't found your horse, it seems."

"No, I'm sure I'll find them first," he smiled. "Not until I see you safely on your way past the city gates, however. I don't want… whatever those things were… to find you again."

"Ratlings," the Maiden clarified.

"Ratlings?" he returned in confusion. "We must not have them in Avallonis."

"Likely not," the Maiden returned. "Emrallt is quite large, the largest of the seven realms. They have plenty of forests to call home, though they do tend to love the city. Most times I actually pity them. They live in such poverty and squalor. Wicked little things they may be, but…"

The Prince heard genuine empathy in her voice, but he didn't share it. The creatures had not only waylaid her; they had attempted to rob her and were possibly prepared to maim or even kill her.

"They seem to bring much misfortune on themselves," the Prince said, matter-of-factly.

"Perhaps they wouldn't if misfortune was not all they have known," she suggested.

The Prince smiled at her pressing will and insight. "You are quite sympathetic to their plight."

"Well, yes, m'lord," she said. "I'm not unfamiliar with what it feels like to... well, I can understand their situation.

4

A PRINCELY GIFT

The Prince and the Maiden walked the last part of the day together. Well, the Prince walked. He insisted she ride his horse while they perused the city. He escorted her amongst the deserted markets and gardens of the city. They both shared interesting stories and bits of history about the grand courtyards and monuments.

"How do you know so much of a foreign city?" she asked at one point.

The Prince shrugged. "My family has long been close with the Emrallt monarchy. We visit this place fairly often. I came alone this time."

The Maiden noticed the Prince was quite dour when mentioning his lone visit. She attempted to cheer him the only way she knew. She asked that he stop the horse and he escorted her down. They were in a garden, amid a grand variety of blossoms, and the Maiden went to the shrubberies and small trees and picked a small assortment of blooms and pollen. She crushed them in her hands and brought them to the Prince.

"Here, smell," she said, lifting her hands to him.

He breathed in carefully at first, then deeply as the sweet

scent filled his nostrils. A tingly spice followed and was then complemented by a lingering medley that set his senses alight.

"It's amazing…" he said, looking at the colorful potpourri she held. "Where did you learn this?"

The Maiden smiled, "My grandmother. She could work miracles with flowers and pollen.

"Apparently so."

The Maiden plucked a tube-shaped flower from a yellow-and-purple bush.

"Now, it may seem odd, but here… eat this," she said matter-of-factly.

"Eat it?" the Prince asked with a raised eyebrow and slight grimace.

"Yes," she chuckled.

The Prince did as instructed and was surprised at how potent the taste of the flower was. A touch of nectar was in the white flower that danced on his tongue like syrup.

"Are you an alchemist?" he asked sincerely.

She blushed and laughed.

"No, not at all. Sugar, tea, apples; these are all plants, are they not? You just have to know where to look."

"My lady, you are quite a surprise."

"Thank you, Your Grace," she replied with a courteous nod.

She looked to the hills and saw that the sun was balanced just on top, looking as if it were prepared to teeter and fall off either side. She had become distracted with the Prince, and it was truly time for her to leave for home. She apologized to him and expressed a great desire to stay in his company, but her obligations pressed her home. The Prince politely bowed his head.

"Of course."

He helped her atop the horse and, the gentleman that he was, took the reins and walked beside them leading the horse along the way. He told the Maiden he would take her to the edge of town, and she could continue from there. The king and queen may take offense if he were absent much longer.

The Maiden voiced her gratitude and understanding and the Prince made sure before departing that she still had the dagger he'd given her. She folded it into her clothing near the waist to carry, tucked safely in its fine sheath.

"Keep it with you always. I have my guards, but I don't like in the least the idea of leaving you alone to journey home. There are dangerous things in those woods, my lady. Hurry home, and may you travel safely."

The Maiden thanked him for his graciousness and dismounted from his horse. He bade her farewell and kissed her hand gently. She smiled back at him, her blue eyes sparkling. It reminded him of home.

She cast one look back over her shoulder, just to make sure all of this was real. His features were darker than the Knight's. He didn't appear royal, she thought. With his close-cropped hair and amber eyes he had the look of some smith from Vitruvia, a kingdom known for their technology and, of course, the Amber Spire. His eyes were kind, if shadowed, and marred by something he hadn't shared with her.

She had read many stories and tales of sheltered royalty and spoiled princes and princesses. He was quite the opposite—noble, gentlemanly, brave, and just a little bit brash. She still couldn't help but feel a pang of sorrow for the ratlings despite their heinous actions.

The Maiden heard the cheers of the final rounds of the tournament echo among the mostly empty streets. Her Knight was there winning glory and gold—she was sure of it. She smiled, wishing she could see the finale, but her obligations drew her home. It would be several hours to walk at a brisk pace to be home by nightfall at this point.

5

OF CRUEL AND WICKED THINGS

Septer held lands and creatures of immeasurable wonder and beauty, but also contained its share of truly evil things lurking in its depths and shadows. Their ambitions and agendas were varied in scope and grandeur, but they were all sinister and cruel. Books upon books and scrolls in between had been written on the dangerous and mythical things lurking among the thickest woodlands.

The great villains skulked and brooded within their domain of choice. Some feasted in great halls among kings and royalty—whispering their schemes into impressionable ears and pulling strings among the unwary. Others were plotting destruction and chaos in inhospitable places avoided by the common folk.

The worst malefactor, however, called no single place home. True, his favorite lair rested atop an ancient overgrown temple deep in the forests of the Emerald Realm, but he kept many other places to rest and scheme throughout the territory of his unsuspecting kin—against their wishes, of course. This only mattered if they knew of it. Which, he was sure they didn't.

Wyvern had many underlings to carry out his orders. Ratlings, trolls, and even the short, typically good-natured elves could be counted among his minions. He chose those who were eager and capable, but manageable. They knew that his favor brought trinkets and baubles of notable worth, while his wrath was meted out with tooth, claw and fire.

It was an open secret that he preferred feasting on those who failed him—and he never went hungry. Among the wicked and cruel, he was king. Many a knight and slayer had sought to claim his hide, for as long as memory could reach. None had yet been successful. Thankfully, the people of Emrallt rarely ran afoul of Wyvern's whims.

On this very day of the tournament, he sat atop his temple pondering his recent and most ambitious endeavor. For Wyvern, life was easily manipulated; not unlike a long, thorough game of chess—pawns to be moved, sacrificed if need be; kings and queens to be hindered by bishops; front lines to be fortified by rooks; knights to be thrown into battle to shed blood for some noble cause. His clawed hand moving these unknowing and ignorant pieces.

Wyvern thumped his tail in anticipation. He flicked a few bones and rocks from his perch—his current unenviable throne—while waiting for news from two of his more pitiable minions. He huffed in impatience and watched as two tendrils of smoke curled from his nostrils. His sharp ears then heard the pattering of multiple small, padded feet scurrying in his direction.

He flexed his haunches and launched himself into a dense thicket of ancient trees and vines. Though his actions were sudden and Wyvern was no small beast, he was swift and quiet as a thought. He entered his chosen spot to observe who exactly was arriving.

Two small creatures came running recklessly into his crumbling sanctum that was slowly being reclaimed by time and nature. They were small, filthy, and wore cloaks and clothing that were caked with grime.

The ratlings turned about; their twitching snouts lifted in the air as they sniffed about for him. Wyvern did not wish to be found, so he would not be. He needed a moment to prepare his patience to deal with these sycophants. He had many of their kind scouring Emerald Arbor for useful information, particularly about the Maiden. This was the only way they proved useful and that he managed to tolerate them. Were it not for him they would have been dead long ago. Vargr wolves—a larger, more ferocious breed of wolves native to the Emerald Realm—ogres, or even pythons would have feasted on them by now. However, there was use to be found in these small, miserable, and undesirable creatures. They made perfect spies among the humans and their city surrounding the Emerald Spire.

As they continued their fruitless search about his grounds, Wyvern silently removed himself from his hidden roost. He deftly climbed back upon his uppermost rest and looked down upon them.

"You found something," his voice rumbled as though it came from the bowels of the world, "Or you had better. Evening approaches and I have not yet fed," he growled menacingly.

Startled at his sudden appearance, the two miserable creatures shrieked and turned to see him looking down upon them like a snake does its prey.

"White-eye, Moss Blossom—speak!" Wyvern shouted. His patience was thin on an empty stomach.

Moss Blossom shouldered White-eye forward, forcing him to explain the events. Wyvern sat unmoving awaiting their news.

"We... uh..." White-eye began, stuttering. "We find pretty lady. She at big tree-city. Shiny... uh... shiny green stone on top..."

Wyvern's eyes squinted and flared. His throat rumbled in rising aggravation. The ratlings recoiled in fear and White-eye began quickly stammering an explanation.

"We had pretty lady! She find us, we use sharp metal but strong man come, important man in blue clothes, and points big sharp metal at us—we... I... we had to run, no choice... no choice..." his voice becoming more shrill with his rising panic.

Wyvern recognized their broken language and knew that White-eye spoke of more than just a town guard or good-natured passerby. Ratlings cared little for the difference between common humans, merchants, and even nobility. It was only a difference in what goods they could pilfer; however, when a ratling described one as 'important,' that often meant 'royalty'.

"The important man—what did he look like?" Wyvern asked.

The two deplorable rodents looked up at him in confusion. They looked through arms held in front of their faces as if to ward off a pending strike. Wyvern leaned forward on his forelimbs.

"You said he was 'important.' He wore blue clothes. What did he look like? Face, hair—*what?*" he growled with small tongues of fire licking around his teeth.

"Also pretty, like lady!" Moss Blossom squealed. "Nice clothes! Long blue vest with another tower—different shiny stone, blue shiny stone..."

Wyvern growled in frustration. The Blue Prince of Avallonis. The little fop could bring Wyvern no end of misery; an army's worth of misery to be exact. Especially if he had his sights set on the Maiden.

"He threatened you?" Wyvern asked of them.

"Y-yes, with sharp metal. He threaten blood," White-eye answered. Moss Blossom nodded her head vigorously in agreement.

"Indeed, you had no choice but to flee," Wyvern said. "But, rules are rules..." he added with menace.

The ratlings shrieked in terror, but Wyvern had decided, and it was time to feed. It was over quickly. The ratlings were quick, but Wyvern knew their behavior, their mannerisms, and what they would do when panicked. In truth, he detested having to eat them. They were filthy and lean—like starving fish. It did little to satiate his hunger, but he could hunt later.

For the time being, he needed to remind himself of why he risked his life for this girl. She was a waif, a human, and utterly without importance save for precious gift, and it was this gift that Wyvern coveted.

He skulked into and loitered about his trophy room filled with the rarest of rarities. Hung on a wall were the well-preserved antlers of a white stag—only seen once every hundred years and only in the forests of Emrallt.

Set upon a pedestal of gold and diamonds was the Eye of Jotun—Lord of the Ogres. Wyvern had to slay the great brute personally to claim this prize. His eye was the size of a water-melon, and upon the giant's demise, it turned into pure crystal and his green iris changed into a magnificent jade captured just below the crystal's surface. Calling it priceless would be a cheap estimate, but it was valuable for more than its physical proper-ties. It held hidden magics that even Wyvern was so far unable to unlock.

Hung above a roaring fireplace was the Neverdim Blade, which once belonged to Sellum the Silverborn; a knight who many said was not the child of man and woman but sprung from the very core of the world and was made of the pure metal of his namesake. Wyvern never believed such stories. The Silverborn Knight was shown his mortality when Wyvern cast him upon the rocks of a distant mountain and took his prized weapon—which could not be dulled and always reflected light in even the harshest darkness.

Resting on a shelf in the room was a small, unassuming jar that flickered with lightning and fire. This was an artifact of Wyvern's own doing—the Din of Hamner's Bane. Wyvern learned of a powerful creature that lived among the fiery depths of a volcanic mountain in the Ruby Realm. Hamner caused one of his kin incredible unease as it was a powerful, immense being of fire, metal, and stone, and lived without fear in the realm of Wyrm—Wyvern's eldest brother. Hamner's forging caused the quakes and fires in the mountain, and this power alone resulted in Wyvern wanting a piece of it. That it earned his brother's ire only made it more desirable. Wyvern won a wager against Hamner that resulted in his acquiring a mote of the destruction that Hamner's knells wrought. It looked merely tantalizing in the jar, but if opened, would easily destroy Wyvern's temple grounds and possibly miles of the surrounding forest.

Among Wyvern's other trinkets were the petrified wood of an Ent, a birdcage full of Pyremoth fairies, the remainder of the mast of the Valiant, the former flagship of the Gray King, a one-of-a-kind suit of armor fashioned from mirrors, the final cask of a millennium-old wine, the ashes of a phoenix, sealed to inhibit the creature's rebirth, and the bones of an extinct sphinx.

His final stop was to peer within a crystal mirror hung upon the wall. It was framed in platinum and diamonds and was also a great relic to behold. When he looked into the mirror he didn't see himself, but a swirling mist and fog. In the mist was the silhouette of a cloaked and crowned being.

"And how are we today?" Wyvern asked darkly.

The figure rushed toward Wyvern and began banging its fists on the crystal. No form or face could be seen, but it was clear the figure was angry. Wyvern chuckled and went amongst his treasures as though he were taking account of them all.

Wyvern neither possessed nor craved the mountains of gold and gems that his kin favored; no, he craved the rare, the powerful, and the unique. He used these things to gain power or to exhibit the power he already had. Indeed, word had been spreading that he might truly be the cause of the extinction of the majestic sphinxes.

All of this, and it would amount to nothing without his grandest prize: the Maiden.

She had a magnificent gift; one that he didn't yet fully understand. He wanted to understand it. He wanted to study it, to profit from it, to have it.

It—it! He knew not what to call the splendid capability she harnessed. And she knew nothing of *it*. The desire, the overwhelming covetous urge that crawled beneath his scales and writhed in his skin; the jealousy that pricked his heart and the envy that poisoned his soul! Oh, to have it! He would claw it out of her very body if he could!

This was what maddened him the most. His cunning and wits would have to win this challenge for him. These traits turned many trials in his favor before, and would have to do so again. Though even to utilize his wit would require action and his mind grew dull with calculating and conspiring. He left his lair of treasures and launched himself into the sky.

He flew high enough to stay out of sight of onlookers, but low enough to avoid any passing griffon patrols from Avallonis or, even worse, the meddling of his brother Drake, Lord of the Clouds. He glided lazily as he looked down upon the roving hills and forests of the Emerald Realm. He could see the spire even at this distance. It was a splinter on the horizon, but he knew the dangers of approaching too closely and too brazenly. The Green Wizard would be a formidable threat and Wyvern's magic, though strong, could not match a master practitioner of the art.

His minions had informed him of the location of the Maiden's family home. He had managed a trip or two between his hurried flights to stop and observe. It was a defenseless peasant's hovel and not one to be concerned with. The fulfillment of his schemes was a matter of timing—this would be a simple thread in the tapestry of his genius.

According to his information, the Maiden would be returning home soon. It was time to nudge things along—simple positioning of pawns now. Nothing too big or boisterous, but enough of a gesture to continue the game.

Wyvern landed on a grassy slope and made his way to the

Maiden's home. The animals would smell his presence and alert the farmer and his wife so he would have to be quick. He snuck up on the house on all fours, appropriately serpent-like, and as sure as he had predicted, the animals began shrieking in fright in their pens and coops.

The farmer's wife was chopping vegetables at a counter when the commotion started. Her husband left his current chore by the fireplace and began to make his way to the door. His axe was not a weapon of war, but it would make quick work of any thieving predator that came after his livestock.

"Careful, dear—a fox is no matter, but a wolf, or bear, or—" Her lovingly chiding words stopped when she turned back and saw, looking back at her through her window, two fiery cat-like eyes staring back at her.

In her fright, she dropped the large clay bowl that she had been holding. It shattered upon the floor, causing the farmer to suddenly turn. Unfortunately, she didn't have time to scream and the farmer had not yet reached his axe.

6

WYVERN'S GREED

The Maiden enjoyed her walk home. The wind was cool and leaves flippantly whispered the events of the day back to her. She found herself smiling as she looked at the tokens bestowed upon her by the Knight and Prince. They were beautiful, each in their own right—the lovely pennon from the Knight's trappings and the Prince's sleek, steel dagger. Using one to shelter the other, they were worth more than her life's earnings.

She would never sell them, though. Not for the Diamond Spire itself. Her father never did like her traveling alone and without a weapon. "One day we will get a dog that could accompany her," her mother had added.

"Or perhaps a young man?" her father would say, adding to her embarrassment.

The Maiden would not turn away the affections of a good and kind man, but she enjoyed life and all its musings for now. She loved harvesting the wild fruits of the forest and helping her mother cook meals that, though humble and barely enough for the three of them, would satisfy the tastes of a king with their flavor and aroma.

She helped her father with chores such as milking the cows, feeding the goats, chopping wood, and sowing the garden. She never had the heart for skinning and cutting the meat of the animals—she knew it was necessary, but often found ways to avoid the task and offered to help in other ways. It was not fear of blood or some such thing that drove her from these duties, but empathy for life. She always had a tender heart for the living— human and animal both. Even the menacing ratlings. Life was so readily taken for granted; she had long ago decided to recognize its precious and fragile beauty.

Her chores awaited her when she arrived home. It was hard work to keep their farmstead in order. She did all she could to help her dear mother and father. The coin she brought from the markets was her contribution.

As she neared her home she expected the smell of dinner to drift on the air. The warm odor of bread should meet her as she walked over the hill along with the sound of her father working away nearby.

Instead, she heard only silence. No homely smells greeted her. No calls of lazy animals or the sounds of her father chopping wood or repairing their home. The quiet was the most disturbing —not even birds sang in the trees. There was only stillness and shadow. The evening was approaching quickly and seemed to be encroaching upon the small farm amid the hills even swifter than usual. Something was not right and her spirit was ill at ease.

Her parents' cottage came into sight. There was nothing to be seen. The animals were gone. Her parents were gone. She ran as quickly as a spooked deer to her house. Half-skipping down the hillside and once nearly stumbling flat on her face.

When she reached her home, she saw no lights were lit within. She entered with the Prince's dagger drawn.

Dishes, chairs, and other items were broken and strewn about the house. Her father's axe was embedded in one of the walls.

Their oak table, which belonged to her great-grandfather when he first built their home, was overturned and a leg was broken.

A tear fell down her cheek—the Maiden was heartbroken. Her family, her home, was demolished and destitute. She knew not where they were, if they were safe, or even if they were alive. She fell to her knees then sat back to observe the carnage silently and tearfully. What was she to do now?

"Quite sad, to find such a state of things," a deep voice said.

The Maiden startled and turned. She instinctively began backing away as she beheld a creature looking in at her from the open doorway.

At first, she thought a massive viper had made its way to her home, but then she saw the angular head and long neck was attached to a slender, serpentine body. Its forelegs were smaller than its hind legs and ended in five-fingered, clawed hands. The hind legs were powerful and muscular with large, sharp talons. Large wings folded perfectly to its figure. She finally saw the long, prehensile tail flicking behind the beast that ended in a wicked-looking stinger as long as her forearm.

"What—what are you?" the Maiden asked through tear-filled eyes.

"What?" the draconic creature asked without insult. Its yellow-and-red eyes, glowing like brimstone, observed her intelligently. "Who, lass—I am Wyvern."

"I..." she stuttered as she choked back her fear. As the creature spoke she could see its fang-filled maw and the forked tongue within. "I am—"

"I don't need your name," Wyvern interrupted.

He squeezed his lithe body through the massive hole where her front door used to be. He fit what portion of himself he could within the small home; his neck and head rising through the roof and wall, collapsing a portion and making room for himself. She cowered as boards and stone fell perilously close to her. He came to rest next to the Maiden and made himself as comfortable as possible.

"Then—what are you doing here?" the Maiden asked, her voice shaking. "Are you—did you do this?"

"Why would you ask such an awful question?" Wyvern sounded hurt. He looked at her through squinted eyes and thumped his tail.

He lifted his tail and used the blunt side of his stinger to wipe a tear from her eyes. The sharp tip glistened dangerously as it slid past her eyes along her cheek.

"What would I gain from harming such a beautiful treasure?" he hissed.

She didn't believe this foul creature, but what could she do but keep it talking until she could think of an escape?

"What are you?"

"A better question would be: can you help me?" Wyvern added cryptically.

"I don't understand."

"Of course," he began, "you have something that could help me greatly. Something that I want."

His eyes burned as he spoke; his nostrils flared and an acrid-smelling smoke curled from them. He bared his teeth. The Maiden was beginning to feel the cold fear grip her again and she began looking about desperately to seek a means of escape. It was then she noticed a large set of claw marks on one end of her home. They were large gouges made from a clawed five-fingered hand. Something dark stained the stone and wood around the gashes. She noticed more blood, now, following the grisly marks made by this beast.

Her lips quivered, and fear was replaced by grief and anger. "What do you want?"

The draconic creature stared back at her with fiery, knowing eyes. It hissed and its tail hovered over her with its stinger brought forth to strike.

The Maiden grabbed the dagger. She wouldn't let this thing get the better of her. She revered life, but this *thing...* it was naught but death. Death, destruction, and misery given scales of blood and eyes of fire.

"Do not press my patience," Wyvern threatened. His eyes flicked to the pathetic, shiny little pin she held in her hand and then back to her.

She gripped the dagger tightly and swung out wildly with it—hoping to wound Wyvern. Her aim struck true and the dagger bit into Wyvern's flank. He yelped in pain and the Maiden turned to flee.

Wyvern used his tail to pull the dagger from his body and it dripped a precious drop of draconic blood onto the floor. He took the blade with a scaled hand and flung it away.

Lashing out at the Maiden, he was able to secure her with his tail. It wrapped around her like a coiling snake and she screamed at the thought of being crushed to death. She shouted for help out of fear and instinct. She knew that none were nearby who could hear her.

As Wyvern tightened his coil, he used the end of his tail to wrap around her lovely wrists and lift them in front of her. He then took her wrists in a clawed hand, freeing his tail.

"Lively—I would not have expected less. Perhaps more of a fight, though. You know nothing of your talents, do you?"

It dawned on him that she was utterly ignorant of who, or perhaps what, she was. Wyvern's eyes darted to the dagger that lay upon the ground.

"A small weapon to bring to bear against the likes of me; you're quite brave."

He then sneered and flicked his forked tongue at her.

"Squirming?" he scoffed. "It's beneath you."

The Maiden had been staring at Wyvern with the utmost scorn; but upon seeing that wicked stinger lifted before her, her eyes widened with fright, her pupils dilating.

"Yes…" Wyvern hissed sadistically. "That is the reaction I was seeking."

The stinger-tipped end of his tail flicked back and forth in front of her. He was mocking her prior bravery; enticing her dread. He finally stopped playing with his prey.

His eyes fixated on her, and she felt as though that fiery gaze was burning her as she watched. The Maiden desperately wanted to look away, but she feared more what Wyvern would do if she did not see it herself. She saw him lift his stinger in front of her threateningly.

He looked deep into her eyes. Fear widened the pupils, opened the soul. He hoped to see what it was she could offer him.

"I'm very old, you know," he began. "I've gathered treasures the likes no living thing has ever seen or could even imagine. And yet…" He trailed off, squinting and looking as though he were trying to pierce the veil of her being. A low, reverberating growl rumbled within him. She could feel it tremble in her own body. "I feel drawn to you. But I cannot for the life of me discern why. You possess something I must have, but I don't know what it is. It is *maddening*," he roared. The heat of his breath took her own away. He gnashed his teeth and flicked his stinger once again in front of her. She kicked defiantly, landing a blow to his tail and knocking the stinger momentarily out of the way.

"Careful now, not even a touch—my venom would surely kill such a fragile thing as you. I'll make you a deal. I'll put you down. If you so much as attempt to stand, I'll kill you. Unfortunately, it would have to be quick. Out of necessity."

He placed her, surprisingly gently, on the ground. She sat there, shoulders hunched and eyes burning with tears. She had never felt such hurt and anguish in her life, never thought herself capable of such anger. Perhaps, being so close to such a monster brought out the worst in her. Could it be that his evil was so consuming, it spilled over into any living thing nearby? She couldn't let it consume her. She would not let it.

The Maiden gasped. A quick, sharp pain jolted one of her hands. She looked down and saw that nearly half Wyvern's barbed stinger jutted through her hand. She had struck her palm sharply upon it, deciding it best that she die rather than give the wicked thing the pleasure of having whatever it was that he was searching for in her.

Then, she felt acutely dizzy. She knew she was still sitting on the ground. Wyvern had not moved her, she hadn't stood as she was fully at his mercy—but she felt as though she were listing back and forth.

Moments later, a powerful lethargy set in. Her eyes grew heavy and she felt herself falling into unconsciousness. Her last image was that of a determined, flaming gaze.

Wyvern felt the maiden fall limp within the grasp of his tail. He roared in agonized, impotent rage. He did not know the girl was so brash. How could he have known? What fool creation would actually impale itself upon his barb?

He hefted her with his tail intending on smashing her against the wall in fury, but he stopped; he listened. A light pounding, getting slower—fainter. She still felt warm. The sound he heard was that of her heart.

By all that was gracious—she was alive. She slumbered deeply. His venom had not killed her. He didn't know why and he had not time to ponder it.

He now had to take her to where he could keep watch over her. Study her. Unravel what it was she held that was so important. He propelled himself to flight from within the house. Its humble, thatched roof splintered easily against him. The Maiden was tucked safely under him; held firmly against his chest with his foreleg.

This was a glorious time. He would enjoy this flight. He did note the rippling of his scales with anxiety and the unknown potential of his new prize.

Wyvern's flight carried him swiftly back to his temple. He

soared over the fields and hills of Emrallt. He cast his evil shadow over the tail of the southern Veil Mountains that sheltered his temple from prying eyes.

He landed atop the temple, perching gracefully and crawling through a hole created by the ceiling falling through ages ago. Wyvern found a spot to lay the Maiden down safely for her to rest so he could ferret out the mystery of how her gift could be useful to him.

Setting measures in place to secure against her escape, Wyvern retired for the evening. He curled up in a room adjacent to the Maiden's. He faced the wall that separated him from his new prize.

Wyvern closed his eyes, confident in his plans, and allowed himself to rest. As he drifted off to sleep, he saw a soft pin of light in the dark behind his eyelids. Trying to open his eyes, fearing the impossible —that his haven had been found, Wyvern felt his eyes pressed closed. He couldn't open them. He growled in his sleep as the light swelled and took on a bluish hue.

Wyvern saw the Maiden's farm, recently destroyed. A great tree was growing from the ruins of the house. A human-shaped light in a blue crown stood between Wyvern and the tree. The figure held a sword of pure white light that hurt Wyvern to look upon.

The tree began to grow upward, shooting into the sky. The rich, brown bark became smooth, white marble. Wyvern saw the curving, natural shape of the tree become the stalwart Diamond Spire, located in another kingdom easily a hundred miles away, and a core piece in his grand plan.

Wyvern felt his muscles tense and realized he could stand. He lunged after the figure, feeling sudden, burning hate consuming him. The blue-crowned figure stood between Wyvern and his prize. When he came within striking distance of the figure, Wyvern stopped. A pang of fear struck him. This person, this thing, whatever it represented, could lay all his plans to waste.

Wyvern's eyes were drawn to the top of the spire, where a bright green glow radiated from within the upper alcoves. Wyvern looked back to the bluish-white figure as it raised its blade and swung at him.

Wyvern's eyes opened. His heart pounded furiously, anger and fear mingled in a sickening concoction that settled in his stomach. His eyes burned, his breaths came slow and heavy, and he stared at the wall where the Maiden lay unconscious. His treasure no longer felt as safe as he previously thought.

He was a dragon-child. He had a deeper connection to the old, arcane things of the world. This was no mere dream. It was a vision. Something, likely a person but as yet still unclear, was or would be standing between him and his victory.

The vision started at the Maiden's farmhouse. He'd just left that sad little place; just began his rest after a nonstop, exhausting flight. But, he would have to return. Whatever threatened his schemes would either be there now or within a short time. The Maiden wasn't going anywhere. He would be back. First, there was a matter of destiny to attend to.

7

FIRE AND SHADOW

That night was clear and without a single cloud to block the light of stars and moons. Though, oddly, there fell a gentle rain. Those who experienced it would hold witness to the strangeness of the event. As the rain fell upon them a supernatural melancholy overtook their senses. They felt a feeling of deep sorrow that could not be explained. Many of the populace's elders would attest, however, that this was a rare occurrence; albeit not without explanation.

The stars themselves were weeping.

Some tragedy had occurred that saddened the very soul of the world and they may never know what exactly it was. The heart of creation itself was mourning that night and all would share this grief. The haunting rain lasted through the night until dawn. Perhaps then the warmth of daybreak would ease such suffering and the celestial lights would rest their weary glow.

The Knight was subject to his own personal portent that evening. He had dreamt a peculiar dream; he felt himself flying over one of the many great forests of Emrallt. It was quite exhilarating initially. He saw the Emerald Spire in the distance; a great fatherly arbor ever watching, ever vigilant.

He then saw a quaint smallholding with various livestock slumbering and feeding amid their pastures and pens. He began falling quickly, as though a hand clutching him gently had suddenly loosed his person from its grip. After a painful crash onto the ground, his eyes opened groggily to see a twisted, shadowed figure prowling upon the house.

It was an evil thing of roiling shadow and flame that took serpentine form. As it passed the animals wailed and fell—their bodies falling to the ground that had become ash at their feet. They caught fire as the creature gently brushed against them.

What wickedness is this, that bear itself upon such an unsuspecting home? The Knight's altruism was stirred, and the coals of his ire stoked. It stirred him from his pained position—prostrate from the fall. He reached for his blade, but in its place was a charred, still smoldering branch of an unidentifiable tree.

The being had not yet seen him. It was peering through the window of the home like a predatory villain; a curious snake seeking out a victim. He cursed his lack of a weapon, but he would throttle the beast with his bare hands if it came to such.

He began to make his way to that roiling fiend of darkness and fire when he stopped cold in his tracks. He felt an unimaginable burning in his stomach—or was it his chest? He looked down to see that he bore no armor; only a tunic of leaves and vines. It was unlike anything he had seen before and certainly not suited to a knight in battle or even the simple clothes of common folk.

The burning originated from a gaping hole just below his ribcage. It was large enough to fit his fist in, and the brim of which was smoldering in flame. He gasped for air as smoke filled his lungs and poured from the wound. He looked up to see the fiendish shadow was now glaring at him. It had eyes of fire and a structure of bone visible beneath the oily smoke that formed its scales. Where its heart should have been was a pulsating void—deeper than black and more evil than the very core of doom.

It looked at him and he was unable to move. Try as he might he could not will his arms to swing, his legs to run, or his mouth to scream. The creature smiled with a maw full of wicked teeth of gold and silver. It echoed a sound that he believed to be laughter, though a hideous mockery of it.

Fire, blood, and death flashed before his eyes. Just as he felt teeth sinking into his skin, he saw the Maiden he had met by the pool. She was alive, but her eyes were closed and her skin paler than he remembered. She lay amid a grove of lilies, orchids, and sweet alyssum. She seemed at rest, but he knew that all was not right with her. Then the eyes of fire and shadow flashed before him.

He awoke in a cold sweat. Gripping his chest, he felt for the smoldering, smoking wound that yet burned beyond the night-mare. The Knight looked around his empty chambers. A gentle fire warmed his room. The heraldry of Emrallt and the Emerald Spire sat unmoving on his walls as not even the gentlest of winds blew. The sun was just beginning to break over the hills and all was quiet. He could smell the freshly fallen rain and feel the crisp moisture in the air.

He looked out his window to the city below—yet to awaken. It was eerily silent that morning. It seemed as though a solemn vigil was being kept by the land itself. His estate was only begin-ning to see the earliest of attendants milling about. He called for his squire, donned his armor, and instructed the young man to inform anyone seeking him that he had gone to see to a personal matter.

His horse seemed to sense his unease and bucked its feet at his arrival. It huffed in anticipation and the Knight placed a calming hand on its muzzle. He ran his hand through its graceful mane, placating it.

"We ride towards a perilous unknown, old friend," the Knight said to his long-time companion.

All knights in Emrallt raised their colts during their time as a squire to full growth before they could attain knighthood. The Knight's personal horse was well-fed, rigorously trained, and worth his weight in diamonds as far as he was concerned. The warhorse had fared better in battle than any number of knights or other warriors.

The Knight rode swiftly through the near-empty streets. The few passersby that saw him could barely even recall that it was an Emerald Knight that raced down the cobblestones. He was quickly reaching the borders of the city when another rider intercepted him.

The cloaked figure galloped in from a side street and cut him off from the road out of town. The Knight reined in his horse and the beast flung its forelegs into the air with a loud whinny. The other rider's mount did so as well, but the manner in which he stopped the Knight gave the notion that he knew the Knight would be there.

"Clear the way, rider!" the Knight commanded.

The cloaked rider's horse stepped about anxiously. The rider removed the heavy cowl from his head and revealed himself to be the Avallonian Prince.

"Majesty? What business have you at this hour and in this place?" the Knight asked respectfully, though his next question took a more stern tone. "Or, I might ask, with me?"

"I'm coming with you," the Prince stated plainly.

"Majesty, I must respectfully—"

"I hope you'll forgive my cryptic answer, but I simply must. I know where you're going," the Prince interrupted with a raised hand, but he spoke politely.

"How so?"

The Knight could see the hesitation on the Prince's face.

"How?" the Knight asked in a raised tone.

The Prince returned a reproachful glance. "A dream," he sighed.

The Prince waited for the Knight to break into riotous laughter, but instead, the Knight lifted his head, took a deep breath, and said, "Follow me. We can speak as we ride."

Taken aback by the Knight's understanding, the Prince nodded in agreement. Their horses carried them as quickly as their powerful legs could manage. The Knight saw that though the Prince wore a plain, unassuming cloak, his clothes were regal and stately but wrinkled. He, too, must have risen and dressed quickly before rushing out his door.

"You didn't scoff at my vision, or dream, or whatever it was. Nor did you press me for how I knew where to find you," the Prince shouted over the racing hoof beats.

"I had a strange dream, too," was all the Knight said.

The Prince tensed as he recalled the prior night's imaginings.

"A young woman? From yesterday's games?"

The Knight looked his way and nodded.

"I saw an armored figure—shining like silver sunlight, racing among the streets of Emrallt. I couldn't see a face because of how blinding the light was, but I knew it was you. I've never met you in my life—but I knew," the Prince acknowledged.

"What else?" the Knight urged his horse on.

"A road, leading to fire and death," the Prince said gravely.

The Knight looked over in his direction again. The Prince stared straight ahead.

"Yours?" the Knight dared ask.

The Prince pursed his lips and remained silent. He shook his head. "This is insane, isn't it?" he shouted. "Surely, we'll get to her, embarrass ourselves over a dream, and you'll return to Emerald Arbor and I to Avallonis and we'll never speak of this again?"

They knew, however, that it was not a dream. They both knew. It was an instinct. Something buried deep down that they couldn't ignore. These weren't dreams, but visions.

"I saw a small house—a farm with livestock. I know it's some-where in the West Wood, not far from Dunlop Burrows. You saw a road, did you see much else?" the Knight inquired.

The Prince nodded and urged his horse on. "Follow me!" he shouted.

They rode for near a half hour. The Maiden must live several hours walk from town; how she managed this consistently with no horse was quite a feat. They rode beyond hills and meadows. A few stray passersby turned quickly to watch the two as they thundered past.

As they neared the location, the Knight began to recognize some of the surroundings from his dream. They approached a small hill and, once they were atop it, looked down upon a dismal scene.

A portion of the house was still smoldering, though it stood mostly intact. Animals lay dead in their fields—torn and cut by vicious claws. Whatever had caused it was most likely responsible for the large hole left in the thatched roof and stone walls.

The Prince heard the sound of steel being drawn. He looked to see the Knight with his sword ready and his jaw set. The Knight gave the Prince a knowing look. A creeping dread worked its way into their bones like tendrils of morning mist wrapping around trees.

The Prince recognized this as the place from his dream as well, though there was a significant absence for which he was grateful. He dreaded the culmination of his vision, but he didn't believe it, at first. Now, here, in this dark place, he felt the inevitable stealing upon them. He turned to warn the Knight, to tell him what he saw, but before he could, the Knight commanded his horse toward the house.

The Prince shouted in protest to no avail. He drew his blade and followed after him. He muttered to himself about the fool-hardy actions the Knight was taking. He cursed himself for his hesitation. They knew nothing of what they were about to face— though he had a terrible idea.

They drew nearer to the house and there was naught to be heard but the faint crackling of small fires. It smelled of acrid, unnatural smoke. They entered the home and saw the inside was utterly sundered. Every inch was littered with broken pots, splintered chairs, a collapsed wooden beam, and a demolished table.

The Prince kicked through some of the debris for any sign of the cause of this destruction. He looked desperately for a sign of the Maiden. The Knight found a bloodied dagger with the symbol of Avallonis engraved upon the handle.

"Majesty," the Knight said, staring forlornly at the weapon.

The Prince, upon seeing the stained blade, roared in protest and kicked angrily at an already broken bowl—sending it crashing into the wall. He grabbed the blade from the Knight and inspected it much more closely.

"Was this something you gave her?" the Knight asked.

"Yes," the Prince answered. "I was concerned for her safety. I saved her from a pair of ratlings who were threatening her."

"Ratlings?" the Knight sounded intrigued at the mention of the filthy creatures.

"Yes. A male and a female. They were attempting to rob her, but they were taking their time," the Prince said with notable irritation at the memory.

The Knight looked about. He saw the large claw marks on the wall and recalled the poor livestock outside. He looked to the Prince and began to sheathe his blade.

"I may know where she is," the Knight said enthusiastically.

"What? Where?" the Prince was dubious.

"The Emerald Knights have been rooting out the ratlings this last year," the Knight explained as they made their way to their horses. "They've been quite aggressive since we've been pushing them out of the city and into the forests. They've been known to bribe troglodytes to do their heavy lifting," he added, looking to the livestock.

"And you know of a nest?"

The Prince assumed their communities were no different from common rats, though he could be wrong.

"Yes. Not far from here," the Knight began to mount his horse when a swift shadow passed overhead.

A seething voice spoke from behind them. "My, my...it appears I'm too late. I so wanted to clean up before guests arrived."

8

TOOTH AND CLAW

The Prince and the Knight turned to see a draconian creature perched atop what remained of the house. It looked at them with its smoldering eyes and both men felt a familiar pang from their shared dreams. A vision of shadow and flame burst into the Knight's head like a slap to the face, while the Prince saw smoke and death wrapped in burning bones that gripped his heart in dread and, if he were being honest, a moment of panic.

The Knight drew his sword and the Prince quickly followed. They approached the beast with caution; the Knight slowly flanking to his right, the Prince to the left. Wyvern watched them both without concern. His haughty eyes followed the Knight the most closely, and he inhaled deeply, puffing out his chest and showing them he had no fear of their little antics. He sat aloof on top of the ruined home.

"What have you done with this family?" the Knight demanded of Wyvern.

"I spared them a few despondent years in this hovel," Wyvern replied caustically.

The Knight scowled at the beast's contempt. He flexed his

grip and wished to hurl his blade at the beast who sat preening on top of that ruined home.

"And the Maiden?" the Prince asked.

Wyvern loosed a low growl in his scaled throat.

"Let us not ask unwanted questions, whelp," Wyvern warned.

The Prince stood defiantly staring up at the creature, returning Wyvern's baleful glare.

"You're outnumbered, beast. Where is the young woman?" the Knight challenged Wyvern.

The once-indifferent creature dug its claws into what remained of the roof and raised its wings just off its back, flittering them like an agitated crow. He was not happy. He hissed and bared his wicked teeth. His tail flexed and curled in anticipation of a strike.

"You speak to me in such a fashion?" Wyvern shouted. "I will roast you alive in your armor, knight!"

Wyvern, nimble and swift despite his size, took an aggressive posture atop the ruined home. He looked over at once to the Prince who was still watching him carefully from opposite the Knight.

"And you, you garish peacock, you challenge me as well? I have watched the strongest warriors writhe in agony as a result of my wrath. You think your blade in league with this one is enough to overcome me? The hubris, the ignorance born of steel and pride," Wyvern bellowed.

He launched himself from the house. What remained fell in upon itself to no more than a heap of rubble and splinters. The Knight and Prince watched as Wyvern took to the sky.

The winged monstrosity came crashing down on the Prince's horse, killing it instantly and leaving the Avallonian with no means of escape. The Knight's horse whinnied and retreated from the creature, placing a good distance between itself and a fiery death. Wyvern looked toward the Knight's horse, aiming to kill it next and strand them both. The Knight saw the Prince flinch as his horse was slain and Wyvern's head turned to its next victim. The Avallonian was brave, but the Knight was battle-tested and more experienced. He knew if his horse were slain, there would be no hope for either of them. He charged at Wyvern, sword raised and voice howling.

Wyvern roared in anticipation and heaved a breath of flame at the Knight who stopped just short of Wyvern's range, throwing up his arm to shield his face. He still felt the great heat, however, and smelled the same unnatural smoke that tainted the farmhouse.

The Prince ran to engage the beast as well, once the surprise of the Knight's initiative wore off. The Knight was also quite fast despite being clad in steel armor. As he approached he heard blows exchanged by the Knight and Wyvern. Wyvern used alternating blows of his tail and his viciously sharp talons.

Though one couldn't discount any lethality of those claws, it was that venomous stinger which the Knight watched—and feared—most.

"My shield!" the Prince heard the Knight shout.

He hesitated for a moment, and then realized the Knight was calling out for the Prince's aid. He looked over and saw the Knight's horse, whinnying and kicking its feet in defiance. The warhorse had retreated from imminent danger, but would not leave its master during battle., and the Prince was grateful. Strapped to the large saddle, rattling against the horse's flank, he saw the shield the Knight called for. A kite shield colored deep green with a golden oak tree emblazoned on the front.

The Prince calmed the animal, unstrapped the shield, and turned. When his eyes fell on the frenzied skirmish, his vision of the previous night accosted him again. He had seen a man with scales colored like rust with eyes of rolling flame. This man carried a dagger that dripped with liquid fire and stabbed the Knight, driving the blade to the hilt, leaving the Knight to fall. It was here that the Prince's dream ended.

He felt a great wave of fear. He didn't know what to make of the vision, so he hadn't said anything. The Knight had charged the house looking for survivors, and he hadn't told him. Wyvern confronted them, and he hadn't told him. Now, it was upon them and he realized he might be too late. The Knight must have his shield. That was not in the vision. This could have a different outcome.

The Prince immediately ran to the Knight as fast as he could, carrying the shield with both arms. He was not a weakling, but he was not as strong as the Knight. He ran straight for the Knight and was intercepted by Wyvern's tail. The beast saw him out of the corner of its eye and lashed out at him. Thankfully, the blow struck the shield and only sent him sprawling to the ground rather than shattering his bones or impaling him on the stinger.

The Knight feigned left, Wyvern stabbed at him with its tail and pierced only the ground. It gave the Knight an opening to retreat to help the Prince. Wyvern mauled and tore at the ground in rage. He paced back and forth spewing a torrent of fire into the ground before him in frustration.

This Knight was good. Very good. Not since the Silverborn had he faced such a challenge. He had underestimated them. Now in a rage, Wyvern realized he would not be able to beat the humans at their own game—so Wyvern would play by his own rules. He saw them both near the war stallion. He smiled inwardly and began to roar and growl in a bestial tantrum. He stepped slowly aside, seeming to prepare to approach them from another angle, but leaving the road open.

The Knight helped the Prince to his feet.

"Spires-all, that thing is strong," the Prince grunted as the Knight offered a hand.

"Too strong," the Knight added. "We can't hope to defeat him alone."

"What do you suggest?" the Prince panted, handing off the shield.

The Prince followed the Knight's gaze to the horse then to the now-open road. It appeared they had an option.

"We can escape," the Prince suggested, "Return with stronger forces."

"Wyvern will be gone long before we would return. He's not leaving the road open by mistake—he's doing it on purpose," the Knight said.

"A trap, but—how do you know so much about this creature? Is he of this realm?" the Prince was confused.

"Indeed. As his brother, Drake, is of yours… though Wyvern is no benevolent creature. In that, we're not as fortunate as you," the Knight explained. "I'll play his game—otherwise we're both dead. Take my horse and go. Get to the Emerald Spire. The king must know Wyvern is stirring again—crawled out of his hole," the Knight added with heated malice in regard to Wyvern who kneaded his claws on the ground like an anxious cat.

The Prince recalled the scaled man of his dream and a shiver coursed through him. "I… I can't. You have to know…"

"Go—now!" the Knight shouted; he pushed the Prince toward the stallion with such force that it near lifted him off his feet.

"He's going to kill you!"

"He can try."

Wyvern roared with impatience. The Knight ran at the beast with sword held high and shield placed squarely in front. Wyvern heaved a torrent of flame at him. He stepped aside, throwing up his shield, but feeling the heat wash around and over his exposed greaves. Wyvern was the smallest of his kind—had the Knight been fighting Naga, or Hydra, or one of his larger kin he would have been reduced to ash.

The shield was still super-heated by Wyvern's fire, forcing him to drop it. Two quick swipes from Wyvern's tail lashed at him. He fell back, dropping his sword.

From his back, he saw where his weapon landed. Wyvern stabbed at him with the stinger-tipped tail, forcing him to roll once... twice... three times to avoid strike after strike. He remained aware of his positioning and knew his blade was out of reach.

Managing to struggle to his feet, he drew a second, smaller sword from a separate scabbard. He stepped to the side as Wyvern's stinger buried itself in the ground where he had previously been standing. He took the opportunity to react quickly and drive the blade into the beast's tail, pinning it to the ground.

Wyvern howled in pain. This maddening little pest had wounded him, and Wyvern's blood did not spill without cost. Pulling out the sword, he saw the Knight had drawn a third blade. Wyvern reached out to pull the short sword from his tail and nearly lost a clawed finger as the Knight cut a deep gash in his claw straight through the scales.

Wyvern instinctively withdrew his claw, roaring again, and saw that the move was a ploy by the Knight to get his weapon back. The Prince, he noticed, was now well up the road. He would catch up to him soon enough once he was finished with this armored roach.

The Emrallti now held both weapons in his hands. He stepped back slightly, readying himself for battle.

"I now have claws of my own, fiend," he taunted Wyvern. "Let us begin."

Wyvern sneered, accepting his challenge. He breathed another burst of flame at the Knight, attempting to set him off guard. The Knight was not so easily swayed and jumped aside with blades still at the ready.

The tail of the creature whipped around and deflected blows from the Knight. Sparks flew from the curved stinger as it was as solid as any metal. Wyvern took care to do this cautiously, so as not to risk having his tail cut off.

The Knight managed to land two well-placed strikes against Wyvern. The beast mistook his armor to mean he was ponderous and ill-fit for maneuvers. The Knight's armor, however, was perfectly-fit and designed for battle. He moved with the strength, ferocity, and grace of a lion. Fortunately for Wyvern, the deadlier of the two blows deflected off his chest scales. These were thicker and stronger than even the Knight's steel plates.

The other, however, gouged deep into Wyvern's scaled flank. Blood gushed from the wound and the scaled beast opened his fanged maw to unleash a bellow of agony and fire. It had hurt him badly and would require special healing. After the initial shock of the pain, Wyvern became incensed. His anger was palpable. Rearing up, his wound still hemorrhaging, Wyvern vowed to make this armored fool suffer and would revel in doing so.

The Knight took a brief moment to enjoy the small victory he'd had by wounding Wyvern. He buried the blade so deep that he had to heave and grunt to pull it loose from the draconian creature. Wyvern flailed its head and tail—the pain must have been excruciating. The blood was deep red, almost black, and steamed as it fell upon the ground. An acrid, smothering odor emanated from it.

He looked up after removing his blade and saw the creature had quickly recovered from its pain and was now rearing up—its head held aloft and its chest heaving in rage. The fire in its eyes seemed to burn him as he looked into them. He knew that the next few moments would decide the battle's resolution.

"Tooth and claw, beast," the Knight called out, clanging the blunt of his blades together. "Tooth and claw."

The next few moments were a flurry of steel and talon, plate and scale; blood flew from Wyvern's great wound, and after a series of strikes from the creature the Knight had his own blood to add to the fray.

He pressed and withdrew, attacked and repelled.

Tooth and claw. Tooth and claw.

Dust and dirt and fire and blood and steel and sinew.

Wyvern and Knight fought as two who had no purpose to live

but to see the other dead. The Knight summoned a vigorous rush to strike a series of continuous blows against Wyvern. The assault left a deep crack in Wyvern's thick chest scales, exposing the vulnerable flesh beneath.

The creature was prone, bereft of effort, and panted from exertion. Wyvern's chest was exposed. The Knight dropped the smaller of his two blades. He took his sword, shimmering and bloody, and raised it with both hands. He would bear it down upon Wyvern and drive it deep into the beast's heart. He would slay it and rid the kingdom of it.

A flash of rust-colored scales crossed his vision. He felt a burning in his chest. The Knight looked down and saw, to his shame, a curved, wicked stinger driven through his armor.

He tried to breathe but felt a burning fire spread through him as Wyvern's venom entered his blood. He dropped his blade; his hands had gone numb. The venom coursed through him quickly. He felt as though he would combust into flame at any moment.

Wyvern's eyes narrowed. He lifted himself from the ground— quite vigorously for having appeared to be all but spent. He let out a slow, deliberate breath. He looked the Knight up and down —observing his triumph.

The Knight stared back then spat upon Wyvern. It was mostly blood, the Knight noticed, but he would not show this villain any weakness. He had little time left—he would spend it in pain and defiance. He would die with nobility, if not victorious.

Wyvern sneered at the Knight's disrespect.

"You could never defeat me," Wyvern whispered sharply to the Knight, lifting him just inches from Wyvern's face.

Having the Knight securely speared by his stinger, Wyvern smashed him viciously on the ground—one solid strike crushing the Knight's bones. He then flung the lifeless body onto the smoldering remains of the house. The armored body landed with such force that it sent small chunks of rubble and splintered wood into the air.

Wyvern peered down the road that the Prince had taken to escape. He could no longer see him for the hills. He would find him shortly.

Wyvern looked down and saw the bloody remains of the Knight's insult. He ran a sharp talon along the crack that the pitiful man cut into his precious scales. He could still feel the throbbing wound in his flank. His tail throbbed where the short sword had pierced it through. All would have to be taken care of once he had returned to his temple. For now, he would handle the man's spittle that tainted his body.

Wyvern looked down and breathed a quick jet of flame upon the wretched substance. His fire could do no harm to himself—he was a dragon-child. But it burnt the last of the little man's insult away.

He had a sudden inspiration. He limped over to the rubble where the Knight's body lay. With a deep breath, he covered the dirt, wood, stone, and remains in dragonfire. He did so a second time and then stood back for a moment to watch what remained of the Knight, and the Maiden's home melt away—stone and metal included. Now, he had a Prince to chase.

* * *

THE PRINCE SAW the Knight engage Wyvern. He admired the man's unflinching courage and sense of duty. As he mounted the horse he cursed those very same attributes. This was a man of war, however, and by staying he would only endanger him further.

The faster he could ride, the sooner he could return in force. Then, this creature would know fear. He would return with knights, archers, lancers, and the fabled griffon-riders of his own Sapphire Realm.

As he rode away he looked back to see the ferocity with which the Knight and Wyvern were fighting one another. He cursed himself a coward; he should be there cutting the draconian beast to pieces with the Knight. He resisted the thought, knowing the best help he could provide was to press on. He was not trained as the Knight was, and to stay would be to burden the Knight with trying to protect him as well as fight.

Still, it left a bitter taste lingering in the Prince's mouth.

He rode as fast as the horse would carry him. It was a magnificent stallion. Quick, powerful, and loyal. It seemed to ride even harder than before as if it knew its master was in danger.

Reaching the peak of another hill, he saw the edge of the Caedwig. The largest and thickest forest of Emrallt, once inside Wyvern would have difficulty seeing him through the trees. He would also be within reach of the Emerald Spire.

The tingle of hope in his chest didn't last. The Prince heard a harsh cry pierce the air. He looked behind him to see a fiendish shape closing in on him. Two sleek wings propelled Wyvern through the sky with deadly grace. The creature's angular body was built for swiftness and the Prince could not hope to outrun him. He commanded the stallion on—faster and faster—but the mighty horse had reached its limit.

He rode until he could hear the flapping of the beast's wings. He hesitated to look over his shoulder for fear of staring up into that hateful maw. He only pressed harder hoping to reach the treeline, but heard the pounding of wings grow louder and begin to overtake the thundering of the stallion's hooves. He braced, waiting to feel the wall of fire claim him.

The Prince closed his eyes, resigning himself to death at Wyvern's wrath, when he heard a sharp crack followed by a tumultuous thunder. The stallion reared so suddenly at the riotous din that both horse and rider fell to the ground. The Prince, thankfully, was thrown from the saddle and not crushed beneath the large animal.

Wyvern felt as though a thousand mighty hammers had been hurled into his body. A white, searing bolt shot from the horizon and struck him. He was hit with such force that he was felled from the sky and plummeted to the ground.

Magic. Powerful, painful. Infuriating.

The Prince hurried to his feet. The stallion was fleeing from them toward the Caedwig. The powerful force had shaken even the war-ready horse. He looked over to see Wyvern unsteadily rising to his feet. He shook his head and looked menacingly about for the source of the lightning.

Wyvern grimaced when he saw—standing amid scorched ground and shattered stone—the Blue Wizard of Avallonis, who also happened to be the Prince's steward and tutor. Wyvern's attitude quickly changed to one of caution.

It was a rare human that could cause Wyvern to hesitate. Wizards were the most common of these rarities. Only one wizard existed for every spire. Each wizard was powerful and, combined, they held their own council, independent of the realms' ruling families. Wyvern did not wish to engage a practiced mage, as to draw their collective ire would be fatal—even for him.

"Be gracious to your sitter, boy," Wyvern said scathingly and took flight again. The creature flew swiftly away to nurse his wounds. He had the Maiden, the Knight was dead, and the Prince was no threat to him any longer. There was planning that remained. The gift was within his grasp, but he had yet to unleash it. All things considered, Wyvern hailed himself victorious this day.

9

HONOR AND GRATITUDE

T he Prince greeted the Wizard with great appreciation.
"Your timing could not have been more appropriate," the Prince said with relief.

"Fortunate timing had nothing to do with my arrival, Your Grace," the Wizard stated matter-of-factly. "How many times do I have to tell you? I am always watching."

"As you say," the Prince replied between breaths. "Then satiate my curiosity, old friend—why were you not there when Wyvern attacked?"

He didn't ask out of anger or ingratitude. After all, it was the Prince who had pressed his father to allow him to visit their friends and neighbors in the Emerald south. It was the Prince who snuck away after the dream to find the Knight and seek out the figure in their shared vision.

"Remember that protection spell I promised your parents I would perfect?" the Wizard explained. "It's somewhat operational. I'm made aware when you are in danger and so when Wyvern gave chase I came as quickly as I could. Suffice to say, this is the first time the spell has ever triggered in a foreign realm. It took… longer than expected. But once I could locate you I came as quickly as I could."

The Prince looked out over the horizon where the Wizard had arrived in thunderous fashion.

"Quickly, indeed," the Prince said with a smile.

"And quite taxing," the Wizard added, rubbing his stiffened neck and aching shoulders. "Very powerful spell—first time I've ever needed to use it. Hopefully, such a need will not arise again," he added with a stern glance at the Prince.

The Prince took a deep breath and pursed his lips. The Wizard was old and powerful—as practitioners of magic are wont to be—but he still had a proud gait. A well-trimmed beard of brown streaked with grey made him look younger than he truly was. He straightened his finely crafted robes—a deep blue to match his title. He was an imposing figure and the Prince, despite being royalty himself, knew to concede to the Wizard's wisdom.

"I have to agree," the Prince nodded. "You'll have to explain a little more about this spell to me sometime."

"Perhaps," the Wizard replied, pulling his rune-trimmed cowl back over his head. His gray eyes still flickered with residual magic from the spell with which he had assaulted Wyvern.

"What was such a beast doing chasing the Avallonian Prince?" the Wizard inquired.

The Prince looked back in the direction of the Maiden's family farm. He explained the events of the prior two days. The tournament, the Maiden, the dream, the farm; it all seemed quite surreal.

"That does not bode well," the Wizard said plainly.

"Clarification, please?" the Prince asked.

"Wyvern and his kin do not meddle in the affairs of men or other mortals without great need. Wyvern is seeking something or someone of great interest if he risks drawing attention to himself so brazenly."

"His fire does not burn as fiercely as his father, Dragon. He does not have the speed of his brother, Drake, or the wisdom of his sister, Serpent. His brother, Wyrm, is of far greater intellect, and his siblings, Hydra and Naga, were unscrupulous, but far more charming and of greater strength."

"But Wyvern—Wyvern is a cunning and vile one. He more than accounts for these shortcomings with calculation and ambition. He's also ferocious and unyielding. There is no creature living that could match the contemptible nature of that scaled fiend."

"That... doesn't bode well at all," the Prince echoed.

"You traveled alone, unescorted?" the Wizard asked with concern.

The Prince cast him a fallen look. "A Knight was with me. If Wyvern came after me, I can only assume he didn't survive their encounter."

The Prince looked back in the direction from whence Wyvern had given chase. It was highly unlikely that Wyvern would be returning to that place or whatever was left of it. The Knight's remains would surely be there.

"His king would want such a brave man's body returned," the Prince said with sorrow.

"I would imagine so, Your Grace, but..." the Wizard's words trailed off. The Prince knew the old man well. He could sense something was wrong.

"What is it?" the Prince asked.

The Wizard sighed, then looked at him before quickly turning away again. "I wanted to tell you when you returned. There was much to do until you came back. Sending a messenger seemed..."

"Come now, out with it," the Prince said, his anxiety building. He'd never seen the Wizard like this before.

"Your father, Your Grace. He's passed."

The Prince swallowed. For a moment, he thought he'd heard wrong.

"He's been ill for a long time, but..." the Prince whispered. He knew he'd been gone too long. He intended to only stay a day or two, but his trip continued to stretch. He'd told himself that, after the games, he would return home. Now, it was too late. He'd never see his father again.

"It finally caught up with him. I'm very sorry, my boy," the Wizard said gruffly, putting an arm around the young man.

The Prince felt his face grow hot and squeezed his eyes closed to hold back the tears. He took a deep breath, then said, "Let's face this crisis. King Brennen needs to know about the Knight and Wyvern, then we'll head home straight away."

The Wizard squeezed his shoulder comfortingly, like a grandfather would. "Yes. Come, Wyvern will have retreated to lick his wounds, but we should be quick about it."

The Wizard pulled a vial from within his robes. He poured a small amount of a crushed, aromatic leaf into his hands. He held his hand to his mouth, whispered something into it, and then cast the substance to the wind. Within moments the Knight's stallion returned from within the forest. It was galloping towards them and appeared to be in full stride. It galloped with renewed vigor

"You never cease to amaze me," the Prince said as an aside.

They both mounted the horse, the Prince taking the reins, and made their way back to the ruined farm. As they neared the location, the Prince began looking about for any signs of Wyvern. Finding none, they rode up to the smoldering remains of the quaint home.

The Knight's body was gone. A gruesome image of Wyvern devouring the honorable and courageous man made him feel ill. The Prince then saw the molten pile of rock and refuse that was once the house.

He rode over to inspect it and there he saw a shining treasure in the ruin. The Knight's body was surely gone, for the breath of Wyvern could melt stone and metal and turn the hardiest wood to ash, but, here, the Knight's armor remained whole. All other remains had been burned away, but the chest piece, pauldrons, greaves, even the sword were whole and as new.

Lifting the chestpiece from the ashes and rubble, the Prince saw something strange. The Knight was a powerfully built man and physically larger than the Prince. This armor he held, which he was certain was the Knight's, had transformed. It was smaller. It appeared to the Prince that the armor would fit himself perfectly.

"What magic is this…" the Prince wondered aloud.

"I'm not sure," the Wizard said hesitantly, startling the Prince. "But it is wondrous, indeed. I can feel an arcane radiance on these items. Strange times…" he trailed off.

The Prince gathered the rest of the armor and weapon. They were cool to the touch despite having been pulled from smoldering stone. He looked at them for a moment, mourning the loss of such an honorable soldier. When the moment passed, he placed the belongings in the packs on the Knight's stallion. The noble beast seemed to know what had occurred to its master and hung its head sadly, pawing at the dirt. It huffed a complaint and flicked its mane as the armor was placed carefully into the saddlebags and strapped in tightly.

"I will return these. It is the least I can do. The man saved my life," the Prince decided.

"Very good. That would be fitting," the Wizard concurred.

"Wyvern was after the Maiden," the Prince said to the Wizard as they rode off. "I'm sure of it."

The Wizard was hesitant. "How can you be sure it was not something the Maiden had in her possession? Begging your pardon, Your Grace, but how can we know she's still alive?"

The Prince pondered the idea for a moment, but then shook off the notion. "She peddled fragrances and other trinkets. She probably helped her family on their farm—this farm," he indicated the decimated smallholding.

"I doubt she would have had anything of worth to Wyvern.

There must be something else that he wants—but I couldn't begin to guess what."

"This situation unsettles me," the Wizard brooded. "Wyvern, a peasant girl, a Knight's magic armor, and a Prince endangered over portents," he shook his head and contemplated these things further.

The Prince closed his eyes and sighed inwardly. The Knight and Maiden were both gone and Wyvern had tried to kill him, as well. His father was dead. The Wizard was a prudent sage, but he longed to ask his father of these occurrences. The Blue King was knowledgeable and judicious, stern and fair; his son had long taken comfort in his wisdom.

As they rode into the city surrounding the Emerald Spire they saw that the town carried on as usual for the most part; however, something was amiss. There were more guards than there had been prior. They all cast suspicious glances at them and the Prince became aware that they took note of two high-ranking visitors from Avallonis riding a stallion adorned with the heraldry of an Emerald Knight. That situation the Prince had not considered.

It was not long before they were finally stopped.

"Greetings, Your Grace!" the captain of the guard, accompanied by an entourage of soldiers, rode up to them with an open-palmed hand held aloft. "I mean no affront, majesty, but, tell me —why do you come to us on the stallion of one of our own?" he asked, looking at the horse and its trappings.

The Prince returned a genuine look of respect and concern. "I have urgent news for your king. Please, take us to him."

The captain returned a discontented look and continued to regard the horse and the Wizard.

"The former master of this horse was slain by Wyvern as he defended a homestead against the beast, alone. He also saved the Prince from such a death. We return with his belongings to offer to the Green King Brennen, with respect and gratitude," the Wizard replied sternly, with a hint of rebuke tinging his hoarse voice. "Now, is there anything further you wish yourself privy to before your king?" he added in veiled warning.

The captain balked, considering the words. He finally bade the two follow him. They rode through the streets at a brisk gallop, finally arriving at the renowned plaza in the base of the Emerald Spire.

The captain dismounted and asked that the Prince and Wizard do the same. The Prince gathered the fallen Knight's belongings to take to the Green King as the captain led them into the plaza. The men who had escorted the captain, meanwhile, attended to the horses. The Prince and Wizard approached a heavily guarded, elegant stairway near the center of the square. With a shout from the captain, they were immediately allowed passage.

The three of them walked up a tall, wide flight of stairs that wound up the inner walls of the spire. It occurred to the Prince that, should they follow this stairway to the top of the spire where the King held court, it would be a very long walk.

As he imagined this, the stairs came to an abrupt end. A wall of carved, ornamented bark, roots, and vines were blocking their path. The captain raised his right hand and, for the first time, the Prince saw that a delicate bronze chain attached to the gauntlet. A beautiful jade tree hung from the chain.

He took the jeweled tree in hand and gently ran it over a specific section of the ancient writing on one of the vines. The trailing plants moved out of the way of their own accord. The bark-covered wall rearranged itself so that a doorway was present; there, beyond that newly-formed door, was the receiving chamber for the Emerald King's court.

They stepped inside and the door closed behind them. The royal guards at the door the court were adorned in functional, but ceremoniously appropriate, garb and armor. Their large, shining halberds stood high beside them. A simple nod and they acknowledged the party that had arrived for the king.

They stepped into the court—a large, magnificent hallway decorated with the green, gold, and earthen-colored heraldry of Emrallt, and statues of kings past. The Prince knew the court to be one of the highest rooms in the tower yet they had barely been ascending the stairs before reaching the doorway. The Emerald Spire must have a similar magical, and defensible, entrance as Avallonis' own spire.

King Brennen rose and greeted them openly. There were no hostilities between the two realms and there had not been for many generations. Though he was only vaguely familiar with the king and queen of Emrallt, the Prince's father made him well aware that they were honorable and just rulers of their kingdom and loved by their people. His visit, though brief and interrupted, had shown this to be true.

"Young Prince," the king said with a smile. "It's good to see you safe. Your absence this morning worried us; even though your father mentioned your penchant for spontaneous journeys."

"I apologize, Your Grace," the Prince said sincerely. He laid down the packs he had been carrying that contained the Knight's belongings, with the sword strapped to the side.

"What is this you bring us?" the king asked with a furrowed brow. "It bears the symbol of Emrallt's royal knighted house."

"Majesty, I bring ill news. My absence this morning was due to an encounter I had with one of your own Emerald Knights, as you have observed. Together, we found Wyvern active in the countryside," the Prince explained.

The king gripped the sides of his throne, his shoulders rising and falling as he adjusted in his seat. He was distraught at the news. Wyvern's presence had not been seen for many decades. Whenever he reared his foul head, death and chaos swiftly followed.

"Where was this?" the king asked.

"At a smallholding outside the borders of the western woods. A farm had been razed and destroyed by him."

The king shook his head. "Strange. Wyvern's actions have often shown little structure or sense, but to ransack a small farm?"

"He was looking for a young woman who lived there; a maiden who often visited the plaza and sold her wares," the Prince attempted to clarify. He realized he had just described dozens, if not hundreds, of young women that visit the spire on a daily basis. He wished he could offer more, but he simply did not know what Wyvern wanted with the Maiden—yet. And he was wholly unwilling to divulge his and the Knight's shared visions.

"Stranger still," the king added.

"The Knight whose belongings I carry, he fought Wyvern... held him at bay while I rode for reinforcements. Wyvern was victorious against him and gave chase after me. My court Wizard intercepted him, otherwise Wyvern would have claimed another victim."

The Prince hung his head in shame. As he shared the events he felt even more cowardly, no matter how logical the plan sounded.

"We returned to find the cottage fully destroyed and burned by dragonfire. The very stone was melted and smoldering, but the Knight's armor, his sword—these were all intact and sitting atop the wreckage," the Prince explained the miracle.

The king nodded in approval. He sighed heavily and ran his hand over his brown beard, streaked with gray from age. "An acknowledgment of his sacrifice. The spires have seen fit to honor him."

"His stallion survived as well. It was this steed that returned us here safely," the Prince concluded.

The king seemed to ponder over this for a moment. He looked at the armor and weapon that sat on the stone floor before him. It was radiant even in the limited light of the room. It looked as though it were fresh from the forge and the blade gleamed dangerously.

"His sword will remain here—adorning the halls of the spire he swore to protect and gave his life in so doing," the king declared, regarding the Prince with admiration and gratitude. "And I would have you take the armor and the stallion. The actions of you both have borne witness to the capability of Emrallt and Avallonis and the alliance we share. I have no doubt it will bring your father pride and honor for you to carry such remnants of one of our best men. I have no doubt you will do his legacy justice. Our court smith can provide your spire's symbol for the armor."

The Prince felt the honor was not due him; but he beheld the pack wherein lay the armor that belonged to the Knight. It had not only been reforged, but refitted. Some miracle, some unseen arcane providence had put that armor in his hands, which he turned over to whom he thought was the rightful owner. Now, they were being offered to him by that very person. The king who sat in power within the Emerald Spire. The spire the Knight had died protecting. This was more than coincidence.

"The honor is mine, Your Grace," the Prince said. "The Knight was a great man. I swear to you, Wyvern will suffer vengeance for his actions."

"Indeed he will. I would know of this maiden he seeks as well," Brennen replied.

The Prince offered what little he knew. "I met the young woman at the tournament. She was lovely, kind, but unre-markable."

A half-truth.

"I could only imagine a fiend like Wyvern would despise such virtue and seek to destroy it in all its forms—but that seems rather trivial. I truly don't know what he wants with her. But it will not do for your people or mine to live in fear of him. He likely won't stop with one simple farm."

Before the king could speak, the doors to the court opened quickly, prompting the guards to grip their weapons. They saw it was only a messenger from the plaza.

"Your Grace, an envoy has arrived from Avallonis with a message," she said urgently. The king and queen looked at one another. The Blue Prince was here with them, what could such a message be?

The king waved her forward. She walked passed the Prince and Wizard, casting them a sad glance. The Prince's brows furrowed as he realized the news she must bear. King Brennen spoke to her quietly for a moment and many of those in the room noticed him lower his head sadly. The king looked at the Prince with heavy eyes.

"I'm so sorry to have to tell you this, Your Grace," the king began, "but, it appears your father has passed. I know he was ill."

The Prince grimaced. "I was just made aware earlier today, King Brennen," he said with a look to the Wizard. "I came to you today," the Prince continued, "to inform you of Wyvern and the loss of your Knight, and planned to return to Avallonis immediately after to settle my father's affairs."

The king pursed his lips and nodded his head. "I wish you well on your way, Prince."

King Brennen looked to the Wizard and cleared his throat. "I apologize that we were unable to do more. Merana tells me you were speaking often."

"No apologies, necessary, Your Grace. You have one of the best healers among us. There was simply nothing to be done."

The king was referring to his own court wizardess, Merana. The Blue Wizard and the Green Wizardess conferred countless times in the last few years, attempting to find some cure for what ailed the Avallonian king. Merana had the most knowledge of healing balms and treatments among the wizards and wizardesses of the kingdoms.

The Prince and the Wizard would have to take their leave. Their griffons would carry them swiftly home and there he would see to his throne and prepare riders to return and assist Emrallt in routing Wyvern. He turned to the messenger and asked for them to be escorted to and the envoy and their griffon.

"Griffon, majesty?" the messenger replied. "your envoy came by horseback," she clarified.

The Prince and the Wizard exchanged confused and worried glances.

"Take us to them," the Prince ordered.

"Did you send the messenger?" the Prince asked quietly to the Wizard.

"No. I was going to tell you when you returned, remember? I had no reason to send a rider," the Wizard replied.

The Wizard felt deep grief for the Prince and the loss of the king. The young man left his home, clashed with Wyvern, and watched an Emrallti knight die. To then find out his father died while he was away?

But, the Prince survived. He would be more than ready to deal with his father's court. When they came outside the plaza they found the rider from their home kingdom waiting. As the messenger stated, next to her stood a muscular grey horse with Avallonian heraldry. The envoy approached and bowed to them.

"Majesty, I rode here immediately with dire news," she began.

"I know about my father," the Prince said plainly, attempting to hide his pain. "I'll return immediately. Where is your griffon?"

The rider looked about nervously. She stuttered a moment, hesitating to speak. The Prince began to show signs of frustration.

"Oh, out with it, lass!" the Wizard barked.

"Sire, they—they left. Flew away to the horizon. Each and

every one," the rider spoke quickly as though it were some fault of her own.

"Why? Did their speaker explain?" the Prince asked. Though he had never personally seen the Speaker of the Griffons, the Blue King had assured him it was custom and tradition that every anointed king of the Sapphire Realm since his grandfather's grandfather was personally greeted by the speaker in a private conference. If the griffons had fled, surely they would have given a reason.

The rider shook her head. "No, majesty. With the king's passing and the absence of his heir, the regent called into question your family's ability to effectively rule."

"Did he now?" the Prince said with anger. "You think perhaps that drove them to flee?"

"I—I can't say..." the rider replied, despondent, and hung her head.

The Prince attempted to alleviate her guilt and assured her it was no fault of hers. She had fulfilled her duty and should return immediately and inform the regent that the heir of Avallonis, the Sapphire Realm was returning with the Blue Wizard. "Ride ahead and inform the council I'll be returning. Ride quickly. I'll be right behind you."

The rider bowed and climbed atop her horse, riding away in a rush.

"Thank King Brennen for his hospitality," the Prince said to the Emrallti messenger. "Inform him that I shall return to speak of the issues we were discussing. For now, I must return home immediately."

The messenger bowed, "Your Grace."

The Prince and the Wizard looked north toward their homeland. Clouds were moving in on the horizon. No doubt a harsh wind was blowing, bringing rain to their lands.

"Had I known your wanderlust would have taken you two days ride away I would have severely strengthened the geas," the

Wizard remarked in jest. If the Prince could be leashed by any magic, it would be another miracle.

"I'm afraid my good humor could use some strengthening at the moment," the Prince sighed.

The Wizard nodded. "Indeed, Prince. Those clouds are surely portents for what we ride into."

"Then let us ride, mage. One foe at a time," the Prince remarked, using an old adage of his grandfather's.

10

THE SAPPHIRE SPIRE

Unbeknownst to the Prince, the Speaker of the Griffons was well aware of the situation brewing in the lands of the spires. She had met with Wyvern, personally. The fiend had stolen the griffon's eggs and held them somewhere dark and secret.

Before the Blue King had passed, Wyvern summoned the Speaker to a rendezvous, urging she come with only her most trusted bodyguards. He sent the message with pieces of a griffon eggshell. The Speaker arrived at the meeting place, where Wyvern made it clear if the griffons moved against him in any way in the coming days he would order the eggs crushed and their remains returned to the griffons—entire generations lost. The Speaker did not doubt Wyvern's capability or his cruelty. However, she would not forsake her oath to the Blue King lightly.

Wyvern was aware of this and, though she knew the eggs were missing, she still challenged him on his word as to whether he was truly in control of the eggs. Wyvern's response was chilling and heartbreaking. He produced more of the crushed eggs—many pieces that had been licked clean.

"They are very delightful on the palate," Wyvern chuckled.

The Speaker, through tears heavy with grief and hot with anger, cursed the fiend and agreed to his terms. Thus, the fabled Avallonian riders would be devoid of their griffon companions. The king and his court, Wyvern added, would be none the wiser regarding Wyvern's involvement, at least during the early, critical stages of his plan—lest his feasting begin.

The griffons remained within the borders of Avallonis. It wasn't a common occurrence to see a griffon rider leave the borders of the Blue Kingdom except, perhaps, in times of war. The griffon riders were the most elite of Avallonis' forces and were too few to send out without great need – such as retrieving the Prince, personally.

No sooner had the king passed, than the Blue Wizard left to find the Prince. The Speaker had a deep and terrible foreboding. The king's council had been disruptive and bickered among each other day and night. Now, with the king dead and the court wizard seeking out the Prince, the Speaker could think only of the eggs and the horrible fate Wyvern planned for them.

The Speaker agonized over her decision but chose in favor of protecting their unborn. All griffons were order to return to their mountaintop homes where they could discuss how to find their eggs and possibly return to their allies. For now, however, the Avallonians would have to make do without them—and it broke her heart.

* * *

ACKALON TAPPED A RINGED finger on an open window, looking out over the city below. Blue and silver flags fluttered in the breeze atop high walls of chiseled stone in the distance.

"Changes are needed. The royal family has held the throne for only three generations. Such a short time and already they weaken the realm," the regent fumed.

"The king is deceased, succumbed to his illness. The Prince is off gallivanting in a neighboring kingdom and the court wizard suddenly disappears?"

The regent was pacing next to the throne; a magnificent creation of quartz with a silver arch rising over it. At its apex, a magnificent sapphire.

"We're vulnerable!" he began shouting in frustration.

A dark-robed woman emerged from the shadows of the echoing chamber. She walked with the grace and intent of a viper.

"Vulnerable against what?" Morgæna asked with an amused tone denoting her lack of concern. "Nothing moves against us. The Spires are at peace, as they have been for eons. No ogre tribes marching, no monstrosities loom over us, and the only sorceress of any regard that could challenge the Blue Wizard is quite busy ruling over her own kingdom—full of swamps and trolls."

Her voice was warm velvet hiding cold knives underneath. She approached her lover and placed her hand on the back of his shoulder.

"There have been rumors," the regent said ominously.

"Oh, Ackalon," Morgæna scoffed, "your mind lingers on dead threats and conspiracies. The Black Griffon has been deceased for generations."

"The Black Griffon was a demon—a creature to be feared, not understood. King Aeuralius became near-mythical after he slew the thing. The hold his family has had on the throne is finally called into question during the reign of his grandson—and now, coincidentally, rumors of the black beast abound."

Ackalon continued his pacing. Morgæna sat in a cushioned chair and sipped casually from a crystal goblet. There were no others present in the court at the time—all of them having been dismissed. She poured herself more wine from a crystal carafe. She was unsure if she was annoyed or amused by the regent's incessant fretting.

"Then decide like a man, not a fussing child," she chided, swirling the deep reddish-purple liquid.

Ackalon came to a standstill. He looked over at Morgæna, her long hair pulled into an intricate braid, resting like a coil of gold along her shoulder. Her looks belied her age—she was youthful despite her forty-plus years. He approached her and cupped her chin in his hands.

"My love, you are right," he said softly. "I have behaved like a child. Share with me your wisdom."

She smiled up at him and took his hands in hers.

"The Prince and the Blue Wizard will no doubt be returning by tomorrow's end. Before then, we show his knights, his people, his nobles that the king's son is not fit to take his place. As he is genuinely unfit, the truth will be our weapon." She stood and stroked the regent's long, graying hair.

"The truth," she repeated, "will be our weapon."

That morning, Ackalon called the people of the city together. He stood on a tier overlooking the town center below. Throngs of people filled the streets; from one end to another, wall to wall, building to building. Their hushed murmurs still echoed like a dull roar. They looked up as the regent and his golden-haired lady approached from within the spire. He stood where the king would always address his people

He held his hands aloft and the crowd silenced quickly. Not even the rattling of the armor of the guards posted about could be heard. When he saw he had their attention he spoke with authority.

"People of Avallonis, of Eidalohn, home to the Sapphire Spire; where is your king?" he began. There was no answer, only some hushed murmurs rolling about the crowd.

"Where is your Prince? Where is the Blue Wizard of this court? They have gone!" His words grew feverish and his voice broke with his fervor.

"Our gracious king has passed from us—he has succumbed to

his illness," a riotous and panicked roar erupted from the crowd. The whispers they had been sharing had been validated.

"His wizard, a sworn protector of this spire," Ackalon continued, "has gone chasing his son—your prince! Who has himself gone off to a foreign land to revel in another king's court; chasing maidens and drinking at tournaments!"

The crowd became riled. Many gasped in shock and others in disbelief. Some cried foul while others shook their heads in disgust at the Prince's actions.

"Those of you who doubt, I hear you. I understand. I didn't want to believe it, myself," Ackalon called out, responding to various jeers heard among the people. "Look around you—who protects you now? Who commanded the armored men of the Sapphire Spire to watch over this gathering and keep it safe? Who has sent riders far and wide to find our griffons? Who remains in this very spire of majesty and honor to see that our realm is secure and that you, its lifeblood, continue to prosper? It was not the royal family! It was not the court protector! It was I!"

The crowd was further provoked. Many were now cheering for the regent, though there remained a noticeable number of loyalists.

"I do not seek to overthrow our Prince, our king. I am no traitor. I seek only that he answer for the well-being of his people, of his throne, that he has left empty in such a dangerous time. Rumors of the Black Griffon have surfaced. Brigands lurk among our lands. The spire's armies have no king to command them. Where is the Prince to guide his kingdom?" the regent entreated them.

He noticed that as more began to see his point of view, even some of the guardsmen began striking their spears on the ground in agreement.

"Let him answer for his actions. The truth shall be our weapon," Ackalon concluded. He retreated back within the spire to the cheers of the populace. Inside, their muffled shouts brought him great happiness. He felt his blood on fire.

"You are quite a speaker, my lord," Morgæna cooed. She adjusted the folds of his attire and straightened his silken collar. "You won them over quite easily."

"With your wisdom to guide me," he returned. "You will make a wonderful Blue Wizard."

"Sorceress," Morgæna clarified.

"Yes—the Blue Sorceress of the Sapphire Spire. You will be stunning and you will be beloved," Ackalon said while gazing at her.

She wrapped her hand around the back of his head and kissed him. She held back the grimace that sought to wrinkle her face. A means to an end.

"Come, my love," she said, turning her back to him. He stared at her exposed shoulders and the deep cut of her dress robes. "We have work to do."

That day, messengers on horseback were sent throughout Avallonis. They spread the word that the Prince and the Wizard had all but abandoned their realm in its time of need. They posted notices of the Black Griffon rumors and the dangers of traveling. The populace was urged to practice excessive caution until the regent and the wizard's proxy, a humble but talented Morgæna, could establish effective patrols.

By the day's end, every town in Avallonis was aware of the Prince's travel to Emrallt and the Wizard's sudden absence. The people were convinced that a spoiled child was abusing the throne and the court Wizard was a self-absorbed, eccentric old man who cared nothing for the duties of his position.

After receiving word from the final messenger of the propaganda's distribution, the regent and his lady retired for the evening. In his chambers, Ackalon fell joyously into slumber as Morgæna lay next to him stroking his hair and whispering sweetly into his ear.

* * *

THE PRINCE and Wizard rode swiftly to their homeland. The Wizard had been graciously given a horse from King Brennen's stables.

"It's a magnificent animal," the Wizard remarked on the Prince's steed as they rode. They slowed long enough to allow the stallions a rest.

The Prince regarded the muscular horse. He scarcely knew the Knight, but he had felt a bond with him. Perhaps it was due to the man saving his life or perhaps that they faced a common foe and shared visions. No matter the source, the Knight's king felt it necessary to grant the magnificent stallion and consecrated armor to the Prince. He would take such gifts and made an oath to himself that they be used in honor of the memory of the man they served before.

He had named the stallion Ceffyl since he didn't know what the Knight had called him. He patted Ceffyl's powerful neck.

"Indeed he is. He will serve me well, and I will see to it I do my best to honor his former master.," the Prince said.

"You are too hard on yourself, my Prince," the Wizard retorted. "The Knight knew of the peril in which he placed himself. So was he trained, so was his duty."

"Of course," the Prince remarked, unconvinced.

After a full day's ride they neared the first town on their road to Eidalohn, just within the borders of Avallonis. They noticed that the town guard was eyeing them suspiciously. Surely they recognized their prince? They slowed their horses to a trot; the Wizard placed himself in front of the Prince and held a hand up in greeting.

"Hello, there," he called out. "We have arrived in Devonshire, have we not?"

"Aye. And in no swift fashion, either," the guard replied

sharply. He stood there unmoving. He did not return their greeting or bow to his lord.

The Prince did not consider himself a man of hubris—but defiance of this kind showed a disregard for the man's duty and disrespect to the king. He was sworn to protect spire, crown, and realm. The Prince's father was a respected king and he was a Prince known to the people and did not draw nor attempt to warrant their indignation.

"Soon to be your king," the Wizard added sternly. "Show some respect for your lord and your duty, soldier."

"Apologies, Your Grace," the guard said, though his indignation was thinly veiled. "What with winged demons about and bandits owning the roads..."

The Prince saw the Wizard tense at the guard's tone. The Wizard began to urge his horse forward to confrontation when the Prince intervened by spurring his horse forward to cut short the Wizard's path and spoke above the men's anger.

"Winged demons?" the Prince asked. "Bandits owning the roads? Where did you hear such information?"

The guard nodded in the direction of a large document nailed to a lamppost nearby.

"Recent notices going out. The magisters have taken it upon themselves to mobilize the king's men and take back the people's lands," the guard explained.

The Prince and Wizard dismounted and approached the parchment nailed to the post.. The 'winged demons' were referring to the Black Griffon, also called the Demon of Black Rock. The Wizard had insisted the Prince learn his history inside and out and this legend had a personal connection to his own family. It was a beast easily twice the size of the largest griffon ever seen. Those who saw it spoke of feathers as black as night and a beak stained red from the blood of its kills.

A typical griffon prowled the mountains with the powerful body of a lion and ruled the skies with the head and wings of a proud eagle. Though there were slight variations in size and color, their physical properties were as constant and unwavering as their loyalty. The wilder griffons were known for their strength and temperamental nature. The royal griffons of the Sapphire Spire were led by their Speaker and were an unusual and remarkable silvery-white in color. They were more intelligent and domesticated than their wild cousins and capable of understanding human speech, and obeyed their Speaker's orders to assist the kings of Avallonis. The Speaker was also blessed with the Tongue of the Magi—capable of speaking with other creatures versed in magic.

Conversely, The Black Griffon was a singular monstrosity of unknown origins. Some dared say the mate of the Speaker of the Griffons, but according to the Prince's father, she vehemently denies such rumors. The Prince's grandfather led the previous king's armies against the creature when it established itself as the alpha leader of the wild griffons.

Though griffons are skilled and brutish fighters, the Black Griffon was exceptionally vicious. Its cry was not proud, but a baleful screech that froze the blood. Its massive paws bore talons that scored stone and pierced breastplates; the wickedly curved spurs of the Black Griffon were as ebon sickles that were ever covered in blood and viscera.

The Speaker, the very same who spoke for the griffons still, being longer-lived even for a griffon, warned Charles, king at that time, that griffons who feasted on the blood of men for too long bore the risk of being driven to a blood-madness. The Demon of Black Rock knew this, was likely mad himself, and was turning the wild griffons to his cause. They would want more, and would soon launch attacks on every hamlet, town, and city in an attempt to slake a bloodthirst that would never end.

The Prince's grandfather—first knight and general of the Avallonian armies—tracked the beast to its original lair in a particular part of the eastern mountains where sharp, black stones cut through the earth.

He brought with him a contingent of heavy cavalry and archers, as well as the sitting king's heir who insisted on aiding the general in protecting his kingdom. The general left the griffon riders to protect the Sapphire Spire and the king. The Black Griffon met his army with its personal retinue of blood-mad wild griffons.

Two days after, the general returned to the City of the Sapphire Spire with the Black Griffon's body—pierced by a thousand arrows and spears they say. He returned with only a third of the force he had left with. When the king and queen rode out to meet the victorious soldiers they saw lying next to the monstrous remains, the body of their son, heir to the throne, slain by the Black Griffon itself during the battle.

The heir insisted on riding into battle, against the wishes of both the king and the general, but Charles's son was much like his father, argued his case, and it was decided that he would go with the general to establish his worth to sit the throne one day. Charles relented and his son rode to battle. The Prince's grandfather informed the king that the heir fought with bravery unmatched by any that day. The heir's confrontation with the Demon of Black Rock was directly responsible for its inevitable fall. His son had, no doubt, saved hundreds if not thousands of his people's lives.

The aging king, now without an heir, named the Prince's grandfather as his successor. It wasn't long after that the king and queen passed and the Prince's family acquired the throne and the Prince, in turn, acquired a legacy of bravery and honor. The people of Avallonis acquired a new tale of heroism and also a new monster to fear, for some could not let go of the tale that a black egg lay nestled and warm in those ebon stones waiting to hatch.

The Wizard ripped the page from its post. The notice was

genuine; a wax mound pressed with the seal of a particular magister—Ackalon. That arrogant steward could not have sanctioned such an announcement without the consent of the rest of the council. It appeared those once loyal to the king were now working against the Prince.

The Prince looked at the guardsman, who returned the gesture with disinterest.

"And what do the spire-knights say of this?" the Prince asked with a raised brow. He was referring to the famed armored griffon riders.

The guard laughed. "Gone they are. The griffons. All of 'em. Word's spreadin' that the knights hold their posts on the spire alone."

The Prince took a breath. He wanted to acknowledge the man without showing his concern or anger.

"I'm aware the griffons are gone. That doesn't diminish the authority of the spire-knights as peers of the council in matters involving ruling in the absence of the king... or myself."

The guard scratched the stubble on his chin. "Word is, they ain't too happy about it. But, without their griffons the council don't take them as seriously."

The Wizard crossed his arms and glared a the guard. "How do you know all this?"

The guard smirked. "Word travels fast among us common-folk. Especially when the council is real loud about it."

The Prince felt his anger rising. The griffon riders were the best of the king's soldiers. Strong and loyal, they protected the realm in tandem with the magisters. Only those rare soldiers christened as griffon riders would be paired with a griffon and granted the title of spire-knight. There are only seven at any given time, along with seven magisters. When one of those stations is empty—through death or withdrawal—another is chosen.

According to the guard, the spire-knights—ever vigilant and

honorable—remained on their watch at the height of the Sapphire Spire protecting the jewel of Avallonis and its king's court without their griffons. The magisters were tasked with seeing to the other affairs of the court: finances and general governance.

One group stood loyal and one in defiance. At least this is what appeared to be the case from the Prince's current knowledge.

"We must ride quickly," the Prince said to the Wizard whilst regarding the notice.

"Agreed," the Wizard hastily replied.

As they rode through town after town they were met with equal disdain. The guards kept the people at a distance, though most of the eyes turned their way were filled with barely disguised scowls. Some even dared spit in their direction.

The council had managed to turn the people against the Prince in a matter of days. How did they manage to incite such a zealous furor in so short a time? The Wizard had his suspicions, but he hesitated to comment until he could see the situation at the spire.

Each town bore numerous copies of the notice. It was with great fervor that Ackalon and his conspirators had been at work. The Prince wondered what the griffon riders thought of these actions.

After an eternity of expeditious riding, they finally came upon Eidalohn, capital of Avallonis. Large stone walls encircled the entire city. Great steel gates emblazoned with the griffon-and-blade symbol of the kingdom were guarded by armored men and protected those within.

The spire itself was one of equal beauty to all the others. It was made of white-and-blue marbled granite that was polished smooth. It reached into the heavens that it so gloriously identified with; white and blue, and there, at the top of the spire, sat the great sapphire.

This tower differed from that of Emrallt in that its exterior was laced with beautiful terraces and outdoor verandas for the various magisters and aeries for the griffon riders who were granted personal chambers within the spire.

The Prince had been raised the whole of his life within these walls, but he still found the sight breathtaking. The green hills and plains surrounding the castle were patched with farms and were constantly graced with flocks of beautiful blue sparrows that were commonplace in the kingdom. The cry of the occasional hawk pierced the air and the wind blew the sweet scent of honeyed barley from the brewery that had been established nearby.

"I am home," the Prince said, as he always did when he rode upon that vista.

"Yes... but we both know it will not be welcoming," the Wizard added, sobering the Prince.

"It's truly pleasant to have you along," the Prince said sarcastically.

The Wizard looked with his piercing eyes at the castle walls.

"You may find yourself glad that I am here."

As they approached the gates, the guards recognized him immediately and raised the massive steel portcullis. They rode inside unabated and made directly for the spire. As they rode through the large, circular basilica in front they could hear jeering from all sides—nobles and peasants alike.

"I suppose here they would be most mindful of my absence," the Prince noted.

"More like they are the most within earshot of Ackalon," the Wizard clarified sardonically.

The Prince found he lacked a response to the accusation.

They reached the castle entry and stopped their horses. A stable hand took their stallions to feed and water them. The Prince took with him the packs containing the Knight's armor. With the Wizard by his side, they both entered the great hall.

They found attendants and nobles present, but the magisters were nowhere to be seen. At the sight of the Prince, the people appeared taken aback. The Prince cautiously glanced over each of them. Their expressions were a mix of shock, confusion, and even scorn.

The Prince saw Lord Monmouth, a family friend, among them. His eyes had heavy bags underneath and his face drooped with sorrow and concern; however, he seemed to brighten somewhat when he saw the prince. The Prince approached the lord and drew him aside.

"Majesty," Monmouth said. He appeared to be searching for words.

"Where are the magisters?" the Prince asked. He was straightforward—Ackalon and his companions had many things to answer for.

"Majesty, where have you been?" Monmouth asked, disregarding the question, "The magisters have been deliberating in the court for the past two days."

"I have only been gone six days," the Prince said in exasperation, "What is so urgent that they have to deliberate?"

"Yes, but without informing anyone. The nobles have heard word of your father's death. The magisters and the riders know of it. Your disappearance seemed both ill-timed and self-absorbed; if I may be so candid," Monmouth said with a slight bow.

"You may, and though my journey may have been ill-timed, it wasn't taken with malefic intent," the Prince replied.

"Now may be a good time to state as much, Your Grace," the lord suggested.

The Prince looked around. Most of the company had moved on to speculating on the Prince's reasons for returning, or what was occurring in the royal family. Others were still regarding him with suspicion.

"I need to see the council," he said to the lord, then looked to the Wizard, "Immediately."

The Wizard nodded and turned to the guests. "My lords and ladies, the Prince will speak to you shortly. For now, he wishes to see his magisters. Please, enjoy the fruits of the king's generosity," he emphasized the last part with a very accommodating tone.

11

THE SAPPHIRE SWORD

The Wizard and the Prince departed, thanking Lord Monmouth for his information. They approached two large wooden doors at the north of the great hall. Two guards in blue and grey heraldry stood unmoving with their spears. The Prince opened the doors and they both approached a large mechanism attached to two powerful oxen.

The mechanism was a lift that could take them to any level of the spire. The powerful oxen would be prodded into turning a massive stone wheel that would carry them to their destination.

"The throne room," the Prince said with urgency.

The steward of the lift and master of the oxen, also adorned in Avallonian heraldry, replied with a quick, "Yes, Your Grace," and hurried the oxen into motion. The steward, knowing the appropriate floor because of the number of rotations the oxen had made, stopped them with remarkable precision just at the floor they asked for.

They stepped off the elaborate contraption and onto a receiving terrace. This being the throne room, the terrace was elaborately decorated and greatly protected. The steward would not have even granted them access to such a terrace had he not recognized the Prince and the Blue Wizard.

They entered into the grand chamber and saw each of the magisters there. Only the commander of the spire-knights, First Knight Lady Gwinn, was present. From the sounds of their conversation, Gwinn was none too pleased with the magisters.

"Your Grace!" she called out upon seeing the doors swing open. "You've returned!" She approached the Prince and knelt before him. She then rose and greeted the Wizard as well.

"It's good to see you both back safely," she said, smiling.

"Lady Gwinn," the Prince returned her greeting, though his irritation could be easily heard in his voice. "Why is it that the people, their guards, and my court have all represented themselves as though I were off to war? I was traveling to a neighboring, and friendly, realm."

The Prince's eyes then darted accusingly toward the magisters —one in particular.

"Ackalon?" he stated as much as asked. "Care to explain this state of affairs?"

Ackalon came to the forefront of the magisters. He and the others were all adorned in the well-tailored robes of state, but it was he who bore a level of arrogance on par with his fine clothes. The Prince noted that he was escorted by the Lady Morgæna— whom he recognized as a noblewoman.

"Lady Gwinn is quite upset at the withdrawal of her riders' griffons. You must allow her some room to vent her frustrations," he said with an oily tone.

"Where are the griffons, Ackalon?" the Prince asked sternly.

"Departed, Your Grace. They took flight the morning of your father's passing," the magister answered.

"Why did they leave?" the Prince pressed.

"Perhaps you should ask yourself that," Ackalon sneered. "You are now so intrigued by the affairs of state? No more tournaments to attend to?"

The Wizard bristled at the magister's disrespect. The Prince was not an impulsive child who used the spire's gold and reputation to satisfy his whims. He had for years now been a young man engaged in affairs of his realm—albeit with slightly more bravado than his father, but he had the spirit of youth still fueling him. This preening snake was hiding something. The Wizard noted he still dodged the Prince's question.

"You flirt with treason..." the Wizard began.

"He is not a king until coronation," Ackalon interrupted.

"You will defer to your king, magister!" the Wizard bellowed.

"I will not yield to an absent juvenile!" Ackalon returned.

Both men appeared coiled to strike. A sudden wind whipped the Wizard's robes and tossed the magister's garments. The Prince noticed that Morgæna stood back warily regarding what unfolded. He drew his blade and Lady Gwinn did the same; she and the knights ready to aid their Prince if necessary.

The Prince watched all of this unfold. Ackalon was committing open sedition. He'd never liked the pompous aristocrat, but this was beyond what Ackalon was capable of. Something was wrong in his court. There, among all the royal court present, he shouted them down.

"Enough with this foolishness!" he yelled. "I will not abide this treasonous behavior," he said with a look to the magister, "in my father's court and that of my grandfather!"

The Prince continued to stare at Ackalon. "Wyvern is active again. With Hydra and Naga having not been seen for centuries, he is the most dangerous foe the kingdoms have encountered. None know what he could be scheming, but we all know that whatever it is it will affect us all. Each and every spire could be in danger."

"We do not, in fact, know that," Ackalon rebutted. "Wyvern is a wicked son of father Dragon, but he is of the forest realm in the Emerald Spire. He could be seeking treasure among its hills or perhaps have a vendetta against King Brennen; no matter the case it is an issue for Emrallt—not Avallonis."

"It is the king's duty to assist his allies if he is compelled to do so," the Prince continued relentlessly.

"And you are not yet king!" Ackalon refuted vigorously.

The Prince drew his blade, well-made and well-honed, and held it before Ackalon and the magisters to behold. It was made by his father and used by the former king in battle before being passed to his son. The Prince regarded them all, though mainly the Wizard and the magister, and addressed them.

"Behold the sword of my father, King Uther; passed to his son upon his ascension to the throne," the Prince tossed it down to the ground. It echoed through the hall as all those present gasped. "I lay it down before you, the court of the Sapphire Spire, before taking my grandfather's blade as my own and claiming my sovereignty."

The magister scoffed at the display.

"Petty dramatics will not win favors here, Your Grace. The full court must be present for your coronation to proceed. Unless, of course, you wish to defile the laws laid down by the ancient kings of the spire—those not among your family," he said derisively.

The Prince regarded him with open contempt. Oh, that he could do such a thing to spite this miserable traitor. He would not begin his rule in such a fashion. He focused on the coming victory—the greater victory—and that would suffice for now.

"No. Summon the magisters and the knights. The coronation will occur as the spire's law has established," the Prince said calmly.

"They will arrive tomorrow, Prince," a magister said with a bow.

Ackalon turned to leave with a handful of the magisters following. The Prince and Wizard noticed that Morgæna was watching them in disapproval. She left with Ackalon, smiling and talking while caressing the back of his neck with her long, shimmering fingernails.

"I do not trust that one," the Wizard said as he approached the Prince and returned his blade.

"I do not trust either of them," the Prince added. "Ackalon is ambitious—but he's no traitor. Something more is amiss here. Lady Morgæna—I do not recall much of her in father's court."

The Wizard nodded.

The Prince continued to watch the magisters leave the hall to summon their cohorts.

The Wizard smiled at the Prince. A man in his twenties, he would be taking the throne earlier than his father—much earlier. He was, however, already beginning to show the wisdom of his forebears. He should make a fine king and the Wizard counted himself fortunate to serve under him.

"Come with me, majesty. I want to show you something," the Wizard said.

The Prince cast him a dubious look. "Very well."

The Prince had Lady Gwinn return her spire-knights to their posts. The Wizard led the Prince up a flight of stairs that was located directly behind the throne.

"My father and mother would never allow me into this portion of the spire," the Prince noted on their way up the stairs.

"Nor should you allow your children," the Wizard commented.

"I suppose this leads to the Sapphire overlook."

Inside, the Prince was quite thrilled. He had never been allowed to the seat of the Sapphire which sat atop the spire. It was considered almost holy to the people of Avallonis.

All spires regarded their jewels as each having some symbolic significance for their realm. For instance, the kings and queens of Avallonis held a unique vigil for their coronations. The Prince was never given the full details of what transpired. He knew only that the Blue Wizard would inform him when it was necessary.

They ascended the stairway, broad and tall steps of stone and granite, to the peak of the spire. They reached a large doorway in the ceiling. As the Prince began to ponder how they might open it, the Wizard reached to his right and pulled a lever. The door lowered, held by two chains attached to two pulleys, and they walked upon it to their destination.

The pinnacle of the Sapphire Spire was perfectly circular. Surrounding the battlements along the edge, stood three knighted griffon riders. Typically they would have been seated on their magnificent white griffons. They still held their vigil with loyalty and pride: three during the day, three during the night

Despite reaching so far into the sky, there was only a gentle breeze at the top of this gilded tower. The Prince looked out and saw the whole of his kingdom—from border to border and horizon and horizon.

"Is this some sort of spell?" he wondered in awe. "How is it I can see such a distance from here—even here?"

The Wizard smiled. He had always enjoyed this majestic roost at the top of the world. "A spell? Perhaps. The spires are older than imagining, save for some minor tinkering of men such as our lift. Its magic is beyond even my understanding, however. Regardless, it has always been that the kings and queens of the Sapphire realm could see all that which the sapphire sees."

The Prince took in the majesty of the sight and he was humbled. This realm was in his charge. He would not want to be known as the Absent King, but he would not have Wyvern torment his allies and then turn against his people.

The Wizard turned the Prince's attention to the center of the spiretop. There, seated in a hollow of steel, stone, and granite, sat the Great Sapphire. It reflected the clouds and even, it seemed, the wind itself.

The sun glistened off its azure surface, as flawless as a noon sky. It was secure in its holdings, but these were situated only at its base. They reached no further than the bottom portion of the jewel. The Prince felt an urge to reach out and support it lest it tumbled to its destruction below, but there it sat—unmoving and unflinching.

"This is the most wonderful thing I have ever seen..." the Prince marveled.

It was then he noticed, within the confines of the sapphire, a blade that looked incredibly familiar. It was designed flawlessly— its pommel both strong and beautiful, the blade as straight as an arrow and sharp as a griffon's claw.

"Calibern," the Wizard said to him. "The sword of your fathers."

"How did it get here?" the Prince asked.

"Indeed, this is the core of why I brought you here," the Wizard explained.

The two of them approached the Great Sapphire and beheld the sword within it.

"It has always been that the Blue Wizard of Avallonis conveys the heritage of Calibern to the next king. So it was before your grandfather was handed the throne; so it shall be with your heirs and my successors.

Tomorrow, in view of the entire court as witnesses, you will remove the sword and claim your heritage. Ackalon can bemoan any facet of your family or methods that he chooses, but once you withdraw the sword he cannot deny you as king."

The Prince nodded. "I understand. But—can no one else remove the sword?"

"None," the Wizard replied simply. "Only the true heir of the throne. When King Aeuralius announced your grandfather as the inheritor the sword returned to its place in the sapphire upon Aeuralius's death, as it always does. Your grandfather removed it. He was king."

"None can simply take it? Breach the castle? Destroy the jewel?" the Prince inquired.

The Wizard ushered the Prince back a distance and placed himself between the Prince and the sapphire.

"Behold," the Wizard said.

The Wizard's lips moved, but the Prince heard nothing. He whispered the ancient words that both bound and released the magical essences of the world. Whatever utterance he had made, the sky soon filled with clouds.

The Wizard continued and the Prince saw, to his amazement, the clouds begin to take shape. A slender, muscular humanoid form began to emerge. Soon feathered wings coalesced and formed on its back. It grew the facial features of a strong, handsome woman. The cotton texture of the clouds soon became as smooth as marble. The woman was protected with the ancient armor their ancestors once wore, the ornate but resilient panoply, and held a hammer in her hand. She seemed to float there among the clouds and held aloft by some mighty wind.

The Wizard finished his spell, his eyes opening wide and with a flourish of his hands.

The winged woman flung her hammer and it crashed upon the stone. It rang out as though a mountain of iron had been struck. The riders, watching in wonder and fear, had drawn their weapons by this time, but shielded their ears against the sound and their eyes against the violent flash that followed.

The sound of a resounding thunder echoed around them at the top of the spire. When the Prince was able to open his eyes, the shape was receding, merging back into the clouds. The riders were looking about in disbelief.

The Prince looked again to the sapphire and saw it unscathed. Not even the stone around it was touched. Not one pebble had moved.

"None can 'simply' take it," the Wizard said, breathing heavily.

The Prince realized he was holding his breath.

"How…" he began, but he found the words came with difficulty. He'd never seen such magic before. "How did you do that?"

The Wizard coughed and then smirked; a weary but sly gesture. It was a small detail that had never arisen in their conversations.

"Wizards are stronger near their spires," he explained, "and here, I am practically touching the source of my power. Simple, really."

They heard the door to the court opening. Turning, they saw Lady Gwinn emerging with her weapon drawn. When she saw that everyone, especially the Prince, was safe, she sheathed her blade.

"Your Grace," she said, bowing, "I feared you were under attack, or, spires-all, possibly thrown from the tower..." She was truly at a loss for how to explain what she heard, and now to see the relative calm before her only further confused her.

"What did happen here?" she asked the Wizard.

The Wizard straightened his robes.

"I was merely explaining to the Prince the safety of Calibern within the sapphire... with the help of an aspara."

"Aspara?" the Prince asked.

"A cloud spirit," Lady Gwinn said in irritation. "You are going to kill the new king with your conjuring!" she chided.

"I assure you I am not," the Wizard said, seeming to take offense at the suggestion. "Come, let us rest. We have the Prince's coronation tomorrow."

The Prince agreed and Lady Gwinn insisted on escorting him as well. She also suggested posting guards at his chamber, given the hostilities earlier.

"You need not be a doting hen over him, Lady Gwinn," the Wizard remarked.

"I do not dote on him," she said, looking at the Prince. "Unlike the magister Ackalon I know he's no child. However, the magister's pandering to the people's fears has shown he is not as loyal as we would have believed and I do not wish to see him successfully take his ambitions to dangerous levels."

The Prince agreed. He would be seen as neither a coward nor a fool. He asked for additional guards to be posted for a single night only. After tomorrow's coronation, they would be dismissed from that duty and the Prince would manage his court appropriately.

12

THE PRINCE'S BLADE

The two guards stood in front of the door to the king's chamber, now in use by the Prince. Situated high in the spire, it was easily defensible and also provided an unmatched view from the balcony—save for what he had earlier seen at the spire's pinnacle.

The guards were fresh on their shift, having just replaced the previous four. They stood unflinching, not speaking, and appearing as armored statues supported by their shining spears. It did not take long, however, for one of them to show signs of bleariness.

One of the guards raised his hand to his helmet and let out a long, audible yawn. Breaking his vigil, the guard quickly returned to his unmoving post. No more than a few seconds passed before he was yawning again.

"Enough of that!" the other guard hissed. "We have only just begun our watch."

"Aye, and I slept like a tavern drunk before our watch," the tired guard protested. "Why am I so tired..." he complained.

Then the other guard shook his head, as he felt a sudden sleep coming on as well. It washed over them as they regarded each other with confusion. They had little time to say anything as they slouched to the ground in a deep slumber.

A slim, shadowed figure slipped past them and quietly allowed itself into the bedchamber. The well-tended door did not so much as squeak. The figure closed it carefully in silence.

Moonlight filtered into the room from the terrace window. The intruder was still cloaked in shadow as no candles burned. The Prince was exhausted from the previous day and found himself quickly falling to sleep earlier that evening. The figure roamed freely and quietly about the room and came quickly to his bed.

It sat ever so gently on the edge nearest the Prince. So graceful was the intruder that the Prince did not stir in his sleep or rise to defend himself. A slender hand reached down and began to gently, soothingly stroke the Prince's hair.

A whispered voice began to speak in his ear. The words crawled like a spider's legs among his sleeping thoughts. They tethered his will with greasy strands to the intruder's whims.

The words were beautiful and lulling, unlike their purpose. The graceful hand caressed the hair and face of the Prince, causing barely a stir.

Without another word the intruder silently departed the chamber. The guards, still slumbering, woke shortly after. They rose to their feet, stretched their aching limbs and necks, and resumed their post as though naught had occurred at all. They remembered nothing of their slumber or the shadow that walked amongst them.

* * *

MORNING CAME WITHOUT INCIDENT. The Prince awoke to bright sunlight cascading into his chambers through the window. The guards greeted him as he opened the door. He ascended to the great court where tables had been arrayed with breads, cheeses, and sugared fruits for breakfast.

The Wizard greeted him and inquired about his evening.

"Uneventful," the Prince said plainly.

He didn't come bearing the fine clothing of royalty. He donned the chest piece of the Knight's sacred armor. His sword was sheathed in its scabbard at his side. He wore the undergarments of war—tooled leather and chainmail. He carried the helmet his father would wear if he rode to war. He also donned the cloak worn by a king when he rode to combat—deep blue with the symbol of Avallonis in bright gray. A shadow of thick stubble adorned his cheeks and chin. His father had always had a beard, and to the Prince, this appeared kingly. He decided to follow suit.

Many of the magisters remarked over him with concern or cast him odd looks. His griffon riders, however, looked on with approval, even pride. Lady Gwinn had a particularly pleased look. Ackalon seemed almost disgusted.

"You look as though we are at war, my Prince," Ackalon said: the first words he said to his new king. "Do you not think this will cause unrest among the people? Among your court?"

The Prince paid him little regard. "As I said, we likely already are. I will make this clear once the coronation is over."

Ackalon sneered, "Very well. Let us ascend."

The Blue Wizard, head of the ceremony, led the court and the Prince to the top of the spire using the same, and only, stairway they used the previous afternoon. The spiretop was exactly as they had left it yesterday—with perhaps a few more clouds.

When they arrived the Wizard noticed the Prince hesitated. He looked over to see the Prince regarding the spire's pinnacle as though seeing it for the first time.

The Prince looked around in amazement. A long, red carpet had been run along the length of the spiretop to the Great Sapphire. A small portable stairway of wood had been placed before a raised stone dais in front of the seat of the jewel. Calla lilies, the royal flower of Avallonis, were placed by the dozens about the area.

The people of Eidalohn were gathered about the base of the tower. It is known that once the king is crowned, the Great Sapphire will glow a brilliant blue for the remainder of the day, marking the event. The new king and his court would then emerge from the spire and greet the people. They all observed in anticipation.

The riders stood at attention on one side of the flower-lined aisle. The magisters stood opposite them. Seven to the right, seven to the left; flanking their king. Might and intellect, guided by wisdom and authority. This was the way of things.

A precious few dignitaries, Lady Morgæna included, stood aside by the entrance. They had a distinct and rare honor to be here. There were but a handful, and they stood enraptured by the sight—even Morgæna.

The Prince approached the sapphire wherein lay Calibern, the sword of his fathers. All present watched eagerly. The magisters turned their heads to view the stone. The riders, in trained fashion, held a forward and focused gaze.

The Prince reached the top of the dais. He was staring into the facets of the gem reflecting a perfect sky. However, as he grew closer it also seemed to waver as the surface of a calm pool that had been disturbed.

He reached out and touched the surface of the sapphire. It was cool and as solid as he thought a stone should feel, yet it rippled at his fingertips. He began to push into the stone, expecting to reach in and grasp the blade. However, just as his fingers breached the very surface, they were stopped. Suddenly all was solid. He could not reach any further. The rippling pond had turned to ice.

He pulled his hand away, observing it in shocked confusion. Nothing appeared abnormal. He tried again and found his hand was halted by the stone. He tried with his other hand and, again, to no avail.

There was an audible gasping among the crowd.

Ackalon looked on and was beaming.

"He is not king..."Ackalon whispered to himself. "He is not king!"

The horrible words echoed among the magisters. Soon, some of the riders were repeating it in disbelief.

"This cannot be..." Lady Gwinn said to herself.

She turned to look at the Wizard who was maintaining his physical composure, but there was a fire in his eyes and his face was wrought with concern. His eyes met hers and he gestured to the sapphire. Lady Gwinn knew what he asked.

She approached the sapphire and respectfully ushered the Prince out of the way. She touched the stone and saw no reaction. It was a cold, solid sapphire—as impenetrable as she had seen the previous day against the might of the aspara.

The Prince stepped back. He looked at his hands in failure. He then turned his curiosity and torment inward—seeking a reason in his soul for this horrendous outcome. His father was king. His mother was queen. Why did the sword refuse him?

The Wizard watched as the riders and magisters huddled about the stone. The magisters stepped upon the dais and were attempting to touch and press upon the sapphire in search of any answer. The riders clustered near Gwinn and the Prince— protecting them and simultaneously attempting to see what came of the commotion. Ackalon, he noticed, stood near the back.

He cast a quick, inconspicuous glance at Lady Morgæna. While the other dignitaries were looking about in worry and fervently discussing what unfolded before them, she stood there calmly. Her hands were tucked in the cuffs of her expensive gown. Her eyes focused on the sapphire.

Then the Wizard saw the number of hands grasping and pressing on the stone. They truly appeared to be pressing against a solid, unwelcoming surface. The Great Sapphire flickered and rippled at the Prince's touch yet his hand could reach slightly within; historically, it was all or nothing.

The Wizard swiftly approached the small throng. Seeing it was the Blue Wizard, the riders stepped aside. He grabbed the Prince by the shoulder and pulled him away. The young man had a troubled look on his face. He was distraught at this bewildering turn of events, but the Wizard did not believe in circumstance.

He believed in what was or was not. Even magic had established rules. He believed that which was set to be was already in motion. Those things that had been established would always be unless they were set upon by foul machinations. What was occurring at the pinnacle of the Sapphire Spire was an establishment set awry.

He took the Prince's chin in his hands. "Look at me," he said sternly.

He cursed himself for what he saw there and had not noticed before. The blacks of the Prince's eyes were overly large. Unnatural light dwelt within and swirled about.

"He's been bewitched," the Wizard said, somewhat to himself. "Step away from the stone!" he called out harshly.

Those that once bustled about the great stone stopped suddenly. They turned to look at the Wizard and saw him with the Prince who gazed about, trying to understand what he'd just heard. The dignitaries turned to look, as well. They all looked to him expectantly.

The Wizard sneered at them. "Our Prince has been hexed—set upon by sinister magic."

"How do you know this?" called out a voice from the gathering.

The Wizard sought out the voice and found it belonged to Lord Kay.

"Very well, who here can say they know something of magic and can authenticate my claim?" the Wizard thundered.

Many of the magisters and riders looked about uncomfortably. It was quite a grave silence.

"I can," a voice declared.

All heads turned to see Lord Gareth. The Wizard had enjoyed his occasional discussions with Gareth. He was a man of common sense and intellect. He was a man of clever thought, not shrewd schemes. Much of Gareth's family, on his mother's side, hailed from the Amethyst realm. They knew much of sorcery.

The Wizard stepped aside. Lord Gareth, a tall man, knelt and looked into the Prince's eyes. It was but a moment that passed before he hung his head and rose to his feet.

"The Blue Wizard speaks truthfully. The Prince has been beset by a spell. This isn't spire magic. It's black magic—possibly Mythestan," Gareth said, referencing the Amethyst Realm's infamy for its dark woods and history of disreputable arcane practices.

The court broke out into a fury of words and accusations.

"Who? Who would do such a thing?" they called out.

"Quiet!" the Wizard declared and held his hands aloft.

He turned his head to the dignitaries. His hands fell and his head rose when he saw Morgæna no longer among them.

"Where is Lady Morgæna?" he asked. He looked specifically at the dignitaries.

They glanced about like lost children. The Wizard stalked furiously towards them. The door to the court was ajar.

"Riders! We must find her," the Wizard shouted.

"Wait!" Ackalon called out.

The riders stopped in spite of their haste; their swords were already drawn.

"What evidence do you have against her?" Ackalon challenged.

The Wizard regarded him with a fury. Truly, what evidence did he have? His suspicions were not enough.

"She has disappeared. Should that not provoke at least a search?" the Wizard replied with urgency.

"That is a pitiable reason to begin a witch hunt." Ackalon retorted sarcastically.

"What a choice of words..." the Wizard began.

"Do you imply such a thing, conjurer?" Ackalon interrupted, stalking towards him.

The two men approached each other menacingly. Suddenly a brilliant blue glow filled the area. The Wizard and Ackalon were forced to cover their eyes as were all those around them. They all turned and there, amid the fading light, stood the Prince. His old sword still sheathed, he held within his hand the blade, Calibern. It reflected the light of the sapphire and the stone itself dazzled with light like a thundercloud.

As it all faded they stood in the sight of the King of the Sapphire Spire. Near him stood Lord Gareth.

"Majesty... the spell?" the Wizard asked, confused.

"Has been broken," the Prince explained, "Lord Gareth is quite skilled."

"Your Grace..." Ackalon began to speak. He was stopped as the king raised his hand.

"Find the Lady Morgæna," the Prince ordered.

"Immediately, Your Grace," Lady Gwinn remarked. She and a number of the riders ran for the court.

The Prince ordered Ackalon held by the riders as he and the Wizard followed Lady Gwinn. They descended into the court to find the riders cornering Morgæna. She had been trapped by a railing near an open balcony.

Facing the blades of the best soldiers in Avallonis, Morgæna looked down at the crowd below. They were cheering; having seen the azure glow of the Great Sapphire they all hailed their king. They were fully ignorant of that which transpired above them.

The riders approached her cautiously, slowly closing in.

Morgæna thrust a hand in their direction. Black, coiling tendrils snaked from her hand. They took the form of ghostly vipers—snapping and hissing at the soldiers.

"Stay back!" she shouted.

The Wizard pushed his way through them as they slowly retreated to a safer distance. He stood there before the witch and regarded her twisting vipers with scorn.

"Dark magic, indeed," he sneered.

His hand shot forth and let loose a bolt of sparks and thunder. To his surprise, she used her vipers to subdue and neutralize the magic—although at the cost of the spectral snakes themselves which disappeared in a puff of oily smoke.

"The king's court is no place for a mage's battle—wouldn't you agree?" Morgæna taunted. "Would you risk the lives of everyone here to destroy me, Wizard?"

"Fool witch!" the Wizard cursed, though he knew she was right.

Morgæna looked over them all. She didn't have the look of one frightened or desperate. She held a cold, unforgiving refinement about her. She backed ever closer to the railing.

"You're correct, Prince. Wyvern is coming," she said snidely, "and he will take what is his."

Spitting her final words at them, she threw herself over the edge. The Wizard and Prince rushed to the railing followed quickly by Gwinn. They leaned over to see Morgæna falling, endlessly falling, to the terrified crowd below.

The riders, not without foresight, had called the lift. The Prince, Wizard, and Gwinn were carried down to ground level. They rushed out the front door to be greeted by a throng of confused and frightened people. The city guard had them placated and under control. The captain walked swiftly to greet the three.

He carried with him a large cloak that they recognized as the one worn by Lady Morgæna. It was all that he'd found. There was no sign of the sorceress.

"There's no blood… nothing…" the Prince remarked. "Where is her body?"

The captain beheld the Prince with a mingling of fear and misunderstanding.

"We all saw her—everyone here, we saw the body fall from the tower and tumble through the sky. When she landed, this… this is all there was—nothing more."

He handed the empty cloak to the Wizard.

"She's fled with her magic," the Wizard explained.

The Prince's face grew shadowed. "Wyvern has allies, even among my court."

The Prince and Wizard regarded each other with growing concern. What scheme had Wyvern laid out? What was it he sought?

The Prince took the cloak and looked into it as though it held these answers. The Wizard took the opportunity to refocus and rally the crowd.

"All hail the king!" he shouted.

"Hail!" the voices rose together.

The Prince drew Calibern and held it before the crowd to see. They cheered and the Prince urged them to return home, that life would continue, stability would remain, and justice would be done. The Prince then excused himself and returned to the spire with his still-loyal court in tow.

Many hours passed. The new king thought on the events of that day while seated on his throne. The Wizard came to him in the early hours of the afternoon.

"Do you bring counsel?" the new king asked, his heart heavy.

"I only come that you may ask it of me if you see fit, my king," the Wizard replied.

The Prince scoffed. "I return to a broken court; a divided throne. My people greeted me with avarice and distrust. My magisters the same. Even my riders had doubted me before Gwinn spoke on my behalf. Now even their griffons are gone."

"I have never known you to sulk, Your Grace," the Wizard remarked.

"I do not sulk," the Prince corrected. "I speak of the current state of my rule. I am no king; not yet. Until Morgæna is returned to justice and the threat of Wyvern is no more."

"An admirable goal, though not without a good measure of peril," the Wizard was curious about the Prince's plan of action.

"Yes. Avallonis can't face Wyvern alone. Morale is damaged and our knights weakened. I will not be just like the fallen prince that resulted in my grandfather gaining the throne. He was brave, but his bravery lacked the support to maintain his kingdom. The Knight was a great warrior. I want to learn to fight like him. It wouldn't hurt if I could find an army of those just like him and perhaps persuade them to join our cause," the Prince leaned forward and creased his brow in thought.

The Wizard, already having such warriors in mind, nodded in agreement with the Prince.

"A legendary army," the Wizard added.

The Prince regarded him dubiously. "You know of such warriors?"

"Indeed, I do," the cryptic old man walked to one of the open windows. There he held out his hand gently. A small bird, with feathers red as blood and black as night, landed and chirped vigorously on his hand. He whispered something to it and then sent it off flying.

"What trickery are you up to?" the Prince asked.

"It's no trickery. Rather, a message. You travel tonight," the Wizard explained.

"Tonight? What of the city? Who will sit in my place? Avallonis was nearly in open revolt over the last little trip I took. I make mistakes, but I don't like making the some mistake twice," the Prince asked sardonically. The Wizard provided no further insight.

"I'm not staying. I have questions of my own involving these events. I will call the Wizard's Council together. Lady Gwinn, however, has proven her exceeding loyalty. As First Knight, she would suit well the role of Avallonis's steward."

The Prince nodded. "Agreed. The magisters proved inept at the task. The riders will have their hour. Without their griffons, they'll be grounded here, as is. They can watch over Eidalohn until I return."

The Wizard thought for a moment. "And what of Ackalon?"

The Prince regarded the Wizard sternly. He quietly considered his options, then nodded when he landed upon an answer. "Send him to the Iron Halls. He can linger there until I return."

The spires, being older than anything currently living, have never had a means of holding prisoners. No dungeons or any similar areas suitable to holding undesirables were present in any of the gilded towers. Each kingdom was tasked with handling its own criminals.

Avallonis constructed the Iron Halls; a large, single-story building of interconnected halls with small rooms large enough for a single person. Much like Emrallt's own Deep Briars, this was where the delinquents of society would spend the rest of their days unless the king decided otherwise.

The Wizard concurred—this was a suitable fate for the former magister.

"Now, Prince, you will ride east. Take the roads following the rising sun until you come to the base of the Veil Mountains. I warn you, majesty, do not attempt to journey through those mountain passes. The cold is enough to freeze a man's breath in his lungs and I'll not go into detail about the frost ogres that call the place home.

You'll need to go beneath the mountains, where it's safe. Before those great peaks is the dwarf-hold of Kalt Dyr. That is where you'll find passage. Upon your arrival, inform the dwarves that you seek the Red Messenger. It's safe to discuss with them the purpose of your travel. You'll know them by the red sparrow pin he wears on his clothing. The Red Messenger will make sure you get to Valgrind, the capital of the kingdom of Edda. There you will find the instruction you seek."

The realm of the Ruby Spire. The Prince's lessons had taught him of all the kingdoms, and Edda was a hard, dry place. He knew of the Veil Mountains and vaguely the time it would take to travel there. He knew of the legendary armies of Edda. He knew of the hellish training they endured. He knew that there he would find the greatest warriors, but he also felt a sudden pang of fear.

"Very well, I will do as you have instructed. When I return, it will be as king," the Prince said.

The Wizard nodded. "Their warriors are the finest in the world. Train with them, speak to the Red King of our plight. I will come to you afterward when your time there is complete."

The Prince and the Wizard gave their instructions to Gwinn. They appropriated their horses. The Prince had become fond of Ceffyl and the horse fond of him. The beast pawed anxiously at the sight of the Prince, ready to begin their journey. The Wizard headed north to a secreted location for the wizards to hold their council. The Prince departed to the east where he would follow the rising sun until he came to the great Veil Mountains and from there to the kingdom of Edda.

13

KALT DYR

The Prince rode beyond the hills and rocks of Avallonis. Above him, soaring unseen, he was watched by the eyes of Drake, the son of father Dragon who dwelt within the peaks of Avallonis and called the sapphire realm home.

The Prince traveled through forest and dale under the swift Drake's watchful gaze. He rode fast and relentlessly. Ceffyl's training and warhorse heritage drove him ever onward when a lesser beast would have fallen aside.

Perhaps this is why the Prince failed to notice the winged shadow that trailed him in the cloudy sky. The good Drake, brother to the vile Wyvern, had heard of his sibling's actions. The children of Dragon were as varied as brothers and sisters come; each having their separate strengths and weaknesses to abide.

Drake was swift; among the fastest of any creature. However, he lacked the cunning and guile of Wyvern and would not deign to assume what his brother sought with his scheme.

At this time the Prince rode alone and Drake did not want to see the errant king come to harm. The Prince simply urged his stallion along the eastern roads. He did not stop except to rest at an unassuming tavern along the road. He did not sleep; stopping only to drink, eat, and rest his horse.

Though the Prince remained unaware, Drake noticed the wild beasts and brigands scatter at the dragonchild's shadow. Drake wondered why the heir rode alone—no guards, no escort—and why the Blue Wizard would abide such? Had he not just been called by a self-imposed geas to the Prince when his brother sought the young man's destruction?

Perhaps, Drake concluded, that the Blue Wizard—wisest among the magi, in his opinion—knew that Drake would be inevitably drawn to the curiosity of such an action and the Prince would be safe in the vicinity of this distant, looming guardian.

Drake soared above the Prince and Ceffyl. He watched as they rode on. Why would Wyvern cause such a stir among the realms? Where was the Prince going with such reckless haste?

The night came and Drake was now soaring in the moonlight. The dark of night did not encumber his vision. He could clearly see the stallion Ceffyl racing along the roads. He could also see packs of wolves and other creatures being drawn to the rider.

A roar would have readily frightened them away. A burst of his flaming breath would also do. However, he wished his presence to remain unknown to the Prince and, knowing that the beasts of the wild would both smell and sense his presence, Drake swooped low with the wind and passed by the stalking creatures. They scattered and fled, and the Prince was safe on his course.

Day came and by early morning the Prince approached the Veil Mountains. More specifically, Drake noticed, he rode to Kalt Dyr. The dwarf-hold kept a constant vigil over the freezing mountain pass. Beyond, the blizzards and storms gave way to a sheer cliff of unimaginable size. Thereafter lay the deserts of Edda, the Ruby Realm and home to his brother, Wyrm.

Wyrm was not as overtly vicious as their sibling Wyvern, but he was quite solitary and had a distaste for being disturbed. He preferred to scour the most ancient of tomes and scrolls and deemed himself a keeper of knowledge and a scholar on all things.

Drake needn't fear the Prince's mistreatment at the claws of Wyrm (as he most likely would never see him in this life or any other) and the men of the Edding armies were among the greatest in the world. They were also men of great honor and wouldn't harm visiting royalty who came on peaceful terms.

Drake found a perch high among the peaks of the Veil Mountains. He looked down as the Prince and Ceffyl arrived at the gates of Kalt Dyr. They were greeted and led inside by the dwarves who dwelt there.

The Prince having safely arrived, Drake flew on to his lair where once resided the white griffons and their Speaker—his dearest friend. Recently they had left the comfortable mountainous dwelling and not returned. It was curious to Drake, but not yet alarming. He was more concerned with the stirrings among the spires.

* * *

THE PRINCE WAS MET by a dwarf with bright red hair caked in dirt. A red sparrow pin sparkled on his broad chest.

"Are you the Red Messenger?" the Prince asked.

The dwarf smiled, his round cheeks pushing his eyes into a squint. The Prince explained his need to travel under the Veil Mountains to Edda. The dwarf gestured for the Prince to enter into the yawning mountain door and was escorted into a bunkhouse for the night. It was a simple room and not well-tended. It smelled of sweat and old bread, and the bed had recently been slept in.

"You'll have to forgive the lodgings, majesty. Don't get many visitors this way; much less royal ones," the old dwarf explained. His thick, wet lips flapped like landed fish in his long, lanky beard. He had to crane his neck to speak to the Prince.

He waddled as he led the Prince about their fortress and smelled of smoke, pitch, and other, more unscrupulous odors. The sharp, spicy smells stung the Prince's nose.

The Prince had never met a dwarf, personally, and all he knew of them were from his academic lessons. They inhabited only the Veil Mountains, and these mighty crags stretched along the larger portion of the spire-realms eastern lands and their roots run deep into the earth.

Dwarves valued work and toil. They never stopped and were rumored to sleep for only an hour or two a day. They ate as they worked, and this lead to rumors that they had developed a taste for minerals, stones, and mortar.

The Prince would have greatly enjoyed to stay and learn more of them, but as soon as he lay down on that filthy bed he fell fast to sleep. He dreamt of nothing during that time, awakening only to the sound of another dwarf snoring in a bunk nearby. He was surprised the constant sounds of tinkering and mining didn't wake him, but he was exhausted.

He rose and dusted the debris, crumbs, and dust off his clothing. When he exited the bunkhouse he was offered a plate of bread and what he thought was meat, but he could barely tell from the soot and grease that covered it all. He politely declined. He instead insisted that he and his horse needed to be on their way.

The dwarf escorting him nodded and began eating away at the portions. The halls they traveled were within the mountain. The dwarf explained that a raging blizzard was tossing about within the valley—a never-ending storm that would kill anything shy of a frost giant. The very fortress he entered was built by dwarves to allow safe passage between the mountains. The Prince would require escort due to the hazards of the continual construction of new tunnels and passageways.

After an hour of travel in the large tunnelways, the Prince was witness to one such hazard when a large mass of boulders collapsed beneath them and they nearly tumbled several dozen feet to solid ground below.

His guide peered into the tunnel and bellowed to the dwarves below. "Ho! You stunted tunnel rats! You near killed a king and worse still, me!"

They traded brief insults in what the Prince could only assume was Dwarvish, and then his guide shouted for the pit to be cordoned off to prevent accidents.

"They'll ne'er finish the blasted road to Djupa Hem at this rate!" the dwarf grumbled as they rode.

"Djupa Hem?" the Prince asked.

"Aye. A quaint little town. You should visit sometime, Your Grace." The dwarf said, his mustache rising as he smiled.

"There's a city below here?" the Prince asked in surprise.

"Well, I wouldn't say 'city'," the dwarf corrected. "Only perhaps seven-hundred or so dwarves there. A few displaced gnomes from the tunneling."

The Prince was dumbfounded. Whole towns and cities within the mountains—it was beyond his imagination. He certainly would have to return someday to see these places; though he would still avoid the food.

A few more hours and they arrived at their destination. The tunnel opened into a large cavern that had been reformed into a grand terrace. He could hear water running and as they drew further into the terrace he saw that a dwarf-cut causeway was carved into the stone, allowing a large flow of water to come from a tunnel within the mountain.

Even more amazing, the water flowed onto a raised, stonework rivulet not unlike what was seen at logging camps. This, however, was many times larger. It ran out into the horizon beyond sight.

"Spires-all..." the Prince cursed.

"Beautiful, is she not?" the dwarf remarked proudly. "Been maintained by us since Ragnarok."

"Ragnarok?" the Prince asked aloud. He'd never heard of that before.

"Oh, well…" the dwarf mumbled, "that, uh, may be… I'm more of an expert on the Dwarf-waters. That's probably a question best left for your guide."

He seemed uncomfortable with the question. The Prince had others for him, though.

"What are the Dwarf-waters?" the Prince asked.

The dwarf explained the wonder of the Dwarf-waters. A masterpiece of engineering, they were remarkably similar to logging sluices commonly found in mills. These were much larger, however, and carried small sailboats, called logboats, and were propelled by water flowing from massive underground water mills, also constructed by the dwarves. They were held aloft by giant support beam networks so they could run up into the high mountain caves safely away from the threats of the desert floor.

As they were currently at the first logboat port in the mountains entering Edda, they were over a hundred feet off the ground. The Dwarf-water sluice snaked out into the desert like an artificial river, traveling beyond sight into the horizon.

The sands of Edda were harsh and unforgiving. The men of the Ruby Spire and their king came to an accord with the dwarves many centuries ago: that they would trade freely, and aid each other in times of war for the use of these systems.

Travel could be made between most major cities within the Red Kingdom by use of the logboats, and the chutes also provided a source of water in the desert. Travel was faster and safer and a beneficial alliance was maintained.

The Prince beheld the awe-inspiring sight of the Dwarf-waters reaching out into the desert of Edda before him. Hundreds of feet below the sheer rock face, a ceaseless desert spread before the Prince's eyes. He would take one of these logboats through the desert to Valgrind, the City of the Ruby Spire, and there he would ask for the aid of the Red King.

They loaded one of the large logboats into the quick-flowing waters. It was held in place by a pair of stones attached to chains which would be removed once they were prepared to depart.

The logboat was just that—a log from the massive drassil trees that grew in the mountains and was carved to fit up to ten men. It required only two small rectangular sails in the event the waters ran slowly. The boat was carved with dwarven insignias and heralds and at the front of the boat was the effigy of a dwarf woman holding forth a lantern commonly used by their proud miners.

The Prince was marveling at the ingenuity and natural beauty of the system when a voice spoke from behind him.

"And you are the Prince of Avallonis, errant King of the Sapphire Spire."

The Prince turned, ready to draw Calibern when he saw another man standing a safe distance from him. The chainmail of his hauberk glinted in the harsh desert light from the hole in the mountainside. Under his mail, a cream-colored long-sleeve shirt that protected his arms from the harsh sun whipped in the sudden breezes that came and went sporadically.

The armor was nicked and scratched. It bore the marks of years of use. A white tabard worn over his chainmail bore the symbol of the Ruby Kingdom—a circular rune-like symbol, similar to the shape of the Great Ruby, set ablaze. A large sword was sheathed on his back and two small war axes were attached to a leather belt that he wore. He also carried an over-sized waterskin.

His long blond hair, woven into thick braids, was permanently tousled from the wind and sand of his kingdom. His eyes were a piercing blue that reminded him of the Maiden's and sat heavy in a face that bore several scars. He was intimidating, of this there was no doubt, but the Prince couldn't let his first impression be one of weakness.

"Let's say 'yes,' for brevity's sake. And you are?" he asked plainly.

"I bear many names in my land," the man said, walking toward the Prince. "The Eastern Dirge. The Biting Wind. The Many-Blades."

"I suppose the last one is my favorite," the Prince said sardonically.

"You," the man said, coming to a stop before the Prince, "will call me 'sir' until such time that I find it unnecessary."

"I thought the Red Messenger would be escorting me to Valgrind?" The Prince stood looking at him, eye to eye, though the younger Prince was forced to look up, somewhat, at the surly man.

"Your wizard sent word to the Red Wizardess that you were coming. The messenger brought you here, I insisted on taking you the rest of the way."

The man acted the way the Prince imagined one who trained soldiers for battle would. He might make a good instructor for his own training.

"I see," the Prince returned. "Does Edda treat all royal visitors with such hostility?"

The Warrior continued to glare at him disdainfully.

"Royalty," the Warrior said. He seemed to roll the word in his mouth, seeing if he wanted to spit it back at him or not.

"You have not fully taken the title of The Blue King for yourself. You are therefore not fully a prince, as well. I say that makes you neither. You don't know who you are and I can't decide how to receive you. Much like our recruits. So, you will call me—"

"Sir," the Prince cut him off. "Very well. Let's see how I measure up to your standards."

The Prince knew the Eddings were a warrior culture and their harsh environment had made them even harder people. He would play things their way. If they were going to assist him, he'd need their respect, not their friendship.

The Warrior instructed him to board the logboat. It would be a lengthy trip to the Ruby Spire and the Prince would be given some instruction during the travel.

They loaded up on the boat; the two of them as well as Ceffyl. The Prince said farewell to the dwarven guide, informing him that someday the Prince would return a king to see that which the dwarf's people had built below the earth and stone.

The boat didn't rock as much as the Prince expected. It sat firmly in place as though nestled between firm rocks. The dwarf bellowed something in his language and the sounds of clattering chains was followed by sight of the stones holding the logboat back lifting out of the water, causing the boat to rock gently as it fully settled into the artificial river. Freed from its moorings, the logboat began its course on the massive sluice. The Prince and the Warrior felt themselves moving faster and faster until their speed beat that of any fleeing horse.

14

THE RED CITY

The Dwarf-waters moved them high above the desert and the Prince could see the endless dunes of sand passing below them.

"Such inhospitable land. Why do your people still linger here? How do you even survive?" the Prince asked.

The Warrior looked out over his homeland. "Hard land. Harder people."

"Was it always this way?"

"Not always," the Warrior replied gruffly.

"The dwarf mentioned something I am curious about; Ragnarok, I think it was."

The Warrior stared ahead for a moment. His gaze lost among the endless sea of dunes. He eventually replied in a hoarse whisper, "Yes. A story for later."

"You're right. We are quite busy," the Prince said, smiling. The dwarf-water channel they rode stretched out to the horizon. No others could be seen to the left or right, and he could see for miles.

"I don't feel like discussing it with an outsider. Being king of a foreign land doesn't make you privy to an explanation of generations of suffering for my people."

The Prince grimaced. Things were different in Edda. A desert realm of tyrannical heat and adversity shut off from the world by a wall of mountains, oppressive cold, and snowstorms.

"I apologize. I'm out of my element. If I may ask, where is this channel taking us?"

"Valgrind, the Red City. There you'll see how my people survive this wasteland."

The Prince was both eager and hesitant. If the Warrior was representative of the populace as a whole, then the people were indeed as hard as the land. They traveled for quite some time without speaking a word to each other until Warrior broke the silence.

"Your training will begin upon arrival. You'll undergo that which every Edding warrior endures. Enjoy this journey, Prince; it is one that few others ever partake in. Your training will try everything that you are, and many things you are not—but if you can endure, you will be a better warrior than any found in other kingdoms."

The Prince regarded the Warrior with as much confidence as he could muster. He reminded himself of what drove him here; Wyvern, the Maiden, the Knight. To return in failure would be to shame those depending on him and to give credence to his enemies. Success was the only acceptable outcome. He would return a king, with allies to face Wyvern, or he would not return at all.

* * *

VALGRIND WAS the only destination on this particular channel of the Dwarf-waters, and it was a magnificent city.

A wall of stone and steel one hundred feet high surrounded the whole of the city. It was also perfectly circular. The Prince could see a scant few entrances at the base of the wall, large bronze doors that glistened in the sun. They were heavily guarded and no one appeared to leave or enter through them. The Dwarf-waters were the only real entrance to the city.

Two other sluices were leading from the north and south-east portions of the city. The northern Dwarf-waters led to another city that could just be seen on the horizon—also encircled by a large wall.

The Prince never thought such a place could exist. Within the wall he could see numerous buildings stacked one upon the other with roads and alleys circling around them and sloping up and down along the interior. Valgrind's people, dressed in light, flowing garments to combat the heat, conducted their business in bustling markets. They spoke openly and to one another, but cast pensive glances and even suspicious stares the Prince's way. Opulent gardens and trees dotted the city and helped the people forget for a moment the relentless and endless desert outside their mighty walls.

The city had to be contained within those walls. The creatures dwelling in the desert were singularly hostile. Without walls, the warriors of Edda would battle the native beasts of this land day and night.

The ground floor was heavily shadowed and dense. The Prince saw fewer people bustling about there. Though it was cool and the harsh sun was filtered by the many sources of shade above, this was where the warriors of Edda made contact with the harsh outside world. The people feared this intimate proximity to the dangerous desert environment.

The city continued to spring up along the interior of the walls until they reached near the top of the spire. Only about one-third of the Ruby Spire jutted from the uppermost ramparts. Great shade-providing canopies stretched like the wings of birds from building to building.

Even with the magnificence of Valgrind, the spire was

grander still. Its stone walls rose into the sky higher than any other of its kind. It was the tallest of the spires. It had no external terraces, but an incredible number of windows. The great ruby atop the spire sat alone—no visible area was present to stand near it—unlike in Eidalohn. It was set in a steel and glass frame styled after the flaming runes of the Edding symbol. The glass and steel caught the sunlight and reflected on the ruby in a manner that made the top of the spire appear to be forever engulfed in flame. The Prince had seen it long before they arrived at the city, and had thought the top of the spire was genuinely on fire like a great lighthouse.

The logboat came to an abrupt stop, resting between two of the large stones in the Dwarf-waters. The Prince and Warrior departed the logboat, which was tended by dwarves even here, and the Warrior led the Prince and Ceffyl to a battlement atop the large wall.

Guards dressed similarly to the Warrior held posts at regular intervals. Here and there were rounded towers providing space for large ballistae. The Prince inquired about the necessity for the large siege weapons and the Warrior explained one of the many dangers of Edda.

He explained that the beasts that resided in the desert were twisted and dangerous. Among them were the jormungandr—massive serpents that lived among the cool sands deep within the ground. They rose only to feed on desert-dwelling creatures and marching armies when hungry. There were also the grendel: monstrous relatives of trolls who inhabited the desert caves.

The ballistae were particularly useful when fending off the manticores—flying monsters whose lionesque bodies bore serpentine wings and a tail covered with foot-long spines sharper than any spear. They grew back when damaged—usually by breaking off into the bodies of their victims—and their man-like faces housed two gaping, unblinking black eyes and many rows of sharp teeth.

The manticores often avoided the walled cities, but the other townships of the desert realm were open to attack. A manticore who attacked an undefended town would often empty it of inhabitants within a week if the Red Warriors couldn't intervene. This is why the Edding warriors trained so fiercely. They must be prepared to traverse hostile environs to face even more hostile creatures.

The Warrior instructed the Prince to follow him to the lower district. There they passed blacksmiths toiling and butchers chopping at their recent shipments. They smelled smoke from various stoves and forges. They heard craftsmen yelling for or at their apprentices. Women herded children away from the bustle as some escaped and engaged in mock combat with sticks and stones.

Two boys, in particular, cut closely in front of the Warrior causing him to halt in his tracks and throw his arms up for balance. The Prince watched warily. The two began swinging large sticks, pretending they were swords. The Warrior turned his gaze to them and shouted, "Both hands, lad! Follow through!" then chuckled as he waved the Prince on.

As they moved through the lower district, the Prince saw that the hard, standoffish people he'd read about in his studies were, in truth, simply disciplined and close-knit. They were rigid in their practices and trade as a means to survive an environment constantly seeking to consume them.

They soon came to a guarded door set into the wall. Recognizing the Warrior, the guards allowed them through. and removed a large iron bar from the thick door. It took two of the guards to move its massive, creaking hinges.

Once inside they walked a torch-lit hallway through the massive innards of the ramparts. The wall was incredibly thick, and housed small bunks for soldiers, guards, and masons working the walls.

They reached the outer doors and the Warrior pulled a small

chain, which was quite unnoticeable unless you knew where to look, and a notch on the door slid open and shut just as quickly.

The door opened to the harsh desert outside. A bright light followed by thick, hot air billowed into the hall. With the Warrior in the lead, they stepped out into a small encampment that was all but unnoticeable on the boat-ride into the city. No more than a firepit and few sheltering tents, the camp contained a handful of other soldiers all garbed in the same chainmail and clothing as the Warrior.

The Warrior greeted one in particular; a man who wore a leather sash across his torso. It was etched with the circle-and-fire symbol of Edda. They exchanged a few words in a foreign tongue and the soldier then saluted and turned away from the Warrior.

"Who was that, may I ask?" the Prince inquired as the Warrior returned to him.

"The leader of this warband. His men will grant us shelter for the time being. There," the Warrior said, pointing to an empty tent.

They entered their tent—a canvas of cloth with two cots and nothing more—and placed their packs on the ground. The Prince sat on the cot and noticed it was quite uncomfortable, but he had the feeling he would ready to sleep in the sand itself come nightfall. The Warrior drank deeply from his waterskin and tossed it to the Prince who drank as well.

"You are going to cook inside that armor," the Warrior stated. "Steel plate, chainmail, and leather underlayers? I'm surprised you're still standing."

"I'm a little warm, but I feel fine," the Prince returned. "although I suppose I could do without the chain or the leather."

"The plate must go. The chain and leather will serve you best," the Warrior explained and gestured to himself.

"I can't remove the plate; that I can assure you," the Prince insisted.

The Warrior approached and examined him. His face bore the look of an experienced veteran preparing to teach his student. He reached out and grasped the breastplate and his demeanor changed to one of surprise. He found the breastplate was quite cool.

"Where did you get this?" he asked in astonishment.

"It was given to me by Brennen, the Green King. One of his knights fell in battle when he and I discovered Wyvern attacking a smallholding. For returning the Knight's belongings he granted me the armor and horse," the Prince explained sadly.

The Warrior nodded.

"A great relic, granted by a noble king. I'll ensure your stallion receives the greatest care. However, I must warn you that the days are hot and the nights short. If the beasts don't take you this armor very well could," the Warrior said. "You still need to be able to move and maneuver—and never, ever slow your horse down. Steel armor can do that."

"If I'm found to have such weakness then let the desert take me. Wyvern will abide no weakness," the Prince said earnestly. He wiped the sweat from his brow.

The Warrior allowed a slight smile, "Then the leather must go."

"The leather must go," the Prince agreed.

* * *

THAT EVENING, they sat around the firepit with the other soldiers. The days in Edda were hot and stagnant. The nights were cold and punctuated with brisk winds. They ate quite differently than earlier that day in the city. Their meal consisted of lizards that were caught and cooked on the open fire. They had a large rodent or two, as well. The Warrior said that outside the walls, survival was achieved minute by minute. Whether it was a few feet from the city for the night, or your fourth day in the wastes, you always behaved the same outside the walls.

The Prince listened as they spoke in their native tongue. The Warrior sat next to him in quiet observance as well. The two of them also sat slightly apart from the others. The Prince noticed that, here and there, the other warriors would cast a glance their way and turn back to their comrades; laughter typically followed.

"What do they speak of?" the Prince asked.

"Your armor," the Warrior answered plainly.

The Prince's brows furrowed, "I'm sure they feel the same as you do."

"Your armor is clean," the Warrior clarified, still focusing on his reptilian dinner. "It doesn't bear the marks of battle. It appears to be unused, untested. As do you."

The Prince looked over at them. They continued to regard him with mocking smiles and laughter. They had the same long hair, and here and there a small braid, as the Warrior and they were dirty from days at the camp.

"So test me," the Prince said, looking at the group.

The soldier stopped and looked at him with indignation. He spoke to him in a thick Edding accent. "I know who you are, Prince," he said derisively. "You come here wanting... what? Honor? Some gold-covered glory that you can carry back to your court? Hailed before your doting magisters like a returning hero?"

The soldier spat on the ground before him. "When you see men bleeding and dying for no other reason than to keep safe a family they will never see again, then you can ask things of me. Otherwise, don't think me a fool to knock the Blue Prince in the dirt and not expect repercussions."

The soldier turned back to the fire-pit. The others regarded the Prince with similar ire.

"What's your name, warrior?" the Prince asked.

The soldier regarded him with mixed curiosity and indignation, "What?"

"What is your name?" the Prince repeated.

"Vidar," he answered with pride.

The Prince rose to his feet. The others regarded him warily and even the Warrior cast a suspicious glance his way. He unsheathed his sword which caused the others to stand swiftly to their feet. The Warrior was content to watch.

He ran his sword into the ground. The group of warriors calmed somewhat. He then looked to the one named Vidar.

"Vidar, behold the sword of my fathers: Calibern, the Sapphire Blade. If I should fail my mentor or his tasks and, in turn, my own people, then you shall have the relics granted me by the Green King, that you may do them honor where I failed. I swear by this blade: the blade of my forefathers granted me by the Sapphire Spire."

Vidar approached the Prince and removed his sword from the ground. He beheld Calibern in the light of the fire and saw it reflected dangerously. He then looked upon the Prince with amused eyes.

"Your oaths are fancy," he returned the blade to the Prince, "but you are beholden to them. We'll see. Should you survive the Seven, we shall see. By the spires," he laughed, "if you complete the Seven I will swear fealty to you myself!"

Vidar and the others returned to their seats where one of his comrades grabbed his shoulder and spoke something in Edding. They both continued laughing.

15

SEVEN TASKS

The Prince sat next to the Warrior and saw the large man was regarding him with a smile.

"You smile too much," the Prince remarked sharply.

"You make a lot of promises, Prince. For one from across the cliffs—soft and pampered—you make perilous oaths to dangerous men," the Warrior said.

The Prince gazed into the firelight and thought on the days to come. "It'll be decided in short enough time. If I don't fulfill them it will be because I'm dead. At that point it won't matter, I suppose."

The Warrior nodded again. "You suppose correctly."

"What is this Seven they speak of?" the Prince asked.

"The Seven?" one of the warriors called out, overhearing their conversation.

He began laughing. "You haven't been told of the Seven?"

The Warrior held up a scarred hand and the whole of the warband quieted.

"The Seven Tasks," the Warrior said to the Prince. "Each Edding man, upon taking up arms, must complete seven tasks that prove his skill and worth as a soldier. That is what these men seek to do—as do we."

"What sort of tasks are undertaken?" the Prince asked.

Vidar was the first to chime in.

"The more dangerous the better," he said, garnering laughter from his fellows.

"My father had slain a jormungandr. He said such a thing should count as two, but his commander refused. So he delivered to him two pieces of the beast—each a full half," one of the soldiers shared.

"What did the commander say?" the Prince asked curiously.

"He still refused to acknowledge two tasks, saying that cutting the beast in two was juvenile at best. My father told him, 'Sir, I used no blade, but my teeth to chew it through!' The commander then relented, granting him the two tasks."

The warband laughed at the tale, as did the Prince and the Warrior. The Warrior didn't mention this was a common joke among those seeking their Seven.

The rest of the evening was filled with tales of the Seven Tasks. Stories of their friends, fathers, grandfathers, even legends of the Red King, himself: Horodir. One man reportedly walked the length of the burning sands with a single waterskin and no shoes. Another told of a man who faked desertion to goad a full company into searching for him. When found he made them all bear witness as he duped a grendel and tricked it into fighting and killing a manticore then slaying the grendel himself—three tasks in one.

Vidar chuckled and took a long pull from his waterskin. No alcohol was allowed during their sojourns into the desert. When the laughter died down, he looked at the Prince and said, "There is one story that is the greatest of them all."

The Prince had yet to say a word this whole time and remained quiet still. He only gazed at Vidar and waited for the tale.

The other warriors were quiet as the still night as Vidar recounted the single greatest feat in living memory; that of the man who had completed all seven tasks in a single go. He'd left with his warband to pursue their Seven—no different than countless others before them. They had trekked across the desert to a settlement huddled alongside the western cliffs. Stories had reached the Red City that a particularly vicious grendel had been killing villagers and stealing their livestock.

After two nights of marching, they had finally reached the small town. The place was half empty and the villagers terrified and unwilling to unbolt their doors even to speak to the warriors. They said the creature would strike in the night and that the soldiers would be the first to go.

Vidar recounted that the warband had rested a day, and at nightfall they had prepared for the beast. They had each taken multiple posts around town, two to each hidden spot. The ground rumbled as massive footsteps could be heard coming into town. Houses were thrashed and stones hurled at the townsfolk attempting to flee. This had been the work of something too large to be a grendel.

As the warband had converged on the sounds of destruction, they saw a sight that turned their insides to water. The warband beheld the frightening Ymir—an ogre from the frozen valleys of the Veil Mountains. The moonlight reflected off skin white as snow and stretched over muscles like rolling steel. He was immune to the cold; in fact, it was necessary for his survival. He ventured into the nearby town at night to take villagers and livestock for food, as few things could live in the eternal blizzard of his home.

The battle had been short, Vidar explained. Although the warriors had not yet earned their Seven, they were certainly not raw recruits, but the mountain ogre was simply too much. It was as fierce, relentless, and unstoppable as the mountain blizzards it slept in.

The few soldiers who weren't killed had been taken back to its lair. One soldier had managed to evade his grasp, and had stalked the ogre to its cavernous home. To avoid the blizzard he'd been forced to take the tunnels into the mountains. No dwarves or gnomes dared to dwell here and it had taken him a full day to track the beast. He'd found it by discovering the piles of discarded bones reaching as high as the cavern's ceiling. The creature had stacked the remains like a macabre throne to its fiendishness.

What the lone warrior found next was even more horrifying. The beast kept the men in cages of ice. The ogre would then run the men through with a sharpened pole and place them out in the blizzard to be frozen, at which point he would then devour them.

The soldier had waited for the ogre to take out the next victims and then had freed the remaining men by hacking away at the ice with his blade. When the ogre returned, the soldier hurried his weak and freezing fellows out through the bone hall-way. He fought the ogre off with the sharpened poles, using his size and the close confines of the cave to his advantage. He managed to run the beast through with multiple sharpened poles, but Ymir had been in a vicious bloodlust and was refusing to fall.

The soldier had baited the ogre to smaller and smaller tunnels until Ymir was trapped by the many poles impaling him. Using the torch he had navigated the tunnels with, the soldier set Ymir ablaze on the gruesome pyre he had made of the creature, and the frost ogre succumbed quickly to the flames, howling in rage and agony.

Vidar explained how the soldier had then led his surviving men back through the tunnels and to the depleted town. Once they became well enough to travel, they returned to the Red City and the soldier had been granted his warrior's right—and had become a legend in his own time.

"Incredible," the Prince remarked, "this soldier, does he yet live?"

"Aye, he lives," answered Vidar huskily, and smiled toward the Prince and Warrior.

The Prince regarded the Warrior with newfound awe.

"You—you accomplished such a feat?" the Prince said, mouth agape.

"Is it so astounding?" the Warrior remarked casually, "I am a warrior of Edda. As many of these men will be. Edding soldiers; we live in honor or we die in pursuit of it."

"A hard land. A harder people," the warriors said in rote fashion. The moment was sobering as they knew not all of them would return from their journey.

"What do you seek here, Prince?" Vidar asked with genuine curiosity. "What brings you from your gentle hills to our burning sands?"

"Wyvern," the Prince replied flatly, "He slew a good man. Kidnapped a gentle young woman and murdered her family. This doesn't seem like much, perhaps, in the grand scheme of things, but that is exactly what concerns me. Why does he bother himself with such things? Wyvern ravaging the countryside is reason enough to hunt him down, but there's more to this; I know it. I will find him, should I survive the Seven Tasks, and I will rid the world of this creature."

"Wyvern? A son of Father Dragon?" Vidar chuckled. "You set your sights on the stars, Prince."

The Warrior rose to his feet, grunting. "Let us sleep. We have only few hours until we awaken before sunrise. We will begin our march then."

16

THE BEAST BY THE SEA

In the cool hours of the night, the troop gathered at a larger exit than the one their small camp was formerly next to. The door beside them opened; the impeccable timing was either incredible discipline or incredible luck—so prompt was it that the Prince could not be sure which.

They must be next to the stables as the Prince could smell stale hay and manure wafting from the gate. Several soldiers led horses out of the city's interior to the warband—one for every man. The Prince recognized Ceffyl among them. He inspected the stallion and saw he was in even better condition than when they had arrived. The Warrior approached his own horse, a cinnamon-hued stallion which he called 'Magni'.

The troop mounted up and began their journey across the darkened sands. The Warrior explained that they would travel the Known Roads—marked by pillars of stone lit by large sconces wherein one was always in sight of another. Traveling a straight path from one to the other ensured avoidance of the underground nests of jormungandr. If the land above their nests were disturbed, they would explode from the sands and devour anything above, such was their hunger and hatred for all things.

The Prince fell in line next to the Warrior. The troop readily grouped into a formation. These were considered the 'unblooded' of their ranks, save for the Warrior who led them. What havoc could a number of their seasoned blades wreak?

The Prince heard a baritone humming come from the group. It was singular and brusque. Following quickly, several others joined him. They seemed to be droning a marching song—one as eerie and gruff as the cold sands. The Warrior, to the Prince's surprise, added words.

THE WAR DRUMS call
>*A thunderous roll*
>*We brave shall gather*
>*A company bold*

>*A bow stretched taut*
>*A sword well-honed*
>*All are marching*
>*Ne'er thoughts of home*

A SEA of fire
>*A chorus din*
>*A war thus borne*
>*Of furious men*

>*The war drums call*
>*A thunderous roll*
>*We brave shall gather*
>*A company bold*

The words were haunting but beautiful in their own way.

Such a life, born into a world with the odds set against you. Horrors in the fields waiting to devour you and all you hold dear. These were men to be respected; men to be feared. The Prince had barely arrived and already he recognized the fortitude of the Edding soldiers.

"To where do we ride?" the Prince questioned.

"A town to the east," the Warrior answered. "We ride to the mountains before daybreak, then follow the mountains to the coast. Villagers have been found mutilated and half-devoured in the surrounding area; some even left in the streets. We go to find their killer."

"East... could we not have taken one of the logboats to a closer city and gone from there? Sparing the horses and the men as well?" the Prince offered, thinking this a good strategy.

Before the Warrior could reply, one of the men, Ullir, offered his explanation.

"Aye, and we could also fill the boat with fresh meats and aged cheeses. Perhaps the finest mead to ease your sand-wrought thirst?"

A number of the troop laughed at his comment. The Prince was unsurprised to hear Vidar join in.

"Watch your tongue, Ullir. This young lad may be my sworn liege by week's end."

Again, more laughter. The Prince searched for a retort, but the Warrior took any chance he had from him by providing a more helpful clarification; the sands were dangerous and wide. The Dwarf-waters had not always been there for their ancestors. They may not always be there for their children and their grandchildren. Their people must never forget how to survive the sands—especially their soldiers. The Warrior also clarified that traversing the sands does not qualify as one of the Seven Tasks in and of itself.

The Prince remained composed and confident. At least outwardly. Within, he was beginning to become a bit ill at ease about the coming days. No matter how slight, he refused to allow this to show. Hearing the braying mockery of Vidar and Ullir from behind only tempered his resolve.

They journeyed the dark sands of the night as swiftly as their stallions could safely carry them. Eventually, the Warrior informed them they had ventured beyond the nests of the jormungandr and could spur their stallions along quicker to reach the village by daybreak.

As the first sliver of light reached the tops of the eastern mountains, they arrived at the cliffs and turned to ride in the shade of the mountain to the coast until they came upon a small, clustered set of houses and farms within sight of the distant sea. They were built among the jutting stones that would run straight to the edge of those rolling waters.

"Clever people. These stones will prove difficult for farming, but they are certainly free from the jormungandr, and manti-cores are not fond of water," the Warrior said as they approached.

"And yet they lose their people to some other monster," the Prince added.

"Perhaps the grendel?" Vidar pondered.

"Perhaps, but they wouldn't have left remains in the streets. They most likely would not have left remains at all," replied the Warrior.

As they approached one of the men from the troop called out to them.

"Another one!" he yelled.

They all turned to see the mangled human remains among the wet stone, red blood barely visible on the dark stones. The Warrior dismounted and approached the grotesque scene. He looked at the poor villager and noticed the gaping wounds and vicious gashes.

"This was no grendel," he said bitterly.

He had an ominous notion as to the nature of this beast, but he must speak with the villagers before he could be certain. The

Warrior returned to his stallion and the troop urged their horses on for the short remainder of their journey.

Upon arrival, they found the lord of the town and he graciously brought them into his hall. They were provided hearty food, spiced drink, and warm fires. As the troop ate, the Warrior leaned in to speak with the lord quietly.

"What knowledge have you of the slayings?" The Warrior asked bluntly.

"Just what I sent to the Red King in my missive; we believe a grendel, perhaps a clan, has taken upon our village to feed on my people," he explained quietly.

The Warrior shook his head gently. "It's no grendel, my lord. The bite marks and other wounds on a victim we recently discovered on the outskirts, are that of a larger beast. It is also one with powerful fangs, not mangled teeth."

The lord's face paled. "Larger than a grendel? What sort of horror plagues our town?"

"You have no livestock; the grendel would be attracted to them first and foremost," the Warrior explained, citing the town's location on a stone-covered stretch of land with nothing for any sort of livestock to graze on. The people of the town had small gardens planted in stone-built containers filled with fertile soil, but their diets otherwise consisted of fish and other creatures from the sea.

"You live near the salt waters," the Warrior continued, "and there are plenty of people fishing its waters. You have a sense of security here away from the jormungandr and manticore. I fear you have attracted the attention of the Barghest."

The lord grew gravely silent. The Prince noticed this and asked the Warrior what sort of creature this barghest was that stalked the town. The Warrior's face grew heavy.

"A wolf-beast the size of a warhorse. It has eyes like a human, not a beast; eyes that glow red with hate. Its teeth are like knives. It can outrun any creature of the desert and even the vicious jormungandrs leave it be. It feasts on grendel when it can't safely haunt a village. This creature is intelligent and ruthless. It exists to hunt and eat."

"How do we kill a barghest?" the Prince asked.

"We've thought them extinct for ages; killed off because they're a terror that die like any other beast. This one is… different.. We don't know what it is or where it comes from. It was first seen nigh a decade ago. As for killing it, we have found nothing can end the creature's existence—only impede it."

"I don't understand—it can't be immune to *all* things," the Prince said.

"We have beheaded it, burned it, buried it. Each time we think it's finished it returns the next season. All we can hope to accomplish here is to deter it from the town."

As they discussed the matter, a loud thud came from the door. The present company startled at the noise. There was one more, louder thud from outside the door—a sharp, sudden sound. The Warrior, Prince, and the rest of the warband drew their weapons and approached the door cautiously. Some of the troop held back with crossbows drawn and ready to fire upon whatever lay outside.

They approached the door from an angle and prepared to open it. The crossbows' line of sight would be clean and their aim would be unimpeded. Those with swords drawn would attack from the side and behind. The Warrior reached out and, swiftly, pulled the door ajar.

Two young children and a woman, likely their mother, fell inside screaming. The crossbowmen immediately lifted their bows, taking their aim off the innocent villagers. The family was terror-stricken and their faces covered in dirt and tears.

"It's outside!" the woman exclaimed, holding her children close and hiding their heads. She backed frantically into the room nearer the fireplace.

The Warrior took her by the shoulders and attempted to calm her.

"What's outside? What did you see?"

"It's outside," she kept screaming, "Close the door! Kill it!" she was shouting hysterically. She kept a wide-eyed, terror-stricken gaze held upon the door.

The crossbows were once again trained on the open frame. The Prince and those of the warband near the door listened and looked outside. A steady rain began to fall. Heavy clouds had moved overhead and darkened the sky and the lord's hall. They heard nothing; saw nothing.

The only noise was that of whimpering children, their mother's frantic breathing, and the staccato pattering of rain. They closed the door and attempted to calm the woman again.

"Easy," the Warrior said. "There is nothing there."

She calmed slightly. Though, now, something else took the place of her terror.

"Dead... my husband... He held the beast off while..."

A thunderous crash cut her explanation short. The beast that crashed through the wall was the size of a large horse and moved with ferocity and purpose.

The Prince was stunned by fear and disbelief. It appeared to be a dog or wolf in some way—though massive in comparison. Its claws and teeth were grotesquely over-large. The hair on its hackles was raised and its fur-covered body was corded in muscle. The beast was as black as night and its growl struck fear into the stoutest of the warband. It had also come through the wall. Was this beast strategizing?

"Barghest!" the Warrior shouted.

He placed himself in front of the woman and her children. The beast had shattered a hole in the side of the hall on its way in. Stone and mortar were sent sprawling across the floor. The rains had become torrential and were beginning to pour into the hall.

The Warrior ordered the lord to take the villagers and retreat to a back room and lock the doors (for what good it would do) and to arm himself once inside. The beast lunged at the closest soldiers and knocked two of them to the ground. Its teeth bit through the chainmail as though it were not there. The Barghest thrashed the soldier about in its maw and finally threw him lifeless out into the rain.

The crossbowmen loosed their bolts at the Barghest and some pierced its tough hide. The creature howled in pain and charged them. Two massive leaps and it was on them. The beast's charge laid them down among the broken stones and knocked their weapons from their hands. The soldiers, bereft of their crossbows, drew their blades and axes.

The Warrior, seeing the lord and the villagers safely retreated, rushed to the Prince's side. The Prince, however, had recovered from his initial fear and was readying himself for an attack.

"Head and appendages—maim and dismember the demon!" the Warrior shouted.

The Prince nodded and they moved to flank the beast. The Barghest, having taken another soldier, turned to attack another. One man hurled a large stone from the rubble at the beast and caught it in the shoulder. It turned just as the Prince stepped in to view.

The Barghest lashed a massive paw out at the Prince—slamming into his arm and cutting deep. The Prince shouted in pain but returned a blow at the creature. He cut naught but air, however. The beast saw the blade, Calibern, and tossed its head about as though it had been wounded. It backed away from the Prince, only to be struck by the Warrior.

A vicious gash was cut along the beast's shoulder. The Warrior saw, just momentarily, that his blade had cut deep into the beast but even this had just managed to get beneath its thick hide. Barely any blood flowed from the wound.

He heard the Prince's moans of pain and looked over to see

the man's arm bleeding freely. Two of his warband gone and his charge was wounded; they were quickly losing this fight.

The Barghest struck him with a back-handed blow and he was flung against a wall. Vidar let out a vicious yell and charged the beast. He, too, was thrown from the ground and knocked unconscious upon landing.

It was then that Ullir and another of the warband attacked the beast. They swung and hacked in a wild attempt to cut the Barghest down. The demon-wolf was too much for their weapons. They cut and marred its armor-like hide, but only furthered the beast's rage. Ullir was quickly clamped between the Barghest's jaws and thrown like the others. The soldier who aided him was kicked by a powerful hind leg, and fell to the ground gasping for air.

The Barghest then looked below and snarled at the Warrior, trapped beneath his massive paws. The Warrior looked up and saw the Barghest, whose human-like eyes held violent sentience; this was no mere beast, but a creature of conscious malevolence. Something else was also present in the beast's telling eyes— something the Warrior could not quite understand.

None of it would matter soon. The horse-sized, wolf-like creature was a mass of brawn and muscle. The Warrior could barely move beneath its weight. He felt about with his hands as the creature growled, preparing to devour him, and finally found a stone he could fit his hand around.

He grabbed it and used what strength he could muster under the crushing power of the Barghest. He brought up the piece of rubble and slammed it against the beast's head again and again. He only managed a few blows before the creature's pained flailing knocked it from his grip. It wasn't enough to force the Barghest to release him. It howled in his face until he felt his head would crumble. Hot spittle and blood flew from its mouth onto his face.

The Barghest finally reared back and prepared to end the

Warrior with its crushing, tooth-filled maw. The Warrior howled back in defiance. He prepared to meet his own end with pride.

A flurry of movement caught the Warrior's eye. Suddenly, the Barghest jumped off of him and began flailing about with the whole of its body. Something was atop the beast fighting it.

* * *

WHILE THE WARBAND was attacking the Barghest, the Prince used what precious time he had after his arm had been lacerated to wrap the wound in some tattered cloth. The bleeding staunched, he looked about and saw the Warrior pinned by the creature. The Barghest let loose a fiendish roar into the face of the Warrior which was returned ferociously by the pinned soldier. The Prince saw the creature rear back for the killing blow. He simply reacted.

Charging the beast, he leaped upon its back. He grabbed hold of the massive, mane-like hackles of the Barghest and held on with all his strength. He saw the ends of a few crossbow bolts jutting out from its fur. He tried unsuccessfully to stab the beast with Calibern.

As he felt his grip failing, he saw the gaping wound the Warrior had managed at the onset of the fight. It bled, but just barely so. The Barghest's hide was remarkably thick, but here was a gap in the armor. Holding on with the strength of his legs —for the scarce moments it would allow—he hefted Calibern into the air and drove it home into the wound. He felt the blade cut through and drive deep into the beast. The placement of the wound with the luck of his strike could have quite possibly driven straight to the heart of the Barghest.

The creature howled, unlike anything the Prince or the Warrior had ever heard. It was both fierce and agonized. The creature fell to the ground, first onto its haunches, then limp to the ground. A gruesome pool formed beneath it.

The Prince hurried to the Warrior and helped him to his feet. The Warrior was still clutching his chest, regaining his breath from the weight of the monster. They looked around to see most of the warband unconscious but alive. Still, they had lost two Sons of Edda this night in their attempt at the Seven Tasks.

They watched the Barghest and saw that it remained unmoving and unbreathing. Blood still pooled beneath it.

"It appears dead," the Prince stated, regarding the Warrior's previous remarks on the creature's apparent immortality.

The Warrior simply shook his head. "It's not. It's only temporary, I assure you. Let us tend to our wounded."

"Should we not watch this monster? Do something with its remains?" the Prince said, bewildered at the Warrior's disregard for the body.

The Warrior approached an unconscious Vidar. "It matters not," is all he offered by way of an explanation.

The Prince allowed himself one more glance at the fearsome thing before attending to Ullir. He helped the fallen warrior to his feet. Ullir was regaining his breath, but was still uneasy upon standing. When Ullir regained his footing, the Prince turned to see nothing but rubble and blood where the Barghest once lay.

He drew his blade again and caused the surviving members of the warband to do the same. The Warrior ran to his side to see what had caused the stir. He quickly lowered his blade when he saw the missing beast.

A howl came from outside; a sound so deep and baleful it sounded as though it originated from the very bowels of the world. All that was left was the sound of the incessant rain.

"It's gone. The town is spared," the Warrior said. He signaled for one of the soldiers to inform the lord and the villagers that it was safe.

"How can we be sure?" the Prince asked. "The beast won't return?"

"Bring wood and wake the blacksmith. We'll need chains and nails," the Warrior said, sending off a number of the warband.

One returned quickly with some broken wood from the hall. The Warrior began cutting away and soon brought out a small dagger from his boot. To the Prince's confusion, he saw that the Warrior had begun whittling.

By the time the others had returned from the blacksmith with spare chains and nails, the Warrior was holding a crude, carved wolf's head. He sat the carving in the large pool of the Barghest's blood, watching as the crimson substance soaked into the wood.

After a few minutes, they took the supplies and left for a spot very near the town where there was soft, muddy soil between the slick stones. In the cold downpour, they raised a tall post with the chain nailed in and situated where the wooden wolf's head effigy could be hung in plain sight. There it swayed in the blustering winds—a grim reminder of the Barghest's assault.

The Warrior stood next to the Prince and talked above the rain and the wind.

"In the decade since its arrival, the Barghest has never visited the same location twice wherein its blood was spilled. It has a revulsion or fear of the smell of its blood. This charm will keep it at bay; perhaps even attract additional townfolk who desire the safety of a town already haunted or refugees from one that was not so fortunate."

The Prince nodded in understanding. They retreated from the elements to the lodge. A hasty repair was made to the damage with blankets and tent canvases. The lord welcomed them to stay in his hall that night. The mother and her children were welcome until they could return safely at dawn to their home—or at least what remained.

The warband made a somber attempt to sleep until dawn. They watched in shifts; listening for the Barghest and hearing only the continuing rain. Very few of them slept much. Having lost comrades, bearing the pain of countless bruises and lacerations, and suffering the bitter cold brought by the ocean-side night through the damaged hall, most of them huddled near the fire as it flickered and offered some manner of warmth.

The Prince and Warrior noted that not one among them offered up a single complaint.

17

THE WARRIOR'S PRIDE

Morning brought the end of the rain but left a sky heavy with clouds. The townspeople skulked out of their homes in frightened clusters. Many made their way to the lord's hall and saw the destruction that had been wrought. A massive hole was torn from the side of the stone building.

Their frightened murmurs caught the ear of the lord who attempted to calm his people. However, they turned their gaze upon the tell-all sigil that swung on a hastily constructed post next to the town. A blood-soaked wooden emblem cast a shadow-filled realization upon them: the Barghest had come.

They took solace in the knowledge that it would not return, and the Warrior was quick to emphasize this. However, it was a cold comfort knowing that the monster had roamed the streets while their children slept.

The Warrior asked who among them had the skills to repair the hall. A pitifully small number of hands rose. He called on those men along with several others and instructed them to begin repairs on the lord's hall.

The lord inquired as to the Warrior's plans for himself and the warband. The Warrior replied that he must confer with his fellows. They came to free this town of the Barghest and that they had done. They would have to decide their next course of action, but not until after they had cared for their dead.

It was their custom to prepare a funeral pyre to respect the fallen warriors. Their bodies were anointed with spices and wine. Their swords rested upon their chests and their helmets were set next to their heads. They were then set alight. After the solemn, sobering rites the Prince approached the Warrior.

"Did you learn anything of the Barghest?" the Prince asked plainly.

"What do you mean?" the Warrior replied stoically.

"You were inches from the beast. Did you observe nothing of use; nothing new?" the Prince clarified.

The Warrior gazed into the cinders for a time. He reimagined that violent evening again—thinking over everything he had seen and heard. It was typical of previous encounters he'd had with the monster. Except...

"The eyes," the Warrior said.

"The eyes?" the Prince repeated, confused.

"Yes. The eyes were something I have never been able to see; nor cared to. Its eyes were sentient—knowing. They were malicious and hateful, but, there was some sort of fog there," the Warrior explained.

The Prince's brows furrowed at this statement. "What sort of fog?"

The Warrior was lost in thought. "I'm not sure. There was a swirling, dull mist that seemed to dance about in the black of the beast's eyes."

The Prince felt his face grow heated with anger. The Wizard had told him of what he'd seen in the Prince's eyes when he discovered Morgæna's hex. Could she truly have such an immense, fearsome beast under her control?

"I fear the issue of this Barghest may go beyond that of a threat to just Edda," the Prince said grimly.

The Warrior regarded him curiously. "How so?"

"The Blue Wizard broke a hex that had been placed on me by an enchantress who sought to manipulate the sapphire throne. A sign of its presence was a dancing haze in my eyes, he told me."

The Warrior's face grew shadowed. "And the Barghest showed a similar ailment. Does the hex increase your aggression? Make you a killer?"

The Prince shook his head. "Not that I'm aware of. All I know is that the hex... twisted things. I wasn't aware of what was happening. The Barghest is evil and that can't be changed. However, it can be controlled, unleashed. Perhaps it could be released from the hex. Though, what that would cause to happen to the beast is beyond me."

The Warrior looked over to the warband who were conversing amongst themselves.

"What do you suggest?" the Warrior asked.

"We must take it alive," the Prince said bleakly, "and return it to the Blue Wizard."

"Alive? The Barghest?" the Warrior scoffed and lay his head back in frustration. "You saved the life of your superior and drove the Barghest from this town—that is two worthy tasks in a night; do you seek to test death itself and add that to your triumphs?"

"I wish to destroy it and rid your people of its menace," the Prince replied in earnest. "Do you wish the same?"

The Warrior regarded him with mingled respect, curiosity, and suspicion. "Of course."

"Then gather the warband. Let us find the beast and capture it."

"We can't simply gather our men and travel in the burning sands. There is a reason we walk the Known Roads guided by their fires; the heat of the day will fell horse and man. We must wait till nightfall."

"We can't effectively track the beast at night," the Prince countered.

The Warrior knew he had a point. He also knew that traveling during the day would be out of the question. The only wise solution was a simple compromise. They would travel in the twilight and early morning hours.

The Warrior, Prince, and warband waited for the cooler winds of the evening before riding from the village. One of the warband, a talented scout, had found pawprints and blood caking the stone and soil leading north. So began their tracking of the Barghest.

For several hours they had followed the markings. The scout would follow the trail, and the warband, in turn, would follow the closest route along the Known Roads. A single, light-footed individual traveling alone was all the Warrior dared risk sending off the safe routes.

They headed north on a straight path. The beast's pace was slow, but it was fleeing the kingdom. The traces of blood were growing thinner and soon there were only tracks to follow. It was as if the Barghest's wounds had healed as its journey progressed.

The Warrior regarded the area in which they found themselves. They were within a stretch of territory generally avoided by the Eddings—the Jotun Foothills. It was thick with jormungandr nests and the Known Roads grew thin. If they traveled much further they could very well find themselves without a road to follow.

The warband decided to make camp for the night. They could go no further in safety and surmised that the Barghest was making its way to the foothills below the cliff walls. Their search could continue when sufficient light was available. The warband established a watch and rested.

The Prince woke to the Warrior calling the warband to gather their belongings. There was a faint light on the horizon and by the time they were prepared to ride there would be enough light to track.

They began riding. Again, they followed the scout as he trailed the markings of the Barghest. It was slow, uneventful, and tiring.

The scout pointed out the beast's trail. It had taken a sudden turn and ventured off in a direction that would lead them from the Known Roads. To follow they would be required to head directly into jormungandr grounds.

"It's escaped again," the Warrior said darkly.

The Prince looked at him in disbelief. "Gone? Have we come so far to give up so easily?"

The Warrior fumed. "I'll suffer your ignorance in that you're foreign to this land. A handful of untested men cannot stand against the monsters in the sand," he said as he cast an open hand to the desert.

"Then test them," the Prince said plainly. "You refuse the safety of the Dwarf-waters for the Seven Tasks. You seek out creatures that crawled from the nightmares of other realms for the Seven Tasks. What's so different now? Risk the jormungandr and let them be Red Warriors of Edda or die in the attempt. Is that not what the tasks are for?" he argued.

"I have no qualms sending brave men to battle; I do take issue with sending them to foolish deaths," the Warrior rebutted.

"Aye," they both heard.

They turned to see a number of the warband approaching them. It was Vidar that had spoken.

"But is it a foolish death if it would rid us of a beast who haunts our lands and kills our own? For what reason do we risk the hot sands and its wicked inhabitants if not to prove that we, too, belong here? It's a hellish, insufferable plot which we call home—but it is our home and that of our ancestors. The soft king is right, let us take it back from that monster."

The warband voiced their enthusiastic agreement. The Warrior looked among them. They were dirty, tired, and had marched until their feet blistered and thoughts of home grew dim—but the yearning for glory in them remained. He would lead these men until they earned their Seven, or died in their efforts. They earned such.

"A hard land..." the Warrior began.

"A harder people," came their reply.

THEY RODE in a loose formation so that, if indeed one of the sand beasts came for them, they could scatter easily. The Jotun Foothills near the northern cliff walls were cooler than the other parts of the kingdom. Hardy grass and shrubs grew here, rooted in the rough soil rather than sand, and made it easier to ride.

If not for the jormungandr, the Eddings would have long cultivated this stretch of land. However, its amiable climate attracted the worst of the beasts in numbers. It would take armies to clear the land enough to inhabit it. The warband had entered likely the most hostile part of an already hostile land.

They could, however, travel easily during the day given the cooler temperatures and the nocturnal natures of many of the beasts. The scout was able to follow the path of the Barghest fairly easily.

It continued northeast to the coast, though no passage could be taken unless the beast chose to swim to the nearest approachable shoreline several miles down. The Veil Mountains' sheer cliffs ran far, and were lined with sharp rocks beaten by harsh waves. Even the Barghest would have a difficult time making such a journey.

The warband traveled as swiftly as the scout could track. Their skin crawled with the thought of what slept below. The hairs of their arms and necks prickled and they felt a thousand unseen eyes on them.

Only the sounds of their clinking armor and saddles could be heard. They traveled with a disciplined silence that was as unnerving as it was tense. These men knew the extent of their plight, however, and even untested they showed the discipline and skill of experienced veterans of other kingdoms.

They rode the foothills until they came to an outcropping of rock that jutted from the ground like brittle bones. As they grew nearer they saw that they were not simply rocks—they were the remains of an ancient fortress of some kind. The stones were so weathered and the grounds so reclaimed by the wild that they appeared to be a natural outcropping.

They stopped at the crest of a hill and looked to the ruin among the sands. It was a dwelling at the end of the world. Once-tended palms were frail husks and cobblestone courtyards were broken and overgrown with now-dead plant life. This place, the Warrior realized, was abandoned even before Ragnarok.

They discussed sending the scout ahead to investigate the ruins. As they talked over their next course of action the Prince felt a strange sensation about them. He held up a hand to quiet them. The warband hushed immediately and began looking about for what had startled the Prince. Then, the Warrior noticed it also; however, he was well aware of what it was.

"Scatter!" he shouted.

No sooner had they begun running than the ground below them burst forth into a spout of sand and rock. A great, scaled creature burst forth from underground. They couldn't tell if the roar that shook the ground came from the beast's churning of the terrain or its fearsome, tooth-filled maw.

"Jormungandr!" one of the warband cried out.

The creature was above ground, slithering across the sand effortlessly with its large and jagged scales. Coarse frills fanned from its neck. Its scale-covered muscles propelled it across the desert as though it were water.

Its roar was shrill and terrifying. It launched itself from the ground and toppled one of the warband who had managed to reach his stallion. Horse and rider were both taken by its horrible maw. The jormungandr spun about as it bit down on the warrior and his horse, disorienting them. It returned to the earth by way of the sinkhole it had created and the rider and his mount were never to be heard from again.

The Prince listened in terror to the eerie silence that fell. They had all climbed atop their stallions; looking and listening for any sign of the creature. Their swords and axes were drawn, but the men were visibly shaken by such a horrifying beast.

"What can be done against them?" the Prince whispered. It was in part to himself, and in part a question to the Warrior.

"Siege weapons," the Warrior said glibly in response to the Prince. "Or the magic of the Red Wizard. A better question would be 'why is it gone?'"

"What?" the Prince replied, confused.

The veteran swordsman looked out across the sands and hills. The fierce monster had disappeared. It was odd, considering jormungandr were known to have a wicked hunger. It should have stayed until all of them were devoured or it was dead.

Why was it satisfied with only one? He wondered.

"This makes no sense," the Warrior thought aloud.

They scoured the horizon and searched the grounds. Soldiers were posted at the sinkhole to listen and feel for the creature's possible return. They were facing both jormungandr and Barghest; the spire's favor wasn't with them this day.

Amid their hushed discussion they didn't hear the scout approach them on foot. The scout almost inadvertently lost his head to a startled Vidar who lifted his blade to strike before he noticed his fellow warrior. Vidar quietly cursed the man for his silence while also admiring the scout's stealth.

"What news have you?" the Warrior asked.

"The Barghest's tracks—they lead directly to the ruins," the scout reported.

"Do they end there," the Warrior asked, "or do they go further?"

The scout shook his head. "I can't say. I dare not venture near those grounds alone—not with the Barghest haunting them."

The Warrior regarded the ruins with foreboding. "I can't fault you for that."

"And I say you're a damn smart one," Vidar remarked flippantly.

The Prince looked to the ruins, as well. The Barghest ventured through the very home of the wurms to these forgotten grounds. The jormungandr would devour anything and anyone, even the fierce Barghest. Why would it leave a safe route to travel here?

"We shouldn't linger here. We must make for the ruins immediately," the Prince said.

"To confront the Barghest while the jormungandr hunt us down?" Vidar scoffed.

"The Barghest hides there, it has to be. It ventures through these same ill-gotten foothills to a pile of ancient stones even though the jormungandr would readily trample all to consume it," the Prince explained tersely.

"And yet they still stand," the Warrior remarked in understanding. "But if there's something there that even the jormungandr fear…"

They suddenly heard shouting from behind them.

"It's coming!" the soldiers were yelling.

They turned to see two of the warband—those tasked with watching the sinkhole—rushing toward them. The rest hurried to meet them, but a large, scaled mass cut through the ground and caused their stallions to rear back and toss the Warrior and the Prince who were at the front of the group.

The two soldiers stumbled and fell back. A vicious head rose from the ground behind them. They turned to behold four black serpentine eyes open and gazing balefully upon them. The creature's mouth was protected by hard, flexible scales when closed; it opened and screeched at the warriors and they all knew it was something that would haunt their dreams.

It opened its many-fold jaws like a dread flower; a bloom of teeth and blackness, each with a separate slender tongue for grasping prey. Its jagged frill fanned once again and its malevolent cry echoed among the hills. The warband backed away; the two guardsmen who fell scrambled to their feet before becoming paralyzed in fear.

The nightmare worsened as a plume of sand burst beneath them. One of the men fell screaming to the ground while the other's cry was drowned out by the blossom-like maw of a second jormungandr closing over him.

"It has a mate..." The Warrior said in hushed terror.

The first jormungandr plunged onto the second soldier who was struggling to his feet. He no more than made it to his knees before he, too, was consumed by the nightmarish wurms.

"Get to the ruins!" the Warrior ordered.

The handful of men that remained spurred their horses furiously. The stallions raced across the loose terrain. The two jormungandrs shrieked an unholy noise and took after them. They flowed through the soil and tore through small grass-covered hills in explosive fury.

Those of the warband talented in horseback archery attempted to stall the monsters by firing haphazard and wayward shots in their direction. The Warrior watched as another of the soldiers was lost in a burst of sand and coiled scales, not even having time to scream.

Their horses' hooves met the grounds of the ruins with what sounded like thunderous applause. Some of them narrowly avoided colliding with stone pillars in their haste. The jormungandr reared back and howled at the surviving warband. They turned to see the vicious things writhing and slithering about, but unwilling to come any further. It was perhaps the closest any Son of Edda had come to actively observing a jormungandr so close and still live.

18

RUINS OF THE AEGIS

The warband watched as the creatures stalked back and forth in seeming impotence. A few of them dared taunt the beasts which caused the jormungandr to roar and spit at them. Deep, guttural hisses sounded from their throats, but they soon returned to the ground and moved on.

The Warrior looked around at the crumbling remains of the lost structure.

"What is this place?" he asked in wonder.

What sort of building—crumbling and broken, easily trampled—did the large jormungandr avoid so? The Warrior ordered everyone to remain together. He reminded them that the Barghest was likely waiting within the halls or shadows and it would be unlikely that it was still wounded.

As they walked the weather-worn arches and exposed courtyard, they began to take note of their surroundings. Ullir, a sharp mind in the history of the Red Kingdom, noticed the layout and architecture of the building was no longer in use by their people.

"These stones are not even from here—they come from deep within the Veil Mountains," he said.

"Dwarven?" the Warrior asked.

"No, too large for dwarves," Ullir said, shaking his head, "and too old."

They entered one of the rooms that lay half-buried in the ground. Ullir was eagerly regarding one of the walls. There were stones set into one side that were larger than any of the others. Chiseled upon their worn faces were runes and rough images.

Ullir looked them over once, twice, and then once again. So enraptured was he in the markings he couldn't hear the others calling out to him.

"Ullir! You false scholar!" the Warrior was shouting. "What do you see?"

Ullir licked his dry lips. He turned to them, forcing himself to tear his gaze from the stones. He regarded them with eyes wide and tried to moisten his parched mouth. He looked as though he were about to speak, but simply looked up and about the room they were in.

"Speak up, man," Vidar prodded.

"We… we are in the walls of a castle. Somewhere within these walls and beneath this floor lies the remains of a god," Ullir said in awe.

Vidar began to approach the walls himself, when he was halted by a raised hand from the Warrior.

"A god? What's on those stones, Ullir?" the Warrior asked dubiously.

Ullir returned to the wall and beckoned the others to follow. They stood behind him as he pointed out the various runes, carvings, and images engraved on the stone.

He pointed at the first of the runes. "These stones—they record the history of Baeol the Aegis; the only man to have ever personally slain one of Father Dragon's children."

This drew the warband closer.

"'Baeol the Aegis, Slayer of Naga," Ullir continued. He then moved on to the images depicting Baeol's exploits. "Here, where he was trained to fight with a sword as a child barely able to

walk. These show him joining the Edding army at twelve. Here...
spires-all... here he is proving his worth to his older comrades."

The warband beheld the birth of the Seven Tasks. A young
Baeol proving that even at several years their younger, he could
fight alongside them as equal. As fate would show them, he was
their superior in every respect.

As the stones progressed, the story unfolded of Baeol driving
the manticores to the cliffsides and off into desolate territory.
They showed him creating an army to protect the citizens against
the monsters under the sands.

Ullir pointed to another stone, one that showed his close
friend, Archimedes, devising and mapping the Known Roads. It
then showed the greatest of Baeol's feats—that which forever
placed him among the pantheon of the greatest of the Sons of
Edda, and the paragon of the Ruby Spire.

Baeol drew the ire of Naga, the capricious sister to Wyrm,
dragon-child of the Ruby Realm. Naga took a liking to the
jormungandr as a species and was furious with Baeol and his
armies for slaughtering them on sight.

Baeol's skill as a fighter and leader grew so that he was
sending his men to seek out the jormungandr and slay them in
their nests. Naga entered Wyrm's territory and convinced him
that Baeol should be kept in check and given a certain perspective, lest he become too powerful for his own good and that of
the spire.

Wyrm was not inclined to engage with the Ruby Realm. He
was legendary for his reclusiveness and was content with his
ages-long studies. He was easily swayed by his sister, however,
and agreed to Naga's request. Naga was free to conduct her
business within his realm, and her only aim was to destroy
Baeol. She gathered to her a number of jormungandr and
offered the manticore a deal that whatever they killed, they
could have. This brought them eagerly to her side. As the
grendel harbored no goodwill toward the 'small men,' they

joined her merely for the opportunity and pleasure of killing as many of them as possible.

Ullir was practically belligerent as he moved on to the stones depicting the actual battle. He read in the stones that Naga marched with many fiends at her command, and her first strike against the mighty king was the doomed city of Naskaro—formerly one of the great, walled cities. It existed prior to the construction of the Dwarf-waters and now, so complete was Naga's destruction that no remnant of the city remains above ground. All the bones of the old structures are covered by sand and legend. Many say that if you take the long-avoided stretch of the Known Roads to Naskaro, during the twilight hours you can see and hear the spirits of the thousands that died there, seeking out their destroyed homes.

Ullir continued his telling; Baeol was crowned the first king of the Edda and was implored by the Edding people to destroy Naga. A long and bloody war whittled away at her forces. Naga called to her brothers and sister to aid her, but they saw the ominous path that Naga had shaped for herself. Even Wyvern told her that she would suffer for her foolish bravado.

Naga marched what remained of her fiends against Baeol and his armies. The siege against the Ruby Spire lasted for seventeen days; tens of thousands lay dead, and the burning sands were soaked with the blood of man and monster alike. Siege weapons lay burning from dragonfire, and the torrid dunes lay pock-marked by jormungandr tunnels.

During one of the final battles in the brutal and desperate attack, Naga herself tossed her jormungandr and manticores against the walls of the City of the Ruby Spire in a desperate attempt to fell the ramparts.

She soared over the wall and faced King Baeol directly. The Red King fought her atop the highest turret of the inner keep within the light of the Great Ruby. After suffering burns and scrapes, and according to one account, losing his shield-arm to

Naga's bite, Baeol felled the great dragoness by cutting her stomach open and then had cast her remains from the wall.

Filled with awe, Ullir continued; Naga's minions, hearing her death throes, retreated in terror. They fled, fractured, and returned to the desert.

Baeol saw his city restored. He ensured his people were safe. He had watched as Naga was put to the pyre. Months later he then succumbed to his wounds. This is where the rune-covered stones ended—with a crowned Baeol bearing sword-and-shield and bathed in light.

"Baeol the Aegis," Ullir concluded. "Slayer of Naga."

"What happened after this? Is this the earliest history of your people?" the Prince asked in interest.

"Our first king," the Warrior corrected. "We've all heard the legends of Baeol the Aegis, Progenitor of the Seven Tasks. This must be his ancestral home before he became king."

"And the jormungandr know it, too, apparently. They fear these very grounds. It may even be the reason they are so prominent and aggressive here. They desperately seek to keep the people of Edda from here," Ullir said.

"Why do you suspect that?" the Prince asked.

"Because," the Warrior answered, "it reminds us they can be beaten."

Many of the soldiers wanted to research the stones further, especially Ullir. Such history, such reverence was owed in this place. The beasts that guarded it were the worst kind of evil. The Warrior stood with the rest of them, quiet and contemplative, when he heard a rumbling. He remained still, fearing the jormungandr had overcome their fear of the place for the sake of destroying them.

A cold fear gripped him; it wasn't rumbling. It was growling. A pair of eyes glittered just within the corner of his vision.

"Barghest!" he shouted as he drew his blade.

The rest of the warband drew their weapons, but the beast

leaped with unnatural speed. They heard a scream as the beast threw his massive weight against the closest soldier: Ullir.

He began punching the monster in the head next to its eyes, attempting to gain some sort of leverage against the beast, but to no avail. The Barghest clamped its massive jaws down upon the warrior and his cries of fear and rage ceased.

A thrown spear bounced off the Barghest's thick hide, barely scratching the creature, and careened off the wall. It turned and stared at Vidar with murder in its disturbing, human-like eyes. It saw their numbers were few. The Prince had a notion that if the monster could smile, it would.

The Barghest charged at Vidar, responsible for the spear, and was greeted with a shout from Vidar and a booming strike from a metal shield to the head. It only agitated the creature and Vidar began swinging with his blade. He was soon joined by the Warrior, the Prince, and the rest of the warband who attempted to overpower the beast.

They cut and hacked at the creature, but it was like striking leather-covered steel. It threw off one then another of the warband. The Prince was caught by the beast's flailing head and thrown bodily into one of the old stone pillars. When he could once again see beyond a disoriented haze, he heard the sound of crumbling rocks and jumped free of the old pillar about to collapse upon him. Crashing into the ground next to the pillar gave him an idea.

He called to the Warrior who looked over to him and saw the Prince standing next to the collapsed rubble.

"The walls! Bring them down!" the Prince called out.

The Warrior nodded in understanding. The soldiers were stumbling to their feet when the Warrior urged them to remain low. Sheathing his sword, he grabbed a large stone, heaving it with both hands, and hurled it with all his might at the beast.

It slammed into the Barghest's hip and resulted in a vicious, pained yelp. It turned and snarled in the direction of the culprit.

The Warrior glared at the beast and drew his blade. He lowered himself into a readied position and bid the beast come for him.

The Barghest, with temper flared and bloodlust burning, charged the Warrior. Barking and snarling, it leaped into the air and lunged for him. The Warrior ducked quickly and left the Barghest to plow directly into the stone wall. It shuddered, but not nearly enough as was needed.

The Warrior slowly backed to one of the larger pillars. The Barghest turned, and the Warrior spit at it.

"Come!" he shouted, clanging the flat of his sword upon the pillar.

The creature galloped then picked up to a charge after him. The Warrior saw renewed caution in the beast's eyes. He wouldn't be able to move until the very last moment. He waited until he could smell the creature's breath and then dropped heavily to the ground and scrambled out of the way.

The Barghest slammed into the pillar. Just as the monster turned, the Warrior could see them beginning to tumble over. The beast, however, didn't notice in time—so infuriated and focused on the Warrior as it was.

It barely managed to move its feet when several hundred pounds of archaic stone fell onto it. A choking cloud of sand and dust billowed into the air and the Warrior slid back from his sitting position to distance himself in the event their plan failed.

The warband gathered with the Prince. As the dust cleared, they saw the Warrior leaning on his arms, not taking his eyes from the fallen stones. They drew weapons in anticipation of the beast's wrath. When the cloud had settled they saw a small pile of fur-covered muscle beneath the stone. It was heaving in ragged, wheezing breaths.

They helped the Warrior to his feet, and he and the Prince approached it and saw it still snarling and snapping. He looked within the Barghest's eyes from a safe distance. Indeed, within those wild eyes were a discernible intelligence and cunning and, also, a dancing, swirling mist as the Warrior had said. The Prince hefted Calibern with both hands and removed the beast's head while he had the chance. This was the only time the beast stopped gnashing at him.

The Warrior approached as he wiped the sweat from his brow.

"We don't have long," he said. "It will revive soon and we don't have the strength to take it down again."

The Prince looked at the creature and its buried body. Their options were limited and their knowledge of the beast even more so.

"I don't where it comes from or who created it, but I do know of one who can place such a hex on it," the Prince said. " "We need to make sure it can't revive. You said you've tried burning it?"

"Yes," the Warrior answered. "we would burn it to ash and scatter it to the wind. The beast would always come back."

The Prince looked at the massive, grotesque head on the ground. He cringed as he thought he saw it trying to move. Simply keeping it headless didn't seem like the best idea.

He thought about the ashes spreading. How long it would take for all the remains to come together, reform, and allow the beast to terrorize again. They let the ashes scatter…

"Perhaps if we burned the body down, but kept the ashes burning to prevent the beast reforming," the Prince thought aloud. "We may be able to keep it down for as long as needed."

"How do we do such a thing?" Vidar asked.

"Oil," the Warrior added, the realization of the plan's merit dawning on him. "We have enough for the lanterns in our packs now that… now that we are down so many. Burn the beast and keep the ashes."

"It's a sound idea," the Prince said.

"Then let's get to it. We need oil, an urn—something metal to hold the fire, and we'll need to lash it to poles so we can carry the load on horseback," the Warrior commanded.

They did as instructed, quickly removing the creature from the pile of stone and burning the remains. After there was nothing but a large pile of ashes they placed them in a makeshift urn made from old braziers within the ruins.

The Prince instructed them to mix the ashes with oil enough to maintain a fire. The result was a slow, flickering burn with a cloying, pungent odor. He informed them that as they traveled they would continue to mix in additional oil to perpetuate the burn until they returned to the Red City.

They would ride as quickly as possible from the Jotun Foothills and, unfortunately, leave their fallen comrades to distract the jormungandr.

"No, that is heinous!" Vidar protested. "They deserve to be buried among their kin!"

The Prince reminded him that they had yet to carry a hot urn filled with burning ash through a hostile desert filled with creatures who want nothing more than to devour each and every one of them. Their brothers-in-arms would provide ample diversion to allow them a chance to escape; it was the only chance they had. If there was any other way, the Prince was open to ideas. He was met with silence.

Their brothers had sacrificed themselves enough already—was Vidar saying he would dishonor their sacrifice by dying so foolishly?

Vidar sneered at the Prince. "You mince words and honor as a poisoner with nightshade and honey. We return with Ullir, at least."

"We can't carry any more weight than we must," the Warrior added. "We will honor our brothers by ensuring this beast is destroyed once and for all."

Vidar turned without another word. The Prince felt a pang of guilt over his tactics. The Edding valued honor, loyalty, and courage. The Prince, a stranger, had used these traditions against Vidar to feed his friends to monsters so that they may live. The Prince told himself it was the right thing to do, but his doubts gnawed at him.

Using lengths of rope, they lashed a small wooden plank to two of the horses who still had riders. The brazier was secured on the plank and would be carried by the two most skilled horsemen back to Valgrind. The rest of them would ride alongside for protection—or distraction. All would ride quickly.

The spare horses would be brought along with them; each one tied to a separate rope. As they rode, there was a morose silence as they heard the jormungandr's roars upon the beasts finding their brothers.

They managed to make a good distance, in no small part due to the skill of the riders carrying the burning urn. It was only a matter of time before the jormungandr turned their attention to the riders, however.

The warband could hear the wurms ominous tunneling over the pounding of their horse's hooves. They broke through the surface of the burning sands like hellish serpents amidst the sea. They turned loose one of the spare horses and the jormungandr, driven by their hunger, diverted to the poor animal immediately.

The jormungandr harried the riders until even the horses began to falter. The warband made a path directly for the rocky shores of the coast. They rode so far, so hard that even the jormungandr began to slow.

The Warrior led them on a path near a rocky outcropping beyond the sands. They would pass very near to yet another danger, but if they continued in their current efforts they would surely perish against the jormungandr.

As they neared the outcropping, the Warrior saw just what he was expecting—cavernous holes within the sides of the stone cliffs.

"What have you done?" Vidar called out. "You've led us straight to a clutch of manticores!"

The Warrior didn't answer. He only spurred his horse on. With nowhere else to go, the warband followed. The Warrior knew his plan was built on desperation, but it had to work.

The thunderous noise of the jormungandr stirred the monsters within the mound. Many winged figures, silhouetted against the sunlight, shot from the caves. A heinous sound, the mix of a lion's roar and human scream, filled the skies.

One of the manticores dove amid the warband, carrying away yet another soldier. The other manticores noticed the greater threat—the jormungandr. As territorial as the sand wurms were, the manticores were doubly so.

The Warrior looked behind him to see the jormungandr covered in winged, furred monstrosities, and both were fighting for their lives. It was the last glance that he took before he spurred his horse on again.

By the time they reached the safety of the stone-covered shore, the horses practically fell into the cool waters. If any of the jormungandr followed them they would have to work for quite some time to dig through the thick rock; however, they had a severe distaste for wet soil and mud.

For now, the warband was safe. The men and the stallions both drank deeply and refilled their water reserves. They checked the rigging on the urn and added oil. The ashes of the Barghest continued to burn and so it appeared to be unable to regenerate itself. At least for now.

As they recuperated from their escape, the Warrior watched the waters rolling against the shore. In terms of peace, it was the most he could ask for. They would follow the rocky shores until they were near the Known Roads. From there they would return to the City of the Ruby Spire.

19

THE RUBY SPIRE

The comforting sight of the walls of the great city lifted a burden from the weary band. Their horses walked with labored steps. Their armor was stained red and their faces were filthy. Their lips were cracked and their muscles sore to their very bones; yet they rode with pride and victory. They returned with the still burning ashes of the great Barghest.

They approached one of the outer doors—the very same one through which they had departed only days earlier. A new warband of young men were waiting to set out to seek their Seven. They approached the remaining members of the incoming group.

"Did you complete the tasks?" one of them asked eagerly.

The Warrior looked at the dented, blackened brazier-turned-urn lashed between the two horses near him. They had faced many tasks; seven was a paltry number by comparison. They would know forever that their tasks would never be called into question—theirs was a Seven paid in blood and brotherhood. He then turned back to the young man who had asked the question.

"I hold their tasks complete. They've faced the burning sands and all the hells it has to offer and returned in glory. And alive.

They are Red Warriors, tried and tested Sons of Edda," the Warrior said with pride and exhaustion.

The Prince understood, but he lacked proper words to explain what the warriors of Edda could endure. Their armies were truly worthy of all the legends surrounding them.

The waiting warband helped the newly anointed soldiers from their stallions. The new Red Warriors didn't stop for food, water, or relief of any sort. They marched a somber procession through the streets of the city carrying with them the ever-burning ashes, as though they bore the remains of their fallen brothers instead of the beast that killed them.

They marched through the market and by the stalls. They ascended to the next district and passed through watchful gatherings. They shuffled through gardens and gateways, tired and bruised. They came, finally, to the towering Ruby Spire.

Guards posted at the door into the lower foyer appeared ready to admit them entrance, seeing fellow warriors; however, the guards hesitated upon seeing the urn, and inspected it. They peered inside and inquired about its contents. They reeled backward upon hearing that it was the smoldering ashes of the Barghest.

For a moment, it appeared they weren't going to let them through. With a stern look from the Warrior, the guards hesitantly waved them along.

Inside, it was more akin to a fortress than a spire. The Warrior led the procession to a large set of iron doors that required multiple men to open. Upon doing so, the Prince saw a set of stairs—not at all uncommon for a spire. However, after the first flight he noticed that the stairs wound ever upward.

"Where do they stop?" he asked the Warrior, who regarded him with a puzzled look.

"At the top," the Warrior answered plainly.

No lifts, no magic—the Edding were a straightforward people. They would walk the numerous stairs to the hall of the

Red King. Though alcoves at regular intervals were available for those who required rest, the warriors bearing the urn continued for flight after flight without complaint or need of rest. The Warrior pointed out that it was often visitors to the spire who required the use of the alcoves and not the people of Edda.

The Prince felt his breathing grow labored. He felt his legs turn to lead, but he refused to show it. He survived the burning, unfamiliar sands of the Red Kingdom, he would not be broken by stairs.

But, were he king of this spire he would have these cursed flights of ever-rising stairs destroyed. Each brick would be broken for every bit of pain in his legs at this moment.

After what seemed like days of ascending the tower stairs, they arrived at a door decorated with the fire-engulfed circle of Edda. These doors were also made entirely of forged iron. The Prince came to the conclusion that with sparse trees, the copious iron from the mountains serviced many of their construction needs. A hard land, a harder people.

"I need to speak with King Horodir for a moment. He needs to know about his son. Vidar, I assume you want to come with me," the Warrior said gruffly.

"Yes," Vidar replied, his voice flat.

The guard opened the door enough for the two men to enter. The Prince could see nothing of the throne room from his vantage point. He could also hear nothing after the large doors shut. All he and the other warriors could do was wait. After several minutes, a knock echoed off the iron doors. The guards in attendance opened the door for the Prince and the remaining warriors, the great hinges groaning like a wounded beast. Inside, large windows were open, allowing the cooler air at this elevation to drift about the room. Gold and red tapestries fluttered in the breeze, and through the windows they could see mountainous dunes, like frozen yellow waves in the distance.

They were escorted to the end of the hall where sat Horodir, the Red King, and Freya, the Red Queen. They stopped before the throne and all kneeled, save for the Prince, who offered a courteous bow.

The Warrior stood next to the king and queen, stoic as always. Vidar glared at the Prince as he and the other warriors approached. A fire burned in Vidar's eyes. The Prince flinched inwardly, hoping the king and queen's first impression of him wasn't too tarnished.

The Prince had never met the Red King, personally. He channeled the strength of his people in his proud demeanor. A crown of red gold sat upon his head, inlaid with rubies but lacking much other adornment. A scarlet sash was wrapped around his face, covering his eyes. The Prince could see a row of scars peeking underneath.

Queen Freya leaned over and began speaking softly to him. She was lovely, with hair like a sunlit waterfall. Her skin was fair, and one would be surprised to learn that she was not much younger than her rugged husband. She had worn a polite smile ever since they entered the throne room, though her eyes were red with recent tears, and now that they were at the foot of her throne they could see that her face was warm and gentle, as well.

"My queen informs me that we have a unique gathering before us," he said, his voice raspy and strong. A smile cut a thin line through his beard, long and red with shoots of gray reaching from the bottom like grasping fingers trying to pull him into his golden years.

"She recognizes the Prince of Avallonis and a number of newly-minted Red Warriors. You bring with you an old urn. I smell fire and ash. What is this?" Horodir asked.

The Warrior spoke for them.

"My king, we bring you the results of this warband's journey into the sands. With the aid of the Blue Prince," he gestured, "we've slain the Barghest and bring with us its ashes."

Queen Freya's smile faded. Like a storm cloud blocking the sun, a shadow crossed over her face.

"Why have you brought them here, Warrior?" she asked. "The Barghest could revive here in our very court, could it not?"

A number of the guards looked uneasy. Some glanced toward the urn as though the beast would come to life then and there.

"Aye, Your Grace, but the Prince has discovered more about the beast. I'll let him explain," the Warrior stepped aside and beckoned the Prince forward.

"Your Grace," the Prince said to Horodir, then looked to Freya, "Your Grace."

He then cast a dour glance at the flames licking at the blackened bronze.

"During our trials in the desert we noticed something particularly odd about the Barghest."

The king chuckled at this. The Prince continued, "Its eyes were alive with intelligence. They were disturbingly human-like. Both your Warrior and I were close enough to look the creature in those eyes and saw something even more disturbing. I believe it's under a similar hex that was placed upon myself in the Sapphire Kingdom very recently. A sorceress infiltrated my court through one of the magisters. I have a suspicion that it may be the very same one who may be responsible for the Barghest's attacks on your people. I don't excuse the Barghest or its actions, but I do believe that it did not ravage your country of its own accord."

The king stroked his bearded chin. It was impossible to judge his feelings on this news. If he had any strong feelings, he kept them guarded. He leaned back on his throne, an imposing seat of stone and iron. Its comfort came from the many manticore hides draped about it.

The warband remained silent as the king pondered. His queen looked first at him with worry and apprehension. She then turned her eyes to the blackened, bent urn resting on the ground.

The ashes within continued to smolder—a thick amalgam of ash, oil, and cinders.

Horodir's hands dropped from his chin. He leaned forward, slowly.

"Your Grace?" the Prince asked.

He didn't respond. His mouth opened and his hands gripped the sides of his throne. Fear gripped his wife and the warband. Then, they noticed the king was watching like he could see something they couldn't. They could all, however, follow his hollow gaze to the urn.

He moved his arms and waved them away from the ashes. The warband backed away and tried desperately to see what their blind king was seeing.

"Let them breathe!" he said in enthusiastic, hushed tones.

Surely, as they stepped away from the urn, the ashes smoldered even hotter. In seconds, it burned with renewed fury as though doused with fresh oil. The warband, the Prince and Warrior included, fell back against the burst of heat. For such a small flame it burned intensely.

The queen stood and grabbed her husband and his guard stepped in front of him with weapons drawn. Horodir moved only to still his wife and calm his guards.

The Red King, through his scarred, useless eyes, could see the glorious sight before him; a birth unseen in ages. He still could not see the room, the urn, or his loving wife beside him. In the endless darkness, he beheld swirling flames before his throne that furled and unfurled like massive wings. The flame took avian form and a phoenix was born of the fire before his eyes.

Only once before had a phoenix risen in the sands of the Ruby Realm—to escort the spirit of Baeol to his final resting place. What, then, would prompt the return of such a magnificent creature?

"Why have you come?" Horodir asked, his voice strained in awe.

The great creature spread its wings, fanning flame and heat about the room. Its feathers sweltered as molten rock. A crest of red fire danced among its head and neck. Its eyes and beak glowed like metal straight from the forge.

It was translucent, as far as Horodir could tell, and within swirled a pulsing eddy of light. The phoenix looked at him, and he heard a voice, though it seemed to come from within the bird itself, as the phoenix's beak did not move to speak.

Horodir, Red King and Lord of the Red Spire; I find myself in the gracious presence of an old friend.

"Who is this that calls me friend?" Horodir asked haltingly.

The once king of Mythesta. Perithane, King of the Amethyst Spire.

Horodir was stricken with doubt. Indeed, the king of the Amethyst Spire had long been his friend and ally. But, he hadn't seen him for nearly ten years; not since the Violet King had received Horodir's family for a winter feast.

"I don't understand, how could this be? Is this magic of the Violet Wizardess?"

No, friend. It's my ashes that burn. I was cursed and found my will no longer my own.

Horodir's face grew red with anger. He pursed his lips in rage. The Prince was right.

"Who has done this?" he fumed. "Say a name, and I will send my warriors to bring them to stand for this crime!"

I have no name to give. I... can't remember. The voice said. The Phoenix ruffled its molten feathers, giving form to Perithane's agitation.

My memories are... broken. I can see flashes of my life. They come and go now. I see pieces of a puzzle but not the finished picture. The Violet Wizardess... she'd taken on an apprentice. One very talented in magic. Beautiful, shrewd and ambitious. Sharp-tongued.

The voice wavered. Fractured sentences slowly fell together like a puzzle.

I... I took a liking to her. My own wife having been gone so long.

Horodir frowned. That winter feast was the first time Perithane had received guests after his wife's passing. The Red King's friend was still hurting, still somber, years later.

I fell for her, but as I began to know her I saw a darkness in her. When my own wizardess came to me with disturbing news of her apprentice, prepared to dismiss her, I confronted the apprentice.

I woke up. I was next to a river in the Misten Woods. I saw my spire through the trees in the distance. I returned to my tower and was attacked on sight. The guards didn't recognize their own king...they were terrified...

"Did you kill any of them? Your own men?" Horodir asked. The phoenix's head hung in shame.

I don't know. Some things I can't remember at all. I remember wallowing by a river, seeing the ghastly reflection looking back at me. It wasn't me, rather some horrifying creature. But it had my eyes... She came to me one day, the apprentice. I tried to attack her, but she held sway over me. Once I had resigned myself to death she lifted my bestial head, ran her hands through that coarse hair, and spoke to me of accepting my new form and submitting to my base nature. Then I began attacking everything I could see. So much rage and bloodthirst...

Horodir clenched his hands upon his knees. "They did not know, my friend... those who have slain you."

I'm grateful for them. They are brave and cunning men; they stopped me before I could kill further. I don't know what kept returning me to life. Perhaps her curse. Without the intervention of your warriors and the Prince, I fear I would never have stopped killing—I brought so much death and sorrow upon your people and for that I am so very sorry.

Horodir shook his head, waving away the Violet King's regret.

"You were bewitched, the deaths are not on your conscience. What of your daughter?" Horodir asked with growing concern.

When she found me in the woods, the apprentice could understand me. Somehow I could talk to her. I asked about my daughter. She said the Violet Wizardess had hidden her... weeks ago. Weeks. Weeks had gone by, Horodir. I can't remember any measure of time.

"It was ten years ago you were first seen among the sands of Edda," Horodir said sorrowfully. He could hear other voices, he thought. They were distant—mere echoes.

Ten years...

The phoenix continued to smolder. The light within grew dim and still. Then, it brightened as Perithane continued speaking, his voice hollow and echoing.

When I was slain this time I saw the phoenix lingering about me. I asked the phoenix why it now saw fit to visit me when I had seen a hundred deaths before. It seems the burning ashes of a wronged king carries the weight to birth one of the creatures.

I implored it to keep me from being dragged back from the darkness into a bloody rage again. It told me that the burning of my ashes prevented the Barghest from regenerating. Whosoever thought of such a scheme is worthy of knighthood—it was that act alone that prevented my return. It told me it would bear me to the worlds beyond but would allow a final word to the living.

"And you came to me instead of your family?" Horodir asked, confused.

The phoenix couldn't find them. The Violet Wizardess hid my daughter well. I next chose to see you, to see that you thanked those who slew me and also give you some closure as to why such a beast haunted your lands.

I also ask you this: do not send your warriors, Horodir. The enchantress likely has my wizardess under her spell, now. If she feels her rule is threatened, she may go after my daughter. If the phoenix couldn't find her, though, she must be in a safe place. Let her be. The enchantress' time will come. Reward your warriors—they have done service to both your realm and mine today.

The light of his friend and king, Perithane, dimmed yet again and the phoenix gave a cry that echoed against the walls of the room. The flapping of its massive wings filled the room with a heat that stole the air from one's lungs. It flew away quickly as flame and cinders danced about the room. Horodir fell back in his seat as the heat overtook him and embers danced about his throne.

It was then silent and cold in the hall. Horodir sat back upon his throne and felt his queen grasping tightly upon his arm.

"Who were you speaking to, Your Grace?" the Warrior asked.

Horodir regarded him warily.

"You couldn't hear him?" he asked.

"Hear who, love?" Freya asked.

They all regarded the king with confusion. Horodir turned his head left and right, his sightless eyes staring into nothing as he sought answers.

"We heard nothing, my king," the Warrior said in disbelief. "The firebird was borne from the ashes and fire and none dared approach it. It merely hovered there, watching you. We heard you speaking, we tried to call out to you, but you didn't respond."

The Red King sat quietly for a moment. It had happened, he was sure. He was not mad. He had spoken to what remained of his friend to the north, protected by one of the rarest of creatures.

Horodir told them of the Barghest and its origins, of the Violet King's torture as he was doomed to kill and be reborn to do the same again and again and again. He finally praised the warband for their efforts saying that their fallen brothers were to be honored greatly. He especially praised the Prince for his guile in keeping the ashes burning.

Vidar pushed his way to the front of the warband; he didn't appear pleased with the king's words.

"You speak so well of the man who caused the death of my brother—then fed his corpse to the jormungandr! You would reward his defilement?" he shouted.

The Prince was surprised to see that the guards didn't flinch at the man who disrespected his king in such a manner.

"Your commander," the king said, facing the Warrior, "spoke highly of Ullir's actions and those of his brothers. He died well—songs will be written about him. If he must die, I'd have it no other way."

"His brothers?" Vidar fumed, his face reddening. "My brother!" He stepped back as the weight of the king's words weighed upon him. "Your son, they fed on him. The jormungandr, those sand devils, they feasted on a prince of Edda... and you praise the man responsible," his words seethed like the hot sands he called home.

The queen raised a lithe hand to her face attempting to conceal her grief. The Prince's eyes widened at Vidar's revelation. He was not aware he had been in the presence of the Edding princes.

"Your brother rode with you and his brothers-in-arms as seekers of the Seven Tasks," Horodir said.

"We were all aware of the risks," he continued, his voice cracking as a fresh tear rolled down the queen's cheek. "Were it not for they, the Barghest would still be ravaging the homes of your people. I hold their tasks complete; their names will be etched upon the outer wall with the names of all their fallen equals."

The Prince approached Horodir and Freya and bowed his head before them. He spoke sincerely, his voice heavy with regret.

"I couldn't return your son to you. I certainly was not aware that he was your son and heir," the Prince began, but Vidar cut him off.

"He was not yours to protect!" Vidar shouted him down. "My father sees you as a hero. I name you coward, errant king!"

"I have spoken!" King Horodir shouted above his son. "Your brother has shown more valor in death than you do now in life—respect his sacrifice, respect the tasks!"

Vidar hung his head in submission, but his anger was palpable. He shouldered past the Prince and Warrior. He stalked off from the audience, his heavy footsteps preceding a great groan as the iron doors were opened and then moaned again as they shut.

The Red King placed a weary hand to his head. The queen sighed heavily. The Warrior continued standing stoically.

"You've done a great service to this realm and your own," the queen said to the Prince. "Ullir was a noble man. He would have understood your actions. We will... grieve his death for some time."

Horodir leaned over to his queen and spoke quietly to her. She rose and left the room.

"Though the Violet King warned me of the dangers befalling his realm, I can't let the actions of this sorceress continue unabated nor allow this enchantress to be a threat against his daughter, who should return to her rightful throne," he said. "I intend to send this very warband to Mythesta as a vanguard. I will have ships ready to sail and meet them with a thousand more if necessary."

The Prince sighed and lowered his head in thought. The warband was not against this. They would be feasting as heroes and after a few days rest and mending they would take the Dwarf-waters to the Veil Mountains and march from there to their destination.

"As prince of a neighboring kingdom, I wouldn't protest. However, I can't join the men immediately."

Horodir chuckled. "You speak as though you're a Red Warrior and not king of another realm. You have duties to attend to as ruler of your own people."

"It has nothing to do with my rule, Your Grace," the Prince interrupted with a raised hand. "I'm greatly suspicious of who this apprentice may be and I will take it upon myself to find out if it's indeed Lady Morgæna. If it is, and I suspect this to be so, then she's responsible for untold murders in your kingdom, regicide in another, and an attempted coup in my own. She will pay for her crimes."

The king grunted in approval and the Prince continued.

"Wyvern is at work here. Even if it's not the same sorceress, she no doubt has ties to the beast if she dares curse a king to take his throne."

"So, where will you go?" Horodir asked.

"Wyvern has behaved strangely since he first reared his head," the Prince thought aloud.

The Prince recalled his and the Knight's visions. He decided it was best not to bring those up to the Red King. He needed Horodir's support, not the king's suspicion that the Prince was mad. "I have reason to believe that Wyvern wants a common woman for some dark purpose. Why a dragon-child would be interested in her is quite baffling. If I'm being honest, Your Grace, I find myself in a bind. I need your warriors to help me fight Wyvern. He gathers allies and I will need my own. I also need to know more of what Wyvern plans, and if I can be certain I have your support, I can focus my efforts on personally investigating Wyvern's motive."

The Red King nodded. "I didn't know your father well. But, word of his people's love and respect for him reached even here. I can hear the conviction in your voice and that tells me more than I could ever see with working eyes. Unfortunately, goodness and wisdom are distinctly separate traits. I hope your choices are as wise as they are well-intended."

"My kingdom is currently overseen by trusted and competent minds, Your Grace," the Prince said, smirking.

"Ah, the fabled griffon riders of Avallonis, it must be. I know you can't possibly be speaking of those perfumed magisters," Horodir laughed.

"I'm afraid after the incident with Lady Morgæna and her manipulation of my council, the riders have indeed been given their time to govern. Lady Gwinn is a capable steward."

"Very good," Horodir replied. "The warriors I've ordered to the Mythestan border will wait there as a defensive measure. That will put them in closer proximity to your own kingdom, as well. If you decide to challenge Wyvern, you need only ask and I will send reinforcements to you from their ranks. This should satisfy both our concerns."

The Prince smiled and bowed in gratitude. "It will, Your Grace. You have my sincere thanks."

Queen Freya returned, carrying with her a bundle wrapped in fine red cloth. She stood before the Prince and smiled at him through eyes red with recent tears.

"I hear the gentle footsteps of my dear wife. I assume she brings the boons I would grant you."

"You assume correctly," she said, smiling at the Prince. Though, her voice was still breaking in grief.

The Prince regarded the bundle curiously. The queen gently placed the folded items on the ground, then lifted the first few folds and revealed a helm made of shining steel; simplistic in design. It was engraved with traditional runes of Edding make. She brought it before the Prince and gave a slight nod. He lowered his head, creasing his brows, and she placed the helmet upon his head.

She knelt and began unwrapping red, silken folds again. This time a broad, stout shield was revealed. It showed a winding, open-mouthed dragon entwining a sword. She handed this to him and, gathering the cloth, returned to her throne.

"King Horodir, Queen Freya… these gifts are too much. I can't possibly…" The Prince trailed off as the Red King interrupted him, smiling broadly.

"They were once mine before I was king. These were made by my own hand—I was quite skilled in smithing; a hobby, really," he smiled even wider.

"I used these during my own tasks. I would now give them to you. If you're to face Wyvern you will do so as both a knight of

Avallonis and a Red Warrior of Edda. In recognition of your services to the Red Realm."

"Shouldn't these go to your son, Your Grace? Remain within your family?" the Prince protested.

"Ha!" Horodir barked a laugh. "I said it was a hobby, Prince. I have plenty of my work to bequeath to Vidar. And more to place at a mural for Ullir."

The mention of his deceased son caused the king to drop his head slightly. He nodded, pursed his lips, and raised his head. Looking in the direction of the Prince, the king gave a smile.

The Prince smiled back, looking at both rulers. "And if you are ever to visit Avallonis, I'll return this favor as king."

The Warrior stepped forward. "Your Grace, I would accompany him, with your leave."

The Red King raised his chin, as though he could see the Warrior.

"Curious. Why would you request such a thing?" he asked of the Warrior.

"What he seeks to accomplish—defeating Wyvern, slaying him and ending his madness—it would benefit all the realms," the Warrior looked to the Prince. "It would benefit the Prince to have a spare sword. Besides, I began his training. It would dishonor me and my brothers in arms if he were to shame us in the field so soon after leaving."

King Horodir barked a sincere laugh. He gestured to the Prince, seeking his input.

"I'd welcome the help, but who will lead your army to the Amethyst Realm?" the Prince replied.

"Vidar," the king answered quickly. He is a capable warrior. You must forgive his outbursts. His brother's death will weigh on us all."

The king spoke haltingly of Ullir. "Now we will see his command capabilities. They'll hold at the Veil Mountains and await this Warrior's return."

The Prince agreed to this course of action. He thanked the Red King for his gifts—the shield and helm of his gloried past. The Prince and Warrior bowed graciously before King Horodir and exchanged their final well-wishes. The Warrior saluted his fellow soldiers as they departed the great hall, sharply striking a fist against their chests, above the heart.

At the base of the Ruby Spire they were brought their horses. Ceffyl appeared quite pleased to see his new master. Having been cleaned and well-fed after their excursion into the desert, the stallion appeared as battle-ready as ever. No doubt he was ready to return to green fields and cool rivers.

"Do we even know where to begin looking for Wyvern?" the Warrior asked dubiously, en route to the dry-port of the Dwarf-waters.

"He stole away the Maiden at her family's smallholding in Emrallt. That's as good a place as any to start."

"And the Blue Wizard? Could he be of any assistance?"

The Prince shook his head, wishing it were otherwise. "He's called a Wizards' Council. They convened following the discovery of Morgæna and her ties to Wyvern. So long as they're in session, he'll be unavailable."

The Warrior looked forward, ever stalwart as he said, "Then, let us hunt.

20

A PIECE OF PARADISE

T he road they travelled was still fraught with uncertainty, but they remained vigilant. The Prince and the Warrior had taken the Dwarf-waters back to the mouth of the Veil Mountains. The cool winds and occasional spray of snow-fed mountain water were refreshing in the desert heat. The Prince marveled yet again at the incredible ingenuity of the dwarves. It appeared their potential as an ally was greatly under-utilized.

They traversed the cavernous tunnels within the mountains with their familiar guide, the gruff and stout dwarf, Gohljen. During the Prince's time amid the burning sands with the Warrior, the dwarves had already made great progress on their new tunnels and the construction of their cities under the mountains. It was odd to both of the men to think that outside and above them was a lethal blizzard fraught with ogres, ice-spiders, and fatal cold. The journey through the mountains, by contrast, was blissfully uneventful.

At the great gates of the dwarf-hold the Prince welcomed the Warrior to the Sapphire Realm. They traversed Avallonis on horseback and avoided towns where possible. They wanted their trip to be swift and unhindered. The errant king of Avallonis and a Red Warrior of Edda would most certainly draw attention, whether for good or ill.

Many times during their trip, the Warrior remarked how pleasant the countryside of Avallonis was, which the Prince appreciated. He also noted that it no doubt raised soft people and spoiled soldiers, which the Prince did not.

"Full of hills and grass—and orchards plenty. Even in the lost era of Edda there was not such abundance," the Warrior remarked at one point.

They followed the River Brim, which wound through Avallonis to Emrallt. The Warrior's horse was frothing at the mouth from exertion, and it made the Prince grateful for Ceffyl. He truly was a one-of-a-kind horse. The Prince's flight to Edda had been taxing on the great stallion and the stable hands of the Ruby Spire informed the Prince that it took the whole of his time there for the poor beast to recover. A lesser horse, they said, would have surely succumbed to such exertion. This ride would take them at least two more days to reach Emrallt.

As they crossed into the Emerald Realm, the land changed from moderately flat with the occasional hill to rolling waves of deep green. The grass grew thicker and taller. Thickets turned to forests. Streams and brooks from the mountains converged into the large Lordbrook River, into which all the smaller rivers and streams of Emrallt flowed. The Warrior felt foreign here. The shrubs and tough grasses, which themselves were sparse in his home realm, were pitiable compared to the thick, soft carpet of Emrallt's lush meadows. The trees grew thick as castle towers and there were more blossoms within reach than could be counted. The smell felt cloying to a man used to crisp, fresh, desert air. The branches and canopies made him feel closed in and almost claustrophobic—especially at night.

With twilight fast approaching, they'd slowed their horses to a walk, found a comfortable place near the river, and made camp for the night. They needed to bathe and wash away the sand and grit and exhaustion of the deserts. They realized that their journey into the Red Wastes had been so all-consuming they were completely unaware of their admittedly poor hygiene. It occurred to them, when they sat down by a crackling fire, of the harrowing nature of the last few days.

The Warrior ran his hands through shrubs and saplings that grew along the riverbanks. The leaves were broad and gentle and each bloom smelled sweet and strong. Simply running your hand through most Edding plants would result in cuts or worse.

"This is a paradise..." he said with wonder. "How could a thing such as Wyvern call this home?"

"Why do any of the dragon-children call their realm home? Perhaps, Wyvern is Emrallt's price to pay for all this beauty. I get the feeling he resides where he chooses, though," the Prince said somberly. "One of the many reasons why we must rid such a place of him."

"I'm still unsure of how exactly you plan to find him," the Warrior said, observing a small number of deer drinking from a small pool formed out of a small cascade near a grove of trees. "I'm with you in this. You did a great service to my realm. Your own came under attack from within, but hunting such a monster... Even the jormungandr pale in comparison to him. He's also far smarter than men, if legends are correct."

"I've seen the creature in person," the Prince recalled. "The legends don't embellish much. Though I'd stress he's more a creature of low cunning. His brother Wyrm is far more intelligent, at least according to scholars."

"Scholars. Legends," the Warrior huffed. "We're fighting foes we know nothing about."

The Prince's thoughts wandered to the Maiden. Wyvern and Morgæna had tried to use his own magisters against him to take the Sapphire Spire from him. The sorceress cursed a king and has spires-know how much influence in Mythesta. The dragon-child was staking claims without waging open war. What did the Maiden have to do with any of this?

"For now we should find and follow the roads," the Prince concluded aloud.

"I thought we planned to follow the river?" the Warrior asked with a furrowed brow.

"Just until we reached Emrallt. We don't want to head too deeply into the forests here. In the Emerald Realm, the deep forests can be as treacherous as your deserts."

The Warrior looked to the harmless, well-fed deer near the pools. The trees covered them like gentle, verdant shields and the water babbled lazily over the stones.

"How could such a place be dangerous?" he thought aloud.

"The deeper we go, the more we wander into the territory of wolves and trolls. Emrallt is beautiful, but all places, no matter how beautiful, have unique evils of their own," the Prince said quietly.

Nodding in agreement, the Warrior stared into the fire. It was quiet for many long moments. The only sound was the gentle rolling of the river's waters.

"It was the end of the world," the Warrior said briskly.

The Prince looked over to see him still staring into the dancing flames. The embers reflected dangerously in his eyes. They pierced the fire, looked through it, and into memories and stories he'd locked away.

"What? The end of the world?" the Prince repeated in confusion.

"Our world."

The Warrior looked up at the Prince. The son of Edda had deep bags under his eyes. Early wrinkles had set in around his eyes and forehead. The Prince saw a man who seemed to have aged years in front of the fire.

"You asked about Ragnarok," the Warrior continued. "You've earned an answer."

He stood and walked over to his horse, removing rations and his waterskin from one of the bags. He handed the Prince some dried, salted meat and sat back down.

"Have you ever wondered why a mountain range covered in spires-forsaken snowstorms leads immediately into a relentless desert?"

He bit and chewed on some of the meat, letting the Prince consider his question. The Prince could only shrug.

"I've read of many wonderous things on this continent. The Amber Realm's clockwork, the ancient ruins of the Opal Realm…"

"Have nothing on a disaster that nearly eliminated an entire people," the Warrior interrupted, his voice harsh. He looked at the meat, sneered, and tossed it aside.

"It was a long time ago. Before my grandfather's grandfather was even born. Every Edding child is told of the Ruby Spire's vengeance: Ragnarok, when our home became a desert waste-land. Some say it was the fault of Wyrm, who hides away in shame in his realm. Others say Edda's dragon-child locked himself away to find a way to counter its effects, and bring back our home to the way it was before—cold, yes, but flourishing with life and cedar trees and cold streams filled with fish. Now, our land only harbors death in many different forms for her people. Little by little, pieces of the story are being lost to us. Scrolls of history lost or damaged. I fear that soon we may forget our tragedy altogether."

"How did it happen?" the Prince asked. "Was it war? A natural disaster?"

The Warrior's eyes glazed back over as he looked at the fire. "That is one of the pieces that we lost. Now, we just learn to live upon the land given us."

"A hard land, a harder people," the Prince said solemnly.

"A harder people," the Warrior returned quietly. He looked out among the trees, black as coal from blocking out the starlight.

The fire spit and crackled, casting orange shadows that danced among the black columns of tree trunks. "When I return, I'll make sure our scholars know of the ruins in the Jotun Foothills we found. We'll run every jormungandr out of that territory and reclaim that knowledge, or die trying."

SURPRISINGLY, they slept easy that night, the exhaustion from the previous weeks finally taking hold. When the sun peeked through the canopies and gentle light dappled the ground, they doused the fire and prepared to be off again. As their horses began to make their way through the brush, the Warrior looked back to that pool. A few of the deer had returned, making their way through the trees to that small piece of paradise.

21

CATCHING A RAT

They quickly came to a small deer trail that cut through the dense trees. They followed the thin, overgrown path until they came to a small crossroads. A wooden signpost was placed squarely in the center. The letters were branded with heated iron and could be easily read.

The markers indicated that the towns of Unfordd and Nerall could be found to the east and west, respectively, but the travelers' destination lay north—Emrallt, the City of the Emerald Spire itself.

"And what do we expect to find there?" the Warrior asked, riding up beside the Prince.

"There's little knowledge to guide us to Wyvern or where he may have taken the Maiden. It has to be here in Emrallt, though. I wouldn't think he'd take her very far from his home realm."

"He cares for her?" the Warrior asked in surprise.

The Prince scoffed. "Doubtful. But, she wasn't among the bodies we found in the ruins of her home."

"That's not very convincing, Prince."

The Prince sighed inwardly and frowned as he replied. "I have... other reasons to believe he finds her valuable."

"Such as?"

The Prince was quiet for a moment. He was suddenly apprehensive about sharing the vision from many nights prior. Those blood-filled images that led him and the Knight to discover the Maiden's smoldering home were seared into his brain with black fire. The Warrior was a pragmatic man and had earned the Prince's respect and, truth be told, his admiration. To say he sought Wyvern due to symbolic visions could likely cost him that hard-earned respect. "The armor I wear, granted me by King Brennen of the Emerald Spire, belonged to the Knight who accompanied me and fought Wyvern," the Prince's hesitation was clear in his tone.

"You've said this before," the Warrior reminded him flatly.

"The Knight and I also shared a vision of sorts. A dream that came to us the night before we encountered Wyvern," the Prince said, sighing in resignation.

The Prince saw, from the corner of his eye, the Warrior's head turn towards him. He could feel the incredulous gaze boring into him already.

"I see," the Warrior replied stoically. His chainmail jingled ever so slightly on the horse, mocking the Prince like a thousand tiny silvered bells.

"Apparently, there were aspects of our dreams that differed. When it came to pass, I realized I foresaw the Knight's death. What makes me certain Wyvern wants the Maiden in good health is another portion of that vision. I saw the avatar of Wyvern in my dream—an oily cloud of black smoke and fire, grasping desperately for a beautiful statue of a woman made of jade. It fit within his palm, but it kept slipping from his grasp."

"You believe the effigy is the Maiden? You're certain?"

"I believe so," the Prince replied. He shuddered at the thought of the vision again. "I truly believe so."

"If you believe so, then you're not certain," the Warrior said plainly.

The Prince's mouth felt dry. After a short time, he replied, "I'm certain."

There was a period of quiet between the two as they followed the road to the Emerald Spire. Finally, the Warrior spoke.

"I've placed great faith in you, Prince. I left my home to help you hunt this threat to all the realms. My king left an army waiting at our borders. I trust you will not show my faith has been ill-placed."

The Prince looked at him, but it was now with confidence. "I assure you, it will not be."

"Good," the Warrior nodded. "Then to what purpose do we ride to Emerald Arbor?"

"The last I visited the city, and the first time I met the Maiden, she had run afoul of two ratlings. From my understanding they are unique to Emrallt; they're intelligent, for their part, and quite adept at self-preservation. They may be of use in locating Wyvern."

"Ratlings?" the Warrior sneered. "That sounds... unpleasant."

"Very much," the Prince added, remembering his encounter with the filthy little creatures.

They reached the City of the Emerald Spire and the Prince found it as pleasant as before—though light a few guards. He noticed the Warrior was quite stiff in his posture as they rode under the large, root-woven arch. Before arriving they both had the foresight to remove their armor and any heraldry of their home realms, wrapping it and burying it outside of town near a distinct grove just inside the treeline. They wore only the simpler clothes under their armor and traveling cloaks from their saddle-bags. Anything adorning the stallions they had also removed and buried with their armor.

They avoided guards and barking shopkeeps alike, quickly making their way to the poorest of areas and began their search for the reclusive ratlings.

After the better part of a day, the shadowed streets of the

paupers district offered no hope of finding one of the creatures. They searched, loitered, and bribed their way about the various streets and alleys to no avail. The stray guard that meandered into the filthy streets paid them little attention, but they knew that the guard's presence would further complicate their search. They also knew that much more of their nosing around would likely alert the guard's suspicions.

They sat in a decrepit tavern, The Bowl and Barrel, for an early supper of what might have been soup but could easily have been gutter water steeped with potato peelings and onion skins. Their mugs were filled with either ale or yet more gutter water.

Finding no appetite for the 'food', the two of them debated a course of action.

"Either they know we're looking for them, or they completely avoid this part of the city altogether," the Warrior complained.

"They're here—it's the only place they could possibly travel in the city without being chased out of town or locked away," the Prince insisted. He stared into his drink, pining for a solution.

"I'm beginning to doubt the validity of the existence of these miserable creatures," the Warrior continued.

"They're very reclusive, but like cockroaches, there's always a few skulking about somewhere in the shadows. Especially in Emerald Arbor. To the best of my knowledge, they steal, pick-pocket, bully..." the Prince thought aloud until he had a realization.

"Come, I know how we'll find them," the Prince said with renewed vigor.

The Warrior looked with disgust into his untouched drink and clapped it down upon the table. He rose to follow the Prince, though he was unsure to what end.

As the Prince explained his plan, the Warrior felt more at ease. "A clever plan," he told the Prince.

They left their horses tied at the tavern and gave some coin to an urchin for a promise to keep them there. A stern look from the Warrior seemed to reaffirm the importance of the horses still being there when they returned.

They found one of the most disreputable portions of the city, even for the paupers district. Everything was covered in soot, mud, garbage, or all three. It created a gray palette of despair and poverty that struck at the Prince. He felt deeply for the poor wretches that called such squalor home.

The Prince meandered a bit, letting his coin purse show, and shuffled slightly. The clinking sound of coin upon coin garnered attention from a few, but the Warrior remained nearby in the event someone was foolish enough to try and rob the disguised Prince.

Soon, the right pickpocket appeared. The Warrior spotted a moving shadow lurking near a pile of rubble and garbage. What he first took to be a pile of dirty rags moved and began to walk towards the Prince. Just as a bony, clawed little hand began to reach out for the purse the Warrior drew his sword on the tatters, placing the point firmly against the rags, but not enough to cut.

"One flinch and I cut it off," the Warrior whispered harshly. The hand was visibly shaking.

The Prince turned and pointed Calibern at the filthy rags. The Warrior sheathed his sword and picked up the thing by the scruff of its neck. A high pitched squeal escaped from the rags. No one paid them any attention as they regarded the grimy, reprehensible thing that squirmed in the Warrior's grasp. They swiftly moved around a corner to a darker alley and the Warrior pulled down the hood of the creature.

What appeared beneath was all manner of muck and misery. It appeared to the Warrior to be a giant rat, for all intents and purposes. However, its muzzle was blunted and it had surprisingly humanoid features about the eyes and mouth. It was thin to the point of emaciation and matted, coarse gray hair covered its body.

"Spires-all," he quietly cursed, "what manner of wretchedness has been permanently visited upon this thing?"

The creature sneered, baring irregular, yellowed teeth, but recoiled in fear at the same time. A foul stench emanated from the creature, but from whether it came from its clothes, breath, or body could not be determined. The two men dared guess it was all three.

"Put it down! Please!" it shrilled.

The Prince shushed the ratling and pressed Calibern closer.

"I've seen your kind before. You're not dangerous and you're not welcome here. We could slit your throat, leave you for dead, and none would care," the Prince said menacingly.

The Warrior looked to him and raised a brow. Such a threat was quite unlike the Prince he had spent the last month with.

The defiance on the creature's face had turned to one of terror. It frowned and whimpered pathetically. The Prince removed his sword and spoke more accommodatingly.

"However, I can offer you gold and food for your help."

The creature stopped squirming and looked at the Prince with wet, sickly eyes.

"H-how? How can it help?" it asked haltingly.

"What rumors have you heard of the great Wyvern that lurks among your forests? You live among the deep parts of the Emerald forests, skulking in darkness; what whispers are among them of this monster?"

The jaundiced eyes darted about, and its nose twitched. "I know nothing about Wyvern—nothing about winged monster…"

"It's lying," the Warrior said flatly. "It stiffened up nicely when you mentioned the beast."

The ratling squeaked at the accusation.

"I have neither the time nor the inclination to cause you any manner of harm. I'm no monster like Wyvern. I offer you food and money for your help, or I can turn you over to the guards for pickpocketing."

The Prince put his sword away. "The choice is yours, friend."

"Truly—Scuffle knows nothing!" the creature pleaded. "Scuffle knows Wyvern bad... seen him in forest many nights ago —many nights! Knows nothing about where he be now."

The Prince looked at the deplorable thing. It was staring at him, pleadingly, though there was an anger in its furled brows. It was dejected and detested—such an existence surely made it a hardened, unforgiving thing. Though it looked at him with hands raised and without further flinching.

"Put him down. This one can't help us," the Prince said with agitation.

The Warrior promptly dropped the creature onto the cobble-stones. It picked itself up and began correcting its disheveled rags.

"Yes... Scuffle know nothing about nasty Moss Blossom and mean White-eye."

The Prince turned quickly and the ratling looked up at him and cocked its head in misunderstanding.

"Grab him!" the Prince shouted.

Scuffle made a noise between a hiss, yelp, and squeal. It turned to flee along the walls much like the other two the Prince had encountered.

With astounding speed, the Warrior plucked Scuffle seem-ingly from midair and held him by both the creature's arms, immobilizing him.

Scuffle squealed again, "You... you give money and food now?" he said miserably.

"I never used those names. I do know who Moss Blossom is, though, and the other one did have quite a nasty white eye," the Prince said menacingly. "I do not appreciate being lied to, Scuffle."

"Oh..." Scuffle shrank back into his filthy clothing.

"The truth, wretch," the Warrior threatened.

The ratling mumbled and hesitated for a moment, unwilling to speak.

He was terrified, the Prince realized. Wyvern had them fearful for their very lives, and possibly the existence of their kind as a whole.

"Look," the Prince began, gesturing to himself and the Warrior, "Strong men, smart men—we're going to kill Wyvern; stop the monster. Help us stop him."

The ugly eyes continued to dart back and forth between them.

"If he's dead," the Prince continued, "he can't hurt you. No more working for Wyvern, no more dying and slaving and scraping for Wyvern. We are going to make him dead, but we need Scuffle's help."

Scuffle finally calmed enough to speak. A determination set into his eyes like a pig settling in mud. It spoke in a stern, if shaking, voice.

"White-eye and Moss Blossom—they go to see Wyvern. Say he had reward for them finding pretty lady. They never come back..."

A flash of fear crossed over its face, quick as a shadow.

"That won't happen anymore," the Prince reassured the creature.

"Wyvern says, when we find something or need to tell him something, go to old stones and wait," Scuffle said.

"Old stones?" the Warrior wondered.

"Where are these old stones?" the Prince asked.

Scuffle sneered and turned his head away. "Put Scuffle down."

The Warrior and Prince shared a knowing look. The Warrior placed Scuffle on the ground and they both braced for it to flee. To their surprise, the creature merely looked up them, its shoulders back and head high, and Scuffle held out his hand.

"Food and money. You said food and money."

The Prince grimaced, but the creature was right. He pulled some coins from his pouch and handed them to the ratling. He entreated upon the Warrior to get a small number of their rations from their packs. The Warrior returned a displeased look. Not that he was offended at the Prince's request itself, but at the thought of being manipulated by the little weasel.

The Warrior returned shortly with the soup and ale from the inn. Surprisingly, it was still on their table—colder and more repulsive than before. Scuffle pocketed the coins and began devouring the meal in the most nauseating manner possible, slurping the soup and drinking the ale messily.

When he was finished, he began describing the way to the old stones that he had spoken of. It wasn't a difficult route or a magical one. It was simply isolated far and away from any civilized point in Emrallt. It was deeper in the great forests of the Emerald Realm than many dared to go. The Prince took a map from within his cloak and showed it to Scuffle. Scuffle was able to point out the approximate location of the old stones with a wrinkled, knobby finger.

"That will be quite a way to travel," the Warrior commented.

"And through territory mostly unknown," the Prince added. "Go, and thank you for your help."

Scuffle snatched up the bowls that contained the soup and rushed off into the shadows.

"Oily little filth, aren't they?" the Warrior commented, wiping his hands on his thighs. "I doubt I'll ever wash the stink out."

The Warrior reflexively wiped his hands again, sniffing them afterward and recoiling at the musky odor. "Spires-all," he grumbled.

22

THE HYNEFOL

They found their horses—the urchin nowhere in sight—and climbed atop them ready to begin their hunt in earnest. They checked their rations, weapons, and all other provisions. They could buy what was necessary at the market before they departed. If luck was with them, they would find Wyvern, and the Prince could return to his people as a worthy king.

As they approached the outer edge of the bustling city, a figure was standing in the road before them. The silhouette of a cloaked human seemed to be looking at them, unmoving.

The figure crossed their arms. Were they waiting? The Warrior put himself just ahead of the Prince and drew his sword. His large stallion snorted slightly at the familiar sound.

"Put the weapon away, Son of Edda. Even a Red Warrior couldn't best me," a familiar voice called out confidently, with a hint of humor under the surface.

The Prince approached and saw the trim of fine blue robes. Gloved hands pulled back the gray cowl to reveal a brown, if graying, beard.

"Well," the Prince chuckled, "you finally return."

The Blue Wizard furrowed his thick brows. "Are you saying I took my time, my young ward?"

"I dare not guess at the games of mages," the Prince replied with a smirk.

"Games!" the Wizard scoffed. "The Wizards' Council... games!" he huffed.

"Your spire wizard, I assume," the Warrior said.

The Wizard bowed slightly. "My pleasure. It was I who sent word to your own Red Wizard of my Prince's coming. Were you among those of the warband he accompanied?"

"I was," the stoic man replied, "and your Prince showed ample ability in combat. He's improving. Though, not us much as I like," the Warrior said plainly, provoking a side glance from the Prince. "Though, I have seen his keen mind at work, as well."

The Wizard smiled. "I suppose you would have."

The Wizard bade them continue and they walked their horses slowly so the Wizard could keep up with them on foot.

"I'm surprised you've come so far so quickly. When exactly have you had time to practice with your sword?" the old mentor asked.

"Whenever we can," the Prince replied. "When we camped at night, mostly. Though, I have to admit that much of my training has been very... hands on. More of a 'fight' or 'die' approach."

His response was tinged with sarcasm, but genuine. The Warrior smiled, while the Wizard cast a reproachful glance that landed against the Warrior's unyielding shrug like dull knives.

"It's very effective," he said casually. The Wizard snorted his disapproval.

"What have you discovered on the whereabouts of Wyvern?" the Wizard asked.

"A ratling told us of some 'old stones' where Wyvern hides his lair in Emrallt," the Prince replied.

"And you go alone? You return from Edda, home of the Red Warriors, and you bring *a* Red Warrior?" the Wizard pointed out.

"The Red King has sent a large force to his northern border with Mythesta. By his command those troops will reinforce us when we have need of them. Now, we need to discover Wyvern's motives before we can move against him. We're traveling through the old forests and bringing an army would be cumbersome and slow moving," the Prince explained.

"As are old wizards who don't have a horse," the Warrior quipped.

"Ah, yes. That would be an issue," the 'old wizard' replied, and pulled a small vial from within his robes. The Prince noted he traveled with more packs about his person than when they last met. Had he not returned to the Sapphire Spire before seeking him out here?

The vial the Wizard produced was filled with a lavender-hued liquid that seemed to contain a sparkling smoke. The Wizard opened the vial and, pouring it upon the ground, whispered some indecipherable words. What started as a few wisps of smoke grew to one resembling a billowing green fire. They could then hear the pounding of hooves quickly closing in on them.

Before their eyes, a stallion emerged from the smoke and violet substance along the ground. It was a smoky gray with an otherworldly black-and-violet mane. Its eyes were pitch black and held a strange intelligence in them. As the smoke cleared they saw that no evidence of the violet liquid remained on the ground.

"Confounded sorcery," the Warrior remarked. "Nothing wrong with a normal horse."

"No, but this one is quite convenient and equally fast," the Wizard rebutted.

The Prince took a level of joy in seeing the Warrior's chagrin at the antics of the Wizard. The conjurer climbed atop his arcane stallion and, together, they rode for the sweeping, wild forests.

The patches of trees and winding roads eventually led to the border of the old forest of Hynefol, where all the paths ended.

The Prince's studies spoke little of the Hynefol save for myth and legend. The Warrior knew nothing of this place or the lands surrounding it. The Wizard, however, had read many things about these woods.

These ancient forests were the source of many tales, often embellished, but the legend of the beautiful dryads that tended the lakes and trees were most certainly true. A few accounts still existed in the Avallonian archives of travelers, woodsmen, and treasure-hunters who ventured into the woods and vowed never to return. Some accounts made a point to mention that some parties returned a few men short. To cut a branch or harvest a tree would be met with swift vengeance by the creatures. Only with good reason and great need should one dare to take from the bounty of the Hynefol.

For Wyvern to nest within its borders shows either great hubris or great power. Most likely, being Wyvern, it was equal amounts of both in copious measure. The Wizard warned them ahead of time to neither shoot the game within the Hynefol's borders nor pluck the fruit from its trees. If they grew hungry, it would be best to use the rations at hand. Only once those were exhausted would it be safe to harvest from the Hynefol. In the Hynefol, you must eat of need, not out of curiosity or pleasure.

Even the animals under the boughs knew the laws of the dryads. More than once had the three men seen a number of wolves follow them, but the creatures didn't approach.

Scaled and feathered cockatrices—feared among the northern towns of Emrallt for their venomous tails and eyes that could turn men to stone—darted among the brush but avoided the companions much like the wolves.

Thankfully, none of these creatures must have been hungry or they would have been free to attack. There was no need to be territorial in this most ancient of forests. Even the animals were aware. The dryads protected every creature, tree, and flower. The three men would have been able to defend themselves, but packs of wolves and cockatrices are not encounters that would have ended without grievous harm.

The ratlings, disgusting though they may have been, were still creatures of nature. They would be welcome here if nowhere else. The dryads cared not for social status or wealth. It was no wonder the socially-outcast ratlings made their many hidden hovels within the Hynefol.

The Warrior was compelled to ask, "Why would such grand and well-guarded beauty deign to allow Wyvern to dwell within its borders?"

"Whatever the reason, the answer doesn't bode well," the Wizard explained. "It's enough to know that it further proves how dangerous that dragon-child is."

After some time, the Prince asked the Wizard, "What did the Wizards' Council have to say?"

The Wizard curled his lips as if he'd bitten into a sour apple. A low growl came from his throat before he spoke.

"They're 'sympathetic' to our plight, but they're bloody wizards. The Green and Red Wizards were quick to speak in favor of taking action, but the others wanted to gather more information. Especially Vacini, that aloof old fool. The Amber Spire... *pah*."

The Prince smiled at the thought of the old rivalry but was disconcerted at where the Wizard's conclusion was headed.

"The other wizards wanted to gather information from their archives, try to find meaning behind Wyvern's habits, and this Maiden he desires so badly. They'll be digging through folklore, legends, myths, and prophecies until the day I die. Those few wizards who have dragon-children left in their realms will likely seek them out, hoping for a word," the Wizards voice grew low.

The Prince pursed his lips in thought. "Have you conferred with Drake? Surely, the Avallonian dragon-child would grant you an audience?"

"I've been unable to reach him," the Wizard said sadly, "he and his sister are most likely looking into their brother's actions, themselves."

They rode at a steady pace but were hindered from traveling as fast as they would have liked by the trees. Packs of animals were always watching, just out of sight. Some darted in the shadows of the large trees.

Fleeting, flying, snarling, and calling; the creatures of the Hynefol lacked only a desire to feed. Even their protective instincts were quelled by the dryads of the wood. The three companions had grown so accustomed to their presence that they soon ignored the fact they were even there. Then the Wizard abruptly stopped his horse. The Prince and Warrior, seeing him halt in near mid-stride, did the same. Their horses whinnied in protest.

"What is it?" the Prince asked with concern.

He rode closer to the Wizard as the blue-shrouded old man looked about as if searching for something.

The sound of the Warrior drawing his blade echoed among the trees.

"Does something approach?" he asked, the leather of his blade's grip squeaking in his tight grasp.

The Wizard continued to look about. "No—nothing approaches... nothing."

The Prince then realized what it was the Wizard spoke of; quite literally nothing was nearby. The wolves, crows, bucks, badgers, and eagles had stopped following them. Not even the chittering of insects could be heard.

What, then, had the Warrior just seen dart beyond the treeline?

He turned to see naught but sunlight dappled through the heavy autumn-colored canopy. Leaves fell gently to the grassy floor. The canopy was thick, as were the trunks of the many trees. However, they were well-enough dispersed to see for some distance and it would seem their branches held firmly to a height roughly two stories high. It was a hauntingly beautiful location in which they had found themselves so suddenly afraid.

The Warrior wanted to blame the fear on simple traveler's fatigue, but he couldn't shake the cold grasp the silence and stillness had on him. The Wizard had not yet stopped peering around at the enchanting copses. He could feel the magic permeating the air. It crawled along the base of his spine. It whispered into his ears. He then realized he could, indeed, hear something. Giggling came from among the boughs. Passing breaths teased his ears. Fingers traced the veins of his hands.

The Prince still had yet to discover what had his companions so distraught. The Warrior was staring into the woods and the Wizard was twitching about awkwardly. He had neither seen nor heard anything unusual—at least no more unusual than what they had encountered so far. Then he saw a tree move slightly.

It was the scarcest of movement. At first, he didn't believe it had happened, that the light through the canopy was playing tricks on his eyes. Then he saw eyes among the trees… dozens of them. His heart stopped momentarily then fluttered back to life as one of the trees 'smiled' at him.

He drew Calibern and upon doing so the light in the Hynefol cast upon the blade and set it ablaze in light, revealing the magic within. There was a slight hush of wind that the three of them quickly realized was a collective gasp.

"Put away the sword, Prince," a voice said. It sounded like honeyed wine.

He looked to the direction from which it came and found nothing.

"No harm will come to you here—none that is not deserved," another voice added, fluttering like the wings of a hummingbird.

He sheathed his weapon, feeling almost compelled to do so. The Warrior was not so easily swayed.

"It will take more than kind words to disarm me, phantom," he challenged.

A gentle hand pressed upon his fist that was tightly gripped about his weapon until his knuckles turned white.

"Then, perhaps, a council?" said a third voice.

The Warrior, under any other circumstances, would have swung about and cut down the owner of said hand. The warmth of the tender touch instead left him overwhelmed with an eerie calmness. He looked down to see a lithe, flawless hand. It was the color of oaken trees and his eyes followed it up to an arm equally as lovely.

The woman—if he could call her such—that spoke to him, was beautiful in a way that only poets could hope to define. Her body was clothed in silk and vines that clung effortlessly to her curves as though they were a part of her. Her face was like carved marble, perfected by artisans, and framed by hair like a sunlit waterfall. Her eyes—by the spires, her eyes—must have been carved of the purest quartz and set with flawless diamonds.

He put his weapon away, her hand guiding his the whole way. Her sisters, as the Prince and Wizard had heard them called at some point in this dreamscape, were inspecting them like they were some sort of creatures from legend. The three companions were each being scrutinized by a different dryad, each as unique as the leaves among the trees or the ripples upon a stream.

"We're in no immediate danger, lads," the Wizard finally spoke, attempting to shake the spell cast over him. Their haunting allure made them dangerous, but the Wizard could help dispel its effects. They would indeed do them no harm so long as they made their way through the Hynefol without harming the forest. "They won't harm us so long as we make our way and leave well enough alone."

One of them looked at the Wizard, giving him a wry smile. "Maybe."

"Guards of the Hynefol," the Warrior said, looking at each of them.

"Guard?" another said, chuckling. "Our Hynefol needs no

protection from you; it's more you who need protecting from the Hynefol."

The dryads bade them come down from their stallions. The three complied with only slight hesitation. They were led to a grove and their horses were tended by more of the magnificent creatures. The Wizard knew of these beings, and was cautious, but he understood them to be quite friendly if not provoked.

The Prince's mind constantly veered to suspicion; however, when he thought to voice it he was constantly admonished by outward forces to calm his fears.

Once they entered the clutch of smaller trees they were given handfuls of fruit and carafes of water from massive lily blossoms. His eyes had become accustomed to their beauty, and the Warrior saw that the bark, leaves, silk, and other things adorning them were not clothing per se, but were, in fact, a part of their very bodies.

"What are you?" he asked bluntly.

He stared at the flawless skin of another of the dryad's bare shoulders. Flakes of bark formed along her chest and threadlike vines of ivy decorated her figure. Her skin was pale as snow and her lips like rose petals.

She smiled at him and the gesture warmed his soul. "We're the keepers of the wild and free things. We tend to the wild beasts and the ancient soil."

"Dryads," the Wizard added without thought.

The dryad accompanying the Prince laughed. "Yes, we've heard that name. A curious one—but not entirely unlovely."

The Prince took a drink of water from the lily. It was sweet and clean and unlike anything he had drunk before, like nectar and honey

"Do you have names?"

One with hair like sea foam looked at him curiously. "Is 'dryad' not sufficient? Do you have multiple names?"

The Prince found himself stuttering, to his humiliation. "No, I mean, do you have individual names? To identify each of you among yourselves?"

"A funny idea, like naming the trees. They are unique but don't desire names; why should we?" one of them inquired.

"The trees do, in fact, have names," the Wizard said, standing and approaching one. "This is what my people call an oak."

"That," he said, pointing to another, "is called an ash."

The dryads seemed both amused and intrigued by this. "Oak —it sounds like you let frogs name things where you're from," chuckled one.

"And ash—like what remains after a fire? That seems quite gruesome," another said, grimacing.

The Wizard chuckled. "Well, I didn't name them. And not all trees have different names. Just the ones that look similar."

"Then why aren't you all named 'human'?" the third one asked.

"That would solve many problems," the Prince pondered.

The Wizard saw that they were gaining favor with the dryads. This could greatly help them in navigating the Hynefol.

The one covered in bark and ivy stood and approached a nearby tree that was just a sapling.

"I like these names. It breeds a… familiarity. What other names do your people have for trees?"

The Wizard shrugged. "Well, there are many. Fir, spruce, pine, beech, willow…"

"Yes, I like that one," bark-and-ivory said, interrupting him. "You may call me Willow."

"Agreed," said the snow-skinned dryad. "I would love a name, too."

She lifted her hands to the Prince, as though she were holding something infinitely delicate within her palms. She opened them before him, and he saw a flower sprout from between her fingers and tiny vines curl about her fingers.

"What do you call this?" she asked.

The Prince hesitated a moment, caught off-guard by the magic before him.

"I believe that's a lily," he said haltingly.

"Lily. I like it," she nodded her head in resolution.

The third, seated next to the Warrior, looked at him and smiled. "You've remained very quiet, human. What sort of names do your people have for the beasts and trees and blossoms?"

"My people don't have trees or blossoms," he said curtly.

"Oh," she said, cocking her head. "How awful."

The Warrior looked at her. Her short hair was the color of autumn leaves, her skin the hue of a deep sunset. Her sad eyes regarded him with pity. Was it even possible for dryads to exist in the harsh sands of his home?

"Well," he said, "we do have birds."

The Prince stifled a smile. The sunset dryad's eyes lit up.

"They live near the Morning Sea, snatching fish among the stones."

"What are they called?" she asked eagerly.

"Killdeer."

Her eyebrows raised and her eyes widened. The Wizard chuckled at the sheer awkwardness of the situation. The Prince cleared his throat.

"Surely... those... aren't the only birds you have in Edda?"

The Warrior thought for a moment, clearly uncomfortable. Then, his face softened. He watched the stream running through the clearing as he spoke.

"Once, when I was a boy, my mother took me to the market with her. I heard a sound and I kept asking her, 'mother, what is that?' and she took me to see. It was a stall, filled with cages, and a man was selling birds. So many different kinds; my mother didn't even know what they all were. I pointed to one, the one with the song I liked so much. She did know that one. It was a desert oriole. It could only be found on an island off the southern coasts. Its feathers were unlike anything I'd ever seen. Orange and yellow and blue... like an autumn sunrise."

"Wait... a what?" asked the dryad. "What did the bird look like?"

"Um... an autumn sunrise?"

"Yes!" she said, clapping her hands. "Autumn. I love it. I choose Autumn."

"Well," the Wizard said, opening his arms as if presenting a newly wedded couple, "we have named the dryads," he smiled, clapping his hands together, "no small feat."

"We're but a few," Willow spoke up from her seat in a tree, though none remembered seeing her climb it. "Many are listening, many are watching. We'll spread the word of these names to the others. Perhaps they will choose names of their own."

Autumn stood next to the Warrior and bid him stand as well. "You've given us a unique gift—and for that, we would offer you a boon."

"What would you ask of us?" Lily said, smiling. "What would you ask of Autumn, Lily, and Willow?"

The Prince and Wizard shared a knowing glance. He approached and stood next to the Warrior.

"Are you familiar with Wyvern?"

23

THE LICH AND THE CAVE

A dark shadow fell over their beautiful faces. Willow's eyes flickered dangerously. The lacy, ivy vines of Lily appeared to twitch and recoil slightly. Even the lovely Autumn spit into the dirt.

"That name is forbidden among these boughs," Willow said harshly. Her words carried the same eerie resonance as when the three men first heard the voice of the dryads.

"What power does he hold over you?" the Wizard asked sincerely. "You outnumber him, you wield the power of the Hynefol."

Autumn, with furrowed brow, looked at the Wizard and her face softened ever so slightly. "He's a child of Father Dragon. He's the youngest of his kin, but where we draw power from the Hynefol and are content with our home; he feeds off something else; something old and evil. He gathers relics, treasures, and artifacts of the rarest kind. Once, he unleashed the power of one his artifacts upon our Hynefol and nearly destroyed our home..."

Tears slipped from Autumn's eyes and Lily finished her words. "A plague of rot and death fell upon our lands. The rivers, those that didn't dry to their very beds, ran with disease and filth."

"The trees withered and fruit fell to the ground, rotted to the core," Willow interjected.

It soon came to sound as though they spoke as one. As they spoke, the trees wilted about them. The words they spoke were given life, as the forest around them twisted to match their memories.

"The animals turned on one another, cannibalizing their own kind; their hearts full of wanton killing and viciousness, their bellies gorged on venom and blood. They ignored our commands, ignored the will of the Hynefol."

The once exquisite trill of Lily stood out for a moment, "A shadow fell upon all, day turned to darkness and night was an impenetrable blackness."

It grew so dark, the Prince would barely see the Warrior next to him. Lily's voice was replaced by Autumn's.

"The air smelled of death and water became as poison. Then he came."

The companions' blood ran cold, as they saw a figure walk among the trees. It must have been at least seven feet tall. Draped in robes that were either black or so rotten their original color could no longer be discerned, it held a staff in its skeletal hands. The eyes burned with a green light and pinpricks of yellow: the fires of undeath. Once a human wizard consumed with the desire for eternal life and incredible power, now bound by horrible rites that granted the wizard their wishes. Their only weakness being that what remained of their soul would be sealed in an urn carved from onyx—known as a phylactery. The wizard—the human—was no more. They were now and forevermore a lich; one of the darkest and vilest creatures in creation.

"It took all of us to take back our land from the lich," Willow said. Her eyes had gone white, along with her sisters, and the color had drained from them. They looked like trees burned nearly to ash.

"It was he who made a throne from the rot and bones and set himself as liege of the fallen Hynefol. It was a battle unknown to the world; we keepers of the loam were left broken and scarred in a tainted home after all was done. The lich was defeated when the greatest of us cast his phylactery upon the very walls of Wyvern's wretched temple."

An image of a dryad appeared, holding what looked like an urn. The Wizard knew this to be the lich's phylactery

Their voices began to separate and they stopped speaking in unison. Slivers of sunlight once again touched upon the forest floor. Willow looked at the Wizard, her eyes filled with mourning.

"The forest has yet to fully recover."

The Warrior, the Prince, the Wizard—all were enthralled in the dryad's tale of their fight against the lich—among the rarest and oldest of the world's evils.

It was a creature few cared to speak of; powerful wizards shunned by the kingdoms, and some say the spires themselves, that, in their wrath and jealousy, undertook dark rituals to render themselves immortal yet bereft of life. Their power grew, their years lingered, but their body withered away until naught was left but bone and ancient sinew.

"So, that's why he yet remains in his lair," the Wizard thought aloud.

"We showed him that we were not to be defeated without great cost. We also learned that same lesson about Wyvern," Autumn said. "You must understand this, if you seek him out."

The Prince realized his forehead was covered in a cold sweat. He wiped his forehead with his hands. The Wizard felt a flutter in his chest and felt the hairs of his arms and neck standing on end. The Warrior realized he had been gripping the hilt of sword almost painfully during the recounting of their story.

Lily, seeing their discomfort, added: "It was a long time ago, at least, I think it was. The Great Rot and its lich liege were powerful, and their essence yet lingers, if only slightly. It's expected to feel such horror at its unnatural decay. It's left even us scarred, both inside and out."

"This is among the most beautiful places I've ever seen, even in my dreams. How can such a taint still linger? Where are the scars?" the Prince asked in disbelief.

The three dryads smiled at his compliments, looking wistfully at their home around them. Willow offered him an explanation.

"Its presence will never be forgotten. The trees groan and the rivers weep at the memories. If you think it beautiful now, it was once breathtaking."

"And us?" Lily continued, "Well, we can only approach you now because of the scars it left on us. Once, just the sight of us would have you clawing your eyes out. Drowning yourself in the rivers," she said with a dark smile.

"Now?" Autumn said, gesturing to herself, a vision of beauty the likes the Prince doubted they'd ever see again, "We're more disfigured than the forest. The lich took much from us."

The lich. The damned lich. If Wyvern controlled such a thing what else could he have stowed away in those ruins of his? The Wizard would have much more to consider before they reached their destination. Could he have underestimated the dragonchild so much?

"Why do you seek Wyvern?" Willow asked of them, interested in their reason for seeking out such a vile thing.

The Prince was quick to answer her. "It killed a man, a knight of the Emerald Spire, who was seeking vengeance for a family murdered by the creature. Wyvern set a witch among my court to take my throne and harm those I have come to call friends. And he holds a woman prisoner, for reasons yet to be explained. At least, we hope he holds her prisoner. Otherwise she's certainly dead."

The dryads were visibly distressed at his description of Wyvern's actions.

"We will find him. We will kill him. And we'll rid the world of his evil. This I promise," the Prince assured them, "but we do need your help."

"I'm sure you do," Willow said, her green eyes flicking back and forth between them. "A large task for an army of three."

"So I've been told," the Prince returned, looking to the Warrior.

"We need to find his lair. We understand it's among some ruins near here. Do you know of them?"

Lily glanced at Willow. "We do."

"We can show you the way, but only as far as the edge of the Hynefol," Willow clarified. "I'm afraid it's all we can do."

"Unfortunate. I'd hate to see the big one die," Autumn said coyly, smirking at the Warrior. He sniffed in discomfort, shifting in his armor. The Prince smiled and put his hand on the Warrior's shoulder.

"Show us the way. We ask no more," the Prince said.

Autumn gave them a large smile and her brown eyes lingered on the Warrior, making him uncomfortable.

The three climbed atop their stallions and were about to offer the dryads to ride with them. However, a rustling from the brush and grasses preceded the arrival of a lumbering bear, giant elk, and a massive wolf.

The Warrior instinctively went for his blade, but a tight grip from a soft hand stayed his actions. Lily went to the wolf, pet its muzzle, and kissed its forehead. She climbed atop its muscular shoulders and they saw that the beasts would carry the dryads to their destinations.

"Spires-all..." the Wizard breathed an oath.

Willow climbed atop the bear while Autumn rode the elk. They bade the three follow them closely as the Hynefol contained no roads.

Both tamed stallion and wild beast rode among the boughs of the ancient forest for the remainder of the day. It was an endless forest with only the scarce hill or moss-covered rocky outcropping piercing the tree-covered landscape. As they rode deeper into the forest, the trees themselves grew as thick as a fortress.

As if out of nowhere they suddenly found themselves facing a steep wall of stone. It took close observation to discern that the wall was not artificial. It was smooth to the touch and covered almost completely by vines, moss, and leafy growths. They looked up to see the wall stretching above the trees.

"That will pose a modest hindrance," the Prince quipped.

The Warrior looked to the Wizard. "I don't suppose you can fly?"

The Wizard returned a reproachful glare.

"There will be no need for flying," Autumn said plainly. "The stone runs from shore to shore here in the Hynefol, but there's a reason we brought you here."

She came down from her seat upon the back of the great elk. After she approached the wall she stopped at a cluster of blood-red flowers. There was no other patch of these particular flowers anywhere in the vicinity. They were quite unique. She splayed the fingers of her right hand open wide and placed her palm next to the flowers, pinky finger touching them. She then splayed the fingers of her left hand and placed it next to the other, thumbs touching. She looked like she was about to push on the wall. Then, she moved her right next to the left, pinky touching pinky.

She repeated the steps, crossing her hands and putting them next to each other like she trying to find her way across the wall, thumb touching thumb and pinky touching pinky. The Wizard counted. She did this ten times, over and over again. He realized she was measuring by hand lengths.

Finally, she grabbed a handful of thick, curling vines and pulled them aside, revealing a small tunnel. It would never have been found unless they decided to poke and prod every inch of the wall.

"Wyvern's ways are many and secret," the Prince said with a smile.

"Come again?" the Warrior asked.

"An old nursery rhyme, friend," the Prince replied:

WYVERN'S WAYS *are many and secret*
  Each treasure he covets and kills to keep it

THE WIZARD FINISHED THE LULLABY:

HOT BURNS *his fire and swift comes his wrath*
  Hurry home sweet child, leave not the path

"A HIDEOUS RHYME," Willow said with a scowl.

"Almost as hideous as he whom it was written about," Lily added. "We wish you success. Go forth with our goodwill. Your horses must stay, but they will be well cared for. Leave them, if need be. They will love the Hynefol."

The Warrior was hesitant, but Autumn offered him comfort. "They can't travel the tunnels. Don't worry, we won't let them come to harm."

"This leads to Wyvern's ruins?" the Wizard asked uncertainly.

"It leads to the road that will take you to it. An old temple, I believe," Willow replied. "The ratlings he is so fond of often use this passage to get to him. The dragon-child thinks he can hide such things in our Hynefol. His hubris is astonishing."

"Or perhaps," said the Prince, "he's not concerned that you know of it."

Willow sighed deeply. "And that is a far more terrifying possibility."

They parted ways there, among the trees and stones. The Wizard thanked the dryads again for their hospitality and expressed their hope to see them again upon their return; if they indeed returned.

"As do we, young magi," Willow said, offering her last farewell.

"You will always be welcome in the Hynefol," Autumn said wryly. The Warrior nodded stiffly and led the way into the mountain.

As the three entered the tunnel they looked back to see the Hynefol for what they hoped would not be the last time.

There were a noticeable number of dryads present that they hadn't seen before. They were as plentiful as the trees themselves. Parting from the magic of the Hynefol and its dryads left them with sharp pangs of sorrow. They were compelled to stay. The Wizard knew this was magical in origin. He placed firm but gentle hands on the shoulders of the Prince and Warrior to guide them away from the arcane temptation and toward the tunnel.

The Warrior looked back over his shoulder, a frown creasing his face. The warmth of the forest beckoned, while only darkness lay ahead. The Prince squeezed past him. A flicker of light whipped across his vision and lingered on the Prince's sword, Calibern. It spread over the blade until it glowed as bright as a torch.

"You're full of surprises, good sir," the Prince said, indicating for the Warrior to follow.

"What do you mean?"

"Ah, my warrior-poet. Come, this walk may be long. Let us speak of autumn sunrises."

The Wizard chortled, leading the other two into laughter. Another small light in the darkness.

* * *

THE TUNNELS WERE rank with moss and mildew. Tiny mushrooms and lichens shimmered and glowed in the darkness, providing a mystifying but inadequate light.

Though the three men were able to stand upright, the cold, winding passages were painfully narrow. The Warrior had the greatest difficulty navigating them. His large frame constantly caught on the sharp rocks that jutted from the walls. His height resulted in more than a few bruises about his head. His broad shoulders could scarcely fit through certain areas and he was forced to edge sidelong through the narrowest portions.

To add to their misery, the tunnel wasn't what one would call dry. Moisture lined much of the surface, and water from some unknown source trickled through the crevices and cracks. They stepped in numerous puddles, some of which bore a dubious odor. They were consistently reminded of the ratlings that frequented here and shuddered at the thought of things they couldn't see in the claustrophobic black.

They had to make their way slowly and could discern neither time nor distance in their current condition. They began to fear they were lost within some sort of underground warren when the Wizard spoke from behind them.

"Air—I smell fresh air!" he exclaimed. "By the spires, it is the loveliest thing I could imagine!"

Within a few moments they saw light before them—small, still some distance away. They marched toward what they hoped was an opening and found their hopes fulfilled. The exit from the tunnel faced into a tight valley. They were atop a small cliff face; the valley opening up before them. It was filled with trees unlike those that spread amongst the Hynefol. These were much more familiar. The Warrior still saw it as enough greenery to last many lifetimes. Another valley of paradise.

There, among the foliage, they could see the weathered stones and toppled pillars of a lost ruin—Wyvern's lair.

24

BEAUTIFUL SLUMBER

As they surveyed the small valley, they saw that it was nearly a box canyon with the steep cliffs surrounding it on all but a small southern shoreline. The view of the beach from the cave was little more than a keyhole in the wall of stone.

A strong wind blew at the mouth of the tunnel. Immediately next to them was a trail that meandered gently down to the valley below. They began their descent but immediately placed their hands on their respective weapons. They were now fully in Wyvern's territory. He was most likely watching them at this very moment.

The Wizard squinted on their way down the trail. They had traveled the better part of a day in the Hynefol. Though they couldn't track time in the tunnel, they had surely spent several hours making their way through it. Yet, the sun was still high in the sky.

Such innate magic in the Hynefol. Everything was different, even the air, he thought to himself. Perhaps even time had different rules in the heart of Emrallt's greatest forest?

It took a short while to reach the floor of the valley. The path must have been one used by the ratlings to travel to the temple. It was more a deer trail of worn grass than an actual road. Here the plants were of a much more familiar variety. The Hynefol was a lush paradise, whereas this forest, like all others, held briars and poison oak, snakes and spiders.

"Let's hope we do not encounter any wolf packs *here...*" the Warrior emphasized, realizing they were outside the dryad's influence.

They continued on the path until the temple came into view. It was still quite magnificent to look at. It was once a many-terraced building of majesty. Now it was reduced to two stories of scarcely walled-in space and the rest residing in pieces. Vines wrapped around toppled pillars as non-functioning fountains lay full of lily pads and algae.

One thing stood out amongst all else—the quiet. They heard crickets and the occasional frog, but nothing else. Was it the stillness before the ambush or was Wyvern not here?

They drew their weapons and the Wizard remained alert, readying his magical arsenal. They crept upon the grounds while attempting to remain hidden among the many stones and large pieces of rubble. Still, no roars of draconic anger permeated the air.

They searched about the first floor and found nothing in any of the rooms. The majority of the temple was an open-air court with many of the ceilings and terraces having collapsed. Near one such terrace, they found a stairway that would still provide a manner of cover. They took the stairs one quiet step at a time, until they reached the next story. It was smaller than the first, with most rooms exposed by collapsed walls.

The Wizard noticed a flickering light along a particular wall. He hissed at his companions and caught their attention. He pointed to the room and the Warrior nodded in understanding. He gestured for the Prince to stay back momentarily as he approached the open archway. The Wizard's hands began to crackle as lightning danced among his fingers.

As they approached the doorway, multiple shadows were cast upon the wall. The Warrior raised his sword, prepared to strike, and the Prince did the same. The Wizard raised his staff and his thunder-infused hand. The archway was large enough for Wyvern to fit through, so it would easily fit the three of them as they charged inside.

What they found was a room devoid of Wyvern, but filled with other things of wonder. The fire that the Wizard had seen was actually a cage of Pyremoth fairies hanging in the fireplace. The room itself was fairly large and the Wizard could not begin to account for the things that he saw organized there.

"Some of these relics—I never thought such a collection existed..." he breathed in wonder.

He noted the Pyremoth fairies, the sphinx bones, and the beautiful mirror on the wall filled with swirling mist. He approached it and looked inside, seeing not his own reflection but instead saw through the mirror as though it were merely cloudy glass. He would have looked much longer had a voice not interrupted him.

"He's been collecting his trinkets for countless years," the small voice said.

The Wizard recognized the tiny voice of one of the fairies. He looked into the cage, but not too closely—the creatures burned hotter than smoldering coals. Through the haze of light and heat, he could see the fiery outline of a winged young woman. There were at least three others with her, perhaps more.

"How long have you been here?" he asked.

He couldn't make out any expression on her face, but he did see her head drop as she spoke. "As long as any of us can remember. He feeds us well. He uses us for light and warmth."

He reached out a hand to unlock the cage when the tiny thing flitted about erratically and held a hand up to him.

"No!" she yelped. "It's deadman's iron, it would kill you."

The Wizard cursed Wyvern. Of course, it wouldn't be simple. Deadman's iron was the result of minotaur's blood heated by dragonfire to a point it solidified, the magic of the minotaur's blood and a dragon's breath acting as a catalyst. Once cooled it became poisonous to the touch and was all but completely resistant to fire. And incredibly rare.

"Where does he keep the key?" the Wizard asked.

"Do you see any door on our prison?" she replied miserably.

The Wizard was convinced that he could free them. Pyremoth fairies are quite friendly and had aided him in the past. He wouldn't leave them to their fates here with Wyvern.

"By the spires…" the Prince said, catching their attention.

The Warrior rushed over to the Prince and the Wizard looked to him.

"What have you found?" the Wizard asked.

"Her. I found the Maiden," the Prince said in hushed surprise.

A portcullis had been erected that blocked the way into the adjoining room. Alone, with nothing more than a chair and bucket of water, was the Maiden. She had been carefully placed onto a finely crafted table, something else that must have some sort of value to Wyvern. Her head rested on a pillow and her arms had been laid at her sides. Her garments were still covered in blood and soot. Her hair was tousled with twigs and ash from her home.

"Is she dead?" the Warrior asked in dismay.

"No, she can't be!" the Prince shouted.

THE WIZARD CAME OVER to investigate the Maiden's condition. Why was she laid upon a bed and not eaten or left in the woods for the animals if she wasn't alive? How had her body not decayed? The only way they would have answers would be to open the portcullis.

"Little one," the Wizard asked as he walked back to the fairies, "did Wyvern forge the portcullis himself?"

The creature shrugged. "He brought it back with him and set it into the stone with his fire."

Then it's not poisoned, the Wizard surmised. Wyvern would not risk the fumes of freshly forged deadman's iron with the Maiden.

The Wizard had an idea to remove the thick steel bars preventing their access to the Maiden. However, it would involve freeing the fairies. The creatures, being creatures of magic like Wyvern, were resistant to the effects of the deadman's iron; however, they would fall into a deep unconsciousness and, being far too hot to even touch, melt through the stones of the temple and the very ground itself, falling through the earth.

The only thing the Pyremoth fairies had to rest upon in the cage was a small bed made of the only thing their burning forms could not ignite—the bark of a redwood tree, which Wyvern likely took from their home. This provided little in the way of breaking the cage. The redwood was still just that—wood against the might of iron. The Wizard had a troubling conundrum.

He then recalled a peculiar spell from an old tome the Red Wizardess had once shown him in a former council. It might work, though it was difficult magic to conjure. He would also need an item difficult to find in their immediate vicinity.

"I need sand," the Wizard bluntly announced.

"Sand?" the Prince replied.

"Yes; not much, but I can't imagine where any would be here and we don't have time to go the shoreline…"

The Wizard stopped suddenly. He was staring at something. The Prince and Warrior followed his gaze.

"Remove your boots," he said to the Warrior.

The large man raised a brow at him. "Excuse me?"

"Your boots! Remove them, please, quickly!" the Wizard urged.

The Warrior removed one of his leather boots. Worn with age and faded from the sun, they were still thick and comfortable and served their purpose. As he set it on the ground the Wizard quickly snatched it up and turned it upside down, shaking it furiously.

The Warrior and the Prince watched as small amounts of sand fell from the folds and creases. It had remained there amid their journey.

"This will do," the Wizard stated, halting the Warrior from removing his other boot. "Keep it on, please."

The Warrior stepped back, equally confused and curious.

The Wizard scooped the sand up in his hand. He pooled it into one palm and with his fingers, he picked up a small amount. Trickling it into his hand, he whispered a string of near inaudible words. The Prince caught a small number of them but didn't understand them in the slightest. They sounded thick and muddled, one word running into the other.

The Wizard finished the phrases and as the last of the grains fell from his fingertips, the Wizard carefully approached the fairies cage.

"Move away, little ones," he cautioned. "You do not want this to touch you."

The small, ever-burning figures hovered back in the iron cage. The Wizard blew sharply into his hand. The sand fell on the tightly woven bars and even trickled onto the redwood bed. The bed immediately began to dry, crack, and then rot and fall away as though it aged decades in mere seconds.

The deadman's iron wasn't affected immediately. For a moment the Wizard thought he may not have made the spell strong enough. Then a small amount of dust fell from the cage. Then, small flakes, followed by large flakes. Gradually, whole chunks of metal begin to fall from the bars. The Wizard stepped away quickly, not daring to touch the pieces. Within moments a large hole was left in the cage where the sand had been.

"Wonderful little spell," the Wizard commented.

"Impressive," the Warrior said, nodding his head in approval.

The Pyremoth fairies fluttered out of their cage, free for the first time in decades—perhaps centuries. The one that had previously spoken to the Wizard hovered up to him as close as she could without causing him harm.

She thanked him profusely and was overwhelmed with joy at her freedom. The Wizard smiled, happy to release the magical creatures from their vile captivity as pets or trinkets or whatever horrid reason Wyvern held them in their cage.

He asked the small being for a favor, to which she readily agreed. Gathering her friends, the fairies flittered about the top and bottom of the portcullis. They grappled the bars, wrapping their arms and legs about them as much as they could, and their tremendous heat began melting away the iron. The bars heated to a dull red, radiating out from the fairies. An orange glow was followed by a bright yellow, and the liquefied metal poured on the floor and began cooling and solidifying immediately.

The Prince and the Warrior grabbed the bars as they began to tilt and pulled them free. Within moments, a multitude of bars lay on the floor still burning red-hot on each end.

"Thank you, friends," the Wizard said. He had an affinity for magical creatures—especially those as carefree and innocent as the fairies.

The three of them stepped over the cooling remains of the gate and entered the room where the Maiden lay unmoving. The room was without decoration or adornment of any kind. She was left lying on the table on thick blanket. The Prince recognized an old coat-of-arms fading on the fabric, but couldn't place where it was from. Wyvern had left her sleeping somewhat comfortably, at least.

The Prince felt a pang of sorrow, almost a physical wound in his stomach. The Warrior, close behind him, looked her over for any sign of life. Her chest didn't rise and fall with breath. Her eyes didn't flutter and her hands didn't twitch. The Wizard saw nothing, as well. Not even the slightest flicker of life emanated from her. None of them knew her, save for the Prince, but the Wizard and Warrior still, for a reason unbeknownst to them, felt a deep sorrow at seeing her there.

No wind stirred in that cloistered chamber. It was dank, lit by rusted sconces, and smelled musty and thick. It was as if death had already moved in upon her, but couldn't take her; so, it pouted and groused as it hung about her, waiting for its chance to claim its victim. Oddly, her face hadn't grown pale but maintained its youthful glow. Her lips weren't drained of color, but still full and rosy. What they saw next only perplexed them further.

The Prince saw a bit of blood on the side of the table. On further inspection he saw that her hand was wrapped in linens and a dark stain showed through. He lifted her limp forearm and removed the bandaging. Letting the soiled cloth slip away, his breath caught at the sight of her wound.

He saw a small scar the size of his thumb in the palm of her hand. It appeared to be healing well, but at some point must have run through her hand as she had a similar scar on the opposite side.

The Prince shook his head in disbelief.

"Do you think it's possible...?" he began, not wanting to finish his question.

The Wizard's eyes were dark and tired as he gazed upon the wound. "She was stung by Wyvern. She is... most certainly dead," he said, forlornly.

The Prince placed her hand back at her side. None of this was making sense.

"She's not dead," a little voice spoke.

One of the Pyremoth fairies flittered out from behind the Wizard. She'd stayed behind, remaining out of earshot.

"What do you mean, little one?" the Wizard asked, surprised

to see she remained. "She neither moves nor breathes. Her hand was pierced by Wyvern's barb."

"She's still warm with life," the fairy said. "I can see it. I can feel it. She is very much alive."

"I don't understand," the Warrior questioned. "How do you know this?"

"I know," the fairy said. "Simple as that. I can see the warmth of life in her body. It's cooler than yours, but it burns still."

The Prince looked at her. The Maiden was alive and it was a truth as beautiful as she. He didn't fully comprehend how, but he dared not question it. He took her uninjured hand in his. He felt it now—the warmth of life in her touch. Her skin wasn't pale; her hands weren't cold. He held her hand and knelt over her. He gently touched his forehead to hers.

"What misfortune has fallen upon you, that you attract the schemes of Wyvern? Where are you now, as you yet cling to life?"

25

A DREAM OF DYING

A t first, all was lost in mist and time. She knew not the day, nor the hour, nor the season. For a short time, she'd forgotten her very name. Her senses eluded her; she couldn't smell anything, taste anything, feel anything. There was no sound; only vapor and darkness.

The Maiden felt no sense of danger, either. She'd lost any sense of purpose, or peace, or turmoil. She simply was, and wondered, *Is this what lay beyond?* She always felt herself to be a good person; or at least, she tried very hard. Is this what good people are granted: an emotionless trance? Are the wicked, then, tormented by torrents of undesirable emotion forever? Are we all, regardless, doomed to wander this nothing?

She couldn't tell how much time had passed as she walked on solid darkness when, through the mists, she could see a murky silhouette. She couldn't tell if it was a person or an object, but she was delighted to see it nonetheless.

She approached slowly.

"Hello?" she called out.

There was no answer. As she drew near she—at last—heard a noise and recognized her own footsteps. She looked down and was able to make out the cracked cobblestones of a well-traveled street beneath a thin veil of the swirling mists.

When she looked back to the silhouette it was now lit by the sun, which was beginning to break through the foggy nothingness. It was a pillar with painted stones lining either side. One side bore stones of an orange-yellow and the other side, stones of blue. Both also had a sigil of some kind painted on them. Marked upon the blue stones was a white blade enclosed in ivy branches. The orange-colored stones bore a strikingly simple symbol: a white triangle, nothing more.

She was on the border of Avallonis—she recognized the well-known symbol of the Prince's kingdom. The other was strange to her. This was, perhaps, a border-marker with the symbol of yet another kingdom, but she had never heard of this one.

Having focused her attention on the small pillar, she failed to notice that the mist had all but vanished. She was now in full daylight and looked about her to see that she was amid a mass of steep, rolling hills. The road she stood upon ran north to south, judging by the position of the sun—and it was also roughly midmorning.

She felt something tickle the skin of her forearm and then her neck and she startled slightly. She reached and felt something there just below her ear. Opening her hand, she saw a magnificent monarch butterfly—one such as she had never seen before. She then noticed that the sensation on her arm was another smaller one.

She then noticed there were several flittering about her. It wasn't a swarm of them—a few dozen perhaps—but it was still the largest gathering of such that she had ever seen. Even in Emrallt, where the beautiful things are found frequently, she'd never seen such a number.

They danced about in the air; some rested upon her and then took flight again. She found herself smiling—it was both fantastic and peculiar. Having enjoyed the unique experience, she began following the road south on the side of the blue-painted stones. She assumed this meant she was in the Sapphire Realm and would find someone who may perhaps be able to help her return home.

A host of memories returned. Home, she remembered, was no longer there. A flash of scales and fire, sharp, unimaginable pain in her hand, a short sensation of being lifted into the air...

She looked down and saw nothing on her palm where it throbbed in pain. As the memory faded so did the dreadful sensation. She remembered her mother and father; gnashed and torn by that great fiend. Her home and fields burned until nothing was left but black, ashen scars.

She fell to her knees, tears falling from her eyes. She wept and felt her soul torn. They were memories; something she had lived through. But, being flooded by such emotions where before there was nothing was like having the wounds torn anew. She didn't know how long she let her tears fall there on the open road.

She felt a familiar tingling sensation upon her hands. She looked down and saw the winged monarchs there again. Looking about, she saw they'd all followed her. Her surroundings were alight with fluttering wings of black and amber. In her grief, she batted them away in frustration. They quickly returned and she tried to shoo them away again, only to fail once more. She cried out and desperately attempted to wave them off. They continued to relentlessly land about her on the ground and all over her person.

She fell forward and reached out, stopping her fall with outstretched hands. One of the creatures landed on her hand, and she was about to shake it away when she noticed something truly peculiar.

Her hand and clothing around it were remarkably transparent. She could see the cobblestones through them. She quickly stood to her feet and took a moment to look carefully at herself. Her body was equally translucent. She felt her chest tighten, and her hands began to shake. She ran down the road as fast as she could in a panic.

In her fright, she stumbled upon her dress and fell onto the cobblestone road. She cried out and, turning reflexively to see behind her, she saw that the stone pillar was as close now as it had ever been. It was as though she had not been running at all.

She turned and sat back—emotionally and physically stretched. The butterflies returned, their gentle touch soothing once again. She felt tears coming on once more, when a kind voice spoke to her.

"Easy, young Maiden," it said.

She looked about and saw a robed and hooded figure standing next to the pillar. Seeing her shocked expression, the figure held up a calming hand.

"I won't hurt you, child. Quite the opposite, in fact," he said.

The figure wore heavy robes colored a deep orange with black and gray underclothes and strange symbols embroidered on them all. He wore a necklace of gold attached to a simple triangular symbol fashioned of amber or some similar substance. His cowl covered his face and prevented her from discerning his age or any other features. His voice was healthy and strong but echoed with age and power.

"I ran until... how can I still be here?" the Maiden asked in confusion.

"You're here because I sought you out. I brought you to this place. It's private and safe," he answered.

"You find yourself on the border of Avallonis, the Sapphire Realm, and Vitruvia, the Amber Realm. I'm the Auburn Wizard," he added with a slight bow. "Some refer to me as the Lord of Dreams. I fancy that name, myself."

"The Lord of Dreams?" the Maiden repeated. She looked again at her hands and body. "Then that—"

"Would explain your curious metaphysical state, yes," he interrupted.

Seeing the Maiden's uncomprehending stare, he explained, "Your transparent appearance."

"I… I don't understand. Wyvern had me. I stung myself on his barb. I can't be alive," she rambled in confusion.

"I'm a master of my craft; aware of my power and its limits. I'm quite adept at conversing with those who slumber, but the dead are far beyond my reach. Therefore, you are most certainly alive," he said plainly.

The Maiden rested her head in her hands. "So I'm not dead? But not alive?"

The hooded figure shrugged. "Something like that. You *should* be dead, let's make that clear. But you're not. Your body still remains alive… somewhere. You are trapped in that place that most closely connects life with death," he spread his arms slightly, palms up as though to present her surroundings to her, "the dominion of dreams."

The Maiden looked around. The wizard could tell she wasn't convinced.

"When you awoke you felt little, if anything, correct?" he asked.

She nodded and he continued.

"You were confused, disoriented, and remained so until I arrived?"

"Perhaps I just panicked?" she added, slightly exasperated.

The hooded head didn't move, seeming to contemplate the answer. "An overly-simplified conclusion, perhaps, but relevant."

"My family is gone; Wyvern destroyed my home. I'm left with nothing…" the Maiden said, despondently.

The cowl of the Lord of Dreams lowered slightly. He pitied her and felt her sorrow. A certain level of uncanny empathy accompanied his wanderings and meddling in the slumbering thoughts of others. He felt a great mourning with her. But, he also noted the presence of the butterflies. This, he found most curious.

"You're accompanied by a great many winged monarchs," he observed.

The Maiden wiped the tears from her face. "Yes," she sighed, "I have no idea why."

The wizard reached out gently and allowed one to land upon his bare hand.

The butterflies were harriers of spirits and the ethereal. The Auburn Wizard suspected she was unconscious somewhere, but the sleep wasn't natural. It wasn't even magical. It was something more that kept her here. It was this that drew him to her. She radiated a powerful light in the darkness. The dominion of dreams was fickle and as stable as a leaf upon rushing waters. One rarely dreamed of places so accurately if they'd never been there. If the Maiden didn't know where she was, how was it that she could recreate this place in her memory?

"I can't answer that for you—at least for the time being," the Wizard said. The Maiden lowered her head despondently.

"But, I will wander with you for a time, if you like" he added softly.

He approached her and offered his hand. She accepted gratefully. There could have been no greater difference among them. Hers were the hands of beauty, youth, and grace. He had the strength of youth but as his fingers wrapped around her hand she felt as though she were being aided by someone many decades her elder.

"Where exactly will we go?" she asked.

The Auburn Wizard made a slight flourish with his fingers. Orange and white smoke swirled about his hand and arm forming a small column, and then dissipated leaving behind an ornate brass staff topped with a triangular cut piece of amber. He held gently to her hand. Words were spoken from the darkness within his cowl.

"Hold fast to my hand and close your eyes," he instructed.

The Maiden did as he said and she heard him whispering something. It was quite lengthy and he spoke feverishly.

"You may open them," he said, releasing her hand.

She opened her eyes and beheld many wondrous sights. Her jaw slackened and her eyes widened. Perhaps she had indeed died at Wyvern's sting, and gone to someplace truly magnificent, after all.

26

THE AMBER SPIRE

The road before her was well-kept and paved with polished stone. The houses, buildings, and towers about her were maintained impeccably. The people were dressed in clean, lavish clothing.

She turned and saw before her another of the looming, ancient spires. They were standing before the Amber Tower of Vitruvia if all the Auburn Wizard said was true.

This tower was a wholly different kind of magnificent.. It was fashioned of solid bronze reinforced by polished steel. Small, individual towers hung from the side of the spire by ornate support structures. Small bridges lined with polished parapets led to the hanging towers and gave the spire the appearance of some sort of technological and engineering marvel.

The area surrounding the tower was dotted with magnificent fountains of all shapes and sizes. Ladies of the city sat about and talked in the presence of the dancing waters. She overheard merchants and nobles discussing various business arrangements. From time to time she even heard the laughter of children darting about the gardens.

One of the playful young ones was running from a friend.

They were playing tag, apparently, and the Maiden was so enraptured by all that surrounded her that she was too late to step away from the child. They must not have noticed her, either.

The child barreled into the young woman just as she saw them. The Maiden yelped, expecting to be knocked down, but the young boy ran right through the Maiden as though she were made of air. She startled, but quickly realized that the child never knew she was there. The other child shouted, "Mommy, butterflies!" and came running. The butterflies had returned.

The mother commented on how lovely the monarchs were and cautioned her child against grabbing and hurting them. The Maiden stepped away, next to one of the fountains, and the butterflies quickly followed. The children followed them and attempted to touch or catch them. Seeing them play about her invisible form was unnerving and unsettling for the Maiden, so she continuously moved away. The butterflies followed, as did the children.

The wizard noted her discomfort and politely asked the children to leave, telling them that the monarchs were lovely creatures to be viewed from afar and allowed to fly unperturbed.

"The wizard!" one of them said aloud.

They obeyed as a child would a court official or guardsmen. They didn't seem afraid of him; however, they quickly obeyed.

"They noticed you?" the Maiden asked in confusion.

The cowl nodded. "I'm not asleep. I'm free to wander as I will among my spire-realm. I'm visible to some degree. I can also summon the consciousness of one who sleeps to a place they're familiar with. Usually for a friendly conversation. However, never before have I met one who can travel to someplace they've never been. It is very intriguing."

The Maiden looked to the wizard, the realization setting in.

"I would appreciate you stop using me for whatever experimentation it is you're conducting! You only brought me here as a test!" she accused.

The Auburn Wizard straightened, slightly offended but also pleased with her astute observation.

"You're safest here among my people for now," he clarified. "My power is strongest here, and Vitruvians are quite accustomed to the eccentric."

"What would I need protection from?" the Maiden asked. "My body was taken by Wyvern to spires-know-where. Do you have me here? My... my body, I mean."

"I do not," he replied. "Unfortunately. I can say for certain that your physical self is in good health as here you are speaking with me. But, unharmed? I'm afraid I can't be certain."

"Can you not find my body as you found—this?" she said, gesturing to her ephemeral self.

"No more than a man can find a particular star in the sky. You're but one of tens of thousands sleeping. I merely found you as your light shined brightest among them—and brightest by far. It was no small margin that set you apart. I can only assume that with such metaphysical brilliance, Wyvern is keeping you locked away safely and secretly. I can find your spirit, but your body is lost to me."

The Maiden sighed in exasperation. "What is this beast that covets me? For what purpose?"

The cowl, again, shook in a negative response. "You've never heard of Wyvern? You are from Emrallt, are you not?"

"Only fairy tales. Nursery rhymes," she explained. She tried casually kicking a rock in frustration but it merely passed through her foot. "Wyvern bad, stay away. That sort of thing," she groused.

"Well, I truly don't know what he could want and for me, the lack of knowledge is the greatest aggravation. If I could discover his intentions, I would. But, Wyvern's cunning is renowned—as is his cruelty."

The Maiden looked about at the waters before her that were still out of reach. She sat on the stones of a fountain and noticed that she felt it only as a familiarity; her spirit had no need to sit or rest. The monarchs perched upon them and, to her unending curiosity and dismay, also rested upon her. How must this look to the passersby?

"Do they not hear you; see you reacting to someone who isn't there?" she asked of the Dream Lord.

"I suppose they do, though in the realm of slumber a whisper can echo among the farthest mountains. I don't have to speak vociferously to communicate with you. As for my shuffling about, it's my understanding that the people of the Amber Realm see me as aloof and peculiar. I'm not averse to that perception."

She thought she heard a smile in his voice.

"Most of them don't notice as I wander among these streets. Most of them don't notice each other for that matter—so enraptured they are in their own affairs. This is the first lengthy conversation I've had in some months."

She gifted him with a warm smile. She was alive and the Auburn Wizard was kind enough to keep her company, but this couldn't last forever.

"Can I return to myself? My body? Could I even find it?" the Maiden asked him.

"Not until you awaken; if there's some other method, I have yet to discover it."

The Maiden looked about with a renewed vigor.

There must be some way, she thought to herself.

She can't simply wander about the world cloaked in butter-flies for days, or weeks, or—spires forbid—years.

The Auburn Wizard walked with her and showed her a number of the sights about the City of the Amber Spire, or Dawnforge, as the Auburn Wizard clarified.

Beyond the garden concourse that lay before the spire were markets, halls, and forges plenty. The Vitruvians were quite fond of metallurgy and blacksmithing. She saw wonders that she never thought possible. Had she not known otherwise, this would certainly have felt like a dream. He led her back through the concourse and its fountains large and small to the heart of the city; the Amber Spire.

There they passed through doors that seemingly opened of their own accord. A loud clunk preceded a rapid clinking noise. The doors slid open, and within were two guards who saluted the wizard as he entered. They, too, failed to notice the Maiden.

Above the two great doors was the great arch of the Amber Spire. It was forged of polished bronze with gold and silver filigree so ornate that it seemed too impossible to be real. A strange language was engraved on the arch, and the Maiden asked the wizard what it meant.

"You know child, for all our intellect and study, all the power and the mystery and books and scrolls—we scarcely know what it is we are reading! Those words are magic, certainly, but older than anything the Wizards Council has ever seen. And it's only here, on the arch of the Amber Spire, that such characters are written. It's my greatest challenge, one I hope to complete before I pass on into my own eternal dreams."

She could hear the age in his voice, as he spoke of the arcane language he couldn't decipher. He continued to walk with her. He talked of magic, which she found interesting. She'd never spoken to a true wizard before. Hedge wizards, perhaps, but never someone as knowledgeable and powerful as a spire wizard.

"We know what the end result of our words and actions create, but we know little of their actual meaning," he sighed deeply and forlornly. "What things we could accomplish if we could only understand that which has been lost to time. There's been no new magic for many, many centuries. What we know now has been passed down from master to apprentice. We simply memorize the words, their flow, their nuances."

"How, then, did you learn your spells?" she asked. "If no one knew them to begin with?"

"Heritage. Teachings. Those before us remember their intonations and outcomes, but over eons we've lost the language itself. Nothing remains of the original language of magic in our mountainous texts and codices."

He seemed frustrated at this and waved off the idea with his hand.

They proceeded inside the spire, which was curious, indeed. Only a single hall lay before them. No doors or alcoves were seen as she walked to the singular door at the end. Once they arrived, the wizard opened a door much like any other. Within, however, was a whole other world to the Maiden's eyes.

Cogs and mechanisms turned and steamed and hissed. The Auburn Wizard pulled a lever that lay off to the side and she cried out when the floor beneath her moved.

To her surprise, a portion of the floor beneath their feet picked up off the ground and began to ascend. She could see no one attending any ropes or other mechanisms to hoist the lift—was it moving on its own?

As the lift moved higher they were eventually enveloped in darkness. Quickly, however, a pillar of light was cast about her. She looked up to see they were approaching a bright patch in the darkness. This was revealed to be the first true floor of the spire. As the lift came to a stop they were greeted by additional guards. The two—or, rather, the wizard, with her in tow—were escorted from a large receiving alcove into an area with many people of various stations and age.

The large, hexagonal room was lit through large windows adorning the ceiling. There were yet more fountains and plants from around the world filling the antechamber. Several windows lined the walls of the beautiful room, as well. An odd-looking device was attached near the windows and the Maiden looked at it curiously.

She saw that it was a long, metallic tube—larger on one end and tapering down smaller and smaller. There was glass attached at each end and she decided to look through it. All she saw was blue.

"It's a telescope," the wizard explained. "Things that are far away can be viewed as though they are at arm's length."

He politely took the device from her. He swiveled it on its narrow stand and twisted a small device that seemed to hold it in place. He then bade the Maiden look through again.

She did as instructed and gazed upon the happenings in a small hamlet. The people went about their lives and all seemed normal.

When she took her eye from the telescope she looked out the window toward where the device was pointed. She could see the village now as just a patch of shapes outside the city.

"That is amazing..." she said in awe. She looked about and found other curiosities.

"How do the fountains work so high within the tower?" she asked. "And the lift—it moved of its own accord."

"Just a few of the things that we as Vitruvians have discovered," he said with a smile. "The miracle of our medicines; you would be awed at what could be achieved with the flora grown within these walls; disease cured within days, the ill allowed to live comfortably. The lift—that is powered by steam; water heated such that it produces a physical power to be harnessed."

The Maiden marveled at these things. "I've never even heard of such things—why would you not share these with the other realms? So many would benefit from the wonders you could share."

The wizard's cowl nodded. "Indeed, they could. Not even all of Vitruvia is aware of what this gilded spire hides."

The Auburn Wizard walked to one of the larger trees. It was adorned with colorful blossoms of various sizes. He touched one of the broad, green leaves and spoke softly.

"The people within this very room don't know all of its mysteries. This tree, for example. The pollen from its flowers can be pressed and mixed with warm water; its paste can draw the most wicked of poisons—even that of the Mythestan Glow Adder. If combined with the honey of a dapperquill—here," he said, pointing out a small flowering vine with trumpet-shaped white petals, "it can be consumed to slow bleeding and prevent one from dying even from dismemberment."

"That's incredible," the Maiden said.

"Yes, very. The petals of this tree's blossom can also be mistaken for one much more common in the hills and plains of many realms: kettlenip."

The Maiden nodded in understanding. "A very common tea. I harvest it in my garden."

"Then you know it has a very strong flavor and is often sweetened with sugar and cinnamon."

"It is," she agreed.

"Making it difficult to discern minor additions—like the slight touch of nectar from this particular blossom which can be added to the kettlenip and would be indistinguishable either in looks or flavor. The victim, however, will soon choke to death in a matter of seconds."

The Maiden's eyes widened in disbelief. "It's such a lovely flower… yet so dangerous."

"A valuable lesson, then," the wizard cautioned. "Beauty is often evil's favorite deception."

"I'd love to know more," she wondered, looking at plants both familiar and foreign. "What more has Vitruvia discovered?"

"Much of what we have discovered is merely one result of multiple possibilities. Most of our discoveries have been born of curiosity or even a wonderous mistake. However, as you can see, sinister practices are a part of the nature of men—so it has always been and may always be," he explained. His voice grew heavy.

"The greatest potential we can abide is hope—that minds will change and hearts will turn. Until then, young lady, the kingdoms of men are not ready for that which we have found."

"You're withholding such knowledge because you await a change in the hearts of men?" the Maiden said with bewilderment. "Are the Vitruvians not men? Did they not create these wondrous things?"

"We of the Amber Spire hold our knowledge very dear to us. We don't wish to see it used for evil; we can't say the same for those of Mythesta or Edda or Avallonis," he replied frankly.

"But you allow suffering to occur just by hiding the medicines and miracles that could help so many!" she argued.

"Medicines and miracles that could readily become poisons and weapons," the Auburn Wizard countered. "Could you imagine if Wyvern were to acquire such things?"

The Maiden hesitated. Did Wyvern not find and take what he wanted, anyway?

"Do you not accept such a risk before creating these things?" she said with an inward sigh.

The Lord of Dreams stood still before her. The people in the room surrounding them carried on in their hushed conversations. The Maiden continued to forget that she was incorporeal to them. The hooded wizard remained silent and unmoving for a time. Though only seconds, it seemed like hours to them both. He finally heaved a heavy sigh.

It was with surprising humor that he answered her. "You're wise beyond your years, my lady. I wish the decision was my own. For all my knowledge and power I, like my brothers and sisters in the arcane, defer to my king and it is the Auburn King who decrees the withholding of our knowledge. The great bronze spire you now stand in is protected by seals that I have personally manufactured."

He turned to face the room and its visitors. "You saw one such seal when you were on the road at the border of the realm."

"The stone pillar," she whispered.

"Yes. It's true when I said I brought you here and it is I that keep you. The pillars are enchanted with a ward of travel. Any person, physical or otherwise, who traverses beyond the stones can walk for days or weeks; they can run as fast as is possible or spur their horse until the beast can run no further. The end result is always the same—they will turn to find they are no more than a few steps from the pillar. This protects our people and our knowledge."

"A traveling ward?" she replied, her eyes revealing her newfound mistrust of the Auburn Wizard. "Are your people restricted by such a ward? Are they not allowed to travel beyond their own borders?"

"Absolutely not," he answered with a raised hand, attempting to quell her rising disdain. "The people are free to travel as they will. They are, after all, our people—my people—not prisoners. Even others may travel into the kingdom unhindered. Unwanted visitors or invaders, however, can be swiftly returned to the wards at my command."

"Yet another wonder that could protect and save others—why not provide this to protect villages and farmlands from brigands or monsters or worse?"

"It's yet another creation that belongs to me personally, I'm afraid. As it is my magic I wouldn't see it misused," he replied flatly; his tone made it apparent that he would not be persuaded otherwise.

The wizard offered an open hand to the Maiden. "Please, take my hand," he said politely.

The Maiden did so, but not without hesitation. He hadn't yet given her reason to vilify him, but her trust in him was now shaken. She found his power misspent and ideals misguided, but he and his king ruled as they best saw fit. Their people were content and that would have to suit her, as well. There was nothing much she could do as it was—no matter if she was physically present or not.

He guided her to a section of the room that divided into three recesses that each appeared to be separate lifts of their own. The one he ushered her to was marked by the ever-present triangle. Walking inside, she stood next to him as he pulled a lever and she heard a sharp hiss as they ascended into the tower. Doors opened above them and they came to a stop at the very pinnacle of the spire.

The Maiden's breath caught. She slowly covered her mouth and beheld the sight of the lands of Vitruvia before her. The top of the spire was an open aerie that held a massive, triangle-cut amber—The Great Amber of Vitruvia, as it were.

It sat atop two impossibly thin bronze supports that shouldn't have been able to bear such a weight. They were engraved in elegant patterns from the very same bronze of the tower, and the supports rose from a still pool of water set in the flooring. The light from the waters danced off of the facets of the great gem and the amber created luminescent flickers of color and light in the pool

"A parting gift, young Maiden," the wizard said to her.

"What? A parting gift?"

The Auburn Wizard approached her; his hooded face still hidden.

"You've asked many questions, all of which still remain unanswerable, at least to me. I felt compelled to see what the brilliant star was that journeyed among so many other slumbering lights. In our time together I've learned much, but not all that I would have liked. You're distraught, and rightfully so, at your lack of understanding as to what Wyvern seeks from you—this gift he so desperately covets. Again, I can't begin to guess what it truly is. Although I have no doubt you've some kind of power he's after. A soul as luminescent as your own certainly harbors something he wants to control for himself. As you wander here in the domain of dreams you prove that even Wyvern's sting cannot take you. You denied death for some unknown but vital purpose. This is part of the power Wyvern seeks, I'm sure of it."

The Maiden remained silent, pondering the Lord of Dream's insight.

"It raises so many more questions," she finally said.

The Auburn Wizard nodded sympathetically.

"Regretfully so—you're quite perplexing, my lady. I would greatly like to talk with you further, but I'm already rudely absent from a gathering of my brethren. I must return to them. Before we part, I offer you a glimpse of our great stone; it may very well be the rarest sight in the land. No outsider has ever gazed upon it, nor have very many Vitruvians."

"I'm grateful, my lord," she said.

The wizard nodded. "I'll return you to the place of our meeting. You'll remember nothing, I might add. The wards will assure that. Mythesta lies to the east and Avallonis to the south; that should suffice."

The Maiden looked at him in disbelief. "You... are going to just abandon me in the wilderness again?"

She wasn't afraid, only confused by the fact that this seemingly kind man would oust her from the realm and leave her bereft of even the knowledge of where she'd been.

"You're incorporeal; a being of the ether," he said, another smile in his voice. "I assure you nothing can harm you. I can't speak for the state of your physical body, however. And I think it best that you seek it out. Should I discover more, and should you still wander the landscape of dreams, I'll certainly find you."

The Lord of Dreams turned from her and she reached out to stay his departure. However, before she could fully raise a hand she found herself surrounded by hills and trees.

How did she get here? She vaguely recalled a man whose face was shrouded by a cowl. She knew that she faced east and to head back westward would be pointless. Strangely, she didn't know the hour, the time, or the place.

27

THE PIEBALD SWAMP

The Maiden wandered for a time. Sometimes it felt like she was lost in a daydream and would come to her senses not knowing how long she had been walking. This happened reflexively, just like a dream, and she would feel a sudden pang of déjà vu.

She found herself surrounded by a forest. One that was different from those of her homeland. It was ominous and mystifying, dense and humid. She heard bird calls both beautiful and menacing, that were pierced intermittently with the shrill calls of frogs. The butterflies that constantly accompanied her fluttered less persistently now. They were less inclined to rest upon what should have been her incorporeal form. They did, however, have no trouble landing upon her arms and shoulders—tickling her hands and neck.

The roads here appeared to be far less traveled than others. The blossoms were of striking colors and variety: deep crimson, bright blue, stark yellow, and dark lavender. She was enraptured by the sight and smell of the blooms. Small creatures climbed and jumped about the trees and their chittering presence grew more frequent as she walked deeper into the realm.

Small animals similar to squirrels but with webbings of skin connecting their arms and legs glided about the canopy. Horned rabbits darted across the pathways, and birds with glowing plumage nested in the dark wooden trestles, their markings looking like leering faces. She began to wonder if any of this was real.

She was harshly reminded of reality when she noticed a foul smell permeating the air. She also noticed that the air had become more humid—it carried a weight and musk. A light fog hung about and congealed like thick soup at her feet. Fireflies flickered about the air and she startled at a large snake she suddenly noticed draping from a tree branch.

When had the forest become so ghastly? The smell reminded her of a swamp, but worse. The songs of the birds were gone; countless crickets ceaselessly played in their place. The high-pitched frogs were replaced by the deep croaking of fattened toads. When she heard a lazy splash she looked down to see one of the toads swimming beneath her feet—she was standing on the water.

Then she noticed something else. She could feel; feel the air, the moisture, the cool shade. She could also smell musk and mold and wet trees. Her earlier memories recalled no sensations at all.

She looked around, sharply taking in not only the sights and sounds but also the smells and sensations; here and there, up and down. Indeed, she had managed to make her way into a swamp. Had she stumbled so far from the road?

Attempting to retrace her steps, she was unable to find the road she had once walked. She felt a pang of fear as her dream-like wanderings left her lost in some spires-forsaken mire. Attempting to retrace her steps, she only roamed deeper into the woods and, as a result, more lost with each step.

She heard voices, and for a moment felt relieved. Then she reminded herself that no one could see or hear her. Downtrodden, she decided to at least see if the owners of the voices were near a road of some kind. She walked through the ferns and trees as though they weren't there until she came upon the source of the voices and was taken aback at what she saw.

A small pack of boglins was going about their business next to their hovels. They were fairly few in number, but more than just a single family lived here. There were three large huts of mud, branches, and fronds encircling a sizeable bonfire. She counted near twelve of the creatures.

They were short, spindly things with long drooping ears. Their skin was the color of the swamp water. Thin legs were attached to drooping pot-bellies. The males were bald, but had a wiry tuft of hair sprouting from their chins—the females shared this trait. They spoke among themselves in the common tongue and appeared to be harvesting some sort of foul-looking mushrooms from the muck and mire about their homes.

Their clothes were tattered and stained. Only a small number of them wore boots of any kind. The females adorned their matted, mangy hair with the local blossoms and fungi, but the flowers were long-since dead.

She observed them silently and pitied the creatures for their misfortune. They scraped among the trees for moss to add to their harvest and poured collected water from vessel-shaped plants. She retched slightly as the one collecting the water plucked some sort of insect from it and readily devoured the thing.

One of the boglins suddenly raised a hand and silenced those who were conversing nearby. He stood up and began sniffing the air. The Maiden, concerned, began to look about for signs of trouble. He began walking and sniffing in the Maiden's direction. Her heart began to race—certainly, they didn't smell her?

As he drew nearer the Maiden prepared to flee; then his eyes stopped directly on her. She froze momentarily and then saw that the boglin was not looking at her, per se. He slowly reached a long, bony hand in her direction and with one of his disproportionately long fingers coaxed a butterfly onto his hand.

He sniffed it, smiled, and covered it with his other hand. Two more of the boglins raced over to him and came to a slippery stop. They began asking him so many questions so fast that the Maiden couldn't discern what was being said.

Finally, he quieted them all with a barked, "Shut it! Shut up!"

He turned and revealed to them his find. The other two stared, dumbfounded, and one began scratching her beard.

"Wot's it?" she asked.

"Yeh, wot's the flippering thin' doin'?" questioned the other.

The one with the butterfly shook his head vigorously but continued smiling. "I's can't tell—but we's be findin' out!"

"How?" asked the female.

"The witch!" he blurted out, drawing attention from the rest of the crowd.

The female slugged him in the jaw nearly causing him to lose the butterfly. She looked back worried that the others had heard.

"Quiet!" she whispered harshly. "You's get tha others good 'en scared…"

The one with the now swollen lip moaned in pain but continued smiling his broken-toothed grin.

"She's be knowin' what 't is!" he said. "She's be willin' t' pay, maybe with meat 'r veggies!"

The eyes of the other two lit up at his statement.

"Yes… yes! Maybe she's be willin'!" the other male chimed in.

What were these pitiful things doing cavorting with a witch, the Maiden wondered? Desperation had driven them to deal with her, obviously, but there was nothing the Maiden could do. However, this may lead her to something that could help her find her way from this fetid swamp.

When the eager boglins began to scamper away with their prize, the Maiden quickly followed. She found that the effects of running were no different than walking: not a leaf stirred from her passing. The creatures were clumsy and quite unlike the ratlings of Emrallt. She had no trouble keeping pace with them, as they seemed to trip over the mist itself in their rush.

They stumbled around a sharp bend and the Maiden feared she may lose them in the in the swamp if not for their crashing and cursing. Passing effortlessly through the dense growth, she soon came out onto an empty road. She looked back to see if she had possibly outpaced them, but there was nothing there.

However, she'd found a road. She could now make her way to a more civilized location and attempt to find her resting body.

She then looked ahead and saw the flickering shadows of three fleeing shapes toward what appeared to be a lit structure—a small, humble hovel nestled in a dank grove. Curiosity overcame her and she raced toward them and caught up as the boglins neared the hut.

She stopped as she entered the grove and attempted to catch her breath. She then thought to herself—why do I struggle to breathe? Remembering that she wasn't actually a physical, breathing being she caught her breath, as it were, and listened to the three boglins bicker about who was going to knock and summon the witch. They pushed, shoved, and even attempted a bite or two.

Finally, one male who had been mostly silent since the Maiden had first encountered them, snatched the butterfly and hurried to the door. The Maiden walked closer, anxious to see what occurred.

Having further entered the grove, she saw that it bore a few differences from the rest of the swamp. It was drier, certainly, and the trees were less gnarled. There were also several green vines curling up about the trunks of the trees. They were covered with the typical thorns and brambles she had seen so far, but these also sported blooms akin to those in the more pleasant areas she had first seen before the forest turned into a swamp.

What sort of haggard person would call this home? The Maiden wondered as she glanced about the place.

The door to the dwelling creaked open and the Maiden moved closer. A voice called out to the boglins and a delicate hand began shooing them away.

"Off! Off with you now!" it was shouting. "I told you, nothing more from here!"

The boglins fled, releasing the butterfly in the process. It fluttered about for a moment and when the door opened fully, the home's owner stepped into the dim light of the grove.

A beautiful woman with hair as dark as night and bright, blue eyes stood in the doorway. She wore magnificent violet clothes adorned with lace and silver filigree. The Maiden thought that it must be some sort of witch's trick. Why would such a beautiful woman in such fine clothes be in the midst of a swamp?

The boglins scurried past the Maiden in a frightful mass. She looked up to see the witch standing in the doorway watching them flee. The Maiden dared to walk closer, attempting to better see this mysterious woman. Her 'breath' caught when she saw the witch was not watching the boglins; the witch was staring at *her*.

28

THE SYBIL'S GRACE

"My, my," she said with a voice like crystal. "It appears Vacini has fallen victim to his curiosities again."

The Maiden nervously fidgeted with her clothing. The witch's stare was becoming uncomfortable. She observed the Maiden as though she were some sort of oddity or strange animal.

"What exactly are you doing here?" the witch asked curiously.

"I was wondering the same about you," the Maiden returned meekly.

"Well, I believe I did ask first," she said in a playfully haughty tone.

"The boglins mentioned a witch. I felt I would at least be able to find a road or some manner of way out of the swamp by following them."

"Do witches tend to live near roads, now?" she chuckled.

"I suppose not."

The witch nodded her head. "Well, found one you did," she commented. "And… you still followed them here?"

"Yes… I saw your house and… and curiosity overcame me."

"And do you still think me a witch?" the woman asked.

The Maiden looked at her for a moment. The witch lifted a curious brow as she awaited her answer.

"You certainly don't appear to be a witch," the Maiden said meekly.

"I would hope not. But witches are not all warts and cauldrons—you would do well to remember that, young lady," the woman admonished her.

"Yes, ma'am," the Maiden acknowledged. "Then may I ask: what are you? Doing here, I mean..." she continued to stumble. Then she remembered that she should not have been visible at all. "And how can you see me?"

"First, I live here. Second, I am a Sybil. And what makes you so sure that you shouldn't be able to be seen?" she asked firmly.

"A Sybil? I don't think I've ever heard of such—"

"Ah-ah-ah," she chided gently, "I answered your questions. Now you answer mine: why should I need magic to see you?"

The Maiden self-consciously looked down at herself. The Sybil said nothing so the Maiden explained.

"I believe you can see through me, can't you?" she asked with genuine curiosity.

The Sybil regarded her again with scrutiny until she finally raised a single, inquisitive brow. "I do find your intangibility... intriguing. Though as I've already stated quite clearly unless I most uncharacteristically stuttered: I believe Vacini has been up to his old habits again. He should've explained everything to you and not sent his little dream friends my way."

The Maiden looked at her in confusion. This Sybil was indeed an eccentric one.

"I'm afraid I don't quite understand," the Maiden replied.

The Sybil sighed, but graciously invited the Maiden into her modest home and offered to explain things further. The Maiden, accepting her invitation with equal grace, walked through the gnarled, wooden door. She saw the Sybil pouring tea at an elegant table surrounded by comfortable, cushioned chairs.

"Would you like some tea, dear?" the Sybil offered. Her tone was like that of nobility. She sounded so proper and polite.

"I can't... no, thank you," the Maiden said

The Sybil chuckled, "Oh, right."

The Maiden looked about the interior of the humble dwelling. It was far different on the inside than its murky exterior. The floor was made of smooth cobblestones with large, plush rugs providing comfort. The small number of dressers and end tables were made of dark cherry wood and the fireplace was elegantly crafted. The chairs were soft and inviting.

The quarters were small but almost lavish in their make. Only one other room was apparent and it was shut behind a door. The Maiden assumed this was the Sybil's bed chamber.

"Such a strange home..." the Maiden remarked, not realizing she said so aloud.

"Strange?" the Sybil replied. "I feel I've done rather well with what I have to work with. Swamp rot is a sure problem with the furniture. And the plant life—oh, so difficult to make a palatable tea; it took me many years to grow what you saw outside."

The Maiden was quick to apologize. "Oh, no, I'm sorry! I meant that, you see, this is indeed a lovely home. In the swamp it seems so out of place. And, pardon my saying, but, so do you. How did you manage to get this all here? Or find this hut? Or, for that matter, how did you come to be here?"

The Sybil took a lingering sip of her tea. When she was done she let out a long sigh.

"Well, the simplest of those answers is my home itself. I, like my mother and sisters, am quite the accomplished enchantress. The hovel was already here when I arrived as were most of its contents. I merely shaped them to my liking. You wouldn't want to see them when I'm gone..."

"Where is your family, then?"

The Sybil sipped her tea. "That answer is much more complicated. My mother has long since passed to the hereafter. My sisters and I weren't from a poor home. We had the means and the capability to care for ourselves and all our needs were more than met."

The Sybil approached one of the windows and looked outside where it had begun to rain. "They wanted for much, however—my sisters—they aren't the best of people."

The Maiden looked about at the Sybil's home. "They drove you here? They forced you from your home?"

The Sybil chuckled in her lovely tone again. "My, no, dear. I came here of my own accord. I'm a Sybil. That has its own... complications. Most people have gut instincts. I have, well, gut assurances, I suppose. I get hints and intimations that I know will come to be in some form or another."

She dropped a cube of sugar in her tea and stirred it, staring into the cup forlornly.

"I had such a feeling about my sisters. Something dark. I chose to ignore it. I didn't want to believe it. After I witnessed what they were becoming... their ambition turned black. They sought power beyond that which was already granted them. They wanted more. But they were still my sisters, after all. My gift drew their jealousy. You can't learn what I have, no matter your skill. They hated me for it. I knew if I were to stay, that a difficult decision would be put upon me and I wouldn't have the strength to see it through. Therefore, I took my leave."

"How terrible..." the Maiden replied.

"Not so terrible, I think," the Sybil said as she sat on one of the thick-cushioned chairs. "I've made a happy life here. Though it seems the actions of my eldest sibling have wrought a growing misfortune on the land."

"What do you mean?"

"The swamps. Mythesta was not always so haggard. Once a lush forest teeming with life and beauty grew here."

"So that's where I am. Mythesta, the Amethyst Realm? If

everything was once similar to the forests I first encountered on your borders, it must have been quite entrancing."

"Yes—perhaps the magical contamination of my sister has not yet reached the outer confines of Mythesta. This land is tied greatly to the arcane. That's one reason I wasn't so surprised to see you, dear."

"You see many spirits roaming the swamps?" the Maiden asked.

"Spirits? No. You're not a spirit. I can see things many others cannot—even wizards. Another of my gifts as a Sybil."

"Then... what am I? I know I'm alive... somewhere. I'm just not sure *how* I know." The Maiden groaned and ran a hand through her hair. "I have memories that I can't quite grasp... things I *know* but can't quite grasp..."

The Sybil huffed, "Spires-all, Vacini."

"You keep saying that name. Who is Vacini?"

"The Auburn Wizard, dear. Wizards have their curious pursuits, but Vacini dabbles often in the world of spirits and dreams. 'The Lord of Dreams', ha!"

The Sybil poured herself another cup of tea, smiling as she stirred in the sugar this time.

"Well, I have no doubt he's the one who sent you here and wiped your memory with his precocious wards."

"Why would he do that?"

"Vitruvians are notoriously reclusive. Even I can't manage to travel to the Amber Realm without coming out with a headache and a lingering desire to give him several pieces of my mind."

"So, I could've been there for days and not known?"

"Unlikely. Even he can't stop time and as curious a fellow as he is, he wouldn't keep you for long. I wouldn't take it personally, dear. He's under king's orders to keep their secrets. There's not much he can keep from me, though," she said with a wry smile. "I retain a little more than most others."

The Maiden's eyes widened. "So, you could take me back?"

"It wouldn't do any good I'm afraid," the Sybil replied in disappointment. "If he could've helped, he would have already."

"I see," the Maiden sighed. "Well," she continued, her tone rising with hope, "you have unique powers, right? Maybe you can help me figure out what's going on with... this."

"I assure you I don't quite know what's 'going on', but a spirit belongs to one recently or not-so-recently deceased. You're quite different. You're more free-willed; more conscious of your state of being. I've had many encounters with spirits and the like in these woods; Mythesta is a realm of esoteric magic. It holds close ties to such things. Maybe that's what drew you here. It called to your, well, not-quite-alive-but-not-quite-dead self."

The Maiden grimaced. "All of this, then," she said and made a sweeping gesture to the surrounding lands, "is the work of your sister?"

"The eldest of us, yes," the Sybil corrected. "It is she who sits in power within the Amethyst Spire. Unfortunately, I don't know what happened to our king."

"You can't help them—your sisters?"

The Sybil's face became shadowed and she lowered head in shame.

"I've never tried. My sisters have much in common: dark, cruel, and powerful. And dangerous, most of all."

"They rule together?" the Maiden asked.

"No, only my eldest sister sits in power. She's the Violet Queen and her sorcery has spread its corruption throughout all of Mythesta. I might have tried to... maybe I could have stopped her... many years ago," the Sybil stuttered, quite unlike what the Maiden had seen of her so far.

"I didn't think she would have truly set her sights on the spire. My other sister, Morgæna, returned from a journey with power unlike either of us had seen before. She shared it with our eldest sister and then departed again. She offered it to me, but it smacked of evil and I wanted nothing of it. My eldest sister was then more powerful than I and by the time she sat upon the throne I couldn't stop her."

The Maiden saw that the Sybil was deeply saddened. She wasn't sure if it was for the fate of her sister or if she felt there was more that could have been done. Or both. If she was able she would have offered a gentle hand of comfort.

"Why do you share all this with me, a complete stranger?"

The Sybil shrugged and stirred her tea half-heartedly. "It gets quite lonely out here. Besides, what will it matter what an isolated swamp witch shares with a young lady wandering the domain of dreams?"

The Maiden grimaced and crossed her arms.

The Sybil turned to her and smiled. "Okay, maybe that's not entirely accurate," she sighed, then continued, "The truth is, I knew you were coming. Well, not you, exactly, but someone. I didn't expect a spirit-ish person," she corrected quickly when she saw the Maiden wince.

"But I did know that someone was coming here, to me, and I had to be here for them. My mind... stirred... after a very strange occurrence. One morning I woke to find it raining, but this wasn't just a typical gentle rain. It felt... sorrowful. I realized something that made me very sad, myself; the world was weeping. It was... extraordinary, heart-wrenching, and it was all about you."

The Maiden's eyes widened. "About me? That can't be true..."

"It is, I'm sure of it," the Sybil replied earnestly. "You're a powerful young woman. What power is this? I don't know, but it's enough that I was given forewarning of your coming...and that a great evil is after you."

The Maiden hadn't told her about Wyvern... it was one weight of many that pressed on her right now. How much did the Sybil know?

"You're surprised that I know that?" the Sybil said. She chuckled. "Don't worry—you're safe with me. No one is going to think to look for you here," she sighed as she looked out to the mire and tangled, drooping willows that lay beyond the window. She grimaced, then yawned loudly.

"It's getting late. We'll rest tonight, or, well, I will. I still need sleep, after all. But, tomorrow we'll find out just why you came here. Until then, my dear, I'm afraid I'll just find some things to keep you busy until the morning. I do apologize."

"It alright—I think I can manage one more night," the Maiden replied warmly.

As the Sybil finished her tea, the Maiden's eyes looked about her belongings. There were some vases containing some of the more beautiful flowers from the Mythestan forests. A few trinkets here and there. It was comfortable, but it lacked the feeling of a home.

"Why do you stay here? Do you have no other family?" the Maiden asked, hoping not to offend.

The Sybil took another sip of her tea before answering.

"Our parents have long since passed. Besides, I may not have the powerful magicks of my siblings, but I have another talent. One that I'm sure either one would seek to exploit. My magic is strongest here in my spire-realm and I hide here so that the Violet Queen can't find me."

The Maiden ventured one more question, grinning as she asked, "Would you dare share this talent with a stranger?"

The Sybil returned a slight smile. "I'm sure it will be fine. Call it one of my 'gut-assurances'. Come, dear. I'll show you."

The Sybil led the Maiden along the destitute path next to the hovel. After a short walk, they turned sharply into a glen that would have been easily missed had the Sybil not known it was there. As they entered, the Maiden saw two small orbs of light hovering lazily about near the twisting vines and gnarled trees.

"What are those?" the Maiden asked.

Feeling her guest's arm tense, the Sybil gave a quick explanation.

"Those are wisps. They're invisible to most everyone, even most wizards. Very interesting that you can see them," she said, raising an eyebrow at the Maiden and then smirked. "I knew I was right about you"

The Maiden relaxed, seeing that they were harmless. "I shouldn't be able to see them?"

"No, but you must wander the same form of existence they do; not *beyond* time and existence, but coursing through its ebb and flows... oh my..." the Sybil said, her breath catching.

The Maiden watched as one orb after another materialized or floated from around trees. They appeared in all shapes in sizes. It was as though the two women were surrounded by stars

"I've never seen so many at once," the Sybil whispered in awe. The seemed to focus and congregate around the Maiden.

One of them approached her and traveled up her arm. It felt warm and soothing, even friendly. The Sybil watched the small orb carefully.

"This one must have something for you."

The Maiden looked at her with mixed confusion and caution. "Have something?"

"Wisps carry visions of things from the past, present, and sometimes even the future. If they choose, they can reveal something. I've been gifted many interesting sights from them... save for the actions of my sisters. Go on, dear—peer into the wisp and see what it has to say."

The Maiden looked into the glowing, swirling trails of light. It was impossibly bright, but it didn't cause her any pain. The glow soon overtook her vision. As she watched, the endless white faded and she was back in the swamp. The Sybil was looking at her expectantly.

"Well? Don't dawdle, dear, what did you see?" the sorceress asked excitedly.

The Maiden hesitated for a moment trying to grasp the

images that flowed through her mind like both vinegar and honey.

"I saw two separate beings, one next to the other. One of them was tall and beautiful, but her soul was dark and stained. The other was a monster—a beast that I first mistook for a wolf but larger and more fearsome than any other I had ever seen; but inside, its soul was, well, not pure but certainly good. Its bones almost seemed a prison for that which was trapped inside."

The Sybil nodded, but her eyes were dark. "That's the Violet Queen and her Barghest," the Sybil's head then perked up quickly.

"You only saw one?"

"One?" the Maiden replied.

"One, yes. Only a single Barghest?"

The Maiden's eyes dashed about as she replayed the vivid images in her head again.

"Yes, I am certain. Only a single one of the beasts was there."

"How odd," the Sybil thought aloud. "Anything else?"

"An—urge. A longing to be there," the Maiden answered.

"Well, then. I suppose you should be on your way," the Sybil said frankly.

"Pardon?" the Maiden questioned.

"If a wisp is generous enough to share anything with you, I find in my experience that it is very much beneficial to do what they say," the Sybil explained.

"It's telling me to go to the Amethyst Spire," the Maiden thought aloud. "I don't even know where it is."

"Well, allow me," the Sybil stated.

She held a gentle, smooth hand out towards the brush and a small, dry branch emerged. It hovered toward them and once it was close enough the Sybil placed her fingers together as though she were holding something and began to write.

"Down here, dear," she said, pointing the Maiden to the

ground. On the dry, dirt path the disembodied branch began to draw a map.

The Sybil drew a rough outline of the Amethyst realm. She drew a circle representing where they currently stood. An 'X' represented the spire. She then began drawing trees, lines, scribbled patches, and various other shapes. One unending line must have represented the road to the spire. The Sybil's instructions started simple enough, then an amalgam of lefts, rights, avoid here, and the occasional—optional—shortcut depending on the season. The Maiden looked at the Sybil with pleading, hopeless eyes.

"Or, perhaps, I could accompany you," the Sybil concluded.

"What of your sister?" the Maiden reminded her.

"You've been given a vision from a wisp. I'll not see it hindered or ignored—it would be against my ethical standards as a sybil. I'll handle my sister if and when such a time arrives."

"Thank you," the Maiden said with a smile.

"Oh, you're quite welcome. Now, let's hurry along. I truly do not enjoy traveling the swamps in the dark."

29

THE AMETHYST SPIRE

Afte several hours, the Maiden was tempted to ask the Sybil if she could simply whisk them away to the Amethyst Spire. It wasn't because she was tired. She couldn't physically feel any pain, yet, but her sense of touch and smell seemed to pick and choose what she felt and smelled. This happened to make the walk even longer; no concentrating on walking, leg pain, or breathing—just one foot in front of the other. It was surprisingly boring.

After a while longer the Sybil informed the Maiden that she would need to rest. It was always dark and tepid within the confines of the gnarled trees, but through the morose canopy, she saw that daylight was turning dim. They'd been traveling for a full day. They hadn't seen a single town or village, so the Maiden asked where the Sybil expected to stop for the evening.

"Oh, I'm purposely circumventing those."

"What? Why?" the Maiden exclaimed. It just occurred to the Maiden, who'd wandered for days without feeling tired or hungry, that the Sybil brought absolutely nothing with her for the journey.

"Well, dear, I'm a beautiful and well-dressed woman traveling alone save for the company of one invisible apparition," she answered playfully. "I wish to avoid any scrutiny or other unwanted attention."

"I thought you said I wasn't a spirit? And aren't you a powerful sorceress?" the Maiden refuted.

"Until I know what you are, 'apparition' will have to do. And yes, I'm quite talented. It's still foolish and arrogant to think I'm safe from any harm."

"What about wild animals?"

"I can deal with them much easier than brutish thugs."

The Maiden agreed by remaining silent. She still didn't know how they would find shelter. She was of a mind to ask when she saw the Sybil remove a brooch from her robes. The Maiden noticed it was in the shape of the Sybil's hut. The Sybil approached a tangle of vines draped like a foul curtain among some low-hanging tree limbs. She clasped the brooch to one of the smaller vines. To the Maiden's surprise, she parted the vines like a set of drapes and behind them was the inside of the Sybil's home.

"Come, dear. I need to get warm."

The Maiden, mouth agape, entered the home. It was the very same one she had stepped into earlier in the day. She looked back, and outside lay the swamp they had been traversing moments earlier.

"Spires-all…" she cursed breathlessly.

"Amazing, is it not?" the Sybil chuckled. "I worked for quite some time for a charm such as this."

The Sybil made tea and removed some vegetables from a basket, placing them in a pot of water. She had tea and soup that evening, then rested while the Maiden simply perused her collection of books.

When early morning finally arrived, the Maiden was reading pages from books the Sybil had left open for her during the night, the Maiden being unable to turn the pages. The Sybil was ready quite quickly and they exited through the strange door of tangled vines. The Sybil removed the brooch and pinned it back upon her robes. The Maiden could then see just through the vines to the remainder of the swamp behind it—the spell was no more.

Their journey to the tower was quite unremarkable. The Maiden wasn't sure if the Sybil had enchanted them with invisibility or if she simply knew the safest routes in and out of the swamp. Possibly both, knowing the eccentric enchantress.

As they walked, the trails through the mire became less like a sponge. The Maiden could hear the Sybil's footsteps as they squished into the saturated ground, and once in a while her senses returned momentarily and she had the sensation of stepping on wet cloth. Eventually, it felt more like the usual muddy trails she was used to hearing after a hard rain.

The change, though still stifling and muck-filled, must have been a relief to the Sybil, the Maiden assumed. Her fine clothes must be constantly caked in mud and other things the Maiden didn't care to think about. Her eyes followed her thoughts to the hems of the enchantress' velvet robes.

"How do they do that?" the Maiden wondered aloud.

"How does what do what, dear?" the Sybil responded, still looking forward.

"Your clothes—we've traversed through muck and slime for two days and yet your clothes are as new as they were yesterday."

The Sybil regarded herself with elegant detachment. "Well, I want them to stay that way. I am an enchantress, dear. Keeping clothing stain-free is somewhat of a trivial task.."

"That's… quite handy," the Maiden mused.

"I would imagine being ethereal is doubly so," the Sybil remarked.

The Maiden sighed. "It has its downfalls."

"Well, perhaps answers lie within the black halls of the Amethyst Spire."

It would seem the Sybil timed her remark perfectly. They just reached the crest of a hill and in the valley below the Maiden could see the broken majesty of the Amethyst Spire rising amidst a great clearing of the surrounding swamplands. Here a number of small lakes dotted the land around the spire. Numerous hamlets, appearing abandoned and unlit, sprung up intermittently between the lakes. The land was either dry and barren or, by contrast, soggy marshland.

The Spire itself appeared to be made of a charred, blackened material. It didn't shimmer or reflect the dour sunlight in any way. Gray clouds hung about the sky and sat there heavy, cold, and hateful. Bright light tinged the sullen, morose blanket as the sun fought to find its way past. The great Amethyst atop the spire floated there seemingly without support. To the Maiden's surprise, it even listed slightly to one side—appearing as if it were on the verge of falling into the pinnacle of the spire.

"We must head directly to the tower," the Sybil whispered, as though her sister could hear within its walls from here. "There is no shelter when we leave the swamps. The Violet Queen or her Ebonguard will surely know we approach."

"I understand," the Maiden assured her.

They began their walk along the snaking road. It was dry and at one point looked heavily traveled. The Violet Queen's hold on the realm of Mythesta had soured the magic of the spire which was more closely tied to the land than any other spire-realm— even Emrallt. The land was sick because of her.

The effects of the Queen's coup and the darkness of her magicks spread from the spire like an infected wound. In the time since she had taken the throne for herself and the disappearance of the king, the taint had spread almost to the borders. There, the effects would cease as the power of the neighboring spires would repel the darkness; but it would forever bite and grasp for those territories out of reach.

The Blue and Auburn Wizards would never allow such black magic to cross into their realm. Mythesta's southern borders were lined by the Veil Mountains and beyond that, Edda. The Violet Queen cared nothing for the mountains and its inhabitants, be they monstrous or dwarven. The harsh deserts of Edda were unappealing and so the Violet Queen's greed was tempered, and weakened near the Ruby Realm. Regardless, the Red Wizardess also held her at bay.

Thus far, no other realm had challenged the Violet Queen's usurpation for fear of damaging the structure of the spire further. A single spire falling could hold disastrous results for realms as a whole. The queen held the spire and its land hostage.

The Sybil had seen the queen's onslaught for years, and felt powerless against it. Her power was not obtained through practice and skill. The 'gift' granted her from Morgæna reeked of malevolence. The Sybil was yet unaware of the true boundaries of her eldest sister's power.

The Maiden saw first-hand and for the first time the befouled spire's effect on the people. The Maiden and the Sybil had no choice but to pass near a few of the villages. She saw that they weren't actually abandoned—only inhabited by fearful, cold, and hungry people. No guards were present, as no one was fit enough to stir trouble and threaten rebellion. Withered crops were harvested by withered people. The tilled fields were as bogs themselves.

This was evil near equal to Wyvern himself, the Maiden thought. The dark soul of the wisp-shared vision could not convey the actual presence of the foulness itself.

When they reached the massive courtyard surrounding the spire it was in surprisingly good condition. The stonework was clean and solid. The fountains poured forth pure water. The large rose bushes and decorative, pink blossomed trees were sparsely blooming, but blooming nonetheless. And, of course, there were guards.

Four of them, imposing brutes heavily armored with breastplates and faulds, and adorned with purple sashes and cloaks, formally approached them. Their armor clanked and their swords rattled. They stopped mere inches from the two, and the one in front spoke in a gravelly baritone that resonated through the visor of his metal helmet.

"No spells, madam," he ordered, grabbing the Sybil by the arm.

A second one grabbed her by the other arm and the last two followed behind. None of them noticed the Maiden. In fact, one of the following escorts walked right through her. The Maiden stayed close and once tried to talk to the Sybil, but noticed she remained silent.

Upon entering the Spire was a stark change from the outside. It was dark—unnaturally dark. The only light came from large, brightly burning sconces. The ghostly greenish flame was also unnatural and didn't provide much light. The Maiden, though, could still see things outside the darkness. She saw the essence and life of those within. Guards paced about near the sconces. Hallways and open arches coursed about this entry-level floor. It would be quite open if not for the cloying, horrible darkness.

"The taint is heavy here. The Queen coats her throne in darkness to protect herself," the Sybil said quietly.

"Quiet," the lead guard ordered stiffly.

"Well, you're both so quiet, I figured I might as well talk with myself," the Sybil quipped.

The Maiden smiled, though the Sybil couldn't see it for being walked briskly by the guards.

"*Quiet,*" he said again, this time more tersely.

They marched along a hallway lit by the ghostly sconces until they reached an area so thick with darkness that even the Maiden couldn't see through it. She could hear the lead guard counting quietly under his breath. They were reduced to walking from one dim green glow to another, not even able to see the ground beneath their feet for the dark. Walking one stiff step at a time, they abruptly emerged into an instantly recognizable great hall.

At the end rested a throne of carved onyx and charoite, a purple stone streaked with black, and less so with white.

The Sybil recognized her sister sitting there, as though the throne belonged to her. The self-titled Violet Queen looked remarkably similar to her middling sister. The Maiden would have trouble telling them apart if not for the queen's sharper features and larger eyes. Except, where the Sybil appeared graceful and kind, the queen was harsh and forbidding. Her face was etched like cold marble, and her smile at seeing her younger sibling cut her face like a knife. The Sybil's eyes were mysterious and alluring. The queen's, although equally enthralling, held no mystery. They were as obviously dangerous as a brigand pulling a knife on their victim. Clad in garments fashioned for royalty, she lounged in the throne like a bored cat. Next to her sat a monster whose fearsome appearance was second only to Wyvern. It was a barghest, a creature once thought extinct.

The Sybil heard, through the wisps and whispers of magic, her sister's horrible rise to power. The witch-sister, among her many other faults, had coveted the spire greatly. She'd wanted to see the ancient tower and its realm torn asunder if she couldn't have it, such was her jealousy and greed. The king, she knew, would be simple enough to overpower if she could gain access to him. The Violet Wizardess would be another issue entirely. Her magical prowess was beyond that of the witch, but her weakness lay in her love for the royal family, who had maintained peace between the humans and the fey for nearly two generations. Control the king, and the wizardess would fall.

Her other sibling, Morgæna, had returned some days after with news of her journey. She had set out on a quest to discover ways to augment their power and she had found it. One of the dragon-children was offering them relics of great power if they were to swear an oath to him—one that they would be beholden to beyond death should they attempt to deceive him. The witch-sister was more than eager to ally with Morgæna and Wyvern.

Morgæna revealed to Jezæla two lockets. Inside were two stones. One was a sapphire; a dark, midnight hue. The other was an amethyst; this one a deep red-violet that reminded her of tainted blood. These stones were to remind them of the realms they were to maintain control over by proxy for Wyvern until he called. He would bequeath to them the power of lost tomes and ancient magic even the council was unaware of, but should the sisters betray Wyvern or seek to abandon him he could snuff out their life with a breath and draw their own essence into the stones forever to be gifted again as he chose.

Jezæla had used her newfound power to take the throne for herself—and Wyvern. Once she'd transformed the king into one of the horrible creatures and sicced him on Edda to disrupt and distract the Red Kingdom, she turned on the Violet Wizardess and did the same. It appeared to the Sybil she kept the Violet Wizardess nearby as some terrible punishment. A tortured existence as Jezæla's pet.

The Maiden was stricken by fear, but also a sharp sense of pity. The Violet Queen smiled maliciously as they approached. Her one hand gracefully held a goblet of wine while the other scratched the shoulder of the powerful Barghest next to her.

"At last you pay me a visit, sister," the queen mocked.

"I never brought you a housewarming gift, Jezæla. As you know, I'm ever-hesitant to be perceived as rude," the Sybil returned flatly.

"Yet it seems you arrive empty-handed."

"I said I was hesitant. Not incapable."

The Violet Queen chuckled.

"I see you still have your pets," the Sybil said, changing the subject.

"Pet," the queen corrected. "One has been missing for some time. I wouldn't suppose you had anything to do with that?"

The Sybil raised a hurt brow. "Dear sister, I would never hurt any creature so magnificent as... well, whatever they are."

"I hear 'Barghest' has become a popular name," the Violet Queen added with dark humor.

"How appropriate," the Sybil replied derisively. "You gave an old folktale life."

As the two sibling sorceresses bantered, the Maiden had time to observe their surroundings. This room, though still dimly lit and unwelcoming, was far brighter than the rest of the spire that they'd been escorted through.

The four Ebonguards stood unflinching in a semi-circular pattern around the Sybil. They no longer restrained her; possibly assuming that their queen could handle her younger sibling if a conflict arose.

The most interesting thing of note was the massive Barghest. The wolf-like creature's eyes were chillingly, disturbingly intelligent. She would almost dare to say "human" if not for their sickly yellow color. The most distressing aspect of all was that the creature was not just looking at her, but staring at her—pleadingly and forlornly.

The Maiden slowly made her way towards it. She kept a watchful eye on the Violet Queen and also the Sybil, noting that neither paid her any attention. The Barghest, however, continued to watch her closely.

As the Maiden neared the beast it spoke.

What are you? it said.

The Maiden stopped reflexively raising a hand. She heard a voice, but the creature's mouth didn't move.

"I'm a peasant, from Emrallt," the Maiden replied haltingly.

If it were so simple I shouldn't be able to see you. No—you're not just a peasant from the Emrallt region. The Barghest corrected, continuing to look at her.

"And who are you, talking beast who can see invisible women?" the Maiden challenged.

I am a soul trapped in this beastly body of bristling fur and anger. My king and I watched over the Amethyst Spire before the witch came.

"The Witch? The Sybil's sister?" the Maiden said. "She created you?"

Turned us. We were human. She turned us into these beasts with her dark magic, and now we're bound to her.

"What do you mean bound to her?"

She holds sway over us; our minds and actions are not our own. I see, I feel, but I can't act or speak. She commands that someone die and we obey.

"How long has this been so?" the Maiden asked, heartbroken.

No less than a decade. I've lost count. I haven't even been able to keep track of the time my king has been missing. His bestial form left at the behest of the witch some time ago. She ordered him off to Edda, that's the last I've seen or heard of him.

Why would she command such a thing?" the Maiden wondered aloud.

I believe she herself was ordered to do so by the dragon-child, Wyvern. I heard them speaking not long after we had been turned. It is he that gave the witch Morgæna her power and instructed that the dark magic be shared with the Violet Queen. She's indebted to him, so as he commands, she obeys.

The Maiden became deeply troubled. "What sort of schemes is Wyvern planning? That creature wants something from me, as well. He told me this himself. The Auburn Wizard, the Sybil... they both see it, but can't explain it. Wyvern is also granting powers to these sorceresses... what else has he done?"

I only know that he spoke to the Violet Queen of an army; one that includes evils from all the reaches of the spire-realms. The Violet Queen also received word, as I'm sure all the kings and queens of the spires did, that the king of the Diamond Spire had disappeared. I've no doubt Wyvern is at fault.

Before the Barghest could continue, the Violet Queen shouted at the Sybil. The seething words from the queen caused the Barghest to begin snarling and barking at the Sybil, who reflexively stepped back and put a defensive hand up. Purple strings of lightning flickered between her fingers.

"How could you do this?" the Sybil was saying. "It's treason, Jezæla!"

"A sudden shift in authority, dear sister, nothing more," the queen cooed.

"So long as his daughter survives, your rule is challenged. You can't hide here in the spire and pretend to rule forever," the Sybil pleaded. The magic that danced among her fingers disappeared.

"Yes. That wizardess hid her from me well. No matter how creative my interrogations became, she refused to tell me where the princess was. I'll find her, in time. I have powerful allies of my own, you know. Besides, the wizardess tried to hide from me, too, and I found her soon enough."

The Violet Queen's smile turned particularly wicked, and she ran a telling hand gently along the side of the Barghest's face. The Sybil's eyes widened and brimmed with barely contained tears.

"And I'm not afraid of sharing such a fate with my cherished family..."

After the queen made her threat clear, the conversation returned to a more 'civil' tone. The Maiden grimaced at the Sybil's heartbreak.

"You're the Violet Wizardess?" the Maiden asked the Barghest, understanding who was now speaking to her.

I am... was.

"Would that I had the ability, I would take this curse from you," she said forlornly.

Not expecting to be able to offer any comfort she reached a hand out to the beast and felt something odd. The fur felt strange —like a thick fog. The beast was a physical creature, that much was certain seeing that the queen was consistently running her hands through the thick fur. The Maiden expected her hand to move through the creature much as it had everything else she'd touched. Except this time, there was a slight tingling sensation on her skin; as a light, misty rain. She continued to reach inside the Barghest and an eddying, dancing light formed at her touch near the beast's heart. At first, it listed about lazily, almost apathetically. Once her fingertips reached it the light grew brighter and began to coalesce into crackling sparks.

How are you doing this? the Barghest asked in wonder.

"I'm not sure what exactly it is I'm doing," the Maiden replied tentatively.

I feel as though I've been mired in oil and grasping for safety for so long; only now do I truly feel the hand of another—I can't truly describe it...

The Maiden's eyes widened with understanding. "Then take my hand..." she whispered in rising awe, "take my hand!"

She 'grasped' the light—feeling a subtle physical resistance against her grip as she tried to hold on to anything tangible of the shimmering substance. She pulled at first with one hand and then grabbed more of the corporeal glow with a second. As she pulled she felt the substance strain to hold to the form of the Barghest.

Hearing an odd groan, the Violet Queen looked over to her pet and saw its eyes starting to roll into the back of its head. The Barghest's mouth hung open and its slack tongue dripped globs of saliva upon the ground.

"What magic is this?" she demanded, glaring at the Sybil.

The Ebonguard drew swords and took a readied stance in a semi-circle around the Sybil. They were ready to kill her at a word from the Violet Queen.

The Sybil, genuinely shocked, replied, "I'm not at fault for this! I'm as confused as you!"

The Sybil looked to the Maiden for the first time. She appeared to be pulling over the beast, which was astonishing in and of itself. However, upon looking closer she saw the Maiden's arms were buried nearly up to her elbows into the creature.

"Spires-all..." the Sybil whispered out loud.

The Maiden continued to pull. Whatever this was—the soul,

embodiment, or essence of the wizardess—she was no longer speaking. Only the baritone rumblings of the Barghest could be heard. Finally, with a great heave, the glow gave way. The Maiden pulled it from the Barghest and the life went out of its eyes. With a final moan, it fell limp to the floor with a massive thud.

The light began to take on a heavy weight. It continued to coalesce and glow, but looked more like a shapeless mass of honey. It became too heavy to hold and the Maiden let it drop to the floor. As the amorphous substance dimmed the light within it grew brighter.

All in the room let out an astonished gasp when tiny sparks began to dance about the floor. At its core, it began to emanate a dull glow. It continued to grow brighter and expand. Soon two tendrils stretched forth and eventually formed a recognizable shape—arms and hands. The same occurred opposite these limbs and became legs.

At this, the Violet Queen stood quickly from her throne. The Sybil looked at her and saw fear grip her face though she attempted to cover it with a scowl. The queen held forth a single, pointing finger and ordered her guards to slay it.

The guards exchanged hesitant glances. Finally, the leader among them drew his sword and brought it down onto the figure which continued to look more and more human with each passing second. They all quickly retreated from the figure when his powerful blow struck the floor and rang out loudly. His blade did no more damage to this glowing figure than it would sunlight.

The queen removed a ring from her finger—one with a dragon's head adorned with rubies for eyes. She began whispering incoherently and the ring floated from her hand. Red lightning flickered within the confines of the ring. She grabbed the ring between two of her fingers and returned it to her hand. Red-tinged bolts of lightning caressed her hand.

The glowing figure, now having taken the full shape of a

woman, began to stand. The Violet Queen opened her palm toward the figure and all the power that had engulfed her hand was let loose. It crackled and thundered, the force reverberating in the Maiden's chest. The crimson forks of energy bounced off the glowing figure harmlessly.

The figure stood tall and approached the throne. There she grabbed a robe that had been draped over the side. She placed it around herself and as she did so the bright glow began to ebb and her human features could be seen. She had the handsome features of an elegant, older woman. She had a regal bearing that commanded attention and the Violet Queen's hands trembled.

The Ebonguard, all having viewed the last few seconds in rapt silence, dropped to one knee. They bowed before her. The Violet Wizardess, Tytania, stood with the cloak wrapped tightly about her. Until the king or his daughter returned, she was stewardess to the Amethyst Spire and one of the most powerful of her kind.

Her brown hair, heavily streaked with gray, was cut short and, coupled with her round face, gave her the appearance of a fey queen from Mythesta's deepest forests. Her deep brown eyes flickered with inner power. Those eyes focused on the treacherous wretch before them, and that power seethed.

THE VIOLET WIZARDESS

Tytania fastened the cloak as tightly as she could. It would have to do until she could get some proper clothes. She made a subtle, beckoning motion toward the Sybil's sister—finally forced to answer for her crimes as a witch. The crown upon the witch-sister's head pulled itself from her locks, causing her to cry out in pain. The crown moved swiftly to the hands of Tytania who, with a flick of her wrist, caused the crown to disappear in swirling wisps of smoke, returning it to its rightful resting place until the king or his daughter returned.

The witch stood with a hate-filled glare at the wizardess. The Maiden saw that as she stood, a dark, oily miasma roiled about the witch. To her surprise, neither the wizardess nor the Sybil reacted to the black aura building around the witch. Did they not see it?

"You filthy cur..." the witch spat at the wizardess. "Wyvern has granted me power beyond your own. Your time as a beast at my command was a mercy—"

The witch's words were cut short by the Violet Wizardess' own magic. Wind and thunder whipped about the throne room lifting the witch from the ground. However, she came to an abrupt stop, holding her own hands out and countering Tytania's spell. Her eyes turned a milky white and she cackled at the wizardess' attempts to harm her.

The Maiden saw the slivers of magic, hurled by the arcane winds of the wizardess, strike harmlessly off the black miasma. Tytania's face was hardened and determined, but marred by confusion at her failed magic.

"You will die!" the witch howled back.

The Sybil pursed her lips and joined in with the wizardess' assault. She began the tell-tale whispering of spell-conjuring. Balls of white fire soared on the wizardess' arcane winds and struck the witch, bursting into a flame that quickly died.

The Maiden could see another event the Sybil could not; hissing, snapping snakes began to form from the miasma. The Sybil's flame only seemed to exacerbate their furor. The witch's hair whipped about wildly and her eyes became as black and dark as her soul yet emanated a fiendish red glow. Her laughter turned maniacal. Something awful was about to happen—all those present could tell, but the Maiden knew doubly so.

Something occurred to the Maiden, but it did not occur without foreboding. She looked to the Sybil who was concentrating on her magic. So, too, was the wizardess. The Ebonguard simply stood back, swords dropped and arms held up to their faces—unable to do anything against a duel of sorceresses.

The Maiden took a deep breath and steeled her resolve. She walked past the wizardess who was no longer able to see her. She walked through the storm of wind and thunder and fire untouched and unaffected. She approached the cackling witch and her coiling serpents. Only the snakes appeared to notice her and they recoiled at her presence. She was prepared for them to strike, but the attack never came. The arcane creatures actually appeared afraid of her. They hissed and coiled about in their miasma attempting to avoid or even escape her.

This not only reassured the Maiden, but also emboldened her. She reached out and grabbed the nearest serpent and pulled it from the oily mire. She felt it go limp almost immediately. She tossed it aside and watched as it turned to ash, whipped away by the roiling winds. She did so again and again; each serpent's death causing the witch's miasma to wane.

The witch became sharply aware of this when one of the wizardess' barbs pierced her arm and drew blood. She cried out in pain and her laughter ceased. Another barb and then another made its way through her defenses. Her sleeve erupted into flame as one of the Sybil's spells pierced through. The Maiden continued to peel serpents away—their ashes filling the air about her and the witch.

The witch's laughter turned to screams of fury and impotence as she attempted to augment Wyvern's gifted magic with her own. It wasn't nearly enough.

Seeing their magic finally striking the witch, the Sybil and the wizardess poured all their effort into a thunderous onslaught of combined arcane power. The barbs alone would have sufficed to kill the fallen queen, but the multiple eruptions of the Sybil's white fire had set the witch ablaze. The wind quickly blew out the flames, but it was too late. The serpents and their miasma had dissipated and the witch fell into a heap on the ground.

The Sybil ran forward to her sister. Smoke coiled from what remained of her clothing and her skin glowed red with residual magic between the cracks of its charred black surface. The Violet Wizardess approached more cautiously, but no pity was to be found in her eyes—at least not for the witch. She placed a hand on the Sybil's shoulder, but the Sybil found no tears left for her sister.

"I have no words to say..." the Violet Wizardess offered.

She couldn't in earnest say she was sorry for the loss of such a villain. However, she did feel for the Sybil and her loss of family.

"It... it's alright," the Sybil said, dry-eyed. "I can't mourn for a woman such as this. My sister was not a kind person. She was beyond redemption. Unfortunately, this is how she's always been. She brought this end upon herself."

"I saw a young woman earlier; as the Barghest," Tytania said, feeling as though she was regurgitating the last words.

"Oh, yes," the Sybil exclaimed, her spirits seemingly rose at talk of the Maiden. "She's, well, she's still here. Right there, actually."

She nodded to where the Maiden stood just a few steps back from the body of the witch. The wizardess looked in the Maiden's direction. Though she had the general location correct it was all but impossible for her to speak to the Maiden directly.

"Thank you, whoever you are. The kingdom can finally begin to heal," the wizardess said, speaking to empty air.

"What exactly happened, dear? Did you have something to do with my sister's succumbing to our magic?" the Sybil asked the Maiden.

The wizardess heard nothing; she only saw the Sybil speaking and responding to herself.

"I see. Oh, dear. Serpents?"

The wizardess' brow furrowed. "What does she say?"

The Sybil touched a gentle hand to her lips. She thought for a moment before she spoke. She explained all the Maiden had told her; everything that happened with the witch that the Sybil and wizardess couldn't see.

"My sister spoke of the dragon-child. Morgæna's power, the gift she said had given her all her power... It was from Wyvern."

The Sybil hung her head in shame. Her sisters were in league with the monster and she had done nothing to stop it.

"He didn't give them such power without something in return. I heard many conversations between the witch and Morgæna. Wyvern visited the Amethyst Spire a time or two. They've been beholden to him for their power. He uses them to further his plans, nothing more," the wizardess explained.

"She discussed such things within earshot of you?" the Sybil asked doubtfully.

"Perhaps she didn't fully understand the effects of my transformation. At the very least I'm sure she didn't expect me to ever regain my humanity."

"Perhaps."

The Sybil found her sister's hubris unthinkable. At least here, her evil was curbed by her arrogance. It sounded as though Morgæna was not only more powerful and just as wicked as her sister but had also been more shrewd and calculating with her schemes.

The wizardess watched as the Sybil looked to her side as though listening to the apparition again. The Sybil's eyes winced in apprehension and her lips parted in concern.

The Sybil looked to the wizardess. "He has an army?"

Tytania held her breath for a moment, a telling sign of her worry.

"Only words. I saw nothing to confirm such a thing. I only heard talk between him and the witch."

"Wyvern does not merely talk. He doesn't waste time with empty words," the Sybil pointed out.

"I didn't hear much, I'm afraid," explained the wizardess, "he merely mentioned the Diamond Spire and constantly reminded the witch of what she owed to him. He stressed the importance of maintaining the hex upon my king and me."

Tytania had ruled alongside Perithane as more than just a wizardess. The Amethyst Spire, as with all the others, was governed by a king or queen, defended by his or her armies, and protected and advised by a court wizard. The Violet Wizardess was not just a sorceress, but an ambassador from the fey people from Mythesta's arcane forests. With the power of her charm and wisdom, she became the chief advisor of the Amethyst Spire's king. Soon thereafter, she became the Violet Wizardess—practically ruling alongside the king and queen. She was trusted, and the Sybil's sister had used and betrayed that trust.

Tytania shuddered as she recalled the day that the witch had forced her way into the throne room. Her ascent through the spire was so swift and unexpected that they hadn't even known until it was too late. A number of the king's honor guard were with her, physically wounded and having switched loyalties. It would only be later that the wizardess would learn that the witch could enchant others in many ways—not solely by turning them into beasts.

The newly formed Ebonguard had seized her king, and the wizardess had attempted and failed to fight against the witch. She watched as Perithane was magically wrenched into a coma by the loathsome woman. Only by relinquishing the throne would they be spared, the witch said. So the wizardess, out of anguish for her king, stood down. The witch turned Perithane into a beast before her eyes.

It broke her heart, but Tytania knew she only a moment to decide what to do. Using her own fey magic, less theatrical and more innate than that of human magic, she disappeared from the room. Her last image of her king was his grotesque body in mid-transformation.

Tytania went immediately to the Violet Princess and found her in her chambers. Tytania gripped the princess' arm tightly and before the girl could say a word, the wizardess and fey queen had transported them both to a safe place among Tytania's people. At her command, the fey would protect the princess and ward her against the witch.

When all precautions were in place, Tytania returned to the castle. She meant only to scout the spire, hidden by fey magic, but Wyvern's gifts had greatly empowered Jezæla. The witch had already laid a trap for the wizardess, and Tytania was discovered. The last thing the wizardess could recall, before her mind was no longer her own, was the feeling of fur growing upon her own skin.

Now, the witch, the self-titled 'Violet Queen', lay in a smoldering heap. The locket was burned into her skin and no longer a beautiful piece of jewelry but as dark and twisted as its former owner. The malignant bond wrought by the tainted stone was no longer effective. Any magic it once contained was dissipated and destroyed.

The Ebonguard had so far remained silent. What was Tytania to do with them? She looked to the one in front with the sashes denoting his leadership. The witch had forced her and the king to do horrible, unthinkable things as the Barghests. Had the same occurred with them?

The leader of the Ebonguard slowly reached his hands upward. The wizardess raised her open hand, readying her magic. The armored figure halted momentarily then continued to grab the menacing helmet that hid his face. He removed it, revealing the familiar visage of the king's former guards that were present when the witch usurped the throne. He threw the helmet unceremoniously to the ground. He tore off his sashes and cloak and tossed them aside. He then removed his sword—black and twisted from the witch's influence—and cast it upon the ground with the rest of the accouterments.

"My lady, my will is again my own. I would return to your service if you would have me," he said, kneeling to the ground.

The three other guards did the same—first removing their helmets and tossing them aside as their captain did. They knelt before her and she felt a twinge of doubt and pity.

The Maiden saw that there was no longer a pall about them. The shadow that had been doused upon the spire and those within it was dissipating like mist against a morning sun. She looked to the Sybil and told her this. The Sybil then explained to Tytania. These men were no longer tainted by the witch-sister's dark charms.

The wizardess looked back to them; all four kneeling before her. "I welcome you back into your rightful service. Let us be no longer beholden to that wretched creature."

The wizardess, now Stewardess of the Violet Throne, ordered them to dispose of the witch—she would be burned to ashes and buried in a silver urn sealed with magic fire. Nothing would return her to this world ever again.

31

A SWIFT SHADOW

As the guards removed the body, the wizardess and the Sybil exchanged mournful glances. What should have been a triumphant day had somehow remained marred by misery. Then a subtle, glistening spark flitted through an open window. The Maiden thought the butterflies had returned. She hadn't seen them since her encounter with the boglins. The spark began to glow brightly and took on a more solid, circular shape. The Sybil looked over, also noticing the arrival of the wisp.

What could this be? she wondered.

"What is it? What do you see?" asked Tytania, seeing the look upon the Sybil's face.

The Sybil, distracted by the wisp, actually hushed the wizardess whose eyes widened in disbelief at the Sybil's bold nerve. The orb danced as though cast about in a breeze despite there being none in the room. It made its way over to the Maiden where it slowed to a stop before her. The Maiden's eyes reflected the sharp light of the creature. It disappeared even more quickly than it had arrived—winking out of existence. The Maiden found herself breathing heavily.

"What, dear—what did it show you?" the Sybil asked impatiently.

"A tower... the Diamond Spire..." The Maiden flinched in pain. "It hurts..." she winced and grabbed her head. "I don't..." her words ended as she fell to the floor.

The Sybil, shocked, covered her open mouth with her hand. She was surprised the Maiden didn't fall right through the floor. A spirit, or whatever the Maiden was, shouldn't feel pain at all. The worried Tytania asked what had happened. Before the Sybil could explain the Maiden was already returning to consciousness.

The Sybil walked swiftly to kneel by her side. "What happened, dear?"

The Maiden stood unsteadily, unable to be helped by anyone, and pulled her hair from her face.

"That... was quite painful," the Maiden said wearily.

"What was? What did you see besides the Diamond Spire?" asked the Sybil.

She recalled the memory; her eyes filled with fear and her breathing grew heavy. "It was... beautiful at first. The Great Diamond glistened like a torch in the sun. I'd never seen this spire before, then... then it was covered in shadow and fire. Burning eyes looked at me through the uppermost window. It was surrounded by thorn bushes of gnashing fangs and rusted blades. It was horrifying..."

The Sybil spoke all of this to the wizardess as the Maiden explained. The wizardess was deeply disturbed by what she heard.

"Wyvern," Tytania said plainly.

"Yes... Wyvern's goal is the Diamond Spire," the Sybil concluded.

"I fear it may be more than that, but he certainly has his eyes set upon the Diamond Realm," replied the wizardess. "Were that Perithane were here..."

"Do you plan to send scouts to look for him now?"

She shook her head slowly, sadly. "The last I'd heard the witch had sent him to Edda. I'll send an envoy to the Red King. They've been friends since childhood. He'll certainly know if Perithane has been seen in his kingdom."

"I wish there was more that could be done, " the Sybil offered in condolence.

"This is not at all what I wanted," Tytania sighed. "I'll put this kingdom back in order. Make sure the witch's influence is truly gone. When it's safe, I'll return Perithane's daughter to her throne."

The Sybil placed a gentle hand on her shoulder. "It's going to be a long road. I don't envy you, Tytania."

"I could use someone such you," Tytania said to the Sybil, her age for once marring her timeless beauty.

The Sybil offered her a smile, but Tytania could see the reluctance on the Sybil's face. "I think my path has been decided," she said, looking to the Maiden. "I need to help her. Dark things are surrounding her and she needn't be alone."

"Did you see that?" the Maiden said, suddenly.

"What? Another wisp?" the Sybil asked.

The Maiden was looking about the room frantically. "No—the room suddenly darkened for a moment, as though a shadow had passed over us... a large one."

The Sybil's brow furrowed again. "I'm afraid I didn't see anything of the sort, dear."

The Maiden's head quickly darted to another direction of the room. "There! It happened again!"

The Sybil did notice that the Maiden's form had begun to fade. Then the Maiden abruptly vanished. She was gone. No echoing voice or lingering shapes. She ceased to exist.

"Is something wrong?" the wizardess asked, seeing the Sybil's concerned expression.

"The Maiden—she's gone. Awoken from whatever slumber she was in, I assume."

Tytania's eyes followed the Sybil's gaze to the place where the Maiden previously stood, now truly empty to all eyes. She smiled at the thought of the young woman who had released her from the witch's hex but was also saddened at the idea that she may never truly know who she was.

"Thank you," she said, hoping that somehow the Maiden with such a curious and precious gift would know the Amethyst Realm's gratitude.

"Well, that's just simply unacceptable," the Sybil said sharply.

"Excuse me?" the wizardess replied in confusion.

"Too many questions about that young lady; I need answers. Riddles were never my favorite."

The Sybil was speaking quickly and Tytania wondered if she merely thinking aloud or talking to her.

"I'm afraid I don't understand."

"Might I borrow your lovely chaise there, Your Grace?" the Sybil asked indicating a lush seat near a window.

"Um… certainly," the wizardess uncharacteristically stuttered.

The Sybil sat down in her typical lady-like fashion. She ran an inspecting hand over the material and nodded in approval.

"Very lovely. Might I ask one more favor—sorceress to sorceress?"

"Of course."

"Do you mind if I take a small nap here for a few days?"

32

WYVERN'S TEMPLE

The Maiden had seen a shadow pass over the Amethyst Spire. It was too swift to be clouds and not dark enough to be the witch's hex. After the second occurrence, the Maiden found herself growing faint and her head heavy. Her world went black.

It lasted only a moment. A passing kiss of flame, burning eyes, and the dull cold of death. She felt as though she were suffocating with a crushing weight on her chest. After a few brief, horrible seconds she saw a blur of light and color, then awoke confused and startled.

She drew several sharp breaths as the feeling of the lingering nightmare faded. She looked around to see several strangers peering at her from within a poorly-lit room walled with stone. She then felt a wave of relief when her vision cleared and she beheld the familiar face of the Prince.

He was speaking to her, but it sounded hollow as though coming through a wall. The words finally became clear—"You're awake! Are you alright? Are you hurt?"

She meant to throw her arms around him; embrace him and call him the greatest thing she has seen in a week. Was it a week?

Had it been longer? Then she recalled the shadow over the spire, the burning eyes…

What came from her lips fell upon the room like a crushing weight.

"He's coming."

The Maiden saw realization dawn on the aged face of what must have been a wizard next to the Prince. He backed away and looked around the room as if the beast were in there with them.

"Candelyte!" the Maiden heard him call out, and a small fairy that looked like it was on fire darted next to his head.

"Can you see him approaching?" the Wizard asked.

The fairy moved with fascinating speed out of the room and returned almost immediately.

"Did… did you even look, friend?" the Wizard asked incredulously.

The fairy was prepared to protest when a great quake shook the whole of the building. Dust and gravel fell around them.

"He's already here…" the fairy whispered, terrified.

The Prince and Warrior drew their swords, but the Wizard lifted a hand to stay their actions. He reached into his robes and pulled forth something and held it tightly. No one could see what it was that he guarded. He began whispering quickly and his clutched fingers began shaking uncontrollably.

"Foolish," a baritone voice hissed down at them. "Were I not so patient I would roast you all for a good meal."

"And destroy your treasures?" the Prince goaded him.

Wyvern chuckled. "Treasures? A treasure denotes excess, debauchery. Something I'm not above, but I assure you I do not hoard treasures. I have nothing that does not have a purpose. Fearsome, dangerous, destructive—and all unknown to you."

"You do not know who stands against you here, worm!" the Warrior called out.

Outside the ruins, Wyvern perched among the remains of the small tower. He knew there were trespassers when he was closer to where he would land. He could smell them. It was only after coming to perch atop his lair that he could tell who the intruders were.

He inhaled deeply taking in the air. "You are very wrong, son of Edda."

The Warrior exchanged a perplexed look with the Prince.

"I can smell the burning sands. I smell the stain on your weapons. 'The Blood of a Thousand Victories'. You cannot clean that much blood from steel. It's dull, cloying, and acrid—but exhilarating. You do your people proud. I can smell the foul stench of jormungandr within it. Impressive."

Wyvern took a few careful steps toward a walled walkway next to the tower.

"I also smell tanned leather and fine steel. Oh, and the sweet stench of fear—hello, little Prince. The Coward of Avallonis graces my home… and he brings his pet wizard. The cacophony of smells the old man emits is humorous at best."

Wyvern made his way closer to them. He moved with surprising silence and swiftness.

"Ah, and the flowers. The countless scents of blossoms and perfumes—I see the Maiden is still here. Very wise. She is all that prevents your incineration," he threatened.

Those within watched and listened carefully, not knowing what Wyvern planned. Such was the silence that loosened dirt could be heard falling from the ceiling. They waited as the seconds passed like hours. Their hearts beat within their chests like war drums.

A sudden roar ripped through the air as the stones of the wall fell away behind them. Wyvern had launched himself against the crumbling structure and torn away a section of the wall and ceiling. He hissed and growled at them. He glared at the companions as they stepped toward him. Wyvern positioned himself, preparing to lash out with his lethal, barbed tail. He would have burnt them all to ash had he not needed the Maiden.

Two quick strikes were aimed at the Wizard to prevent him from casting any spells he had no doubt prepared. The Warrior, closest to the old man, batted away the stinger with his blade. The second was deflected by the Prince's shield as he smashed into Wyvern's tail. The Wizard stumbled backward and Wyvern went for the kill.

As he pulled his muscular tail back, a searing pain shot through his eye and into his head and face. His vision was blurred by flame and clung to him like a possessed cinder. He recognized the shouts as coming from one of the Pyremoth fairies; the wretches had released them somehow. The fire of the fairies' rage was white-hot and, being a uniquely potent source of magical flame, he felt every moment of it. It was an agony that would be repaid in kind.

Wyvern roared and shook his head viciously. The fairy clung to the scales surrounding his eyes and unleashed her fury—burning brighter with each passing moment. The Prince saw the opportunity to escape and pulled the Maiden from her resting place.

They began descending the rockslide created by the collapsed tower to the path below. As they rushed haphazardly down the debris, the Maiden and Prince fell when Wyvern's lashing tail struck the Prince's leg. A loud crack was heard and the Prince howled in pain as they rolled down what was left of the debris.

At the bottom, the Prince attempted to right himself and fell heavily to the ground, shouting in agony. The Warrior and Wizard assisted him to his feet. As they did, they heard another fiendish roar from Wyvern above. They looked to see him shaking his head violently and clawing at his snout and eyes.

Candelyte was thrown from his face and against a crumbled portion of the tower. A small, straight trail of fire indicated the violence with which she was hurled against the stone like a ray of light. She had no sooner struck the rubble when Wyvern bellowed a vicious blast of dragonfire that engulfed the small fairy along with a large portion of the wall.

The Wizard looked on in impotent fury. The Warrior urged him on, insisting that they retreat while they had the chance. They were in no condition to fight Wyvern in their current state. Just before he turned to flee he saw Wyvern cease what seemed to be an endless current of flame. The Pyremoth fairies, for all their torrid properties, were still no match for dragonfire. Candelyte was gone—destroyed by Wyvern, and not even ashes remained as a memory of her.

The Wizard cursed the beast. So much so that he nearly turned away from his companions and faced the monster. The Prince's sudden cry of pain as he put weight on his leg tempered the Wizard's rage. They had found the Maiden and they now must flee Wyvern's wrath if they were to keep her safe.

33

ALL ARE GATHERED

Above all that was occurring, above the scattered trees, rocks, and ruins, a falcon soared in the clouds. This particular raptor was set apart from others of its kind. Its feathered wings were adorned with deep violet runes. Its light gray plumage hid it from sight as it traveled on the winds of magic at unthinkable speed. It knew it had found what it was seeking when it saw Wyvern in a fit of rage below.

With its keen eyes, it also spotted the four figures escaping along the derelict road that coursed the forgotten woodlands. The four slowed then cut sharply into the woods. Immediately after Wyvern recovered from some sort of malady, momentarily nursing one side of its face, it spit fire in aggravation and pain and then took the skies just above the trees to look for them.

The falcon plunged into a rapid dive, becoming a blurred, grey bolt barely visible in the sky. It coursed along a direct route to the four escapees. Just as it hit the canopy it lifted its wings to halt its flight. In a spectacular display, the four companions stopped short of a mighty gust of wind slamming into the ground and sending leaves and dust swirling into the air. The Maiden recognized the Sybil as her robes slowly settled amid the dissipating vortex.

The Warrior stepped away from the Prince ensuring first that the Wizard could bear his weight alone. He then drew his sword against the newcomer. He stalked toward her carefully in a defensive posture.

"Stay your blade, Warrior—she's a sorceress. Your steel will do little against her magic," the Wizard cautioned.

"No!" the Maiden shouted. "She's no enemy! Put your weapon away."

The Warrior hesitated but obliged. He slowly backed away to the Prince, but he never took his gaze from the Sybil.

"Good to see you again, dear," the Sybil said with a smile. "Now, give me a moment with this rather incensed monstrosity you've crossed."

She reached down and grabbed a handful of leaves from the ground. She began arranging them in her hands.

"No... no... yes, here..." the Sybil mumbled to herself as she arranged the leaves in her hand.

"We should run," the Warrior insisted. "Wyvern has turned his attention to us—he'll be upon on us any moment!"

"Yes, agreed. Come, child," the Wizard said to the Maiden.

"Ah, there! Perfect!" the Sybil shouted.

She threw the leaves into the air, but instead of a sparse few, an explosive plume of vegetation leaped forth from her hands. Everyone recoiled in surprise, expecting to be doused with falling leaves and for Wyvern to head directly towards the fountain of green and gold that shot forth from the forest. To their great surprise, nothing of the sort happened. Not so much as a single leaf fell.

Wyvern saw clearly where the four pests fled into the forests. He found it almost laughable at how easy they would be to apprehend. If necessary he'd simply light the woods ablaze and let them burn in their trap. Then a peculiar thing happened; he lost their scent entirely.

It didn't fade as though they outdistanced him. Nor did it become muddled from some vain tempt to swim or hide under-water or flee underground. It didn't trail off. It simply, completely, disappeared.

Their clumsy forms among the branches could no longer be seen. They'd disappeared as well. Gone from sight, sound, and smell. Wyvern began huffing, smoke pouring from his mouth and nostrils, as the idea of defeat set in. He lost them and they'd stolen his prize. He beat his wings heavily against the air as he hovered above where he last spotted them. He released another roar of renewed frustration.

Contemptible wretches! Thieves! he brooded. He scanned the canopy for them, but his sight was blurred and his vision impaired by the Pyremoth fairy's damage. His other eye pained him greatly and his vision was clouded as the injured eye watered. He couldn't track them in this state.

"Very well, cowards," he seethed as they listened below within the Sybil's magical façade. "The Maiden was important, but not necessary. The Diamond Spire is still mine."

With that, he snorted a puff of flame in contempt. His wings beat faster as he flew away. Within the safety of the trees and the Sybil's enchantment, they observed him returning to his lair. When he left, he carried with him a bundle of rucksacks in his claws.

The Sybil turned to see them attempting to assist the Prince to a fallen log. As they sat him down he winced in pain. A wounded prince, a confused maiden, and an angry wizard. They were quite the gathering. The loyal warrior attempted to remove the Prince's greaves to view the injury.

With Wyvern no longer an immediate concern, it appeared they would be resting here for the night.

34

A SMALL BREAK

Having evaded Wyvern, the group focused their efforts on attending to the injured Prince. The Sybil, with her knowledge in healing arts and herbs, insisted she be allowed to see the injury. The Wizard was still suspicious of her and reluctant to let her anywhere near his Prince.

"And why would I let you near my king?" he challenged.

"I do believe I just saved us all," the Sybil returned derisively.

The Wizard continued to stare at her, his eyes narrow and unrelenting. The Sybil scoffed.

"I also recall her vouching for me," she said with a nod to the Maiden.

The Wizard huffed. "I suppose."

"You suppose? Well, I *suppose* that will do. Now allow me to attend to the young man's wounds you cantankerous old fop," the Sybil said brusquely.

She approached him with her head held high and walked with a grace one would not expect from a lady hiding out in the woods.

"Step aside, please," she said with polite firmness.

The Wizard cast a reproachful look in her direction and

nodded his encouragement to the Prince. The Sybil knelt before him; his face was pallid and he was sweating profusely. She feared the worst; if Wyvern had stung him he would be dead any moment. Looking at the state of his wound, she placed a gentle hand over her lips.

"Oh, dear," she whispered.

"What is it?" the Prince asked through heavy, pained breaths.

"Well, it… it could be worse," the Sybil pointed out with a rising inflection that fooled no one. "You haven't been stung, but… well, you have quite the injury nonetheless."

"Let me see," the Wizard interjected.

He pushed his way forward like a panicked parent to inspect the wound. The Prince saw exasperation fall upon his face. The Wizard pursed his lips and ran his hand along his short beard, noticeably grayer than the Prince remembered.

"It's an ugly break," the Sybil whispered to the Wizard. "You can almost see…"

"Yes, you can," the Wizard interrupted, stopping her from saying it aloud for the Prince to hear.

"It must be set back into place. Otherwise, it won't matter what else I do," the Sybil said with genuine empathy.

"I agree. I'll help," the Wizard said.

The Warrior, who had been listening to the conversation, looked over both of them as they knelt before the Prince.

"No, I'll set the bone," he said, speaking as though he were commanding his Red Warriors.

The two mages turned and looked at him, obviously doubtful. The Warrior looked back and forth between them briefly.

"I don't doubt your skills, but I've set many broken limbs in the field. I can correct the break; you can apply your balms."

The Wizard and Sybil regarded each other for a moment. It was a sound idea. They both readily agreed. The Warrior looked to the Maiden, his eyes firm but gentle.

"Maybe you should assist the Sybil in preparing the salve?" the

Warrior said to her. He knew there'd be cracking, blood, and screaming. She knew he was trying to spare her the sight.

The Maiden shook her head and placed her hand on the Prince's shoulder. "No, I'll stay with him."

She sat next to him and looked him in the eyes. They were squinted and bloodshot from pain and exertion, but they softened when she gave him a soothing smile.

The Warrior removed his belt and doubled it over twice. He gave it to the Prince.

"You'll want to bite on this."

The Maiden reached for the Prince's free hand, but the Warrior quickly grabbed it.

"I wouldn't do that," he said firmly. "If you wish to help, hold his leg, around the thigh—hard, with everything you have."

The Warrior positioned himself and gripped the wounded shin. He looked at the Prince and they both nodded. With a quick, ghastly snap the Warrior felt the bones realign beautifully. It was quite a contradiction to the horrendous screaming coming from the Prince. His howls were muffled by his clenched jaw.

The Maiden flinched at both noises. The Warrior saw that tears had appeared in her eyes. It was not pleasant to hear a pained, screaming man, even for a seasoned warrior. This young woman would have difficulty with such a thing even if she didn't have feelings for the Prince, which the Warrior saw that she quite clearly had.

The Maiden held his leg as best she could. The Prince was strong. Even stronger than the last time they'd met. His leg flexed and writhed in agony before they finally went limp and the screaming stopped. She felt a sharp pang of fear at first, thinking he had succumbed to the wound. She saw his chest moving slowly and rhythmically, thankfully having only lost consciousness from the pain.

The Warrior stood and gave a heavy sigh. "He's strong; lasted longer than others before passing out. We need to wrap the wound. It's time for the mages to do their work."

The Warrior left them. The Sybil and the Wizard were walking among the trees and brush looking for additional items they may need: berries, herbs, and such. The Maiden looked at the Prince and regretted the irony of their situation. How long had he watched her slumber, waiting for her to awaken, and now in only moments their fortunes were reversed?

She stroked his hair—dirty and touched with sweat—and it was still the greatest sensation she had felt in days. It was one of the *only* sensations she had felt in days, actually. How much time had passed while she walked in her ethereal state? Her wanderings were punctuated with empty, black slates of time.

As she questioned her recent experiences she looked down at the Prince's wound. They had narrowly avoided tragedy. The Prince had merely been caught by Wyvern's tail and it was the beast's great strength that snapped his leg. Had he been stung or even scratched by that heinous barb, the Maiden knew he would be dead before he'd come to a stop at the bottom of the rubble.

She reached for his leg, wanting to observe the wound. She gently cupped the bandaged appendage in her hand and steadied it with the other. The bandages were caked with blood and made for a sorrowful sight. It was only a few moments, however, before she felt a tingling in her hand. It wasn't painful or uncomfortable—just a light prickling sensation all along where her skin made contact with the Prince's wound.

She looked on as the color slowly returned to the Prince's leg and, eventually, his face. His sweating stopped and his breathing returned to normal. What just happened?

The Maiden began to unwrap the bandages and then suddenly stopped for fear of hurting the Prince or exacerbating his wounds. She looked up quickly to see him slumbering peacefully. She continued to unravel the sticky bandages until they fell away.

The Prince's shin was covered in the blood from his wrappings. It was difficult to see much at first. Then the Maiden saw... nothing. No wound, nor scar, nor scratch. There was nothing beneath the blood, except for a leg that was as whole and healthy as it had ever been. His wounds had been completely and unquestionably healed by her own hands.

35

REVELATIONS

S he looked at her hands and saw nothing had changed about them. The tingling sensation was quickly ebbing and was soon gone in seconds. Her breathing quickened; she was in utter disbelief. She didn't think she could be surprised by anything anymore—but here she was again. She called to the Sybil and the Wizard who came running towards her.

She pointed to the Prince's healed wound and explained all that had happened. The Sybil seemed to be less surprised than the Wizard, but the Sybil had spent time with the Maiden and was privy to her mysterious gifts. The Wizard only knew her as a trinket peddler.

The Wizard, eyes alight, asked, "Has this happened before?"

The Maiden looked at him and sighed. It was quite apparent in her face that there was much to tell. The Maiden and the Sybil told the Wizard of the events that had occurred in Mythesta. The Maiden explained that some of her memories were still unclear. Flashes of a man in auburn robes and a brass city were slowly coming back to her, but much was still missing before her arrival at the Amethyst Realm. The Wizard grimaced, piecing together that she was likely describing the eccentric wizard of Vitruvia.

She told of the boglins and butterflies, of the Sybil and the swamps. Finally, she told him of the Violet Witch and her black magic.

The Wizard asked for more detail of her encounter at the top of the Amethyst Spire. The Maiden spoke in detail of Tytania and her imprisonment within the Barghest and the disappearance of her king. The Warrior's eyes widened at this.

She told of the witch's black serpents that struck out and devoured the magic the Sybil and Tytania threw at her. She spoke of the serpents' apparent fear of her, their recoiling from her touch, and her ability to pluck them from the oily light that had protected the witch. She explained how they turned to ash at her touch.

It was difficult for the Maiden to judge the Wizard's thoughts of her tale. His eyes burned with inward wonderings but his face wrinkled in apprehension.

"This is startling news. The Lord of Dreams knew of what he spoke when he said you were a unique spirit," the Wizard said to the Maiden, then turned to the Sybil. "I've no doubt he aided you finding the young woman?"

The Sybil crossed her arms in protest. "I am a friend of the Dream Lord, but I'm a sybil, not just a sorceress. I can see many things even you cannot."

She grimaced and scoffed. "But, yes… he did help. A little."

"Did he tell you anything of her gift?"

"No, and I know little more than you do," the Sybil shrugged. "He said she was in a dream-like state. Neither dead nor alive. I assume that scar upon her hand can attest to something magical or supernatural."

The Sybil gestured to the Maiden's hand where a circular scar marred her skin. Having been held by Wyvern, the Sybil deduced that she'd somehow been stung by the monster. It should have killed her, but here she stood.

He looked to the Maiden as she regarded the scar on her

hand. It was a horrible memory and one she wished she could forget, that it would slip away into the black nothing between her wandering memories.

"You are quite a special young woman, aren't you?" the Wizard said, offering a comforting smile.

She forced a smile in return. "I find myself suddenly longing for the mundane."

"So long as Wyvern lives, I fear none of us will ever know anything of the mundane," the Warrior added.

"Indeed. He flies to the Diamond Spire. Assuming he has no other business, he will make it there within a few days," the Wizard sighed.

"Whatever it is that he's scheming, his goal lies there. This is his endgame," the Warrior said darkly.

"Then we must do something. The Violet Wizardess has returned to power, ruling as stewardess until the Violet King returns; surely she has soldiers or apprentices she can send?" the Sybil knew the offer was only half-hearted. Tytania would still be trying to rebuild the realm after the witch's destructive rule.

The Warrior turned to the Sybil, she saw confusion and hurt on his gruff, dirty face. He looked as though he wanted to say something, but had trouble finding the words.

"Your wizardess waits for her king?"

The Sybil's eyes narrowed, "Yes? Why, have you seen him? Is he in Edda as she suspects?"

She sounded hopeful. When she saw the Warrior's face droop even further, a pit formed in her stomach. "What is it?"

The Warrior looked to the Prince, who was still resting. He wished the young ruler was awake and could help him convey the tragic news to the Sybil. The young ruler was much better with words.

"King Perithane is dead. He was cursed..."

"...by my sister," the Sybil interrupted bitterly. "What happened?"

"He was slain," the Warrior spoke slowly, "by us and my warriors. He was trapped in the shape of a beast. He was murdering whole villages. We had to stop him. He was grateful that we did."

The Sybil crossed her arms, trying to hold her emotions together. So much suffering because of her sister. Because she couldn't do what she had needed to.

"The Stewardess of the Violet Throne will need to know," she said calmly, though sadness laced her words. "Let's find this wicked creature and Morgæna, and put a stop to their madness."

"Now that an explanation has been given for the Barghest, the Red Warriors garrisoned near Mythesta will need to be recalled," the Warrior said. "I believe if I go to them, their commander can be convinced to reroute them immediately to face the true threat in the Diamond Realm."

Life or death, the Wizard thought.

Life or death. The plight of the Maiden and Wyvern, as well as their mysterious connection, was beginning to make a level of sense.

"Yes, yes..." the Wizard stammered, shaking a knowing finger at a sudden revelation. "Lead them to the border of the Diamond Realm, but do not enter! Wyvern will know and we mustn't draw his attention."

The Wizard looked to the Sybil and the Maiden. "I have someone I must see; an old friend who may be able to assist us. As soon as the Prince wakes, I want the two of you," he looked to the Maiden and Sybil, "to make for the Diamond Realm. Take the road through Mythesta, it should be safe now, and head north. When you reach the Diamond Realm head west just as you cross its borders. You will find a smallholding with Gnome's Nose growing along the roadside—a lot of it." He addressed the Maiden directly, "You should know the looks of the herb. Stay there until I arrive. You'll be safe."

He looked to the Warrior. "Bring your army. We'll need every advantage we can get." He looked back to the Maiden, "Do you know how to ride, young lady?"

"I do, but…" she tried to speak up but was interrupted.

"Ride?" the Warrior chuckled. "Our horses are on the other side of a mountain, remember?"

In his excitement, the Wizard most certainly did not remember.

"The Hynefol," he mumbled.

"It's ok, the…" the Maiden tried to cut in again.

"The dryads are still tending to them," the Warrior said, finishing the Wizard's thought.

"Dryads? How lovely! I wonder if I could meet them?" the Sybil commented.

"Would you listen to me for one moment?" the Maiden shouted. All heads turned to her, surprised at her uncharacteristic outburst.

"The Prince's leg is healed," she said to the Sybil, reminding her that though he still slept from the exertion and would likely be unconscious for several hours at least, he was no longer maimed.

"How far away is this place?" she continued.

The Wizard and the Warrior looked at one another. It seemed like a lifetime ago when they'd made their way through the narrow, dank, and disorienting tunnel.

"It's difficult to say," the Wizard explained, "but I'd say no more than half a day's travel."

The Maiden shook her head firmly. "Then we'll wake the Prince and make our way through the tunnel. You hurry to where you need to be, Wizard. We'll meet you at the border of the Diamond Realm."

The Wizard looked concerned by her plan. "Are you sure, my lady? Travelling on foot at this moment…"

"Is the only option we have, unless you have horses hidden in your pockets," the Maiden finished for him.

The Wizard's eyes lingered on the Maiden.

"Spires-all, you do, don't you?" she sighed, crossing her arms.

"Only two vials are left," he clarified, feigning insult. "And there's still the issue of the Prince. He's unconscious and will have to be carried through the tunnel. It's already a squeeze as is."

"I can carry him," the Warrior offered, "but it will be slow-going."

"Maybe not," the Sybil chimed in. She retrieved a small feather from an Evening Sparrow, native to Mythesta, from within her robes. She placed the feather under the Prince's breastplate, secured so as not to fall out. She placed her hand on the breast-plate, over where she tucked in the feather. Whispering a few brief words, she removed her hand and then placed both arms under the Prince. She lifted him as though he weighed nothing at all.

The Warriors eyes widened and the Wizard nodded. "Very nice," the old man commented.

"Now," the Sybil said, "this should make carrying him through the tunnel much easier."

She passed the Prince off to the Warrior, who braced for the weight. He was left feeling both surprised and foolish when he discovered the Prince weighed, literally, nothing at all.

The Sybil took a quick breath, like she came to a decision, and began detailing a plan.

"We'll need one of your magic stallions. The Edding can take his own horse. The Maiden can ride the Prince's and I'll ride this sparkly steed of yours. It doesn't seem very princely placing the young man over the back of a horse like a sack of vegetables, but we'll find better transport once we're out of the Hynefol."

Everyone was silent for a moment after the Sybil finished elaborating on their situation. Her eyes flicked between them all. "Well?" she clipped.

"Very well," the Wizard said, and produced one of the smoke-filled vials that would provide the Sybil a ride for their journey

The Wizard looked back and forth between the seasoned fighter and mysterious sorceress he'd only recently become acquainted with. They did owe their lives to her. He folded his hands into the sleeves of his robes and cleared his throat.

"We've only just met, and we owe you our lives. There's powerful magic you're heading into. Please, protect them. The Warrior will have to leave you once you reach the outskirts of the Hynefol. If I'm correct, then what's coming could be devastating to us all."

She smirked and clasped her arms behind her back.

"You're not going to tell me about your hunch, are you?"

He nodded slowly. "If I'm right, I'd rather you not know. I need you focused on getting to my safehouse and wait for me without distraction."

She sighed softly. "No harm will come to her. Or him, so far as we ride together."

The Wizard pursed his lips. The Sybil could see his hesitation and worry. "You have my word, " she said softly.

The Wizard turned and approached the Warrior, still holding the unconscious Prince. The Warrior gave the Wizard a sharp and respectful nod. "Well meet again," the Warrior said confidently.

THE WIZARD PRODUCED the last vial filled with roiling smoke. "I save this for emergencies," he commented. "I'd say this is as good a time as any."

He poured the smoke from the vial, which fell like thin smoke on the ground. It swirled and grew, curling up from the ground. A ghostly whinny echoed around them, and a white stallion coalesced as the smoke faded. As he mounted the very life-like conjuration, the Wizard reminded them each of their responsibility: reroute the Edding army, find his safehouse, and above all, protect the Maiden. The Wizard assured them he would rendezvous with them within a matter of days.

They said their farewells and parted ways.

"Spires help us," the Wizard thought aloud. "The coming days bring great peril; perhaps ruin."

36

THE OPAL SPIRE

The Wizard's road took him beyond Emrallt's verdant hills, which he always found breathtaking. His arcane stallion rode through them like a mote of marble light tracing a rolling sea of jade. He kept the powerful, snow-covered Veil Mountains to his right and followed their natural flow through the recovering countryside of Mythesta. His steed was a creature of magic and wouldn't tire or require rest. He would have to take full advantage of his tireless companion.

He rode continuously until the mountains subsided the draining swamps were replaced with rocky hills. The fallows and forests turned to light grasses and countless small rivers and rocky lakes and ponds. The air grew cool and dry. A light but constant breeze began to blow. He rode until the air smelled of salt and grew humid once again. He had finally arrived in the coastal realm of Upala.

It was written throughout the multitude of tomes and historical documents of the spire-realms that each kingdom was as unique as its people. Each with its own beauties and flaws. It was the balance of the world and was held firm by the spire's influence over its respective realm. The great gems exuded pure magical essence. It was the study of this essence that led to the first wizards. It was their study of the ancient tomes that led to their proficiency in the arcane. The gemstones and their towers were not all-powerful, they discovered. The towers could fall and the jewels be destroyed. It was here in the Opal Realm that such a discovery was first made.

An ancient king in times long ago, his name forgotten but his deeds remaining as a scar of his reign, had sought to move the location of the Opal Spire. He was not pleased with its location on one island amid many just off the coast. He desired to rule from a seat on the mainland. At the recommendation of his advisor, the Viridian Wizard, he attempted to see if the Great Opal could possibly be relocated. At first, the Viridian King used typical methods; wedges, pulleys, and other contraptions.

When this proved futile he returned to the court wizard for additional ideas. The king asked the wizard to scour every tome for spells of every kind: enchantments, incantations, conjurations, and invocations—anything that would move the Great Opal. The wizard studied relentlessly. He examined every spell in the Upaleen libraries and every secret text his predecessor passed to him. He called for aid from the Wizard's Council. None of the other spire-wizards could offer any spell that would safely remove the gemstone.

It was then for the first time in millennia that a wizard attempted to create new magic. He pored over texts unimaginable in size. He crafted his own ink from the galls of oak trees hundreds of years old (rumored to have been taken from the Hynefol itself) and vitriol from master dwarven craftsmen in the Veil Mountains. He cooked it with wine from the king's stores and used a particularly rare and expensive (some would say priceless) vintage that has since been lost to time. He then enchanted the ink with the tears of a weeping, winged horse, and dust of gold. Using as a quill the feather of a rare albino cliff eagle he inscribed the new spell on cured vellum imported from Mythesta.

His heart racing, he felt the spell was ready. The elements of the spell were worth a large fortune and this was only intended to be conjured a single time. On as still a day as was possible in the gusty province, the Viridian Wizard approached the top of the spire. He used the open-arched stairway that led to the stone-paved roof of the gilded tower. He stood there with the king who had come to witness the momentous event he had waited nearly a year for, when the wizard first began to concoct his spell.

The Viridian Wizard approached the massive, elliptical opal as the rays of the sun set its colors afire. He opened the vellum scroll and whispered a spell that set it ablaze. The vellum was untouched, but the words themselves glowed brightly. The wizard read the scroll aloud, and the light of the words engulfed the scroll entirely. The wizard released the vellum as though he had been burned, but found he was unhurt. There was only silence in return.

The king bellowed, accusing the wizard of his greatest failure. The wizard's arms dropped to his sides as he stood there befuddled and embarrassed, his mouth agape. Then, the same light that had engulfed the scribed letters began to glow within the Great Opal. It grew so bright that those present were forced to avert their eyes. After a few moments, there came a rumbling like a clap of distant, tremulous thunder.

A wave of force, a powerful gale burst forth from the Opal. It was accompanied by an explosive din that could be heard for miles around. The Viridian Queen, escorted by her guards, ran to see what occurred. They found the rooftop empty; the force had thrown the mage and the king from the tower. The wizard's body was found shattered on the rocks on the coast adjacent to the spire's northern wall. The king's body was never recovered, likely having been thrown into the ocean. More shocking still, the

Queen saw something no monarch of the spires had ever seen before—a crack marred the surface of the Great Opal.

Fear struck the heart of Septer soon after. The great stones could indeed be damaged. If they could be damaged they could be destroyed. None knew what sort of catastrophe would occur should such a thing come to pass, nor the power required to do so, but after the folly of the Viridian Wizard and the Viridian King none dared trifle with the gems again. No wizard has since attempted the creation of new magic. They repaired what had been damaged by the foolhardy king, including the careful restoration of the quartz mantle on which stood the Great Opal.

The Wizard wondered if such a grievous act was part of Wyvern's plan. If so, why would he risk such a thing? What did it have to do with the Maiden? Why did he use the witch-sisters as pawns to control other realms? Was it total control he wanted? Or total destruction? He had one too many questions needing answers, but he knew it was here he could find them if he were to find them anywhere.

The Diamond Realm had been led by its king to a golden age that surpassed the other realms of this generation. In that sense it held a great measure of power, but Upala was far older than any other realm. It may have very well been the first, but this was beyond the scope of the Wizard's concept of time.

Here, the Wizard would speak of things long forgotten by mortals. He would visit with a friend unique among living creatures. The Wizard found his friend's home near a small mountain that once touched the sky, but had been weathered over eons to a mere outcropping compared to its former self. The old heart of the mountain now raked against the sky like dragon's teeth. The symbolism was not lost on the Wizard.

37

FATHER DRAGON

The gate was as welcoming as ever: two ancient columns, crumbling with age and colored a dull teal from the salt air held aloft two roaring lions. One was missing an outstretched paw. The somewhat humble and decrepit entrance failed to herald what awaited within. The power and magnificence of Father Dragon were as potent as ever.

He entered the primeval halls that had forever been inhabited by the original dragon-kin. The walls were polished smooth and carved with murals and writings by archaic dwarven craftsmen who made a pilgrimage to his home to honor him. Father Dragon had no fear of them or any real creature knowing of his lair—he was the mightiest of beasts. His children were respected, or feared, enough for their own power; who was to question the strength of their father?

The Wizard took a torch from its holding place among the many that lined the walls. These were lit by the Upaleen pilgrims that visited this entryway, thinking that doing so would invoke the blessing of the dragon and bring good fortune.

"And who has come so far to disturb an old god?" a voice thundered from within the throat of the great stone hall.

The Wizard smirked. Father Dragon had most likely smelled the Wizard as soon as he set foot within his lair. He also noted the humor that tinged the voice.

"An equally old friend," The Wizard called out.

"Equally?" Father Dragon scoffed. "You have lived but a blink of an existence, by comparison, friend."

"All perspective," the Wizard said flatly.

Dragon stood with a thunderous rumble coming from his throat as he stretched tight muscles. The Wizard's presence had awoken him from a weeks-long slumber. He opened his tooth-filled maw with a boisterous yawn and the Wizard felt the heat from his gullet even at a good distance. Dragon reared his long neck back and blasted a wave of flame—as hot as molten lead—into the chimney-shaped alcove above him.

The rock of this mountain persisted through the ages because it was a substance known as sunstone; it could be found in the Veil Mountains, as well, but only as small clusters among striations of coal. When Dragon found this particular mountain he could smell a great knot of the sunstone and bore out his home with his all-consuming breath. Now, whenever he desired light, he would bellow a searing lungful into the dragon-made alcove and the mystical stone would alight with the ferocity of a fresh torch, but burn for many hours longer even if submerged in water. With the copious amount of the substance above him the Wizard looked up to see a wondrous sight akin to a chandelier of stars just out of reach.

"You always find the choicest locations," the Wizard remarked.

"Much better than that seaside hovel," Dragon replied.

"The one with the walls littered with turquoise and sparkling quartz? Yes, quite a hovel," the Wizard replied sardonically.

"It was too humid. Surely, you do not visit to discuss my humble warren."

"No, I do not. I come for a more dire reason. A more personal one," the Wizard said sadly.

"My son," Dragon stated matter-of-factly.

The Wizard looked at him. His eyes, burning red-orange, were sad. It didn't need to be said which son he spoke of. Father Dragon was not omnipotent, but he was as intelligent as they came, and had couriers carry news of the realms most important events to him. He mostly preferred to keep to himself, but his intervention might be greatly needed now.

"My lord, we cannot sit by any longer. He's drawn the spires into his game. Why have his brothers and sister not intervened? Do they not feel the need to protect their homes and realms?"

"Such dramatics," Dragon sighed, a sound like a geyser venting steam.

Dragon and his children had, so very long ago, decided it best to parcel the lands of the spires among themselves. Though majestic, powerful, and nigh immortal, those of dragonkind were still creatures of emotion and habit. They desired homes of their own, and were protective of them. To prevent conflicts and disputes Father Dragon had tasked his children with finding a home suitable to them among the realms, but allowed that only one dragon-child may lair within a given realm.

They had each returned within a year. They'd agreed upon their territories of choice and an oath was sworn among them. They would not interfere or encroach upon one another's realms. They were the children of Dragon and they all knew the importance of the ancient gilded towers and the sovereignty of man—who had ever ruled them. Dragon was pleased with his children, including even the boisterous Hydra and devious Wyvern.

"The dragon-children; they act according to their natures to a fault. Hydra and Naga are long dead. I wouldn't find it surprising if Wyvern were involved in some way, though the legends would exonerate him. Drake has been most active in investigating his brother's activities, of course," Dragon explained.

"Of course," agreed the Wizard.

"But, he is true to his word and treads lightly when involved in the affairs and realms of his kin. Wyrm is content in his studies. I have heard nothing from him in ages—longer than your family line has existed, in fact. Even Naga had heard naught from her brother when she appealed to him for aid against the humans in his own realm before being slain."

"Baeol," the Wizard clarified. "He's a legend among we humans."

The dragon sniffed; he didn't blame the humans for the action taken against his fickle and ill-tempered daughter. He wouldn't stoop to call her slayer a 'legend', however.

"Baeol—that is what Drake called him. What would this Baeol have thought if he knew he fought a dragon-child not far from the doorstep of her brother?" Dragon asked the Wizard.

"Her brother, Wyrm?" the Wizard clarified.

Wyrm was as reclusive as any creature came. His purpose within Edda was multi-layered. He enjoyed the solitude that the burning sands provided and constructed his home deep within the ground where it was cool and sheltered. The entrance to his lair was unknown even to his kin. He communicated with Dragon and his other family by equally enigmatic means. Dragon would simply wake to find a rolled vellum, scribed in the intricate writing style of the intellectual Wyrm, tucked away in a bottle made of glass from the Edding desert. This was how Dragon learned of Naga's fate at the hands of Baeol. It was also how he learned of Wyrm's dismay at her passing, but also of the withholding of his support of his sister as she had trespassed on his land and brought war to the Edding people.

This, Father, is proof uncontestable of the capability of the Sons of Edda. The letter had said in closing. None of his children had entered their brother's realm since.

"He knew of what transpired. Naga brought her fate upon

herself and Wyrm was quite correct in his assumptions of man's aptitudes," Dragon said.

"But we did nothing to invoke Wyvern's wrath; and what of Drake and Serpent? Certainly, they do not sit idly by?" the Wizard asked with mounting concern.

"Wyrm's intellect is unrivaled, but Wyvern is cunning and manipulative. No doubt he has conversed with Wyrm and convinced him to remain in his den and tend to his studies. Drake is strong and good-natured, but wit and wisdom were never his greatest faculties. Wyvern will out-think him in any given situation; he possibly has him flying circles in Avallonis as we speak. Serpent... She has her own troubles to attend to. The Gray King and Gray Wizard have gone missing."

The Wizard's brow rose. "And you honestly don't suspect Wyvern has a hand in that?"

Dragon's gaze narrowed. "You speak of my kin as though you know all their comings and goings. Wyvern has forsaken his realm and stirred mischief among your own... all of which will be dealt with in due time."

"Do you not know the extent of your son's actions?" the Wizard said with daring skepticism. "Do you not recall the Hyne-fol? The lich? The otherwise completely unremarkable young woman he obsesses over despite his interest being solely in the unique and nigh-unobtainable? He took two witches under his wing, pardon the expression, and traded power for their obedi-ence. Morgæna was one of them. The other placed a hex on the Violet King and Wizardess. The Amethyst realm was contami-nated by dark magic for a decade; its king terrorized the Edding sands as a mindless beast. Once the actions of the witch-sister were discovered, the Red King sent an army to Mythesta's border to prepare for retaliation. Wyvern is stoking the fires of war among the realms!"

"Enough!" Dragon roared as fire coursed from between his

teeth and out his nostrils. His eyes flared as he looked down upon the Wizard. The walls trembled and the ground shook.

"How is it that I have not been made aware of such things? You are an honorable man, an old friend, and you bring this hearsay to my chamber?" Dragon barked.

"How long have you slumbered? Upala is a peaceful land and you've overseen it wisely, but how much attention have you truly paid to the world around it?"

Dragon thought on this. His children were mature—old enough to handle their own affairs. With certain promises made he could not—would not—have intervened if it was warranted. So, he slept.

"I have been resting for some time," he admitted.

"Wyvern must be stopped. Leave this place; come with me— we must ride to the Diamond Spire," the Wizard beseeched him.

The Dragon appeared suddenly distraught. "The Diamond Spire—Wyvern goes next to the Diamond Spire?"

"Yes... why do you seem so concerned, and so suddenly?" the Wizard asked, feeling a deep foreboding.

"Tell me of this young woman you mentioned," Dragon said.

The Wizard, stuttering slightly at the change of subject but curious as to the Dragon's reasoning, told of his and the Avallonian prince's time with the Maiden. He spoke of the gentle presence she radiated, and the wonders she had performed at Wyvern's temple. The Wizard spoke of the light in her eyes and how her voice spoke with unconditional kindness and compassion. He had truly never met a woman like her or who possessed her gift. She was unquestionably endearing, but otherwise utterly commonplace.

The Wizard stopped suddenly, seeing the Dragon's head wilt in a mournful fashion. The creature's eyes were squinted and pained. It took a few moments, but the Wizard saw the glassy eyes of one prepared to weep. Dragon's tears came slowly and scarcely, and a deep rumble escaped his throat.

"Is what Wyvern plans for the lady so terrible?" the Wizard asked.

"I do not weep for the Maiden," Dragon said softly. "I weep for my son."

"I... don't understand," the Wizard said quietly.

Dragon lifted his head to the alcove above his chamber where the heatstones still burned brightly. He recalled the memories of his dragon-children; noble Drake, beautiful Serpent, scholarly Wyrm, fiery Naga, boastful Hydra, and, of course, the sly Wyvern. Each one of them with their strengths and weaknesses. Wyvern, however, had always been a matter of concern. The smallest of his kin, Wyvern learned quickly to focus on his capacity for manipulation. He could rival Wyrm on many occasions, and though Serpent was gifted with magic unlike any being Dragon had seen, Wyvern possessed an equally astute knowledge of the subject.

Wyvern was not teased by his brothers and sisters. He was not hated or reviled by others. He simply showed a certain... callousness... for life in general. It wasn't that he was filled with loathing, fond of animosity, begrudged certain people, or even sought vengeance of some kind. He simply didn't care. There was an evil nihilism about him that Dragon couldn't understand. When the dragon-children returned with the news of their chosen realms, Dragon felt pity for the people of the Emerald Spire. They did not acquire an ally that day.

"Wyvern is not a caring creature. He is not one who often shows empathy. I never knew his scheming would lead him to this."

"You mean you hoped it never would," the Wizard added candidly.

"Yes," Dragon sighed.

"You can help us now," the Wizard said. "Come with me to the Diamond Realm. I'm certain the Maiden is key to this; I have my theory, but I need your help!"

"If you haven't figured it out already then you are not as wise as I gave you credit for," Dragon retorted. "I cannot help you, friend. I am sorry."

The Wizard was confused and angry. "How can you deny us now? Your son seeks our destruction; his kin, those most capable of stopping him, do not!"

"I will *not* be responsible for the death of another of my children!" Dragon roared, shaking the walls.

The Wizard instinctively shielded himself with his arms. Falling pebbles and dust rained upon him. The walls reverberated and the Wizard feared the place would fall around them, such was Dragon's ire.

"Another?" the Wizard said, regaining his composure.

"Another," Dragon repeated. "Three dragons are no longer present among the spire-realms; two of them dragon-children. My mate has been gone for so long I cannot even remember her face. My daughter, Naga, we know her story. But my son, he... an alternate course of action could have been taken, I think."

Dragon seemed doubtful, regretful. The Wizard had never known him to be either in his long life.

"I only know he was slain by the Vitruvians long ago," The Wizard said gently.

"It took an army," Dragon clarified with a measure of pride.

His son's defeat was an open wound for the old Dragon. It pained him with every mention of his son's name. He told the Wizard of Vitruvia's indifferent attitude toward Hydra. It irritated him. Hydra was impulsive and prideful. A single head was more foolhardy than the rest of Dragon's brood combined and Hydra had seven.

Dragon told of Hydra's attempts to win the respect and favor of Vitruvia. It started with small displays of power and grew until Hydra began showing a more public presence, which his father, brothers, and sisters had warned him against. They were eventually proven right, to their eternal regret. The people of the Amber

Spire didn't respect or venerate Hydra—they feared him. They began sending hunter after hunter, each claiming to be a greater dragonslayer than the previous, to destroy him. Hydra accepted the challenge.

Each time Hydra met the challenger on open ground. When his opponent was defeated Hydra hurled his body back from whence they had come. Surely now, Hydra told his father, they would show more respect to one who bested their own champions.

"He treated it as some sort of macabre tournament!" Dragon bellowed.

The Wizard shook his head in dismay. "They grew tired of sending dragonslayers, I assume."

Dragon scoffed. They not only grew weary of sending single 'champions'; they invented what has become staples of large-scale warfare. Catapults, ballistae, trebuchets; all the siege engines Vitruvia invented were initially a result of their fight against Hydra.

"The Auburn King finally had enough. He wanted no more deaths as a result of this 'Siege of the Seven Heads' as he called it. He sent an emissary to me; the Auburn Wizard."

Dragon grew silent for a moment. The Wizard waited patiently for him to continue. Dragon began again, but spoke softer and more slowly.

"I believed the wizard and I had an understanding," Dragon said. "I told him that they could fling as many stones and fire as many arrows as they wanted, but Hydra would only recover. He was strong. The strongest of my children," Dragon emphasized with pride, "strong, but foolish. I told him I knew of a method that may stay my son's pride and stop his boorish attempts at recognition. Only a dragon's fire may close the wounds of his many necks; or a blade forged in dragonfire. They sent smiths and I aided them in producing a few dozen of the blades. They were small, to a dragon-child, but enough that

I thought it would give Hydra pause. A sting to make him reconsider aggravating the hornet's nest. It was nothing that I thought would kill him. This is what I discussed with the Auburn Wizard."

"They betrayed you," the Wizard said, seeing Dragon's face darken.

"They brought an army against him. One-thousand strong. They brought him to his knees and took his heads one by one until he was slain…"

"I am sorry, old friend," the Wizard was stricken with grief for the majestic creature. He had never been privy to the story of Hydra and he had never dared to ask.

"My desire for vengeance was such that each of my children attempted to quell my thirst. And do you know who eventually was able to subdue my wrath?" Dragon added with a sparkle in his eyes.

"Wyvern," the Wizard stated, his heart sinking.

"Wyvern. He made me see that to take vengeance upon the people of Vitruvia would draw the fear and anger of every other spire. It would be a war that would destroy us all. Do you now see why I will not—cannot—aid again in the fall of another of my own?"

The Wizard thought for a moment. He realized something at that moment. "Wyvern learned something as well…" he began, his eyes widening as the idea became clear. "You, your children, you are some of the most powerful creations in all the world, but the spires—they are older even than you. Many of their secrets remain a mystery even to us—those who sit in power in them; those who control the thrones…"

"Man," Dragon concluded.

"Humanity… we've controlled the spires since before memory can recall," The Wizard added.

"Long before," Dragon clarified. "Only you can reign over the spire-realms as their sovereign rulers. No dwarf or dryad or even

I could sit upon one of the seven thrones. Wyvern could not possibly…" Dragon's eyes shifted, he stared off into the distance.

"The Maiden; you realize it, too, don't you?" the Wizard said. "She has powers that even our own council couldn't harness. She uses it without training, without even knowing exactly what she's doing. It's instinct. Who knows what power she could possess if she had proper training? Perhaps Wyvern knows this. He had what he needed before flying for the Diamond Spire."

"Yes, but only in part," Dragon said, continuing to stare into open space beyond the Wizard and beyond his lair. His eyes sagged once again.

"What, old friend? What are you not telling me?" the Wizard asked softly but impatiently.

"You said this Maiden harnessed powers unknown in magic; that she could see life, bring life where it had all but been snuffed out?"

"Yes… from what I've seen."

"And my son… Wyvern brings only death. In ways only death itself could imagine."

"Yes…" the Wizard said. "Wherever he treads, death follows. But the Maiden… she brings only life."

"Are you understanding now? The Spires are quite mysterious. They are older than I; as old as the world. Some say they are a part of the world itself—that they were never actually constructed by traditional means. One cannot say for certain whether they are merely great constructs or living artifacts with a consciousness all their own. One thing is for certain: they have held the realms in balance for eons."

"What are you saying, Dragon?"

"Life and death… they ultimately maintain balance over all things. But life always holds power over death. Death comes for life, consumes it in small pieces, but life will always create and grow. Death would be nothing without it," Dragon said, turning his back on the Wizard.

"Leave me, now. I must tend to my grief," Dragon said in a sorrowful baritone.

The dragon-sire turned and took his leave. The light of the heatstones began to fade and the Wizard knew it would soon grow dark in the cave. With the stones cooling and the heat of Dragon's breath no longer near, it grew notably colder around the Wizard.

As the Wizard left the confines of the cave he saw the reason behind the chill and the darkness. A rolling thunderhead had moved in and was soon to pour rain upon the seaside realm. The Wizard's magical steed waited for him.

Life.

The stallion looked real. It felt real. Its hair flowed in the breeze and it was warm to the touch. But its chest didn't heave with labored breath as it ran. Its nostrils flared at the sight of the Wizard, but its eyes held no spark. This was a creature of magic, not of life. Everything was coalescing, and he would be carried to the great fight between life and death on a creature that was neither. The irony wasn't lost on him.

The Wizard would ride through rain and cold and all manner of ill weather. The horse could bear him without need for rest, and the Wizard would fight sleep, thirst, and hunger to make the journey. He had a plan, but it would require the Maiden and Wyvern together in one place.

Life and death gathered at the pinnacle of the Diamond Spire amid its golden age. His heart raced faster than the beast that carried him.

38

THE SECRET PLACE

The countryside was truly beautiful. The Prince had awoken to see a land so similar to his own that he thought at first he was in Avallonis. This land held a few striking differences, however. The hills were far rockier, and gentle cascades coursed among them. The flatlands that sprawled between the hills were the site of small hamlets and towns. Massive windmills turned lazily in the wind, and mills churned along the wide, inland rivers. White-sailed boats frequented the rivers like low-flying gulls across their mirrored surfaces.

He was jostled back to reality when the small cart he was in tossed him about. He looked up to see the wagon lashed to two horses—one that looked vaguely familiar, and the other was Ceffyl. Riding them was a proper-looking woman in deep, wine-colored robes, and the Maiden.

The last he remembered, they were fleeing from Wyvern at his temple. Where did this cart come from?

"Where are we?" he asked groggily. "Why... why am I in a cart?"

"We're near the border of the Diamond Realm," a pleasant voice called back.

The Maiden looked over her shoulder to him and shot a quick smile, but had to quickly return her gaze to the road ahead. He could tell they were moving at a steady, but swift pace, as he was occasionally tossed about in the cart as they hit ruts and potholes.

"Where are we going?" he shouted.

"I'm not sure, but wherever it is we are almost there," The Maiden shouted back.

The Prince was too tired and his body ached too much to ask any further questions. He merely lay back onto the hay-filled sack that had been put there for his comfort. At least, it seemed that was its intention.

The Maiden was correct—they arrived shortly after the Prince had awoken. The horse and cart had pulled to a stop and the Prince rose to see a thicket of trees with a field of tall grass and large, white stones strewn about randomly in a tight cluster. They were also surrounded by large patches of a plant that could best be described as homely. It grew in large clutches, with single stalks protruding from a focal point in the dirt. Crowning each deep green stalk was a bulbous growth that could be either a flower or a fruit; the Prince couldn't tell. Each was covered in fine, stiff hairs that stood on end, and each bulb was a varying shade of red and orange.

"Gnome's Nose…" he heard the other woman comment, seemingly to herself.

His senses continued to return and he became aware of the armor he still wore. What sort of spell had he been under to sleep so heavily in chainmail and a breastplate? His body would not be thanking him for it later.

With a grunt, he stood on unsteady legs and pulled the pins holding the door of the cart in place. He hopped down, landing heavily and teetering like a tavern drunk.

The Maiden dismounted and rushed to him, helping to steady him. He accepted her help, his head still clearing. They smiled at each other. He was happy to see her alive. He was happy to see her altogether, really.

The Maiden, feeling the weight of the steel armor and its cold touch pressing through her clothes, was relieved to have him back. It wasn't because she wanted his protection; his smile warmed her and his presence was comforting.

The Sybil approached, and the Prince almost felt he needed to bow in her presence. She carried herself like royalty, but her eyes and smile spoke of a kindness and sincerity that she didn't try very hard to hide.

"Well," she began, a wry smirk creating a sparkle in her eye, "it's good to see you alive and well, Prince." she said cheerily, her voice like sweet wine poured into a crystal glass. "We'll have time to catch up. For now, we need to find this safehouse. Your Wizard was quite adamant about it."

"He would've been," the Prince chuckled.

They gathered at the base of the snow-colored stones and the Prince looked back at the cart that had carried him here.

"Where did you acquire the cart, the rope, the hay...?" he asked.

The Sybil, still observing the stones, answered him quite matter-of-factly. "Your Wizard's not the only one here with magic. Or not here, as it were. He made it quite clear we were to meet him at his 'hidden place'. Which is supposed to be right here. Your Edding friend has gone off to fetch an army for us. Meanwhile, I'm stuck here ferreting out whatever insane magic was cooked into these stones."

She put her hands on her hips, never looking his way as she spoke, and continued to analyze the stones, seemingly growing more frustrated as she rambled.

The Prince looked back to see a tousled array of sticks and branches where the cart once stood. A few vines and blades of grass were included as well. Could she not have conjured a decent pillow?

He ran a hand through his hair and returned his focus to the stones before them. He stood next to the Maiden and offered another smile. She smiled in return and took his hand.

"I'm happy you're safe. We were very worried," she said.

"I still don't remember much. I can only recall being chased by Wyvern and falling, and an awful, horrible pain. Then I woke up in a cart," he rubbed his aching forehead.

"I've questioned if my gifts are a blessing or a curse, and most often I find it the latter, but I'm grateful for it at the moment, at least. It saved you. Your leg was broken—the bone pierced through the skin," she shuddered at the memory. "You would possibly have been laid up in the Sapphire Spire at this moment were it not for me stumbling upon more of my special talents."

Her last few words were laced heavily with sarcasm.

"Then I'm grateful, too," he replied.

He squeezed her hand and she heard a sound she wasn't used to hearing from the Sybil—that of outright frustration.

"Oh, bollocks! Leave it to a wizard…" she grumbled.

The Sybil was looking for something, trouncing around the thick grass and holding the hem of her robes up. She must have checked each stone twice, and stood on several of them. At the peak of her grousing, she even kicked a few.

"Is there something we can do?" the Maiden asked.

"Oh, yes!" the Sybil shouted, though the Maiden and Prince were unsure if she was speaking to them or merely shouting in surprise.

The Sybil began waving them over. "Yes! Here, help lift this."

The three of them pushed and pulled on a smooth, slightly rectangular stone until it stood lengthwise and reached to their thighs. The Sybil walked in long, even strides until she reached another stone. Calling over to them, she'd already begun raising that particular stone. The Prince noted that she even grunted gracefully.

After a short search they lifted two more stones and then two more. All in all there were eight stones, forming a circular pattern.

When all the rectangular white blocks were standing, the Sybil drew the two of them back a few paces.

"Now—behold!" she said, both hands making a grand flourish.

The Prince and the Maiden waited; a few seconds turned to a few seconds more. They heard nothing. They felt nothing. No unusual sight or smell or even a change in the wind.

"Oh, for pity's sake," the Sybil said in exasperation.

She made her way around the inside of the standing stones looking at the ground as she went. She looked here and there and seemed to have all manner of expressions—from approving nods to slight scowls.

"Well, I'm certain that doesn't belong here," she once said, picking a plain, unassuming gray rock off the ground and tossing it outside the ring.

She looked around a bit more before coming to a stop.

"Oh, now I'm just embarrassed," she said to herself, chuckling and chortling. The Maiden looked at the Prince and shrugged. He sighed and crossed his arms.

She lifted her dress with her usual grace and etiquette and pushed on a perfectly rounded stone near the center of the ring. With a final grunt, she stepped back. Just as she did a sound of crumbling rock rattled amongst the air. Stones of the same type that formed the circle began to pile upon one another; some appearing out of mid-air. The sound of scraping stone grew as block after block piled upon one another like ants. They took the shape of walls as perfectly cut planks folded out of nothing to form frames, and furniture—well-made but not too pretentious —materialized next to the Sybil.

The Prince watched with mouth agape. The Maiden was impressed, but she had found herself growing accustomed to such things when the Sybil was present. The Maiden felt the Prince's grip on her hand tighten and she looked over to see him captivated by the sight. A smile crossed her face and the Prince must have seen her looking at him from the corner of his eye. He looked over, realized he was slack-jawed, and closed his mouth quickly. He turned back to see the rest of the event unfold.

It took less than a minute, but the magic involved in creating such a geistheim must have taken the Wizard months of preparation and planning. The Sybil nodded her head in approval once all had been completed. The Prince and the Maiden entered the spacious home and saw it was every bit as accommodating as an actual house—even the fireplace was crackling and alive.

"Is this similar to the spell that your brooch works?" the Maiden asked as she picked up an apple from a bowl of real fruit sitting upon a table.

"Yes, well, this is far more complex and opulent as you no doubt can see," she replied. "Where I can only store so much magic in my tiny brooch to summon the inner confines of my home, the Wizard has built an entire house here and stored its contents within the rocks and their formation. It's quite amazing, actually."

"I would say so..." replied the Prince, who ducked as he entered, waiting for the building to collapse around them.

"What are we to do now?" he asked.

"We wait," the Sybil replied. "That's what the Wizard instructed. I don't know what he has planned or what he fled in such a hurry to do, but we have to trust his guidance for now."

"What if Wyvern finds us? Or his followers?" asked the Maiden.

The Sybil wondered the same thing, though she decided against voicing her concern. She walked to the door and closed it, shutting them all inside. She smiled, then, when she saw a manner of engravings on the back of the door.

"They won't," she chuckled.

You sly old codger, the Sybil thought to herself. Runes similar to those used by the Dream Lord were etched in enchanted ink on the back of the door. Once the door was shut, whoever was not within the confines of the home would see only the broken rubble that the three had seen upon their arrival. No one would know they were there.

They sat that night at a smooth oak table. Sweet fruit that tasted freshly plucked still filled the large bowl that sat in the middle. The Prince returned with a fat cluster of pheasants that were prepared and garnished with the herbs taken from a pantry that never seemed to empty of eggs, flour, and other basic foods. They enjoyed each other's company and, for a time, left their worries outside those enchanted stone walls.

"A wonderful meal if I do say so myself," the Sybil said as they cleared their dishes from the table. "Though, so long as I am here I won't let my charges eat anything less."

"And what exactly are you doing here?" the Prince asked, though he made sure not to sound impolite. "The Maiden trusts you, and therefore so shall I—but, that doesn't tell me why you're helping us."

"It's quite alright. I do understand," the Sybil said, looking to the Maiden with a smile. "I met the young lady, or rather, her spirit of sorts, roaming the swamps around my home in Mythesta."

"*Around* your home?" the Maiden said, then added with a chuckle, "I do believe you lived in those very swamps."

"It was a… temporary relocation of my permanent dwelling, dear, I assure you," she said, her cheeks flushing.

"I wouldn't be surprised to discover you come from a noble family. Am I right?" the Prince asked.

"Well, the Maiden could explain much of that, I suppose… it's not a very exciting story, really," the Sybil said.

After they had cleaned the table and the dishes were washed in a basin of water that remained perpetually clean, the Sybil informed them she would be retiring for the evening. The Prince and the Maiden smiled and said good night. The Sybil left for one of three bedchambers within the house. A circumstantially perfect number.

Once the door had closed, the Prince and Maiden walked to one of the windows and opened it, allowing some fresh air into the room. It was a cool evening and a light breeze blew. Crickets began to sing their songs as the sun began to dip below the horizon.

"May I ask you something?" the Maiden said to the Prince.

"Of course," he replied. "Anything."

"You know me only from the tournament and the market at Emerald Arbor. I'm not ungrateful, but why did you risk your life coming for me? What made the others do so?" She looked out the window onto the darkening horizon.

The Prince looked at her and saw the last rays of light touching her. It was as if the sun itself was saddened by turning its face from her. Was that all that truly drove him to her? Was he smitten with her? Some foolish infatuation? Or were his motives more of benevolence and duty as he had first thought—to destroy Wyvern, avenge the Knight and the realm of Emrallt, and cleanse his own realm of treason? As he looked at her he felt there was more there. They, all of them, were drawn to her. Like fate had tethered them together. His feelings for her were just a joyful consequence.

"Much has happened since then," he said in a low voice. "The man from the east—the Red Warrior—I trained with him to fight. Certainly, I had good instructors in Avallonis, but, as the Wizard pointed out, I needed to fight—to be blooded. I needed to see battle if I had any hope of stopping Wyvern."

"And what drives you to stop him? How did you first encounter that monster?"

The Prince never realized that the Maiden knew only that Wyvern took her—she knew nothing of their first contact with the beast, or the price it cost. He explained to her of the vision. The monster of smoke, blood, and fire. He told her of the shared dream between him and the Knight. He then told her of the Knight's fate.

She was visibly distraught. She covered her mouth to quiet a sob and her eyes grew wet with ready tears. The Prince put a comforting hand on her shoulder. To his surprise, she turned into him. She didn't weep, but it was the first time she'd heard about her home and what happened at the beginning; what seemed like so long ago. It was no doubt overwhelming. He embraced her gently and attempted to reassure her that the Knight fought with skill and bravery that would rival any man he'd seen, even better than several Red Warriors he'd fought and died with. He told her of the Green King's gifts to him to honor the Knight's deeds. He gestured to the breastplate now sitting near the table and told of Ceffyl, his great stallion, that she had been riding.

The Maiden stepped back and looked up to him. A tear had trailed down her face, but she had managed to force a smile.

"The armor you wore to Wyvern's lair," she said, looking over to it then back to the Prince. "It looked quite good on you. You fought well. You honored him."

Her eyes lingered on his, and he was lost in their depth. They drew him in, and he felt something there that was beyond words. It was more than just his feelings for her. He cleared his throat and broke their hold on him.

"So, it seems we've found several others who seek vengeance on Wyvern," she said, turning to look back out the window.

"Among other things. Wyvern's influence has spread over the land like a disease. He empowered two witches that tried to assume control of Avallonis and Mythesta. My very own kingdom is a piece in the creature's game. My council questions my ability to rule. I made it my duty before accepting the crown to return with Wyvern's head."

The Maiden looked at him curiously. "Would having become

king not made it simpler? Take your armies and ride against him?"

"No, it would not. Wyvern had no armies—my understanding was that I would face him alone," the Prince said irritably. "Just a beast and his whims. I found out otherwise, soon enough."

"This Warrior—he rides to gather an army, does he not?"

The Prince nodded. "Yes—hopefully it's enough."

"I'd like to see you return to your throne, Your Grace—I mean, attend the coronation. I've never seen such a thing before," the Maiden said.

"We've all been seeing a lot of new things lately, haven't we?"

They looked to one another and the Maiden smiled—warmth filling her face again. The Prince took her hand and kissed it gently.

"I would very much like you to be there," he returned.

The last of the day's light was gone. Only the gentle shadows of the fire danced about the room. He looked at her and she at him. The fire crackled softly and the breeze dipped through the window, caressing their skin in cool contrast to the nearby flame. The Prince kissed her lips. She fell into him, and were it up to the Prince, he would have never let go.

39

UNWELCOME

The Sybil left her room as the morning's light began to dapple through the curtained windows. She made herself presentable and then began preparing breakfast. As she walked into the great-room, nearly tripping over the Prince's chainmail and breastplate he'd placed by the table, she noticed that the Prince and Maiden had fallen asleep on the plush couch. The Maiden's head rested on his shoulder and his head rested on hers. The Sybil smiled and noted to herself.

As she entered the kitchen she felt a slight draft. Where was it coming from? Her heart skipped and she began looking for the source. She saw a single leaf teetering on the windowsill. She looked up and a slight gasp escaped her lips; how did she not see it before?

The window above the Prince and Maiden was open and a slight breeze slipped through the room. The Sybil woke them shaking the Prince and Maiden both with separate hands.

"Up, you two! Up! We can't tarry here any longer!" she was shouting.

The Prince jumped to his feet, still shaking off the slumber, causing the Maiden to abruptly waken as she fell to the cushions. He was looking about in alarm. The Sybil reminded herself that the recent days haven't been the kind to jostle someone awake from—but current circumstances had required it.

"W—what? What is it?" the Prince asked as he rubbed his weary eyes.

"The window—who left it open?" she asked urgently.

"One of us—why?" he returned, yawning.

The Sybil growled in irritation. "The enchantment—with a portal to the geistheim open it's no longer invisible!"

She cursed herself for not thinking the warn them beforehand to leave the doors and windows closed. How could she have been so foolish?

The Prince quickly shut the window. The Maiden, hearing the hurried exchange, was now quite awake. She rushed over to the window to glance outside. She saw nothing in the fields and no one on the roads.

"No one's there," she said with a sigh of relief.

The Prince picked up his armor and the Maiden assisted him in buckling it. He donned the sheathed Calibern and put on his cloak.

"I prefer not to take chances. I'll go have a look outside," he said.

With a look to the Sybil, he added, "I apologize, my lady, for the foolish mistake."

The Sybil nodded in understanding though her face was marred with concern. The Prince stepped outside. His hand gripped the hilt of his sword. All was calm where his eyes could see. The road was empty and the air still. That was when he realized there were no noises to be heard at all. No birds called. No insects chirped.

"Is something wrong?" he heard the Maiden ask from behind him.

The Maiden and the Sybil stepped outside the confines of the geistheim. The Prince urged them back inside as his eyes and ears peered into the distance. He looked from horizon to horizon

"I wouldn't advise it," a feminine voice trilled behind him.

He turned sharply to see the horrors perched atop the structure. Morgæna, seated atop a black pegasus, was looking down on them with a victorious grin. The evil, winged stallion pawed at the ground and snorted at them. Worse still, around her sat a clutch of women with taloned feet and filthy wings who heeded her commands.

The harpies hailed from Upala and were notoriously illtempered. Wyvern held sway over all manner of wicked beasts, and these were yet another addition to his dark ranks. They were garbed in ragged clothes stolen from victims. In sharp contrast, they also were adorned with many stolen jewels and baubles as well.

Stories had said they were hideous to behold, with their birdlike noses, sharp teeth, and fingers that ended in long, claw-like appendages. Their wings were feathered and frayed, tales telling of them having the traits of both birds and bats. The stories were all true.

"I've been looking all over the realms for you, young lady," Morgæna said to the Maiden. "These things that travel with me are quite a strain on my patience."

A guttural growl escaped one of the bird-women as it looked balefully at the sorceress. They worked for Wyvern, and with each other, but there was apparently no love lost between them.

"It's good I found you. Lovely little trick—the disappearing house," she preened mockingly.

"What do you want with me?" the Maiden shouted in frustration.

"Oh, I care nothing for you," Morgæna said with a flick of her wrist. "I'd let the harpies have you just to rid myself of their squawking for a few minutes. It's Wyvern who wants you. Let's go ask him."

The Maiden's face crinkled in anger. "He said he no longer needed me—he was done with me!"

Morgæna chuckled. It was disturbingly blithe. The similarity between her and the Sybil was very striking.

"Yet you came seeking him, did you not?" Morgæna said.

The Prince drew Calibern and both the pegasus and harpies shrieked at the sight of it. He glanced over to Ceffyl and saw the gifts from the Red King and Queen lashed so temptingly close— the helmet and shield that would serve him so well this moment.

"Put it away, Prince," Morgæna warned through cold eyes. "Even my dear sister knows better than to stand against me."

The Prince turned slowly, letting the light of the sun catch the blade, letting them all see his ancestral weapon. The harpies hissed like angry snakes.

"I've been called a slow learner many times," he said as he glared at the sorceress.

Morgæna scowled. "You're outnumbered and the beasts grow hungry. They prefer human flesh and it's been some time for them. The Maiden would live, unfortunately; sworn as I am on pain of death. However, Wyvern did not specify that she had to be returned whole."

The Maiden now glared at Morgæna. The sorceress could see the internal struggle on the young woman's pained face. She would never let someone die for her. Morgæna's smile widened at the sight of the sweat on the pretentious Prince's brow.

The Prince felt a hand on his shoulder and turned to see the Sybil looking at him with firmness and calm.

"Stay your blade, Prince. All our efforts will have been in vain if we die here."

The Prince kept his gaze on the enemy before him, but he spoke quietly to the Sybil.

"You speak on behalf of your sister?" he said in low, accusatory tones.

"We really didn't catch up, did we..." she returned sadly.

"The Wizard expects us here. How will he know where we've gone?" he asked.

"The Blue Wizard is a man of great guile. He'll find us," she said, with a squeeze on his arm for emphasis.

The Prince looked at the sorceress and her minions. He despised—no, hated—what he was about to do. The Sybil, however, was correct. He wouldn't be a brash fool. He sheathed his weapon and held his head high to Morgæna.

"That's a good little poppet," the sorceress chuckled. "Take them."

The harpies squealed and cackled in delight as they leaped from their perch atop the roof. Their shrill call was so horrendous that the three upon the ground cried out in pain. They instinctively covered their ears and the harpies grabbed their wrists with powerful hands.

The Prince noted that the winged women were incredibly strong. They also reeked of stagnant water, salt, and seaweed. He looked up to see their thin, almost gaunt bodies corded with muscle. Their wings were powerful and capable of lifting the armored Prince off the ground with little effort.

"Any tricks, big sister, and I'll command them to drop you here and now," Morgæna shouted.

The Sybil hung her head in defeat and sorrow. Her little sister —or what had once been her little sister not so long ago—had become a woman of utter darkness and malevolence. Though it was difficult, the Sybil didn't entirely blame herself; it was mostly the outcome of the circumstances and the fateful choices of her sister. She resolved herself to a bitter, necessary conclusion: If fate had not destined the Sybil to die today, but somehow the tables were to be turned, she would do that which she could not do years ago—Morgæna's evil would end with her death at the Sybil's hands.

40

THE WIZARD'S TASK

The Wizard arrived at the site of one of his favorite creations—the geistheim. He spent many years here before his calling to the Sapphire Spire to serve as its court wizard. This, in fact, was the very spell that cemented his place among his comrades. No longer an apprentice, he was now a full wizard and had earned their unrivaled respect.

It would have been a remarkable story he would have shared with those that awaited him... had they been awaiting him. He arrived to see the geistheim fully constructed and visible. The front door was open and being calmly swung about on its hinges by the wind.

The Wizard rushed to the entrance and looked inside. It was clean. Nothing had been toppled or broken. Why was no one inside? Where they all daft enough to leave and not close the front door?

No. He thought. *The Sybil, especially, would never have allowed such.*

Then he felt it. A twinge on the back of his neck. A prickle in his beard. He turned, expecting to see something creeping at him from the aether. Dark magic was here—and it was used recently. Powerful, evil creatures were about his geistheim.

Morgæna.

She had taken them. He was sure of it. He needed to catch them quickly. His arcane steed wouldn't be fast enough and he had never replaced the geas which had once bound him to the Prince. Urgent matters had caused his old mind to forget this important duty. He would have to face those consequences later.

His mind raced for a spell or invocation, any incantation that would speed him along. *Think, you old fool!* He scolded himself. He wished he had the capability to boot himself in the ass.

Boots… boots! He rejoiced inwardly. The Wizard rushed into his home and entered his main bedchamber. He smelled the perfume of the Sybil still lingering within and it pricked at his nose. He went to a picture on the wall of a dragon guarding a large, closed chest. At his touch the picture of the dragon magically recoiled, allowing access to the image of the chest. The Wizard reached within the picture itself and pulled the chest from it. It wasn't a large chest, but big enough to contain several small items.

The Wizard immediately pulled from the chest a pair of black, faded leather boots with bronze buckles. He set them aside and continued to dig through the chest.

Memories of his old studies flooded back to him. A wand that would instantly boil a small pot of water—child's play, really. A leaf that could be coaxed into becoming a full shade tree in seconds. A quill that produced its own ink. Finally, he came upon a small bag. It contained seven different kinds of flowers. Though not necessarily rare, they were of a species unique to each realm, growing only within their respective borders.

Pulling a white rose with blue thorns from the bag, he dropped it into one of the boots (the thorns having been trimmed, of course). These were a special item; a pair that he had used many times as their worn look could attest. Traveling with them wore them down as though their wearer had walked the actual distance on foot, so he saved them for emergency situations and, of course, had forgotten all about them over time. He had dubbed them the "Seven-Step Boots". By placing a special token of the location you wish you travel to and reciting a basic invocation you would be there after taking only seven steps.

It wasn't new magic, *per se*. This was an already known, and difficult, spell. He simply augmented it.

Lifting the boots with his hands, he whispered the incantation. He left the geistheim and closed the front door. Giving seven knocks upon the front door, the house crumbled away, leaving the familiar field of white stones. He put the boots on his feet (they were large enough to fit over those he currently wore) and looked to the east in the direction of the Diamond Spire.

A few more steps. he thought. A few more steps for all to be decided. And so, he began walking.

One, two, three, four, five, six…

THE DIAMOND SPIRE

I t was a terrible, terrifying flight. The harpies gripped the companions' wrists and arms in a monstrous, almost vindictive, vise. They trilled and cawed to one another whenever the Sybil, Prince, or Maiden attempted any sort of communication. They let loose with ear-splitting shrieks and gray-toothed snarls to silence them.

Eventually, the looming majesty of the Diamond Spire appeared ahead. The Prince felt a horribly conflicted rush of relief mingled with dread. Here the three of them would be free of the awful talons and cloying smell of the bird-hags, but dropped into the waiting clutches of Wyvern.

The Prince had only seen detailed sketches and masterful paintings of the Diamond Spire. The Sybil had also read of the great tower, now in its prime, but never seen it. The Maiden only knew of it through word of mouth and awe-inspired whisperings. Now, as they lay eyes on it for the first time, they felt a reverence and wonder that made them forget, momentarily, of the beasts that held them prisoner.

The magnificent Diamond Spire rose from a valley of rivers,

overlooked snowcapped mountains, and basked in the winds from the nearby shores of the glistening western sea. The hillcrest that the spire crowned, rolled gently down to the shore where the Gray King and Queen resided. The capital of Sion, Icostraea. Any other time, such a panorama of beauty and strength would bring one to tears. It seemed as though all the majesty of the ageless spires coalesced here within its marble walls.

Unlike many other spires, the Diamond Spire was separately located from its home city and protected by a citadel known as Sygil, whose aesthetics spoke of power and regality. It was encircled by a septet of towers, equally spaced and connected by quartz-colored walls. Each acted as its own gatehouse. These gates had never been closed since the Wizard could remember, and they remained open now. Wyvern's hubris appeared to be getting the better of his strategic sense.

Icostraea was at the end of a wide road leading from the north-west of Sygil like a ray of light. Known as the Shining Mile, it connected the citadel that protected the spire, to its home city, and allowed for quick travel between them. The Gray King held court here and often met his honored and royal guests at a castle in the heart of Icostraea. Travel along the Shining Mile was an oft-used diplomatic tactic that created a more intimate setting for discussions. The Gray King was never known to mince words.

It was the era of the Diamond Spire, and Sion in all its glory was on display. Amid the beauty, however, a pox was festering. As they drew near the white-walled tower they saw shadowy forms milling around its mighty foundations. A roiling blackness shuffled about in its great courtyard coming within mere feet of its glistening doors. A cacophonous babble rose from the masses of creatures that formed the wretched mass.

Wyvern was attacking. The Prince lamented his inability to ride in with his forces; to muster his knights and lead them with

Lady Gwinn to battle and victory. Damn it, where had his grif-fons gone?

The Sybil's heart broke at the sight before her. How could her sister be involved with this madness? Relishing in it; thriving upon it? She would never have believed it, had she not seen with her own eyes the evil in which her younger sibling had been a part of. The Sybil's magic and enchantments couldn't sway such a bleak tide that stirred below them. It was only her sister that she had resolved herself to stopping; that much could be certain.

The Maiden looked on and felt a powerful, unfamiliar grief. Certainly, this was a travesty to see a wicked horde assaulting the walls of the beautiful spire, but she felt a deeper ache in her soul. It trembled in her heart and froze her blood. She'd never been to the Diamond realm before, much less the Diamond Spire. Why, now, was she so pained by its conflict?

She looked below her and saw a very peculiar sight: a unicorn as white as fresh snow with a horn of gold, strolled in the fields below them, seemingly unaware or disinterested in the events unfolding nearby. Sion was home to many rare beauties and wonders. Unicorns were only ever found here, in the Diamond Realm, and a unicorn hadn't been seen for decades. Now, one meandered about near the world's most dangerous creatures and one of creation's darkest foes. It did, however, seem to be watching intensely...

Closer and closer they came; each beat of the foul harpies' wings bringing them nearer the jeweled pinnacle. They could now make out large windows in the walls. At the foot of the spire, in its courtyard, filled with monstrosities great and small, the spire's Morning Guard stood vigilantly at the doors to the tower itself. They were resplendent; armed with shining swords and glistening spears and armored with thick steel that covered them head to foot. They were cloaked in silvery-white sashes and capes that gave them an air of strength, authority, and immortal fortitude.

It was odd, then, that they didn't strike at the creatures they faced. They merely stood at full attention with their swords sheathed and their spears upright. Their shining helms stared overhead of the creatures shouting before them. They completely ignored them as though they were unaware of their presence and unfazed by the slathering insults and plumes of frothing spittle cast their way.

The true revelation came after a few more beats of the grimy wings. The horde of monsters wasn't assaulting the spire. They were not, in fact, gnashing their teeth and spitting in the direction of the Morning Guard. Their backs were turned to the shining knights. The horde was *guarding* the tower.

What madness has been wrought upon the Diamond Spire? The Prince asked himself. The knights were easily outnumbered a full fifty to one at least, but there was a clear line drawn between them and the masses. A few bodies lay dead within that small, clear stretch; aggressive, stupid creatures that tempted the knights too far or perhaps attempted to enter the tower. From their vantage point in the sky, it looked like a shining shield holding living darkness at bay.

Their destination appeared to be the uppermost room of the spire. Large, open windows allowed them entrance. The harpies swooped through into the almost open-aired room and dropped their cargo unceremoniously upon the floor. The dark pegasus landed much more gracefully.

"Go. Guard the skies with the manticores until his majesty returns," Morgæna ordered the harpies.

"His majesty?" the Prince scoffed.

He looked around to see that, indeed, they were within the throne room of the Diamond Spire. The Prince felt the room was quite indefensible for a king's main audience hall, but he'd learned from his studies that the Morning Guard would typically line the airy hall in a display that appeared ceremonial but was quite functional. The Gray Wizard would also no doubt have various wards and spells to protect the king or queen.

Where was the Gray Wizard for that matter? The Prince had heard nothing of him in all of this. Wyvern would have quite a challenge in besting the Gray King's court wizard to claim this tower.

The Prince no more than finished this thought when he heard the Sybil gasp.

"Oh no..." she said, covering her mouth with a graceful hand.

The Prince followed her gaze to a seat near the throne. It was the seat of the wizard. It was similar to, but smaller than, the throne. In this case, silver-colored linens and cushions filled a seat of carved white marble, flecked with gold and silver. The head of the seat was a quartz mantle carved into a magnificently detailed unicorn's head. Standing next to the seat was a statue of a man in flowing robes, clean-shaven and surprisingly youthful, whose hands were raised in what appeared to be the preparation of a spell—the Gray Wizard. He had been turned into a statue of solid quartz.

"Lovely little decoration, no?" Morgæna chuckled. It was a sound like broken glass—delicate and dangerous.

"The final sign of my power and loyalty to Wyvern. Even the great court wizards cannot stand against me."

The Prince spat at her feet. "Mine did and drove you away like a scurrying rat. And his skill is always growing..."

"As is mine!" Morgæna interrupted, shouting.

She slung an open hand in his direction and black, oily tendrils snaked from her spread fingers. They wrapped tightly around the Prince's neck and knocked him from his feet. Before he could fall she lifted him from the ground. The shadowy coils stretched until the Prince was hanging over a lethal height out of a window.

"Last we met I was forced into a similar situation; shall we see if you, too, can save yourself?" Morgæna seethed.

"No!" the Maiden shouted.

She began to rush to him, but the Sybil grabbed her and held her back, knowing that her sister would readily drop him to see the Maiden suffer.

"Can you fly, Prince? Might your griffons overcome their cowardice and fetch you?" Morgæna said, trying to provoke him.

The tendrils gripped so tightly that the Prince barely managed a pained gurgle. His eyes rolled into his head as he began to lose consciousness.

"Bring him in," a low voice rumbled from behind them.

All turned to see Wyvern entering the fray through another of the windows. As he deftly climbed through the large arch, his tail caressed a mist-filled mirror on the wall. Much of his treasure looked to have been transferred here. Even Morgæna didn't know how long he had secretly been controlling the Diamond Spire.

"There will be time for vengeance, my sorceress. For now, he lives," Wyvern said in a soft, charming tone. The contrast of such a tone coming from the creature was as frightful as it was ominous.

Morgæna brought the Prince just within the walls and dropped him from an uncomfortable height. He hit the floor with a resounding smash and choked for air. The Maiden and Sybil ran to him and helped him to his feet.

Morgæna approached Wyvern. His appearance was quite different from what they had previously seen. His scales had turned from a rusty brown to a deep, blood red. His eyes still burned like fire, but the flame did not rage on the surface so much as consumed him from within, and had waxed a fearsome scarlet color. With his schemes at their penultimate state, he'd unleashed the power of several of his relics and grown stronger. The sorceress that he had called his own, stood next to him and lovingly caressed his large, square jaw.

"I bring you gifts, my love," she said to the dragon-child.

"And what wondrous gifts they are, my lady," he cooed.

A rumble coursed his throat and chilled their veins. He eyed the Prince and scowled at the sword sheathed at his side.

"Calibern… relieve him of it," Wyvern ordered.

Morgæna removed the Prince's buckled sheath and wrenched the blade from him as the Sybil and Maiden glared at her. Smirking, she approached the window he had recently been dangled from. She began to toss the sword from the spire when Wyvern stayed her hand.

"No, place it on the throne. I want it for my collection."

Morgæna shrugged and did as instructed, tossing the sword unceremoniously next to the empty throne. The crossguard clanged unceremoniously as it came to rest at the base of the raised dais.

Wyvern then turned his attention to the Maiden.

"My beautiful Maiden, I have missed you," he hissed.

He stepped towards them, his tail reaching out to her. His wicked stinger caught part of her clothing and he pulled her toward him. She resisted, but his strength was great and she feared for those with her. He drew her close and gazed into her eyes.

"Ah, yes; it's still there. More precious than the diamond atop this very spire," he smiled.

"What?" the Maiden asked in frustration. "What is it that you want from me? Please, just tell me," she begged.

So much death and destruction. So many lives lost and changed forever; and she knew not what this reprehensible, unforgivable creature wanted from her. She would readily give it if he would only say what this gift was. Tears of frustration began to form and make their way down her cheeks. Wyvern's stinger appeared before her face and she was reminded of that dreadful day at her home. A blunt edge of the lethal barb plucked a tear from her face and he presented it before her eyes.

"Certainly not this," he scolded her and flicked the tear away.

He walked haughtily past the Sybil and Prince, who still clutched his throat. Coming to a stop at the edge of one of the windows, he summoned the Maiden over.

"Come see, young Maiden," he said with his back to her. He showed little fear and an aberrant lack of caution.

The Maiden did as he asked. She stood next to Wyvern, half-expecting to be tossed from the tower. He looked out over the beautiful stretch of land before them. The braying and shouting of the horde below just managed to make its way up to them. The throng of gathered evil was such that their racket raised to the peak of the spire.

"Behold my power and influence."

Wyvern was quite proud of this, the Maiden thought. He wallows in his cruelty and delights in the destruction he's caused.

"This," Wyvern continued, "is yet incomplete. There is one more step to tread before my victory. You will help me with this."

The Maiden clenched her fists and set her jaw. Her fear had been crushed by a wave of sudden anger.

"And what could possibly make you think I will be a party to any of this?" she spat at him.

Wyvern regarded her with his burning eyes. He turned and looked back to the Sybil and Prince. He allowed his gaze to linger there for a moment. Long enough for her to follow it and let the realization take hold.

"Call it a hunch," he hissed.

42

THE SERPENT AND THE UNICORN

"Seven," the Wizard whispered.

He took a breath and opened his eyes and beheld chaos. A surging, bellowing, raucous riot of inhuman stench roared before him. He looked on with a weight in his heart and felt the sweat begin to bead upon his brow.

The horde was enormous. Thousands upon thousands of the worst fiends the realms had to offer shouted and spat at the air before them. They were as starved dogs on a short chain. They were all facing away from the tower, which could only mean Wyvern was already inside.

So this is his army, the Wizard thought. Wretched. Loathsome. It fit Wyvern to be followed by such filth.

The bulk of the forces appeared to be comprised of Mythestan boglins—short, wiry, and armed with the crudest of weapons. No doubt they were fodder to allow the more formidable beasts to move in for a kill, though in these numbers the boglins could prove just as deadly. They were a foul, malodorous swarm with rusty stingers of their own.

Towering above them were trolls from Vitruvia and the Avallonian lowlands. They were head and shoulders taller than a man, with thick, leathery skin that was difficult to pierce. Their hideous features were further contorted by their vicious howling and slurs thrown at seemingly everyone and no one.

The Wizard saw, dotted throughout the horde like cancerous growths, ogres from the Veil Mountains. They kicked and slapped at the boglins that prodded and provoked them. They were bloated, piebald, and covered with what the Wizard could only guess was sweat from the exertion of moving their grotesque tonnage about. Despite their corpulent sluggishness, they could crush a horse and rider with their bare hands if they managed to catch them.

These were the least of his worries, unfortunately. These brutes had been fought and slain many times. No doubt Wyvern was quite aware of this. He had augmented his forces with much more fearsome creatures. Thankfully, these more brutal beasts didn't seem to notice him. He was quite far away, and their incandescent rage blinded them to any flights of reason.

Manticores from Edda and harpies from the wind-swept shores of Upala circled the walls of the upper floors of the Diamond Spire like flies about a glorious scepter. Their darting shadows marred the otherwise marvelous skies. The harpies perched on the open windows of the spire, screeching and cawing at the unfamiliar manticores. The lion-like monsters, however, were not content to listen to the bird-women's shrieks. Instead, they chose to glide aimlessly about the spire in between short rests upon its summit.

To the Wizard's growing disgust, he saw more than one of the manticores sweep down when a boglin ventured too far from the horde, and pounce upon the hapless prey from the sky. Multiple manticores would join in on the feeding and nothing would be left but blood-stained ground only minutes later.

Then a true horror stomped from behind the tower. Hailing from the deepest woods of Emrallt, a fire-spewing chimera roared as a small number of manticores flew too closely towards it. Its serpent-headed tail lashed out, nearly striking one and hissing in aggravation. Another of its heads—a gruesome mockery of a lion—spewed flame about the ground, scorching its surroundings in a display of dominance. Its third and final head —that of a hideous goat—attempted to gore the manticores that approached from the ground. The fearsome creature was the size of a merchant's wagon, and after this display it was given plenty of clear ground.

Wyvern had amassed a fearsome lot; what they lacked in finesse they would recover in brute strength and cruelty. The Wizard regarded the land before him. He wouldn't have been surprised if the Warrior disregarded his warning and confronted the horde out of spite for such wickedness. He saw no sign of conflict, though. No remains or fallen weapons. It would be convenient to have an army with him right now, but what could even the Sons of Edda do against such a gathering as this?

Curiously, the Wizard saw from the corner of his eye a blur of movement. He looked over to see a truly astounding sight: a unicorn was racing toward the filthy throng. The sight of such a rare and magnificent creature was breathtaking, but the Wizard also found himself struck with unnatural terror. What chance would the magical beast have against them? Unicorns were incredibly intelligent, some would say even more so than humans. It wouldn't race toward such danger without cause. The Wizard watched with intense curiosity and dread.

A number of the fiends noticed the unicorn and maneuvered to intercept her. A crowd of boglins began to circle the beast and clash their weapons and shields. They were preparing to attack and overwhelm her with numbers. The more intelligent trolls— for it is only when compared to a boglin that a troll could be referred to as intelligent—lingered behind to see what fared of their smaller cousins. The ogres, were too lazy to care. They would what they Wyvern commanded, or, most likely bribed, them to do—nothing more.

The unicorn came to an abrupt halt. She reared back and whinnied loudly, kicking her front hooves to keep them back. The boglins recoiled, intimidated by the display, but only slightly. When the unicorn came down, her hooves hit the ground with a powerful din. A clap of thunder resounded through the forest and fields surrounding the spire. The ground shook such that the Wizard felt it reverberate where he was standing. Trees reeled back as if struck by a strong wind. Most of the boglins were knocked from their feet. The cowardly creatures fled in fear back to their ranks.

Now the trolls came forth. No longer leering at the lesser creatures before them, they snarled and plucked boglins from those retreating and hurled them at the unicorn. She avoided the screaming projectiles as the creatures bounced and careened off the ground. She lifted her front legs and whinnied again, slamming them down with yet another ferocious stomp. This time the ground split and cracked around her golden hooves. The trolls stepped back cautiously, fear finally marring their pocked faces.

The unicorn snorted angrily, kicked her hooves, and tossed her mane in defiance before the numerous fiends. After such a display of the arcane, they recoiled from her presence. Was she trying to herd them? It appeared to be working. The throng moved tightly together and pressed against one another to avoid the angry, magical beast with the thundering hooves.

They clamored over one another—boglin and troll and ogre— until their viciousness overtook them and they began turning on one another. As they drew nearer the tower, the Morning Guard finally showed signs of life within those glistening metal plates. They braced themselves and lowered their weapons whilst raising their shields, becoming a glistening, impenetrable wall. The chimera feasted upon one or two of the creatures who sought to hide within its shadow.

The unicorn was sowing chaos among his ranks and Wyvern would not have it. He looked down upon the bedlam that had become of his army and loosed a fiery roar. It grew suddenly and eerily quiet. The chimera crunching and swallowing its recent catch the last sound to be made. All eyes looked to the top of the tower.

"Watch them," Wyvern commanded Morgæna, referring to his prized captives.

He dropped effortlessly from the windowed arch and spread his wings. He drifted slowly, his shadow cast upon those below him and spreading a cold fear that touched even the ogres. When he was closer to the ground, he perched upon the ledge of a lower window and glared intently at the one who had caused such a tumult.

He saw the unicorn pacing there, snorting and tossing its mane in front of the full might of his army without fear or hesitation. He felt the magic draped about its shining coat. He also recognized a very familiar smell—one he would always recognize. The unicorn must have known he would.

"A cunning plan, sister," Wyvern shouted. "But even you can't stand alone against my army."

The Wizard's brow furrowed. Sister? Could it be? He looked from Wyvern to the unicorn to see, standing in its place, the dragon-child, Serpent. The patron dragon of the Diamond Spire and its realm, Sion. She had dropped the glamour and in a blink, her true form had been revealed. Scales shimmering in the sun. Her eyes were captivating and her mane, her true dragon mane, an array of brilliant blues and striking violets. Her magics were the subject of legends and myths. Her beauty even more so.

"These? This rabble that feared a mere horse?" she countered. "What fear would clutch their hearts at the wrath of a dragon-child?"

She glared at the horde and a deep rumble built in her throat. Her lithe body tensed and coiled and she breathed a wave of fire in the direction of the monsters that scored her spire's ground with her wrath. The boglins were falling over one another in their attempts to flee. Only a barked order from Wyvern returned them to their ranks.

"You will do nothing to my army, sibling!" Wyvern roared. "I have *her* with me. I have others, as well. The Prince of Avallonis himself is among my guests. If you do not wish to see their flayed and burned bodies tossed from the highest of these arches, then you will stand down!"

Serpent hissed and seethed at her brother. She never liked him. She always—*always*—knew he would bring ill will upon anything and anyone cursed with his presence. She begged their father to send him off, banish him from the realms to one of the far continents, but Dragon wouldn't hear it. Now, he sat atop the Diamond Spire with a prince as a hostage and the keystone to his schemes locked away with him.

Then, Wyvern did something that surprised her. She saw his muscles ease. His brow unfurrowed and his snarl relaxed into mere grimace.

"It doesn't have to be this way, sister," he growled.

What is he up to? she wondered. His eyes no longer flared with hatred, but there was still something there; a conflict within himself.

"So long as you threaten my realm, brother, it will have to be."

Wyvern's chest rumbled. "I only need to complete my work. You and Drake can keep your realms. Watch over them as you always have. You will answer to no one but me."

Serpent's eyes narrowed. She growled at the insult of his offer. Wyvern—ruling over the Diamond and Sapphire Realms with her and Drake as his lackeys? She would rather die in the fields surrounding her spire rather than serve under a tyrant who would dominate it.

"I reject your offer, *brother*," she said, injecting venom into the last word.

Wyvern gave a low, aggravated roar and bared his teeth at Serpent. Then, his mouth slowly curled into a sneer. He wouldn't show the pang of regret at her stubbornness. The brief, flickering moment of sorrow that came with knowing he would have to kill both of his siblings. It didn't last long, but he couldn't deny it was there. He steeled his nerve again and watched his sibling from his perch.

"You can come out, Wizard," Serpent said over her shoulder as she continued to look upon the throng.

The Wizard was taken aback. He thought he had remained in quite a good spot out of sight of the display. He should have known better than to hide from a dragon-child, but, then, she had not exactly been a dragon when she had first arrived.

"An honor to be in your presence, my lady," the Wizard said as he emerged from the nearby shadows of the trees.

He came to stand next to Serpent who'd retreated a short distance so as not to provoke her wicked brother.

"I suppose we find ourselves at an impasse," the Wizard sighed.

"No. We do not," Serpent replied frankly.

"No? Not to doubt your abilities, but your brother alone would require your full attention. I'm no apprentice, but I believe there are a few too many…"

The Wizard stopped speaking and listened. He felt it first, but as the seconds passed he began to hear a noise behind the rumbling. He turned to see a sea of armored soldiers upon horseback riding towards them. Their banners were white and red, a rune circled in fire. The Sons of Edda. Ranks of mounted infantry were followed by more ranks of mounted archers. They were led by two men—one he instantly recognized as the Warrior. The other was a young man of similar age who bore a crown atop his head. The Red Prince, Vidar, had followed in the footsteps of his courageous father and rode to battle with his men.

"Red Warriors… hundreds of them…" the Wizard said with relief.

"More akin to thousands," Serpent clarified.

"Much better odds, though we're still outnumbered," the Wizard observed.

Upon his return to Mythesta and seeing the army camped just outside its borders, the Warrior was impressed by the numbers that his prince had mustered and led across the burning sands. When informed of Wyvern's location, the Red Prince was more than ready to reroute the army to the borders of the Diamond Realm. His warriors burned for a fight and had grown tired of standing guard at the border of what was, in their opinion, a swamp realm.

Once there it didn't take long before large wings cast a shadow over their camp. The Sons of Edda gathered and readied themselves to bring arms against whatever fiend had come to them. The Warrior truly thought Wyvern had arrived to destroy them. Then they found themselves captured by the beauty and majesty of Serpent. She came to call on their courage and ferocity to bring to bear against Wyvern. She described the fierce horde he'd gathered to himself at Sygil.

With such praise from the dragon-child, the fiery blood of the warriors had been stoked. They rode with Serpent across plain and valley until they arrived here at the site of the wondrous Diamond Spire to witness the siege firsthand.

"Drake will arrive shortly, my lady. He was spotted by the Red Wizardess through means of her magic," the Warrior said as his large horse strode up to them.

"Good. Does that help the odds, wizard?" she asked.

"Quite," the Wizard replied.

Wyvern looked down and sneered at his siblings' attempt to stand against him. A handful of men and an old conjurer against his armies? His smug sister and oafish brother against him? Did they not think he would prepare for such a thing?

"Your attempts humor me, sister," Wyvern called out to

Serpent. "The screams of their painful last moments will haunt you. Their blood is on your hands."

Serpent was unimpressed. Wyvern attempted to exploit her good nature. Watching him ascend the spire, she feared what he had in store for the Maiden. There was something more at work here.

"Why do the Morning Guard not attack?" the Warrior said, interrupting her thoughts.

"One of his ploys," answered the Wizard.

"More manipulation and low cunning," Serpent commented.

"The Morning Guard are sworn to protect the tower; not necessarily those within it. They're not the king's personal guard, rather defenders of Sygil," the Wizard explained. "So long as the tower stands and the horde remains outside the halls of the spire, they will hold their vigil. The Gray King has been missing along with the Gray Wizard. With Wyvern residing peacefully in the spire, they would not dare lay siege to it."

How Wyvern managed to take residence in the tower was both intriguing and terrifying, the Wizard thought. As he looked upon its stunning walls and saw Wyvern returning to its pinnacle, the Wizard realized what he needed to do.

"I must get inside," he thought aloud.

Serpent continued to look up at her brother. "Yes, the Maiden and the Prince will need you."

"How do you know of her?" the Wizard asked.

Serpent looked at him patiently. "I know all that occurs in my realm. I make it my place to know. Even your geistheim was being observed."

"Then why did you not protect them when they were taken by the beasts?" the Wizard asked almost confrontationally.

"I did not know what my brother wanted with them. That was equally as important as their safety, unfortunately."

The Wizard's next question more poured from his mouth

than was asked in any thoughtful manner. Serpent's ire was as dangerous as Wyvern's, after all.

"How did your brother usurp the spire under your nose?"

A low hiss escaped Serpent's maw. Her nostril's flared, and then she heaved a sigh.

"No one is perfect," she ceded.

"Indeed."

"Now, let's get you in the spire."

43

THE SERPENT AND THE OWL

Serpent stood upon her haunches and stretched herself to her full height.

"Brother!" she called out. "Wyvern!"

Wyvern looked back, just in time to hear a mighty roar pierce the sky. His elder brother, Drake, appeared from the clouds. His muscular frame was held aloft by powerful wings that beat ferociously as he slowed his descent and came to rest next to their sister.

"Your timing is immaculate." Serpent said, smiling at Drake's arrival.

"I would not leave you and the Eddings to fight this battle alone," said the great dragon-child. He and Serpent touched their foreheads in a sign of sibling affection.

Wyvern snorted in derision. "You want me to change my mind now that our dear brother has arrived?"

Serpent narrowed her eyes at him.

"I wish to send an ambassador, that we may avoid so much bloodshed."

Wyvern laughed a deep, genuine laugh that raked Serpent's

patience along burning coals. He turned and looked at her with barely contained contempt.

"I suppose a single man wouldn't be too much trouble. If they should be able to pass my army and the Morning Guard they are welcome to climb to the top!"

Wyvern turned and leaped from his perch on the tower. He flew back to the top of the structure and disappeared within. The stinger of his lithe tail scratching a deep gouge in the marble before disappearing in the highest alcove.

"That was gracious of him," the Wizard said sardonically.

Then, he had an epiphany.

"The boots..." he said, looking back at the thicket he'd emerged from. He had left the boots there, tucked beneath a large, exposed tree root after Serpent called out to him.

"What boots?" Serpent asked.

"Just a small means of travel I keep in my geistheim; or did you not know?" he smiled.

Seeing Serpent's glare, he gestured to their location.

"There. In the brush. Seven steps and they will return me here, to this very spot. Get me in the tower and I can return the Maiden and anyone else in contact with me."

"Could you guarantee the return of the Prince?" Drake asked.

The Wizard thought for a moment, but the tired look in his eyes was not promising.

"I cannot guarantee anyone's safety. Not the Prince's. Not the Maiden's. Not my own. I would be entering Wyvern's lair; a dangerous gamble."

"It's the best we have," Serpent concluded.

She looked at the slavering, stinking horde before her and turned to see the brave gathering behind them. She then looked to her brother. Serpent was wise, but it was Drake who knew the tactics and strategies of the battlefield best among the dragon-children.

"If we can defeat Wyvern, his army may scatter."

"Is that all?" Serpent quipped.

Drake ignored her and continued. "We'll wait before we engage them."

"Fetch your boots, Wizard" Serpent ordered.

Returning from the edge of the woods, the Wizard showed the boots to Serpent.

"It's odd. Almost funny, really," he thought out loud.

"What is that?" Serpent asked, her eyes lingering on the horde.

The Wizard smiled. "That our best plan lies in an old pair of magic boots."

Air huffed through Serpent's nose. The Wizard recognized it as a sigh. Serpent looked down at the Wizard who was putting the boots on and taking a white flower out of the pack that once contained the simple magic item.

"Be quick, Wizard," Serpent said.

She reached down and gripped him in a large clawed hand. The Wizard closed his eyes, not quite sure what to expect from the skilled dragon-sorceress. She gripped his upper torso in her other hand and clutched him gently. She then blew softly into her lovely claws. Violet flame trickled out from her fingers. When she opened her hands a great grey owl flew from her claws and towards the tower.

Serpent, Drake, and the Warrior watched as the owl flew out of sight towards the top. Wyvern's army didn't appear to notice.

"It will not be pleasant if he fails," the Warrior said, craning his neck to stare upwards.

"Does that surprise you?" Drake replied.

"I have seen Wyvern's wrath firsthand. Worse yet, I've seen the relics he hoards. There are none living who could know the full extent of his capabilities. Even you, my lady," he said to Serpent.

Expecting to be rebuked by the proud dragon-child, the Warrior instead saw Serpent peering at him with sad eyes.

"I regretfully agree, young Warrior."

44

THE MIND OF A MONSTER

A t the tower's peak, beneath the Great Diamond shining like a midday star, Wyvern returned to his honored guests. The Prince had recovered, unfortunately, and now placed himself close to the Maiden. How chivalrous and pointless, Wyvern thought.

Morgæna leered and fumed near the statue of the Gray Wizard. She hated the Prince; she had made this clear to Wyvern many times. He surmised that his youthful arrogance, above-average martial skill, and desire to be respected by his people contrasted too much with her own youthful arrogance, above-average magical skill, and desire to be feared by her people. Two sides of the same coin.

Wyvern needed her presence in Avallonis and had tasked her with gaining control of the powerful realm. Having just concluded its own golden age, Avallonis would be quite influential for centuries to come. Wyvern needed it brought to heel.

Ultimately she failed him in this. However, she had proven far more useful than her pathetic sister, Jezæla, the Violet Witch. It was Morgæna who had discovered the ruins in Upala that told of one such as the Maiden. It was Morgæna herself who discovered the Maiden during a visit to Emrallt as a dignitary, spotting her in the city's square. Should she continue to show her usefulness, it would be Morgæna who would be rewarded further. Wyvern would need a queen and she was not unpleasant to the eyes.

The three of them—Maiden, Prince, and Sybil—stood there defiant against him. The arrival of his sister and her little band had set him behind. They'd wasted enough of his time.

"You've waited long enough to find why I have brought you here; what all this has been for. All the suffering. The blood," Wyvern said, seating himself next to Morgæna.

She stroked his snout and smiled at him. Her gaze returned to the three companions and went cold again.

"Humanity is marvelous. So utterly fragile and useless from a natural perspective. Yet you have such fire, such unique cruelty of your own. You not only survive, you prosper. You flourish. You thrive. You rule the very spires themselves."

Wyvern approached the throne of the Diamond Spire. He coiled around it, stopping when he could look upon them all below the dais.

"It fits me... does it not?" he hissed.

"You want the throne? That's your grand scheme?" the Maiden scoffed.

A low rumble escaped his throat.

"It is not merely a throne. Do you know nothing of your history, you stupid ape?" He spat the words at her. The Prince reached for his blade but was quickly reminded it had been wrested from him as he choked on the ground.

"Only humans have ruled the old thrones. The seven spires have forever been held by human kings and queens. Even their wizards have ever been the sons and daughters of man. I cannot simply take the throne for myself..."

"And how can I... oh..." the Maiden remembered.

She remembered surviving Wyvern's sting. She remembered the Lord of Dream's bewilderment at her 'curious metaphysical state'. She remembered seeing the wisps; something only sybils should be able to accomplish and she saw them during her dream-like wanderings. She remembered seeing beyond Jezæla's hex and pulling the Violet Wizardess from the prison of the Barghest. She remembered seeing the same oily, smoking aura surrounding the Violet Witch, and taking her power from her. She remembered the butterflies. Finally, she remembered saving the Prince and how his grievous wound had been healed at her touch.

"Yes..." Wyvern whispered. "I can see it in your eyes. It is beginning to occur to you, finally, how special you are. How many miraculous things have you done since we crossed paths? Have you ever heard of healing magic existing anywhere? At any time in all of history?"

"I... I still don't know what it is I can do for you. You desire to be human? I can't make something into what it's not! I have healed, I have... purified," she said with hesitation, not entirely sure what to call the effect she had on the Violet Witch and Tytania. "I don't understand how you expect me to make you human!"

"I have heard of some of your deeds, Maiden. The Barghest? The queen? You turned a beast human, did you not?" he said slyly.

"I only undid what had been done..." she reasoned.

"There is nothing unnatural about a Barghest. They've been extinct for over a century but they certainly did exist. And what is a hex but a conjuring of magic? Magic is a manipulation of nature, but so are the spires."

The Maiden lowered her eyes. "I cannot make you human—I don't even know where to begin."

She raised her eyes, red with anger and tears, to glare at Wyvern. "And even if I did... I wouldn't."

"You can and you will!" Wyvern shouted, fire escaping his maw. As he rose to look down upon her, a slight blur of movement caught his attention. It was far too small to be his sibling. What creature dared enter Wyvern's throne room?

Suddenly, there was a puff of gray feathers accompanied by the sound of a hundred fluttering wings that simultaneously faded into nothingness. The Wizard was standing in the open court, much to Wyvern's surprise. He was holding a large feather, an owl's feather, and he tossed it casually aside.

"Your sister's magic is quite formidable," the Wizard said calmly.

45

WISDOM AND REGRET

Wyvern saw that the Wizard had appeared, conveniently, beside the Maiden. Wyvern bristled at his intrusion. He hissed and began to rear back to strike the fool when his eyes caught the mage's boots. He could just see the tips of them beneath the Wizard's robes, but they sang to him. They reverberated with powerful magic. It emitted such power that to look at them, for Wyvern, was like seeing them through a shallow pool.

"The boots—remove them, now!" he roared.

The Wizard's eyes narrowed dangerously. He took a deep breath and stepped next to the Maiden. It was one in a needed count of seven. Could he grab the young lady and make the other six fast enough to avoid Wyvern's barb, his breath, or Morgæna's magic?

Wyvern lunged from his place near the dais and, in a flash of blood-colored scales, his tail gripped the Sybil and slammed her against a nearby wall. His tail coiling about her and squeezing the life from her, Wyvern glared at the Wizard without another word. These wretches had tested his patience time and again—enough. He would begin teaching them humility by the most lethal of means. He needed the Prince if he was to manipulate the Maiden. He did not need the mewling Sybil.

Seeing Wyvern's incredible quickness and the ruthless nature in which he'd subdued the Sybil, who now gasped impotently in his coils, the Wizard lowered his head. He looked upon the enchanted boots that were his greatest chance to remove the Maiden from Wyvern's grasp. He might still succeed but at the death of the innocent young woman who was quickly fading in Wyvern's grip. He came to several quick conclusions and hated each of them.

The world could come to great misery if he let Wyvern succeed. The Sybil may not forgive him. Her spirit may haunt him and his choice certainly would, but the Wizard's conscience would be that much heavier if he did not take every chance to destroy Wyvern's grab at dominion over the continent. The Maiden was all that could destroy him. Here, the monster had control. Here, little to nothing could be done to stop the malevolent dragon-child.

The Wizard grabbed the Maiden and whispered, in a moment where it seemed all time had ceased, "Run."

He pulled the Maiden towards a nearby window. Six steps, he reminded himself. Six steps and they would be safe near Serpent and Drake and a thousand angry Red Warriors.

With his second step, he pulled the Maiden in his direction. Wyvern, however, was not slow to react.

By the third step, Wyvern had dropped the Sybil and leaped in their direction.

On the fourth step, Wyvern was soaring over them, propelled by his powerful legs and fueled by rage.

The fifth step had the Wizard yanking the Maiden suddenly in a different direction.

Finally, the sixth step. The next would see them disappear and Wyvern, no doubt, would be howling in frustration. The fate of the Sybil and his own Prince would stay with him for the rest of his days. He could only tell himself that it must be done, for the good of all the realms, not just his own.

He felt himself being pulled by an outward force. He'd never made the journey with open eyes before. He was unsure what effect it would have. He felt himself being lifted from the ground... and suddenly slamming back down onto it.

He gasped for breath and rolled onto his back. He saw the Maiden rising to her feet. Morgæna was scowling viciously at them with her hands coming to rest at her sides. She lifted them again, her open hands crackling with dark magic.

A swift, looming shadow passed over him and he saw Morgæna lifted from the ground by Wyvern's lashing tail. She was hurled against the floor with a painful cry.

Clutching at her body in a panic, she found no blood or wound marring her robes. Wyvern had only struck her. As she attempted to stand on throbbing, shaking limbs she heard his roaring voice directed at her.

"Never touch my prey again, witch!"

She hung her head obediently. She was glad to still be alive after such a mistake. The thought of a horrible, agonizing death from Wyvern's venom had shaken respect and fear of him back into her.

Wyvern breathed a gout of flame at the Wizard's feet. The boots caught fire immediately. The lower hems of his robes soon followed. The Wizard frantically kicked the boots from his feet and stomped at the fire.

The beast then recognized that one of his prisoners was missing. He looked to the throne and his eyes went alight in an all-consuming fire. The Prince, in the skirmish, had made his way to the dais and was now standing, strong and tall, with Calibern drawn and ready. The blade's reflected light burned Wyvern's eyes. The wind dancing off its infused steel resounded painfully in his ears. He smelled the blood of a million vanquished evils upon its edge.

This was enough. His patience had burned away in frustration, pain, and anger. Wyvern rose high on his haunches. The Prince stood tall, but he stood taller. He bared his shining fangs as flame licked his lips and nostrils. He spread his wings and came down upon his forelegs and released a vicious, crashing roar that forced all in the room to cover their ears—except the Prince.

He flinched and gritted his teeth against the sound. It shook his soul and attempted to cow his nerve. He looked into the mouth of hell before him as it spat cinders and bathed him in a fetid stench. Sulfur. This was unlike anything he had ever heard. It occurred to him that Wyvern was not merely attempting to intimidate the Prince; this was a call to battle.

46

BATTLE OF THE DIAMOND SPIRE

The sound from the top of the Diamond Spire was horrendous. At first, Serpent's heart was lifted at the thought that, perhaps, it was the death-cry of her brother. Looking at the plethora of crooked, stained teeth bared at her from Wyvern's hoard, she quickly changed her assumption.

The boglins howled in delight and the trolls banged a single massive fist on their chests. The Warrior recognized the challenge: they were advancing. They began with barely a trot, but as a troll loosed a shrieking cry and an ogre bellowed a deep shout, they bolted into a cacophonous wave of bloodlust.

The Red Prince lifted his blade, shining in the afternoon sun. Without a word, the disciplined archers, still on their horses, nocked their arrows and waited. Vidar swiftly lowered his arm and hundreds of arrows flew over their heads. The silent restraint of the Edding soldiers contrasted against the hateful bellowing of Wyvern's horde. The volley struck the advancing monstrosities, felling boglins one after the other. The arrows bounced harmlessly off the leathery hides of the trolls. The ogres, with their rolling, fat-covered muscles, were enraged by the few arrows that reached them and became embedded in their corpulent bodies.

The putrid tide was barely slowed by the first volley. A second did little more than anger them further. Vidar looked to the Warrior, his eyes alight and determined. He shouted to his men, and the Sons of Edda, in their combined might, returned an indiscernible shout and rode against the horde. The Warrior and Prince Vidar were at their forefront. Horde and army clashed head-on as the mounted warriors rode among the shrieking boglins, chopping and slashing as if they were fighting a wave of filthy water. It had the same effect. Wherever one fell another was there to bite and hack and scratch in its place.

The boglins were voracious; nothing like those met by the Maiden in the swamps of Mythesta. These were driven mad by greed and hate burned into them by Wyvern's promise of boundless riches and endless gluttony. All lies, of course, as Wyvern knew few, if any, would leave the battlefield alive.

The trolls knew Wyvern's plans as well. They took a psychotic glee in knowing the boglins would be fodder for the battle. They were also promised plunder and murder to their black hearts' content. Stomping and barreling their way through boglins dead and alive, their hateful eyes were set on those Red Warriors who were skillfully wedging their way through the filthy mass. The strength and skill of the men were well-beyond the endless swarm of rusted stingers and dull claws. Occasionally, one of the trolls would pick up one of the boglins and hurl it, screaming and flailing, into a horse or rider, which sent both broken bodies to the ground.

The boglins quickly learned to steer clear of the trolls and leave a good bit of room around them. This proved advantageous for the Red Warriors. Their captains called out for their men to ride into the clearings and overwhelm the trolls with numbers. They reared their warhorses which kicked at the monsters with their powerful legs. They pierced and slashed at the leathery hide of the trolls until a small number of them fell to the ground.

However, the beasts' kills outnumbered the warriors'. The trolls, swinging their oversized arms like massive clubs, sent horse and rider flying through the air. Bones crunched and muffled screams came from beneath the feet of the trolls as they stomped through ranks of Red Warriors..

Drake was already in the air when the first troll had fallen. The Sons of Edda had never faced trolls before and were therefore unprepared to face the creatures' most fearsome trait.

Trolls were not a common sight; they rarely bred and fought amongst themselves so often that few survived to adulthood. A fully grown troll, though, had an entirely different mechanism for survival. They could quickly close wounds, mend bones— even regrow limbs if given time enough. These regenerative aspects could only be prevented if the troll was burned with fire. Drake ensured that every fallen troll was awash in flame as soon as it fell to the ground.

It was posed to Drake, shortly before the battle, if he should not just take to the air and roast them where they stood. He made sure to point out that a living troll, enraged by pain and burning with dragonfire would quite likely be more dangerous than they already were. This new plan was quickly formulated.

It was difficult to stay in the air, however. The ogres, not quite capable, or merely unwilling, to engage in any sort of charge were wrenching anything they could from the ground and hurling it at Drake. They grabbed trees, fountains, and statuary to use as ammunition, becoming living, mobile catapults. Drake heaved gouts of flame at them and heard their roars of pain as his breath scorched their deformed bodies. His victory was short-lived as a piece of debris smashed into his ribs. He roared in agony and he felt the muscles powering his wings grow weak. He managed to slow his descent until he was grounded. The boglins quickly swarmed over the downed dragon-child, like foul, stinking ants. He bit and snapped at the creatures, but every breath he drew to bring forth his fire only filled his chest with pain.

The Warrior saw the great Drake on the ground and witnessed the boglins' futile attempts to breach his thick scales with their rusted and makeshift weapons. Most broke, cracked, and chipped while those that did manage to pierce a section of Drake's natural armor found their weapon breaking from its hilt as they pulled and yanked it free. He gripped his blade and charged for the skirmish.

Leaping upon Drake's side, he heard the dragon-child grunt in pain. He slid down Drake's stomach, bringing many boglins with him, and made short work of them. He grabbed at the ones he could reach and tossed them off the great creature. The rest he was content to swing at. Brown, oily blood covered Drake by the time the Warrior had cleared enough room for the dragon-child to stand to his feet. They both looked up in time to see that an ogre had made its way to them. It appeared quite incandescent.

Part of the morbid, obese giant's anger was due to the burned flesh it bore on one of its fatty arms and back. Drake had wounded it, but only enough to fan its rage. Now the ogre was all but on top of them before they had time to notice. Ogres are known for being uniquely ugly. Each one had its own distinctive variation of grotesquery that gave it an advantage in battle. The current hideous bulk of fury that approached them walked with the aid of one meaty fist upon the ground like a sort of ape.

Drake roared at the monstrosity from his wounded and vulnerable position. The Warrior readied his sword, looking for any opening to attack the mass of fat, flesh, and muscle. The ogre slammed its smaller arm on the ground in anger and then raised both fists in the air, hefting the tonnage of its large, malformed hand like a massive hammer.

As Drake and the Warrior glared at the approaching ogre, they saw a blur of movement. The ogre was slammed into the ground howling in pain as Serpent dropped from the sky upon him, her long claws piercing his fat-covered muscle. Her weight and speed felled the monster, Serpent gaining the upper hand and pinning the monster onto the ground. She roared defiantly at the ogre as it shouted in return. She then loosed a ferocious blast of fire, inches from its hideous face. After seconds of bearing the furnace of a dragon's burning wrath, there was nothing left of the ogre's body above the shoulders but a small amount of ash and scored stone.

The ferocity and brutality of the attack drove the nearby boglins and trolls back. Drake could now be helped to his feet as Red Warriors filled the gaps left by the ebbing tide of boglins. Serpent helped her wounded brother, and she did so with maternal care.

"Are you alright, friend?" the Warrior asked.

"I will live," Drake groaned in discomfort as he stood. He looked at the rusted spearheads, blades, and axes that protruded from various parts of his body. He snarled in disgust and with a quick, wheezing breath he washed his body with fire and burned away the remains of the vermin.

They took a moment to breathe and collect themselves, studying the state of the battle. A deep, subtle tremor alarmed the dragon-children. They looked around, concerned, but saw nothing.

"What is it?" the Warrior asked with concern. "What do you see?"

"It's not what I see..." Serpent responded absently. "Do you feel that?"

"Yes..." Drake replied in a hushed, worried tone.

"No," the Warrior said simultaneously.

Then, he felt it. An ominous rumble that grew louder.

"Wait..." the Warrior whispered.

In the heated battle raging around them, none of the other warriors or creatures seemed to notice. The source soon revealed itself. In a thunderous eruption that rained men, fiends, and debris upon the battlefield, a monstrous grey-scaled jormungandr rose from the ground. Two separate heads connected to a massive, black-scaled body. Each set of four sickly, yellow eyes scanned the battlefield. Both maws split apart and roared a challenge to the dragon-children.

"Spires help us…" Serpent whispered.

47

NIDHOGR

The Warrior heard screams both human and inhuman. He smelled the wet dirt raining around them that was pulled from the deep with the creature. He heard the unwholesome roar from a living nightmare that crawled from a cold hell.

A jormungandr was trouble enough. This was the two-headed liege of the monstrous worms—Nidhogr. His arrival to the battle was met with fear from both sides. The boglins ran for fear of being devoured. The remaining trolls shouted in victory and the ogres smiled maliciously. Nidhogr, himself, merely snarled and growled. He owed Wyvern a debt, and had heard the dragon-child's call to battle. Today, Nidhogr would repay that debt with his enemy's blood.

The creature focused one of its heads on each dragon-child. The *hiss* that escaped its throats sounded like steam forcing its way from the bowls of the earth. Nidhogr was massive, even for a jormungandr. The dragon-children's fire would burn. Their fangs would pierce his scales and slice his flesh. They would scream when these things failed them as he rent their bodies into large, bleeding pieces.

Nidhogr noticed the larger of the two was wounded, its head hanging slightly in pain. The human stood protecting the injured dragon-child. The greatest sign was the smell—his fear, his pain. The large one would die first.

Nidhogr's heads roared; one then the other. His powerful muscles and scales dug into the stonework surrounding the Diamond spire and propelled him toward his prey. His mouths opened wide, baring the thousand fangs of a jormungandr. In the case of this monstrosity, a thousand more.

Serpent stepped in front of her brother and breathed fire at the approaching fiend. The Warrior felt utterly useless—what could he do against such a demon? It seemed his fate was revealed to him. It was one that any Son of Edda, any Red Warrior, would accept. He would die a brave, blood-soaked death and make certain his enemy remembered it.

Nidhogr was dazed by the flame that washed over his heads, but it wouldn't last. This gave the Warrior the opportunity to jump on its back. He grabbed hold of a massive dorsal scale and winced in pain. The scales of Nidhogr were sharper than any other jormungandr. They were as teeth of their own, used to cut through the very innards of the world that it called home. The Warrior winced with each handhold, his tough leather gloves tearing against the scales. He climbed up, using the scales to help reach the base of the monster's thrashing necks. Each grasping motion bringing more pain. His boots and gloves having been lacerated from the climb, the Warrior gripped his blade in cut, bloodied hands. He lifted his blade into the air and swung with a strength born of reckless resolve. He was not leaving here alive and, spires-willing, neither was Nidhogr.

When the blow struck the base of one of the beast's necks it felt as though he had hit solid stone. It reverberated through his arms and shot pain through his shoulders.

You old, withered fool! the Warrior cursed himself.

He looked at where his blade landed and saw nothing—no

scratch or chipping of any kind. He then looked directly between Nidhogr's necks where they met his body.

Of course.

There, he saw the scales were thinner, smaller, and weaker than the others in order for his necks to move freely. As Nidhogr lashed about at Drake and Serpent the Warrior saw the scales ripple and bend; less like solid rock and more akin to snakeskin.

He hefted his sword again, one hand gripping tight to a scale, and lifted the blade above his head. He pointed it downward and plunged the sword as hard as he could into the fleshy joint. He met with fierce resistance. These scales were still tough, and the muscle thick and powerful, but he felt his blade pierce its way through. Nidhogr roared in pain. The Warrior's time had become much less abundant. Nidhogr was now not only aware of his presence, but concerned about it.

The two-headed wurm curled and stretched but couldn't reach him. He thrashed and bit but could not shake the Warrior loose. Nidhogr decided that if the human could not be shaken free, he would be pulled free. A human cannot breathe underground with lungs full of dirt. Nidhogr wheeled around and began to make his way back to the tunnel he had created earlier from his arrival.

Serpent saw Nidhogr attempting to flee. She felt a twinge of success at first, then confusion as she felt the battle wasn't greatly favoring her and her brother. Then she saw the Warrior positioned on Nidhogr's back and the blood trailing behind him.

He's going to suffocate him, she realized.

"Brother, can you fly?" she asked urgently.

Drake, hearing the fear in her voice, steeled his resolve, and nodded sharply.

"Yes."

"Then, come!" Serpent shouted, hear hind legs launching her into the air.

Drake gritted his teeth, groaning as sharp pains shot through his side and back, and beat his wings against the wind and pain. He rose slowly at first, but then saw Nidhogr fleeing with the Warrior and doubled his effort. He saw Serpent circle about and come down atop the fleeing jormungandr, grabbing his hard scales with her claws. Nidhogr flailed about like a snake in an eagle's clutches and threw the Warrior from his back. Drake grabbed the flailing tail of Nidhogr and, together, they hefted him screeching into the air.

Lying on his back, pain shooting through every muscle, the Warrior looked up to see an astonishing sight. Peering through the glare of the sun he witnessed two silhouetted, draconic figures carrying a roaring, writhing mass ever higher into the sky. They continued until he felt they would carry the beast to be burned away in the sun. Then, the two dragon-children turned away and carried Nidhogr in the direction of the Diamond Spire.

"There, sister!" Drake shouted.

He gestured in the direction of the spire itself. Serpent cast him a reproachful glare.

"Do you think me insane? I will not throw this filth into the spire!" she reproached.

"Next to the tower, sister," Drake added.

Serpent looked down and immediately saw what her brother suggested. A band of the Red Warriors had circled the second of Wyvern's great monstrosities—the chimera. Its serpent-headed tail lay limp at one side covered in blood and arrows. The horned goat's head thrashed about, attempting to keep the attackers at bay, while the lion's head swallowed what remained of a recently slain warrior. Bodies of boglins and warriors were strewn about the vicinity of the beast—it appeared to kill without much discrimination.

"I see, Drake. Clever, little brother," Serpent smiled.

Flying in tandem they bore Nidhogr in a swift descent upon the melee. The crazed beast was too preoccupied in its rage-fueled tantrum to see the dragon-children carrying it to its doom. Serpent and Drake made certain not to fly too low, lest Nidhogr survive the fall.

The warriors attacking the chimera had lost many in such a short span of fighting. The creature was as fierce as anything they had ever faced and twice as brutal. The serpent's head finally fell only because it lacked the fortitude of the other two. Those that died from being pierced through by its massive fangs were obvious—their bodies lay twisted in agony upon the ground from its venom.

Their captain was prepared to order a retreat when he heard a pair of powerful cries from the sky. They were distant and closing in. He looked up and saw Drake and Serpent flying in their direction with a large, squirming abomination in their claws. He then understood why they were calling out—the captain needed to make good on his former plan.

"Retreat!" he called out. "Sons of Edda, retreat!"

He rallied what men he could, though some couldn't hear over the cacophony of battle. There were also wounded that couldn't flee. He could only lead those he could to safety and hope the rest would be spared.

The men under his command were confused at first. They fled from the chimera's onslaught but only far enough to observe it safely. Why were they not rejoining another skirmish? The chimera, ordered to remain near the spire, watched them flee and roared in victory with its two surviving heads—even the goat's head let out a baleful noise that could barely be recognized as anything belonging to an animal.

The chimera's victory was short-lived. In the midst of its victorious roar, Nidhogr, loosed by the dragon-children, crashed upon it with a thunderous din. The sharp, stone-hard scales tore at the chimera's fur-covered hide. The greatest of the jormungandr, hurled at such speeds and from such a height, nearly tore through the three-headed fiend in a gruesome display. Massive bones cracked like timber and the ground was instantly soaked in vile blood.

The Red Warriors looked on in astonishment. The roars of the dragon-children, the true victors, pierced the skies. As the dust cleared, Nidhogr could be seen feebly lifting one of his heads—broken and dying. The other lay motionless. The end of his tail twitched and the great lord of the jormungandr gurgled a pathetic, impotent cry before falling for the last time. The Sons of Edda cheered at the unfathomable slaying of both creatures before separating ranks to attend the wounded and bolster their brothers in the fray.

48

SYGIL

The Prince glared at Wyvern. The piercing call to war had set in motion a clamor below that could be heard in the great throne room. It was a dull roar heard hundreds of feet below, but it tore at the Prince to know that the grounds of the Diamond Spire would be stained by the fruit of Wyvern's greed.

"All this," the Prince found himself saying aloud. "So you can, what, be human?"

Wyvern's keeled scales bristled again and his eyes narrowed. "Such an impossible desire, boy? Do you think so little of yourself that it's not feasible for a child of Father Dragon to want to be human?"

"I feel it unthinkable that a child of Father Dragon would be so murderous and cruel to attain anything. And, yes, you've been quite disdainful of my people."

Wyvern scoffed. "For all your teachings you apparently know little of my other brother. The dead one."

"I pity your father most; how he must feel knowing that he failed in raising you..."

Wyvern lashed out with his barbed tail, forcing the Prince to drop to a knee to avoid his head being separated from his neck. He barely did so in time.

"You talk too much, boy," Wyvern hissed. There was lethal calm in his eyes. He was angry, but not as furious as the Prince had hoped.

"Enough!" the Maiden shouted. "I can't make you human, fiend! Even if I had such power, I would rather die!"

Wyvern snarled, his fangs gleamed, and with his claws he slapped the Maiden and sent her crashing against a wall. She shouted in pain and the Wizard and Prince both began to race toward her. However, black bolts of lightning struck the ground before the Wizard, sparks cracking and scoring the stone. He halted immediately. Wyvern's claws caught the Prince in a vicious backhand that sent him sprawling to the ground well away from the Maiden.

"Enough? *Enough?*" Wyvern shouted. His hot breath caused the Maiden to recoil.

He stomped to a table that bore his relics. He grabbed what appeared to an ordinary, albeit large, conch shell. He also took a handful of sand, scorched it into crude glass in his hands, and hurled it from the window.

"Very well, Maiden. Enough. I let your friends live. A sign of my mercy to you despite their repeated attempts to destroy me. Now... listen!"

He threw the remaining sand into the conch shell and slammed it to the ground. The Maiden thought it would shatter, but instead, she heard a noise coming from within. Soon it was loud enough for all to hear. Sounds of metal against metal. Sounds of pain and shouts of violence. Orders mingled with indecipherable, guttural bellowing. It was the sound of the conflict below.

"A Heeding Shell..." the Wizard whispered to himself.

None of the shells had been seen for generations. They were crafted by old wizards from Upala. One could hear something occurring hundreds, even thousands of miles away by placing a handful of sand in that location and placing another handful of the same batch of sand in the shell. Wyvern scorched the first bit of sand to ensure it reached the bottom of the tower.

"So many dying..." she whispered, horrified.

"And so many more to come," Wyvern hissed menacingly. "I've spared you. I've spared your friends. In return, I demand the price I have asked. Then I will permit you to leave."

The Maiden looked to him in shock. "Why?"

"Because I never want to see you—or anyone associated with you—ever again," Wyvern said through narrow eyes.

The cunning snake, the Wizard thought.

He was sure the Maiden would be true to her word. Wyvern knew that the Maiden was the only one who held any sort of power that could defy him. In letting her live, though, did he truly know how much? He would indeed let them all leave so that he wouldn't risk open war with all the realms. Not yet.

The comparatively small number of Red Warriors had ridden against him at the behest of Serpent. Drake came of his own will. But, to kill the Sybil, who had gained favor with the Violet Queen, or the Blue Wizard of the council or, spires forbid, the heir of Avallonis, would bring entire realms down upon him.

The Maiden's eyes darted about as she thought over the offer. She didn't know how to give Wyvern his humanity. It wasn't as apparent as the solution had been with the Barghest. There was no soul trapped within Wyvern's mortal frame. She doubted he had anything resembling a soul, but if it would give them their freedom...

A loud clang followed by a reflexive shriek from Wyvern split her thoughts. The Prince had taken the opportunity to strike. Wyvern had all manner of magicks protecting him. But, he was still evil to his core. Caliburn's own benevolent arcane nature would still strike through the heart of such evil.

The Sybil rose to help the Prince and managed to grab a few

bits of crumbled stone to use for a spell. She whispered the incantation and threw the small bits of rock. She expected them to enlarge to the size of a man's head with all the speed with which she had thrown the pebbles. A crushing weight hit her and all her senses were lost.

The Wizard saw the Sybil, in the midst of an incantation, take a blow from Wyvern who had thrashed his tail in pain. She fell unconscious to the floor and nearly rolled out of one of the windows. He grimaced. Again, he couldn't afford to help her. He had to get to the Maiden.

Morgæna saw the Wizard focus on the Maiden. She pulled a sprig of nightshade from within her robes. She whispered into her hand and then, opening it palm up, blew upon the now crumbled, deadly plant. Wispy tendrils of grey smoke coiled and twisted through the air until they reached the Wizard. He covered his mouth quickly with his robes the moment the smell had touched his nostrils, which he knew meant it was already too late. As his lungs began to burn he looked with tear-choked eyes at the Maiden.

Wyvern recoiled in pain and howled at the fire shooting through his tail. He looked down to see blood pooling wherever his tail landed. His stinger was gone.

Looking about frantically he spotted it lying on the floor in a red pool of its own. A loud clang caught his attention. He looked over to see the Prince had acquired a helmet and shield from one of the decorative suits of armor against the wall. The Prince was now fully armored and had crashed his sword against his shield challenging Wyvern.

Wyvern felt the blood in his body grow hot. His scales quivered; not in fear, but rage and hate. He felt his mouth grow hot with eager fire as the grievous pain in his tail faded. Eyeing the Prince, he brought his tail forward and breathed a gout of fire upon the mutilated stub that had once contained his vicious barb. It cauterized the wound and stopped the bleeding, but caused him a deal more of pain, though he didn't flinch in the sight of his enemy.

Enough, the Maiden had said. Enough. Yes, this pup would now bear the wrath he deserved.

The Maiden lay prostrate, agony coursing through her. She was surprised that every bone in her body wasn't broken. She assumed Wyvern knew her abilities would heal her, and slapped her against the wall out of sheer brutality.

From her limited vantage point, she witnessed the Sybil fall to floor unconscious and perilously close to an open archway. She saw the Wizard succumb to a great fit of coughing and look to her with pain-filled eyes. Such suffering. The thought of causing others pain, even the smallest of creatures, went against her being. Her own father would laugh when she took a wandering spider out to find a new home among the brush. But, not Wyvern. He could no longer be suffered to live. He was anathema to all that existed.

"You old wretch," Morgæna seethed, glaring at the Wizard with unrestrained hate.

She stalked towards them. As she raised her hands, black, coiling strands climbed up her arms. She cackled, and it was an evil, chilling sound. Her eyes seemed almost aglow with a hideous, unnatural light. She threw her head back to behold the magic that shifted, angry and restless, about her hands. She lifted her hands higher, preparing to reduce the Wizard to a withered, smoldering husk. The Maiden threw herself over the vulnerable mage.

"Sister..." a feeble voice called out.

Morgæna looked down to see the Sybil clutching at the hems of her robes. Snarling at the pathetic display, she lowered her hands and felt the dark magic tingle as it coursed back into her blood. She cast a glance back to see the Maiden still there, nearly weeping as she protected the dying Wizard.

Morgæna knelt down to look at her injured sister, lying there grasping at her. She gently grabbed the Sybil's wrist and placed her hand beneath her sister's chin inclining it so the Sybil could look upon her.

"Olændra, my sweet, stupid sister. I gave you a chance to be great. You and I were always so much more talented than Jezæla. Mother knew and, I believe, so did you. I do regret that it has come to this—but only just so."

Morgæna smiled a crooked, evil smile at her weakened sister. With a great effort the Sybil came to her knees and threw her arms around her sister. Morgæna scowled at the show of affection. A hug, now? Was she pleading for her life?

Then, Morgæna tensed as she realized that her sister wasn't embracing her. The Sybil was gripping too tightly and Morgæna found it difficult to pull away.

"Goodbye, sister," the Sybil whispered, her eyes filled with tears.

Holding on tightly to the ill-prepared Morgæna, the Sybil, Olændra, with all the strength left in her, fell back and took them both over the perilous edge. The Maiden looked on in shock as Morgæna's screams fell further and further away.

As the wind whipped at her face and her eyes watered, Morgæna began frantically reciting the words to a featherweight spell. She tried clutching at the components in her robes, but Olændra gripped too tightly. Her sister was whispering words of her own: counterspells.

She imagined her older sister was wanting her to remember that she loved her. Olændra had always been sentimental. As her mind raced for ideas to save herself, he eyes saw the roiling battle below them growing closer. She still hated her sister for doing this to her. She hated many things. As time froze for a moment as the ground rose to meet them, Morgæna realized that deep down in the darkest parts of her dwelt a small mote of sadness.

49

OF MONSTERS AND MEN

A weak hand was gripping at the Maiden's clothes. The Wizard, blood trickling from his nose and mouth, was weakly whispering words to her through pained breaths.

"Young lady... my lovely, precious, young lady..." His words were lost in a series of painful, wheezing breaths. "You must do as he asks... Wyvern."

"How?" the Maiden asked, choking on tears. "How can I do this?"

"You must... he needs you to get... what he wants. Wherever he treads... he brings death. Where... wherever you go, you bring life. You can undo anything that he has wrought. I've failed, but you can still undo him. Remember the miracles..."

As the Wizard heaved and tried to catch his breath, the Maiden recalled again the many wonders she found herself performing. They had all been wounds, injustices, hexes wrought by Wyvern in some way—and she had undone them.

"Yes..." the Wizard said, seeing the light in her eyes. "You understand."

The Prince and Wyvern were committed to each other's destruction. They hadn't seen the Sybil's sacrifice to end her sister's evil. They hadn't seen the Maiden counseled by a dying Wizard. The Prince saw only a draconic, twisted beast maimed and enraged. Wyvern saw only a whelp of a man whose skills had, he admitted hesitantly to himself, grown dramatically in the time since they had last met.

The shield he'd grabbed from among the armored suits glowed almost as red as the Great Ruby atop Edda's spire after bearing the brunt of multiple blasts of fire from Wyvern's maw. The Prince was forced to toss it aside when it became too hot to bear. The Prince saw, for the first time, hesitation and even fear in Wyvern as he slashed and cut at the beast with Calibern. Wyvern had been maimed, perhaps for the first time, and was not a foolish creature.

The injury sustained by the cursed Calibern was insulting. Wyvern would not be so brazen again. The whimpering pup sought to be a biting hound, but a filthy mongrel he would ever be. Wyvern still had the strength of his tail to crush him even in his blessed armor. It proved difficult, however, as the Prince out-maneuvered him. Where had he learned these skills?

Wyvern smashed his tail into the Prince intending to catch him in its coil and crush the life from him. The Prince had braced for such an attack and pivoted away from Wyvern's grip. It was difficult for the Prince to see from within the helmet, but he ruled it better that his head be protected. It had been quite useful with the number of falls and blows he had suffered in the battle.

The Prince managed to draw near to his discarded shield, now cooled, and donned it again. Wyvern roared in anger and slashed at the Prince with his claws. Upon feeling his claws hit steel, he lashed at the shield with his mangled tail with such force that it was thrown again from the Prince's arm. The Prince cried out as his forearm was wrenched so awkwardly he thought for a moment it might be broken. Taking advantage of this hesitation, Wyvern brought a massive claw to bear upon him and pinned the Prince against the wall.

Their gaze locked for a moment. Burning, seething hatred from Wyvern pierced through the visor of the Prince's helm. What he saw, staring back at him, were the defiant and courageous eyes of a king. It chilled Wyvern for a moment and the fire in his eyes flickered. None of this mongrel's valor would save him now. Baring his shining fangs, a foreboding growl rumbled in the dragon-child's throat.

"I'll do it," came a steely voice.

It was quiet at first but echoed in his head like a distant horn.

"I will do as you ask, creature," the Maiden repeated.

Wyvern kept his eyes locked on the Prince as he spoke to the Maiden.

"Call off your pet, girl," Wyvern said, referring to the Prince.

The Maiden stood where she could look into the Prince's eyes through his helm.

"Do as I ask, my Prince... please."

The Prince winced at the thought. Had Wyvern won? He looked at the Maiden and saw the determination in her eyes. Very well... he would acquiesce to his Maiden. He would trust her judgment. He sheathed Calibern and cradled his throbbing arm.

"Discard it," Wyvern ordered.

The Prince regarded him with disdain, barely looking Wyvern's way.

"Toss it, dog!" Wyvern shouted.

The Prince looked to the Maiden who nodded slowly. What was she doing, giving in to this monster's demands? He unsheathed his weapon and threw it near the throne. It clanged loudly against the stone floor and rang painfully in his ears.

"I have one condition," the Maiden said firmly.

Wyvern tossed the Prince aside, removing the whelp from his presence. He would do no harm now—he loved the Maiden. Wyvern could smell the stench of affection on him. He would do as his Maiden asked.

"I don't see you in much of a condition to make demands," Wyvern snarled as he turned to the Maiden.

"And without me, your plans are all for naught," she calmly reminded him.

"And what is this condition of yours?" Wyvern growled.

The sorrow and empathy in her eyes sickened Wyvern. Soft and juvenile; a waste of time. What horrid thing was she prepared to ask?

"You have many relics and vast knowledge. Save the Wizard and I shall make you human."

Wyvern narrowed his eyes and looked from her to the Wizard and back again. The old mage lay pale and motionless on the stone floor.

Wyvern laughed. A black, hollow, mirthless sound.

"And now, I fear, it's my turn to deny you. I can't possibly raise the dead!" he said sardonically. "Your power is immense, but even you can't draw on back from the realms of death."

Wyvern didn't doubt the Maiden's conviction. He did doubt her capability. Death was beyond her abilities. Then again, she had saved herself from his barb. She hadn't died—only slept. The Wizard had already passed from the living, however. He had already crossed that veil. This may be too much for her. But, if she could bring him back... her value to Wyvern would be immeasurable.

The Maiden thought on the Wizard's last words. She could undo anything Wyvern had wrought. She approached the Wizard and looked at his pale, still body. It was Morgæna's dark magic that had slain him, but her greatest powers were a 'gift' from Wyvern...

She knelt beside the Wizard. She touched his worn, wise

cheek. It was cold and lifeless. She winced and then saw the blood that had trickled from his nose and mouth. This was not how she remembered him. She remembered a kind man. Stern but gentle in a way that made her smile. Her heart warmed at the thought. She took the other cheek in her hand and lifted his head slightly. Then, with tender care, breathed softly onto his face, letting her breath flow into his mouth and nostrils. She stroked his hair and laid his head back gently.

Wyvern smiled viciously. *Prepare for disappointment, girl,* he thought, *what are you in the face of death?*

The Wizard then gasped and his body tensed. The Maiden took his hand and it gripped painfully onto hers. He looked around in panic as color returned to his face.

"Spires-all..." he said as he regained consciousness.

The old man looked at the Maiden and a light came to his eyes.

"You... you didn't..." he said in disbelief.

The Maiden shook her head softly. "I did," she said with a smile. She stood and turned to Wyvern.

"Now, I will give you what you seek," she said coldly.

She held out a soft hand. Wyvern hesitated, but then approached her carefully. He then leaned his head slowly forward keeping his eyes on the Prince and Wizard. Seeing them both unmoving—the Wizard still frail and the Prince in shock at the seeing the dead return to life—he turned his burning gaze to the Maiden.

She placed her hand on his muzzle. It was hot and prickled her skin to touch. She looked him in the eyes and felt her soul burn under his searing stare. She also saw, within those eyes, that which she could hold onto and strip him of his draconic heritage and make him a man.

"Wyvern, you shall have the humanity you seek. You shall share in our glory, our enduring spirit, our strengths... and our weaknesses."

Wyvern felt a strange, nauseating sensation. He fell to his haunches and shrieked in pain. His scales molted and his skin grew taut. His blood cooled to the point that he felt as though he were dying. The cursed witch! What had she done to him? She would suffer for this!

In a few moments Wyvern felt whole again; different, but whole. He opened his eyes to see the Maiden, Prince, and Wizard staring at him. Their faces were grim, but none more so than the Maiden's.

Wyvern stood and stumbled to the ornate mirror hanging near his relics. It felt awkward to walk. What he saw in the mirror, besides mist upon the other side, was the face of a young and handsome human male.

He chuckled to himself at first, and it quickly grew to victorious, almost maniacal, laughter.

"Yes! Yes! Do you see this, you foolish old man?" he shouted into the mirror.

For the first time, the three companions saw another form in the mirror—not reflected, but within. It was shadowed and shrouded in mist but appeared to be banging on the glass with impunity.

Wyvern continued to laugh in ecstasy. He backed away and turned to look upon his throne. In the back of his mind, a mote of doubt had scratched at his brain. The thought of transforming himself into a human, the only creature on Septer capable of ruling a spire, seemed a great gamble even for him. But, he'd done it. It was the greatest treasure that took him the longest to find, the most dangerous to pursue, the riskiest to use. Human form was granted to him. The great Diamond Spire was his.

His relics would secure his power, as no doubt his army below had been decimated. The sounds from the Heeding Shell had diminished greatly.

He turned back to the mirror and glared at the human shape inside. Wyvern had been mocked and disregarded by his siblings.

He was patient, however, and it had paid greatly. He would destroy them first and if his father would not see to reason, well, it would be a great battle, perhaps even require him going to war, but his father would fall, too.

He would need a queen; a beautiful queen worthy of his side. He would grant her great powers so she could sit as his Gray Wizardess. The Diamond Spire would see a golden age that would never end.

Wyvern suddenly felt a sharp, jarring pain and pressure in his chest. It hurt—abominably. He found himself gasping for air; a new sensation for him. He looked into the mirror and saw not one, but two faces looking back at him. That of the shrouded figure and the Prince.

The pressure he felt upon him was the Prince's arms grappling him, one arm reaching over his shoulder, the other thrusting an impossibly sharp object into his chest. The Prince released him and pushed Wyvern away.

Wyvern landed against the mirror, causing it to sway but not fall from its place on the wall. Wyvern stepped forward feeling his blood heat again. It was soothing and comforting at first; a familiar feeling. Quickly, very quickly, it became unbearable. It felt as though every part of his being was aflame. He looked at the Maiden who bore a pained expression on her face. He looked down to see his own stinger protruding from his chest—precisely where the human heart would reside.

He dropped to his knees screaming in pain and helplessness. His venom was moving quickly through his human blood. The bleeding stump that had once been his fiendish weapon could not be removed. Perhaps the Prince had lodged it so deep or the venom rendered him too weak. He let his hands fall to his sides as his lungs burst and he could scream no longer. A blood-filled haze quickly clouded his vision. The last thing he remembered was the stern, hard look of the Maiden before darkness took him.

The 'human' Wyvern fell lifeless to the floor with a harsh

thud. The Maiden covered her mouth with a lithe hand. The Prince helped the Wizard to his feet, who placed his arm around the Prince's shoulder to help him stand in his weakened state. They came to stand by the Maiden and looked upon the floor at the infamous Wyvern.

"It is done…" the Maiden whispered in disbelief.

50

LOSS

The Maiden looked to the strange mirror on the wall. The shape inside was no longer striking its hands against the walls of its prison. It was now leaning against the glass resting its head and looking, seemingly, in the direction of the fallen dragon-child.

The Maiden saw a strange sheen on the mirror. It reminded her of the Violet Witch's aura, as well as the prison that bound Tytania in the Barghest. She reached out and touched the surface. The figure stepped back as it gave way to her fingertips, clinging to them like spiderwebs. She pulled the veil away like it was a thin sheet. The mist, no longer trapped, poured from the bottom of the mirror like an open door.

As the thick mist wafted from within, the figure stepped forward and climbed from the mystical prison. The Prince and Wizard stared, eyes widened in disbelief. The Gray King was again among them. He breathed deeply of the fresh air in his throne room.

"I have been gone too long," he said, peering about his court.

He saw the statue of the Gray Wizard and sighed deeply.

"My old friend... what have they done to you?" The Gray

King touched the arm of the statue and, indeed, it was solid marble.

"Majesty?" the Maiden said, bowing to the king. "I may be able to help him."

The king nodded and stepped aside, bidding her to do as she will. Something strange occurred to her, but it was a day for strange occurrences. The Maiden took a piece of cloth and poured water from a nearby carafe. She wet the cloth and began to clean the outstretched hand of the statue. Surely, the quartz turned to mud and wiped away at the Maiden's touch leaving healthy, unharmed flesh in its place. She was startled when the hand, once fully clean, began to move.

"Here!" the Prince called out. He had poured the carafe into a larger container and told her to pour it over the statue.

The Maiden dumped the water over the statue and used the Prince's traveling cloak to wipe the mud from the Gray Wizard who fell to the ground as his full form was restored. The mud fell in piles at his feet and his once-pristine robes were still caked with it, but he was alive and well.

"By the spires, what happened?" he asked.

The Blue Wizard approached him with a wry smile. "You have been on quite a vacation, my friend. Let's get you cleaned up and I'll explain. As well as I can, anyway…"

The Maiden grabbed the Heeding Shell where it still sat on the ground. She lifted it and held it close to her ear.

"It's quiet…" The Maiden said, concerned. "Do you think the spell has faded?"

The Prince nodded grimly. "Yes—I think I should get to the battle and see who remains standing."

* * *

THE WIZARDS AIDED the two in getting to the bottom of the spire. Wyvern had interfered with the magic of the spire and traveling to its base would require a re-working of the spells. As they began their task, the Prince and Maiden were given a safe route to the bottom so they could look upon the battle.

They weren't prepared for what they found. As they walked out the great doors of the spire, the Morning Guard parted for them, nodding to the Prince with respect and to the Maiden in etiquette. The towering, armored men should have sprung on them the moment the door to their gilded tower opened, but they must have known of the king's safety and return. How they knew this escaped the two, but they must have known nonetheless.

The blood of a thousand slain fiends soaked the grounds of the Diamond Spire and mingled with the blood of hundreds of Red Warriors. The remnants of the army, including the dragon-children Serpent and Drake, had gathered about their prisoners —dozens of quivering, defeated boglins. Not a single troll or ogre stood. They were, one and all, crushed, perforated, or charred hulks littering the courtyard.

There was one warrior in particular that the Prince and Maiden scoured the group for. Their hearts raced as they sought to discover the fate of their friend. The ranks of blood-stained and weary warriors parted and their own Warrior walked out of the crowd, his hands and face heavily bandaged.

"Make way!" he barked at them.

Seeing his friends alive and well he walked briskly toward them. The Maiden and Prince did so, as well. The Maiden then broke into a run and hugged her friend despite the macabre stains upon his armor. Seeing the Prince, the Warrior gripped the younger man's hand in a firm and happy greeting.

"It's good to see you alive, both of you," the Warrior said.

"Same here, friend," the Prince replied. The Warrior pulled him in for a strong hug.

"You escaped the spire—what of Wyvern?"

The Maiden looked at him and sighed. "He is no more."

The Warriors jaw clenched and he nodded his head in approval, "It is done."

"It is," the Prince echoed.

The Warrior suddenly furrowed his brows. "Where is the Wizard? The Sybil?"

"Olændra!" the Maiden gasped, looking about. "She grabbed Morgæna and… she threw herself and her sister from the top of the spire."

"Come again?" the Warrior said, skeptically.

"It's true. Where did they…" The Prince stopped himself from finishing the question.

The Warrior looked about the scene of the vicious battle. He began barking questions at other soldiers.

"Two women? Wearing robes, look like sorceresses?"

Serpent and Drake approached and inquired about Wyvern. Upon hearing the news Serpent lowered her head sadly while Drake winced, but nothing more. They were then also asked about Olændra and Morgæna.

"Oh," Serpent replied, "I didn't know one of them was your friend…" she trailed off, her head turning back to the spire. "I found them on the northern court. Please, let us bring them."

The Maiden's eyes flowed freely with tears. When Serpent and Drake returned, each carrying one of the sisters, they placed them gently on the ground. Each looked still and serene. When the Maiden saw Olændra, she broke into a fit of sobs.

She fell to her knees and threw her arms around her friend. An eccentric, empathetic soul gone from the world. She cried and called to the Sybil to come back, until her voice grew hoarse. This was no fault of Wyvern's. It was the Sybil who chose to stop her sister's evil and give them a chance against Morgæna's master. The Maiden could do nothing for her. Then, she wept more.

51

RETURN TO GLORY

The Gray King met the warriors and his Morning Guard on the field of battle. With the restored Gray Wizard at his side, he surveyed the destruction and bloodshed that had been wrought at the behest of Wyvern. Seeing the quivering boglin prisoners and their bloodied, spent wardens, the king had made a merciful decree.

He and the warriors both knew that boglins were cowards at heart and most likely followed Wyvern out of sheer terror. He also knew that such fear would work in favor of the Red Warriors. The boglins, he declared, would be allowed to return to their swamps under the condition they clean the remains of Wyvern's army from Sygil's grounds and that every presence of their blood and the blood of their monstrous allies be cleansed from every stone. It did not entirely sit well with the Sons of Edda, who lost many brethren that day, but it pleased them all to observe the boglins undertake the gruesome duty.

The boglins began their work gratefully. In the end, it took two full days for the multitude of boglins to clean the filth and blood from the courtyards, but they worked tirelessly under the watch of the Morning Guard. The massive numbers of slain creatures were thrown upon pyres to burn away. Serpent carried the bodies of the chimera and Nidhogr, separately, far into the ocean to be dumped unceremoniously.

* * *

THE SONS of Edda returned in victory to their homeland. Though they were missing many, the names of the fallen were carved into the walls of the great cities per their custom. They resumed their duties with the vigilance and stoic pride they were known for. The Red Prince became a hero in Edda's history and earned the pride and respect of his father and comrades.

The Warrior returned with them, riding alongside Prince Vidar through the streets of Valgrind as the citizens cheered their return. The crowd roared the names of the two champions, the Red Prince and the Warrior, and those names echoed between the high walls of Valgrind. "Vidar! Sigard!"

Sigard made a promise to the Prince that he would he would visit the young ruler in his own kingdom, meet the Avallonian people as the Prince had met the Warrior's. The Warrior and the Prince gripped each other's hands in brotherhood one more time, with more promises of feasting and celebration to come, when the last days of evil would be swept away.

Many rumors spread, until it became a legend of its own, that Sigard kept a lovely, eternally-blossoming tree in his quarters from the Hynefol itself and that he was often visited by a woman whose beauty could steal a man's breath. He never boasted or even spoke of such a thing and answered any questions regarding the strange rumors with an uncharacteristically warm smile.

* * *

TRUE TO HIS WORD, Prince Arturion, king errant of Avallonis, returned with proof of Wyvern's demise. Though, being that the fiend was human when slain, he returned not with a head but rather the barb that had been the beast's undoing. This was more than enough, he reasoned, as all knew Wyvern would rather die than part with such a thing.

He returned just in time to see the glorious return of the spire's griffons. Their splendid, spread wings were like banners heralding his timely return. The fabled riders of Avallonis were reunited with their loyal mounts now that the griffons were free of Wyvern's vile threat against their eggs. Prince Arturion personally met with the Speaker of the griffons to deeply apologize that such horrible threats were made because of his involvement in the events. The Speaker returned her own regrets, stating that nothing short of Wyvern's threat against their children would have kept the griffons from their timeless oath to the king of Avallonis—errant or no.

The coronation of Arturion, King of Avallonis, was one that would never be outdone. Lady Gwinn and the Avallonian knights were in attendance upon their griffons and in full regalia. Sigard, the Warrior, was present in ceremonial Edding armor. He stood alongside the Blue Wizard, Serulian, and they watched their Prince with pride. The Green King and his queen, along with the Tytania, Steward of the Violet Throne, were among the guests of honor.

52

CORRINA

Tables upon tables of food and a mountain of wine barrels from all over Septer were provided during King Arturion's coronation. A true surprise, however, was the King's guest. The Maiden was there at his side, resplendent in an elaborate gown of green and light blue. Of course, she was uncomfortable in such extravagant clothing, but the Prince insisted. Her beauty and kind nature captivated the people and nobles. Even the magisters were without a snide comment.

Corrina, a maiden from the fields of Emrallt, had captured the hearts and minds of each and every realm. She had defied death. Brought a king back to his people. Returned a man to life. Together, she and Arturion had defeated a dragon-child and saved a continent. The Wizard made sure to remark that this was just as much Corrina's coronation as it was Arturion's.

To end the grand coronation, King Arturion then bent a knee to her. He presented Corrina with a ring of gold. It was in the vague shape of a Wyvern and upon its back were seven brilliant stones—an emerald, sapphire, and ruby, followed by a perfect bit of amber, a cut of amethyst that brought a catch to her throat, and topped with a sparkling diamond. A representation of all she had overcome.

"Be my queen," the King stated. "This ring will forever remind you of your trial and your triumph. It will forever remind you of the times that brought us together and the times we will strive to create."

Corrina, shocked by the proposal, covered her mouth with her hand… if only to hide her smile. It was a terrifyingly long moment for the new King. Certainly, there were those who sneered at the King's proposal to an orphaned peasant Maiden, but they hid their snide remarks and glances as the intimidating Sigard, the wise Blue Wizard, Serulian, and the beaming faces of King Brennen and Tytania looked on in delight at the sight of the two.

"Of course!" the Maiden replied.

King Arturion placed the ring gently on her finger and they embraced for the first time since their harrowing journey had ended. They held one another close and their happiness was profound. Corrina placed a gentle hand on the check of her King, which was quickly growing a rich brown from the beard he felt made him appear 'wiser'.

Sigard smiled and glanced toward the Wizard.

"You know what this means, Serulian," the Warrior said.

The Wizard, still smiling and watching his King and future Queen, replied, "No, I don't."

"You won't have to watch over Arturion quite so closely anymore."

"He's my king, Sigard. I will always watch over him."

"And how will you have time for that, Serulian, when you'll be so busy watching over all their children?"

The Warrior fought to withhold a laugh as the Wizard's smile faded and his eyes briefly winced.

As the wedding planning continued, Serulian took the

Maiden under his wing. She was now curious about the powers she possessed, and the fabled Blue Wizard had much to teach her.

Her lessons, at first, were rudimentary as expected. However, she learned quickly. She seemed a natural at such things. She was the first creature in known history to wield the power of healing magic, and the Wizard's Council spent days at a time with her in discourse over the subject. Before her final days, Corrina would create the first new magic in generations and found the new teachings of healing.

Just days before the wedding, Serulian informed her of his true agenda: she was to replace him. The Maiden was taken aback. She refused the idea at first, but the Wizard was not without his own charm. He was old, he explained, and Arturion would need a wise and kind soul to aid him in his rule. She was both the kindest and wisest individual he had ever known. Her skill would be more than sufficient and she would sit as both the Blue Queen and the Blue Wizardess. She, herself, knew this was not unheard of.

The Maiden acquiesced to his desire, only asking that she visit once more her former home before the wedding.

"Do you not wish to travel with Arturion?" he asked.

"No," she replied, sadness marring her voice. "I want to do this alone."

Serulian granted her request. Using their combined magic, she was carried swiftly to her old home. Once there he stepped away to allow her a moment of privacy and to prepare the spell for their return.

The Maiden looked through the ashes of her former home. The pens and coops were no longer standing at all. The pile of ash and soot and stone that had once been her warmth and safety was beginning to grow over with grass and blossoms.

One thing she noted that stood out quite differently was the presence of a unique tree. It grew through the pile of rubble and pushed aside all that was in its way. It was strong and hardy. Its boughs held broad, heavy leaves and it had grown with amazing swiftness.

In the peace surrounding the former smallholding she could feel a familiar presence. As a breeze rustled through the wondrous tree she could feel the Knight's hands touch her face. She regretted she never grew to know him more. Corrina felt his presence grow warmer and she knew he was at peace, and so should she and Arturion be.

"We never even knew your name..." she whispered. She was so overwhelmed with the events of that day in Emerald Arbor, a lifetime ago, she had forgotten to ask. A soft wind blew, stirring leaves of the Knight's tree.

Wiping a tear from her face, she turned and saw the Wizard standing stoically at the hilltop. He looked older than usual but with that age came even more wisdom and patience. She approached him and said that she was prepared to depart for her new home.

It was evening when they returned, and handmaidens rushed the soon-to-be queen when she arrived. They brushed and tended and hurried as they prepared her for bed and the wedding to come the next day.

When dawn came, Corrina rose to a peculiar sound. She was used to hearing sparrows by this time of the morning. Instead, she heard a calling of a much different bird. Sitting up in bed, she saw a beautiful falcon perched upon her window. She stood slowly from her bed so as not to frighten the creature and approached slowly. The bird cocked its head to her as if asking what she was tarrying about for. The wings were adorned with dark grey feathers and amethyst markings that looked almost like runes. The beautiful red eyes looked at her inquisitively. The Maiden held out a hand and the falcon leaned in and rubbed its head against her hand. The falcon cried out loudly before flying away; its beautiful rune-like markings caught the sunlight.

A short knock preceded the door to the Maiden's chamber

opening. Arturion stepped in still wearing casual clothing, for a king. The Maiden smiled at him, though with a reproachful glint in her eyes.

"I don't believe you're supposed to see me before the ceremony, Your Grace," she quipped.

Arturion put his arms around her and smiled in return.

"I've faced Wyvern for you; I'm not afraid of a little superstition," he declared haughtily.

"What were you looking at through the window? You were quite focused on something," he said.

The Maiden stared off for a moment.

"I'm not certain," was all she said. Then, "I do have a request; for a wedding gift, if I may?"

Arturion's brow furrowed in concern. "Of course, love —anything."

The Maiden returned her gaze to the window. "I'm not certain what sort of visitor I just had—a falcon, for certain, but, something more. I would like to travel to Mythesta, soon. For a visit."

The Prince saw her smiling to herself as she stared out the window. He sighed, not truly wanting to press the subject at the moment, and kissed her gently on the cheek.

"I will see you shortly," he said on his way out.

He left the Maiden's room just as a flurry of handmaidens made their way in. Still looking out at the clear morning sky, the Maiden continued to smile to herself.

The wedding was magnificent, and every guest that had attended the coronation of the king had returned for the event. There were music and camaraderie to be had throughout the City of the Sapphire Spire. Corrina's gown was adorned with blue blossoms and silk, and she felt both self-conscious and splendid all at once.

Corrina was speaking with Lady Gwinn when the Stewardess

of the Violet Throne approached. She was holding a large tome wrapped with a purple silk sash.

"What's this?" Corrina asked.

"A gift, Your Grace," Tytania smiled. "For your wedding day."

Corrina began to raise a protest, but a stern look from the fey sorceress stopped her. "This one is... special. Not just any book of magic."

"How so?"

A weary smile crossed Tytania's face. "This belonged to Olændra."

At the mention of her friend, Corrina's eyes grew red. "Where did it come from?"

Tytania cocked her head sideways. "I'm not just Stewardess of the Violet Throne, *dear*," she said, invoking the Sybil. "The fey that frequented her old home brought it to me. She would want you to have this. A little bird told me," she finished with a smile.

Corrina held the tome close to her chest. All she could manage in return was a heartfelt smile and a nod. Tytania put a warm hand on her shoulder.

After the ceremony, when the king and queen had been announced to the world, Arturion and Corrina had a moment of respite from the well-wishes and festivities in a quiet garden outside the spire. Sigard found them and approached his friends. He handed the King a sprig from a tree.

"It's from her. She couldn't be here for... obvious reasons. She said to plant this piece of our Hynefol tree and it will forever bear fruit for you and your children and every generation thereafter; be it spring or winter. Not that you will ever have the need for such, of course."

Corrina wrapped her arms around Sigard's thick neck. "We will plant it immediately," she said.

And, surely, she did. When the evening's activities concluded they planted the sprig atop a hill nearby. It was a favorite spot of theirs where the Maiden would read to her Prince during quiet moments.

Serulian wished them both the best of years and said he would retire for the evening. Arturion also noted the Wizard's sudden aging. Despite his age, he lived a very long life after his journeys among the realms. Some say it was due to the gift of the Maiden's breath that returned him to life and somehow granted him additional longevity. Regardless, Serulian was grateful for every day he lived among the rolling hills and cobblestone streets of his beloved land and could be the close advisor of his king and queen, his friends, Arturion and Corrina.

The next evening, Arturion and Corrina spent their first day together as king and queen. They sat watching the sunset beneath the boughs of the Hynefol tree; it had grown to a full tree within just a day's time.

The Queen, Corrina, and her King, Arturion, sat once more as Maiden and Prince. This would forever be their place of solace. They would make many great decisions here. They would continue to fall in love here, over and over again. Here, they would sit with their children. As the sun's golden glow descended behind the hills of Avallonis, Corrina and Arturion kissed each other warmly.

They would live a life of love and joy for the remainder of their days.

MEET THE AUTHOR

R ussell Archey has been writing since he was old enough to hold a pencil. His love for narratives, world-building, and story-telling has fed into nearly every aspect of his life: from his video and board game hobbies to pressing his most cherished books onto his unfortunate children (who will, one day, read the Lord of the Rings trilogy whether they like it or not).

When he's not creating new worlds and horrifying things to threaten them with destruction, he's bringing other author's fantastic works to life as an audio book narrator, spending time with his two children, and pressing his dear wife's eternal patience with his quirky habits.

OTHER TITLES

FROM 5 PRINCE PUBLISHING

5PrinceBooks.com
After School Adventure: Into the Desert *Antony Soehner*
At Last *Bernadette Marie*
Masterpiece *Bernadette Marie*
A Tropical Christmas *Bernadette Marie*
Corporate Christmas *Bernadette Marie*
Faith Through Falling Snow *Sandy Sinnett*
After School Adventure: Beyond the Briar Patch *Antony Soehner*
Walker Defense *Bernadette Marie*
Clash of the Cheerleaders *April Marcom*
Stevie-Girl and the Phantom of Forever *Ann Swann*
Assemble the Party *Antony Soehner*
The Last Goodbye *Bernadette Marie*
The Gingerbread Curse *April Marcom*
Stevie-girl and the Phantom of Crybaby Bridge *Ann Swann*
The MacBrides: Hannah & Ash *J.L. Petersen*
Leather and Lies *Celeste Straub*
Beginnings *Bernadette Marie*
Love and Loopholes *Railyn Stone*
Unite the Party *Antony Soehner*

Star Seer *April Marcom*

Totally Devoted *E.M. Bannock*

Bases Loaded *Jena James*

The Tea Shop *Bernadette Marie*

Walker Spirit *Bernadette Marie*

Remains in the Pond *Ann Swann*

Gather the Party *Antony Soehner*

Stevie-girl and the Phantom Pilot *Ann Swann*

Chasing Shadows *Bernadette Marie*

The MacBrides: Logan and RJ *J.L. Petersen*

Never Saw It Coming *Bernadette Marie*

Blissful Disaster *Amy L. Gale*